Bad Attitude

Diamond In The Rough

Doris Parmett

D1563788

13Thirty Books
Print and Digital Editions
Copyright 2017

Discover new and exciting works by Doris Parmett and 13Thirty Books at www.13thirtybooks.com

Print and Digital Edition, License Notes

Copyright © 2017 Doris Parmett

All rights reserved.

ISBN:0692738673
ISBN-13:978-0692738672

DEDICATION

Bad Attitude
This one's for you, Beth, the best sister in the world.

Diamond In The Rough
Thanks, Matthew, for continuously bringing joy into my life.

BAD ATTITUDE

DIAMOND IN THE ROUGH

Bad Attitude

Doris Parmett

CHAPTER ONE

Polly Sweet listened in growing disbelief to the tall, lean, dark-haired Pennsylvania state policeman who stood before the fireplace in the den she'd converted into her office. Detective Reid Cameron had interrupted her at the worst possible moment, while she was writing a tender love scene, a scene she'd struggled with for most of the day. If she didn't stick to her schedule, she couldn't possibly finish the romance novel before school started in the fall. After spending nine months with energetic kindergartners, she'd eagerly looked forward to her summer hiatus.

She would not allow him to ruin her plans with his preposterous scheme.

"No," she said when he finished his explanation. "It's out of the question. I will not allow you to use my house for your command post."

"Ms. Sweet," he said, lowering his voice in contrast to the way she'd raised hers. "You've got the terminology wrong. Your house isn't being used for anything."

"Not according to what you told me."

"I'm obligated to protect you."

She frowned at the thoroughness of his steady gaze, which moved over her as if she were under a microscope. She'd dressed for comfort that morning in a pair of frayed white cutoffs and an old, snug sleeveless cotton top.

"That's a matter of opinion," she retorted, planting her hands at her waist to signal her irritation. "If I say I don't need your protection, I don't. If I say I live a quiet life in the country, take my word for it. Surely you can see I'm far from wealthy. The few pieces of jewelry I own are fake, nothing to tempt a jewel thief. Do you really expect me to buy your absurd story?"

"I expect you to listen to reason," he said as she paced in front of the window.

She turned toward him, scowling. "No jewel thief with an ounce of brains would stash a cache of diamonds here. Why would he choose this place? It isn't easily accessible. You know that, you had to cross my private bridge to get here. I suggest you return to your headquarters and check your facts. If it makes you feel better, you may inform your superiors you've fulfilled your duty by telling me. Thank you and good day."

She marched past him through the homey room, filled with family mementos and the comfortable furniture her parents had loved. Out in the hall she flung open the front door. While she didn't want to appear rude, she couldn't allow herself to get bogged down in conversation. Not with the crucial love scene waiting. When she felt the warm June breeze caress her face and she didn't hear footsteps at her back, she spun around. Nothing. She'd shown herself the door! Marching back into the den, she found Reid Cameron leaning forward, knees slightly bent, peering at a mural her father had painted.

"Detective Cameron, I thought I made myself clear. In case I didn't, I'll repeat myself. My intention when I awoke this glorious morning was to spend the whole day writing, stop around six, prepare dinner, then relax with a cup of chamomile tea while I listen to the evening news. Following that, I would return here to my den, sit at this computer, and edit my day's efforts. This still remains my Thursday goal."

He peered over his shoulder at her and nodded. "Admirable. This is a terrific oil painting. Who did it?"

A special man, she thought. One she'd loved dearly and would always miss. A tall, strong man. A caring man who always found time for his inquisitive daughter. She'd loved watching him dab oils on his sable brush, then lift his hand to bring his vision of their land to life on the canvas.

"My father," she replied, a wistful note creeping into her voice.

Detective Cameron turned around, regarding her thoughtfully. "He's good. He shows an interesting combination of powerful strokes mixed with a lyrical touch."

It surprised her that this stranger found the same beauty in her father's painting as she did. "Yes, he did."

"Did?"

She felt the lump in her throat that always came when she thought of the loss of her father and, shortly afterward, her mother. The two people closest to her had died too young from injuries sustained in an automobile accident.

Blinking back her tears, Polly found herself gazing into a pair of sympathetic dark eyes. "My parents passed away several years ago. My father was a farmer who loved to paint."

"I'm sorry for your loss. I still miss my own dad. Do you set different goals for each day of the week, Ms. Sweet?"

"I'm sorry for your loss, too, Detective Cameron, but surely you have better things to do with your time than discuss my father's artistic abilities or my weekly calendar. It's three o'clock. Three precious hours left for me to accomplish my first draft."

"Your clock's fast. It's ten of three. Three hours and ten precious minutes, to be exact."

Polly caught his faint smile and decided she'd wasted enough time. By habit and nature, she meticulously planned her days. She never forgot a friend's or a relative's birthday. When her school principal asked for lesson plans, she delivered her book promptly. It suited her professional persona; it suited her disposition. Now her brain signaled a warning that unless she quickly got rid of this policeman, he would discover other interesting things in the room to waste her precious time.

"Thank you," she said. "I'll reset my watch after you leave. Again, good day."

A shadow of amused forbearance crossed his face. Without further comment or permission, he sat down on a blue upholstered armchair, then indicated she should sit too.

"I hate putting a damper on your afternoon," he said, "but I'm afraid it doesn't work your way. You can't tell me what to do. I tell you what to do. Now please, sit down."

For a moment she debated getting the baseball bat she kept in the front closet and threatening him with it, but then she'd give him cause to arrest her. Her stomach clenched. She sat down.

He wasn't in uniform, and he didn't look like her idea of a cop. Though maybe on second thought, his rugged face, straight dark brows, and flashing white teeth did. His clothes didn't. He wore a denim jacket over jeans that clung to muscular thighs, and scruffy sneakers green with grass stains.

He leaned forward. "The man we're after, Aaron Grayson, isn't the brains behind the outfit that stole the jewelry. He's one player in what we know is a nationwide ring. The reasons you've given me against his coming here are exactly the reasons why he would use this place.

It's a perfect location to hide jewels, away from prying eyes. Also, he knows this section of western Pennsylvania like the back of his hand. He lived in the neighboring county until after he left high school. And may I remind you that you live alone."

"So what? A lot of women live alone. Right now I wish I were alone."

"Yes, many women live alone, but wouldn't you agree that most women don't live in an isolated location?"

"Don't play the statistics game with me, Detective."

"Ms. Sweet, we know Grayson could have come here without fear of being seen. We're fairly certain he hid the jewels here. Therefore, he'll return for them. Our information is, he will probably head back this way sometime over the next few days. You need me, Ms. Sweet."

She regarded him steadily. He didn't so much as blink. "No, I don't. I prefer to take my chances."

A slight smile lifted the corners of his mouth, the kind of sensual mouth she'd ascribed to the hero in her romance novel. Except her hero was malleable, reasonable. Gallant.

"The choice isn't yours," he said. "Grayson is dangerous. Until he's apprehended, I'm not leaving your side, Ms. Sweet. Day or night."

"What!" She sprang out of her seat. All his talk about missing jewels sounded like a bad movie script.

But his saying he wasn't leaving her side—day or night!—that sounded like real life. She couldn't allow it.

"I told you I live alone. It's the way I intend to live until I choose otherwise. My summers are precious to me. All year long I plan how I'll use my time. Use it, not squander it, to accomplish certain tasks I set for myself. My barn needs repairs. Barring my winning the lottery, which isn't likely, I'm obliged to work. That work requires privacy, solitude. As far as I'm concerned, you may set up all the roadblocks you want, as long as you set them on county property, which is on the other side of my bridge."

"No."

"Yes. I am far too busy to have you camped underfoot on the wild chance there are diamonds on my property. For example, Mr. Soames, a roofer, is coming to fix my barn tomorrow before it caves in. He kindly moved me up in his schedule after seeing how badly the roof needs repair. I'm sure you've noticed how saturated the ground is from our recent heavy rains. More rain is coming, either tomorrow or Saturday."

"Ms. Sweet, I suggest you call Mr. Soames and tell him not to come until next week. If you don't, I will. It's best coming from you. You can say you're leaving town unexpectedly."

His cool arrogance shocked her. "How dare you, Detective Cameron! Not only don't I want to cancel the roofer, you're asking me to tell a lie."

He didn't raise his voice, but calmly said, "That's right. Lie convincingly, but lie."

She shook her head, tossing her unruly blond hair. "Shame on you. And you call yourself a policeman. Some example you set."

"Your faith in police as role models is touching. Call it a cover story. Call it whatever you please. I'm not here to set an example. I'd appreciate the least amount of hassle possible." He paused, then added, "I have a court order to tap your phone."

She leaped out of her chair. "Whaaat?"

He ignored her outcry. "We have Grayson's voice print. If he calls pretending he's someone else, we'll know it's him. The fewer strangers on the property until he's captured, the better. I'm sorry to mess up your plans, but it can't be helped."

She stared at him, her gaze locked with his. There was an exasperating smile on his face, as if he knew, as a state policeman, he was acting within his rights. That by stating his duty was to protect her, he made his wishes supersede hers. He meant what he said. It wasn't fair. A wave of dizziness washed over her.

In seconds strong hands steadied her. Instinctively she

grabbed them, holding on to them, feeling their strength. She experienced a nearly overwhelming desire to stay put and an equally strong desire, stemming from self-preservation, to move away. Aware that the uncommon tingling she felt came from the very person she hoped to get rid of, she disengaged her hands with a snap, flinging her palms up, indicating he was the last person she wanted touching her.

He had the decency to step back from her. "Ms. Sweet, I thought it best to get the bad news out of the way first."

"Did you? What's the good news?"

A grin tugged at his lips. "I'll be gone in a few days."

"If you think that makes me grateful, you're wrong. If you want to see grateful, leave. You barged into my home—"

"I rang the bell."

"Don't be cute. I asked you politely to leave. You refused. You order me around while telling me I should be afraid of a phantom thief. You're tapping my phone without my permission. How can you think that hiding behind the law as you insist on wrecking my privacy will make me feel better?"

"I assure you, whatever actions I take are for your protection."

She couldn't speak, she was that flabbergasted. Not for a minute did she feel her life in danger, unless it was from him. He was stealing her precious freedom. She eyed her computer screen longingly.

That morning she had awakened with such enthusiasm, joyous to see the sun streaming through her window. She'd welcomed a bright blue sky after five days of pounding rain, and had hurried to the barn to milk Horace, a cow incongruously named by Polly's elderly aunt Martha who lived across the road. The cow had been happy to leave the barn's confines after days of being cooped up. Polly's animal was happy; she was happy. Or she had been, until Reid Cameron's unwelcome arrival.

She studied his rough-hewn features. Damn him for resembling the hero in her book! Over lunch at school one-day last month, she had led the conversation onto the kind of man her teacher friends liked to see as heroes. She knew they read romances. They didn't know she was writing one.

Her best friend, Grace Waters, had said, "Give me a gloomy,

complex rebel, put us alone in a room with a single bed, then leave the rest to me."

Joan Daniels, the other kindergarten teacher, said, "Me too. I'll forget grading papers, shopping, taking my kids to the dentist, reminding them to practice piano. I'll forget about bills, carpooling, the works."

Lonni Landis wanted a hero whose burning dark gaze turned smoky with desire. She preferred him formidable, with a great body, yet manly enough to wear an earring. A sexy man, one who carried an aura of danger.

Grace summed it up for the three women. "We wouldn't change our husbands. We're not confusing reality with fantasy. It's harmless to escape for a few hours. What woman doesn't dream of a Rhett Butler striding into her life?"

Polly blinked. Her friends should meet Reid Cameron. His profession met their condition for an element of danger. He was tall and had the requisite midnight-black hair and dark eyes. His broad shoulders tapered to a narrow waist. And he certainly looked formidable, standing before her with his arms folded in front of him, appearing about as movable as a granite statue. Give her a man with blond or light brown hair and blue or hazel eyes. Most important, he must possess a poetic soul, a man like Ashley Wilkes in *Gone With The Wind*.

Ashley was the essence of politeness. Ashley would never treat a lady rudely. She lifted her chin.

"I don't like you, Detective Cameron. I don't want you here. I disapprove of a man who forces his way into my private life, taps my phone, orders me to cancel my roofer, all under the guise of protecting me. So, no, I won't allow you to disrupt my life. Why can't you search the farm, find the jewels, and leave me alone?"

"We're after the whole gang, if possible. The people Grayson is associated with also deal drugs."

"All the more reason to leave me alone," she argued. "Catch him somewhere else."

He shook his head. "This is the best lead we've had in the two years we've been after this gang." He glanced at his watch. "My partner, Fran Mohr, will be here by dinnertime. Before then I'd like to check out the house and grounds."

How could her life get so complicated so quickly?

A teacher's salary didn't go far, and any extra money she had went into the care and upkeep of the house and property she'd inherited from her parents. Her love life was flat. She dated, but there was no one special. Her last serious romance had fizzled out three years ago. Was it any wonder she dreamed of selling her novel, of finally getting a break, of opening new doors?

"Detective Cameron, if you and your partner stay in my house, you'll abide by my rules. Otherwise you sleep outside."

As if he hadn't heard her, he strolled over to her desk and peered at the computer screen.

She grabbed his arm, blocking his view of the monitor. "That's the first rule! Stay away from my computer."

His unexpected smile was startling. It took her aback. The horrid man looked… handsome.

"So you write romances," he said. "My partner is hooked on them. I've never figured out their appeal."

"Figures. If you're trying to make points with me, you're losing. My second rule is that you never—ever—go near my bedroom."

His smile twisted. "When you see me in your bedroom, Ms. Sweet, I assure you it will be on official business."

He walked over to look at a little painting, a tranquil pastoral, that rested on an easel beside an occasional table.

"Your father's too?"

"Yes."

"Talented man." He turned to face her. "Ms. Sweet, just so you and I avoid trouble, let's clear up a few things. I am not your enemy. I know what I've told you hit you like a bolt from the blue."

"That's putting it mildly. It's unreal."

"You're wrong. It's real. Otherwise I'd never invade your privacy. If it helps, I didn't ask for this assignment. No one hopes more than I that we wrap up the case soon. Then"—he grinned—"you can get back to writing your sizzling romance."

"I think you're insufferable."

His smile broadened. "Good. We're off to an auspicious start."

Polly rolled her eyes

"You and Fran will share your bedroom," he went on. "I don't want you left alone. The last time one of our people let a woman he was supposed to be guarding coerce him into leaving her side, an unfortunate accident happened to another trooper."

"What was it?"

"He stopped a bullet meant for her. Had she been where she belonged, he wouldn't have been shot." Polly felt the blood drain from her face. Bullets killed. The man could have died. She stood silently for a few moments, her lips compressed.

"I'm stuck with you, aren't I?" she said finally.

"Yes." He spoke with as much reluctance as she.

"But think, when we return the diamonds to the insurance company, you'll collect a handsome reward."

"However much the check, it won't be enough!"

"Damn," he muttered as he started from the room. "I can see protecting you isn't going to be a bit of fun."

He went over her house like a bloodhound, not leaving a nook or cranny unexplored. He paced off halls, measuring them also for width. He ran up and down her staircase, testing which steps squeaked the most. He checked doors and windows for warping, checked the angles and views from each window. He prowled rooms, moving some furniture in order to have clear paths to the doors. He carried a twin bed from one of the spare rooms into her bedroom for his partner.

"Where is your partner?" Polly asked.

"Busy," he said shortly. Before setting up the bed, he removed his jacket to roll up his shirtsleeves. "She'll bring supplies with her when she comes later."

Polly's eyes widened when she saw the holster at his waist. Naturally he'd wear a gun. Cops wore a firearm. While she adjusted her mind to the unwelcome sight, he finished setting up the bed and said he'd take the room next door.

Polly bit back her smile. The mattress in the other bedroom was old and lumpy. And judging from his height of well over six feet, she guessed his feet would hang over the edge.

"There's one bathroom on this floor," she said, walking back out into the hall. "I'll post a schedule."

He walked into the white tile bathroom. Several of her lacy bras hung on the shower rod, and she snatched them down.

"Are you assuming," he asked, "that nature calls on cue?"

Inhaling a deep breath, she counted to ten as he sauntered

past her into the hall. "I meant if you want to use the shower. Keep up your fresh talk and you can swim in the river. The swift current should take you downstream fast. Providing you make it past the boulders."

He stopped and turned so swiftly, she was barely a few inches away from him. As she stared up into his dark eyes, she was disconcertingly aware of the heat emanating from his hard body.

"Ms. Sweet," he said in a near growl, "we'll get along fine if you stop trying to give me a hard time. For better or worse, you and I will be together for a while. If I swallowed my disappointment at having to do this, I suggest you do the same."

She glared up at him. "My third rule is you're never to try to intimidate me. I'll report you to your superiors."

He gave her a hard look. "For the record I like agreeable women. You are not agreeable. For the record my superiors sent me. For the record I can think of ten other places I'd rather be. Try to understand, I'm not playing games." He turned to the stairs. "Now will you please show me where the cellar is?"

His insult galled her. She tromped down the stairs behind him, then stalked past him into the kitchen and jerked the cellar door open. "Since I'm forced to tolerate you, I'm going to write down a list of rules. I'll insist you follow them."

As if she hadn't spoken, he switched on the cellar light and started down the stairs, leaving her staring at his back.

Her heart sank. He'd made it clear that, for whatever reason, he resented being there as much as she wished he'd leave. Who knows? she thought, applying her writer's imagination. Maybe Detective Cameron and his partner, Fran Mohr, weren't getting along. Maybe they had mixed business with pleasure, and their romance had soured.

She peered out the window. The afternoon sunshine looked enticing. Marshmallow clouds dotted a blue sky. She'd planned on a long walk before dinner, but it looked as if that, too, had gone the way of her writing schedule.

With great reluctance she dialed Mr. Soames. His cheerful voice chilled after she offered Reid's excuse. Yes, he'd reschedule, but he couldn't say when. He'd reshuffled other customers as a special favor to her, he said, laying on the guilt. Then he added that the section of roof directly above the hayloft wasn't leaking. Yet.

She apologized profusely and quickly hung up.

Her hands were shaking. She looked at them in disgust. That was Reid Cameron's fault. He wasn't a figment of her fertile imagination. He was there all right, dark and domineering. What would her friends say if they knew?

Whether he liked it or not, while he was in her home, he'd abide by her guidelines. Taking pencil and paper, she sat down and started her list of rules. She set the times he could prepare his meals. She expected him to leave the kitchen spotless. Whatever he used, she expected him to replenish. If he dirtied the floors by walking around with muddy shoes, he'd be responsible for washing them. No towels on the bathroom floor. The bathroom seat must be left down. No hair in the sink. If he borrowed her tube of toothpaste, he'd better squeeze from the bottom. Better yet, she expected him to use his own.

Polly felt a small degree of perverse satisfaction as she read the list of rules and regulations. Normally she would never have the arrogance to demand that a guest follow such a list. Or any list, for that matter. She prided herself on having many dear friends of long standing. Reid Cameron, though, had pushed himself on her. He'd walked into her life as though he owned her and taken over. That night, he would sleep in the bedroom next to hers. She thought about it with distaste. The walls weren't soundproof.

She heard him rattling around in the cellar, doing who knew what to what. Poking into her things, her life! Grimacing, she sent her pencil racing across the paper with one last rule:

No snoring!

CHAPTER TWO

Reid gazed around the large, neat cellar. Cellars told a lot about people. This one blared that Polly Sweet preferred an orderly life. Everything in its proper place, nothing strewn or scattered on the floor as he'd seen in many homes. Tidy. Polly Sweet liked tidy. Plastic sheeting covered a metal clothes rack with her winter clothes. Her suitcases were lined up like bookends, near a stack of board games. Not a cobweb in sight.

Against one wall was a covered workbench, and the shelf beneath held a variety of saws and hammers. Her father's, he thought, recalling how her eyes had softened when she'd spoken of the loss of her parents. It couldn't be easy for her, living alone, responsible for the upkeep on a large piece of property and the constant repairs needed on a house and a barn. The bridge hadn't sounded sturdy to him.

He walked over to a bookcase. The titles weren't new, indicating Ms. Sweet was also a saver. He ran his finger along one row and pulled out a black leather high school yearbook. Curious about his unwilling hostess, he flipped through it, searching for Polly Sweet's name.

Ms. Polly Sweet. Ms. Polly Sweet with the stormy blue eyes had led the debating team her senior year in high school. Ms. Polly Sweet with the luminous blue eyes had graduated at the top of her class. Ms. Polly Sweet with the spitting-angry blue eyes had been a cheerleader. A very cute cheerleader, he thought as he stared at her in her skimpy uniform. Ms. Polly Sweet's classmates had voted her

Most Popular, claiming her name suited her: Sweet.

Not by a long shot! Her former classmates obviously had never seen Ms. Polly Sweet's temper!

Which she had unwisely aimed at him, instead of Grayson. He supposed it sounded farfetched to think a crook had planted stolen jewelry on her property. Grayson had, though. Ms. Polly Sweet didn't realize that once Grayson made his appearance, she'd be grateful for police protection. Therefore, whether she liked it or not, they were going to establish a working relationship.

They'd gotten off to a lousy start. He hadn't expected her to collapse at his feet with gratitude, but she'd floored him when she'd dismissed the idea of receiving a bundle in reward money. It galled him that he was stuck with a defiant writer who wouldn't take her life as seriously as her precious manuscript!

Sitting down on a metal folding chair, he absent-mindedly massaged his aching thigh. The bullet that had struck him a few months earlier had nicked a nerve, temporarily paralyzing some of the sensation in his right leg. He had required intensive physical therapy before he'd regained full use and full feeling in the leg, but the leg could still ache, his personal weather barometer.

During his first week in the hospital the top brass of the state police had visited, praising him for his quick action. Not only had he stopped a bullet meant for a woman the state police had been assigned to protect, he had single-handedly arrested the shooter. At a bedside ceremony the department brass had presented him with a commendation, which he'd put in a dresser drawer in his Pittsburgh apartment, along with the other ones he'd earned.

While he'd been on leave recuperating, he had considered ending his stint with the police and putting his law degree to use. He had always known his future included practicing law, and he could see himself as a prosecuting attorney, nailing the bad guys. Still, he'd decided practicing law could wait a while longer. It wasn't as if he had a wife and children. He had never met a woman that he wanted to marry. Not enough, that is.

His former steady, the sultry Trisha of the long legs and bedroom eyes and unfaithful body had accused him of having a mistress—his police badge. Apparently she'd decided that if he could have another love, so could she. Five months after she'd moved her lingerie into his dresser drawer, he'd come home early and found her gorgeous legs locked around another man's waist. He'd tossed her, her lover, and their clothes out of his apartment. The clothes went by way of the window. Trisha had been right about one thing, he'd realized. She'd said she couldn't compete with his devotion to duty, and she couldn't.

Tough assignments suited him, and hanging out at Polly Sweet's didn't qualify as a tough assignment. Sure he'd caught a bullet and he'd been lucky, but he didn't want fear as a legacy. That was one of die reasons he'd asked his chief for a different assignment, one with more action. All his protests hadn't gotten him anywhere. So there he sat, wishing for cooperation and knowing he needed to perform a miracle upon Ms. Sweet to get it. Too bad he couldn't speak with her deccased father, get a clue on how to get through to his daughter.

He would have preferred timing his arrival to when the surveillance team tracking Grayson placed him near her home. That would mean gambling, though, and all police personnel knew the best plans often turned on a dime. While he waited for Grayson to show up, he'd make a thorough search for the jewels. If he found them, he would substitute the diamonds with cubic zirconia. No sense letting Grayson have the advantage.

He mulled over his problem with Ms. Sweet, then smiled as an idea came to him. She didn't know it yet, but she was about to become his guide. Not only did she know her home and property, but, considering the annoyed looks he'd seen in the feisty spitfire's eyes, she'd be delighted to get rid of him by speeding the process. Which suited him fine.

He paused at the base of the staircase. He didn't hear noise coming from the kitchen. No doubt she was making good her threat with her silly list of rules. An image of her with a pencil flying over the paper had him grinning. He could think of better uses for her pouty red mouth than telling him off!

Chuckling, he recalled part of what he'd read on her computer.

His hands caressed soft flesh. Her lips tasted like fine wine.
Thirsty, he lowered his head, drinking his fill.

Reid added one more fact to his store of knowledge. The not so sweet Ms. Sweet possessed one hell of a vivid imagination. In a more pleasant frame of mind he switched off the light and mounted the stairs.

"Hello," he said as he entered the kitchen.

She stood up from the table and walked over to him. "Here's your list. Kindly see it's followed."

Without even a glance he dropped the paper on the kitchen counter.

"Aren't you going to read it?"

He turned the cold-water tap on. "Mind if I have a glass of water?"

"You'll find glasses in the cabinet above your head. I want you to read my list."

He filled the glass and drank the water. "I will. I promise to read it later. Or, if you feel it's imperative, you can tell me about it while you show me around outside." He washed, dried, and returned the clean glass to where he'd found it.

She snatched the list from the Formica counter and stuck it on the refrigerator door with a magnet. "Read it!"

His voice laced with humor, he said, "You're tough." His gaze moved from the cotton top stretched across her breasts, past her rib cage, her narrow waistline, and softly curved hips, skimmed over her white shorts and down her bare legs to her white anklets and old sneakers.

"Ready, Ms. Sweet?"

"For what?" she demanded, obviously affronted at his thorough perusal.

"A walk in the sunshine. I want you to show me around."

"No, Detective Cameron, I'm not ready. Go by yourself. Take all the time you need. While you show yourself around, pretend I'm not home. I'll pretend you're not here."

As if she hadn't spoken, he took her arm, propelled her to the back door, and gave her a gentle shove outside.

"Isn't this nice?" he asked.

"It could be."

"How can you stay inside all day?" he said, determined not to let her bother him. He filled his lungs with fresh air.

"Check out this fabulous blue sky," he said. "Look around you at the majestic mountains. The scenery is breathtaking."

She twisted free of his loose grasp. "I live here, remember? Besides, why aren't you looking at it?" She'd caught him.

15

"Your sour face captivates me."

"My sour face! If I look sour, it's because I'm wondering why, if you're supposedly sent to guard me, you aren't nice, polite, and respectful."

He chuckled. "That's easy. Most women in your situation would be grateful, making it simple for me to be nice, polite, and respectful."

She hooted. "Most women haven't met you. Hurling insults is not the way to get in my good graces."

"You're right. Wrong tactic. I apologize. Now, how about a truce?"

She cocked her head. "What's in it for me?"

"Why don't we find out?"

"Do I have a choice?"

"No."

"You're wrong, Detective Cameron." She turned to go.

He leaned close and said very distinctly, "Ms. Sweet, whether you are or are not interested in coming with me is immaterial to me. You will be my cooperative guide while I familiarize myself with your property. If you need an incentive to propel your feet and force polite words from your lovely viperish mouth, I suggest you think of the reward money."

She wheeled to face him, planting her hands on her hips. "I'd rather think of how much less time you'll be here."

"Whatever works. Let's go."

As they started off, Reid inhaled the scent of springtime in western Pennsylvania. Far more appealing than the fumes of Pittsburgh. He felt humbled by the rolling pastoral farmland, ringed by distant mountains tinted in purple and green hues.

"I see why your father chose to paint this."

Polly gazed at him, uncertain of his motives, but realizing the tough cop had a tender spot in his heart for art and nature. It made tramping over fields, wandering past a stand of apple trees, walking the line of fence posts, easier. From time to time he stopped to take his bearings, pivoting slowly until he'd looked in all directions. When she asked him why he was doing that, he replied he was mentally measuring distances from various spots to the house. He asked detailed questions, and listened intently to her replies.

"You're very thorough," she said, impressed. "We've been

walking and talking for more than an hour."

"I hadn't realized." He stopped and gestured to a mound of ladybugs mating on a sycamore leaf. "Nature's grand, isn't it?" he teased.

"Terrific," she muttered.

"Lighten up."

"I was hoping we were done."

"Not a chance. It pays to be thorough. Proper planning and preparation solves most cases. Whatever I can accomplish beforehand will help neutralize any advantage Grayson may have in coming here first."

Polly glanced at Reid. He really believed this Grayson person had hidden diamonds on her property. Despite hearing him talk about it, she couldn't fathom it. She simply couldn't take him seriously. "I still don't know how you can be certain he was here, even after all you've said."

"His whereabouts are being monitored."

"Then why haven't you arrested him?"

"We're after the big fish. Grayson's the bait. As I said, he's a member of a nasty ring of thieves. They deal in more than jewels, drugs primarily. What's over there?" He pointed across a narrow stream.

When she told him it was still her land, he took her hand without asking and helped her across the stream. When they reached the other side, she quickly freed herself.

"The boundary for my land," she said, "is on the other side of the bridge you used to get here. The state and county maintain the river that the bridge crosses."

"Do you fish?" he asked.

"I did with my dad. That is, he fished. I read a book."

She pushed her hair back from her forehead and snuck a look at him. He walked with an easy gait. His hair grew low on the back of his neck, which surprised her. Every police officer she'd ever seen wore his or her hair neat and short. Reid's longer hair defied her conception of departmental correctness. More than that, the longer she studied it, the more she was tempted to touch it, to see if it was crisp or soft, to see if the slight wave in it would curl around her fingers.

Shocked by her thoughts, she jerked her gaze away from him

and desperately sought something to say.

"This area of western Pennsylvania," she began, hoping she didn't sound as flustered as she felt, "has some of the best farmland in the state. Unfortunately, last May's freak late spring frost hurt the apple crop. Another boon for Washington State."

"Why do you say that? We sell plenty of apples. Not as many as we used to. The apples grown in the Northeast taste as good as Washington's, but you've got to give them credit. They market their apples aggressively. As a result, they've cornered the apple market, leaving us with a smaller share. Do you think you'll find the missing jewels?"

"I'm fairly good at getting what I'm after. So, yes, if the diamonds are here, we have high-tech ways to locate them."

"High tech?"

"Good updated, old-fashioned snooping. The insurance company's reward should ease things financially for you. A new roof must be expensive."

"It is. I saved all year for it. I'm lucky it isn't leaking over the hayloft."

She veered left, toward the river. When Reid helped her over a jagged-edge boulder, his strong hands lifting her as if she were a feather, she didn't protest. She told herself it was because she was honoring their truce, not because she liked the feel of his hands on her.

"Ms. Sweet, is there a man in your life?"

She stopped and looked at him suspiciously, ready to forget the truce. "I don't see where my private life is any of your business."

"Don't take this personally, but for the next few days everything about you is my business. Therefore, I'll ask you to answer the question."

She turned the tables on him. "Is there a woman in your life?"

He regarded her impassively. "I'm not the one in possible danger. Please answer the question."

"First tell me why you think my private life is your business."

"You're a beautiful woman." Warmth zinged through her veins, but he ruined the compliment by adding, "I don't need a jealous lover lunging at me in the dark."

"Does a scandalous liaison count?" she asked, continuing to

sidestep her reply.

"You and I aren't out for a springtime stroll in the park," he said, a sarcastic edge seeping into his tone. "Yes, it counts. Any man who touches you in a familiar way counts. Do I make myself clear?"

"Very." She tossed her head. "You think your badge entitles you to snap your fingers and make me jump through a hoop. It doesn't."

She turned her back on him and walked on. Her victory in not answering was small but significant. Anything to shake his imperious attitude.

"I'll answer personal questions," she said, "providing your partner asks them. Are you sure she's coming?"

"Yes."

"She better."

They hiked in the opposite direction from the barn, following a trail overlooking the river. With the recent rains the swiftly flowing river had risen to an unusually high level. Still, many boulders jutted upward.

Reid stared at the wooden bridge a few hundred yards away. "It sounded funny in one spot. When's the last time you had it checked for structural damage?"

"Never."

His brows knit together. "Considering that you live alone, don't you think it's wise to check it? I couldn't help noticing the wood is older than the treated kind used today. It could be rotted. How long is the bridge? About seventy feet?"

"Sixty-eight."

He nodded. "And who lives over there?" He pointed to a white bungalow with green shutters across the road.

"My Aunt Martha."

He turned to her. "Keep her away."

"No," she said, shaking her head. "Don't even think about asking me to do that. In the first place it won't work. In the second place I refuse to worry her. In the third place all of this is probably for nothing. Besides, Martha comes over to see Horace."

"Who?"

"Horace, her pet milk cow."

"Are you serious?"

"Yes. Martha named her. I have a barn, so Horace lives here.

You haven't seen her yet. She's out in the pasture. I'll have to bring her in soon for her radio show."

"They have shows for cows?" Reid asked, his brows raised.

"No. Martha adores Guns N' Roses, and she turned Horace on to their music. Horace refuses to give milk if she doesn't get daily doses of Axl Rose. Fortunately, a local radio station loves Guns N' Roses, too, and does half-hour shows of their music three times a day. Of course, I have to rescue Cuddles before the radio turns on. His ears are too sensitive."

Reid stared at her. "Cuddles?"

"Short for Barracuda. He's another of Aunt Martha's gifts. Cuddles is a Chihuahua. Aren't you glad you dropped in?"

"My God, you're serious. I can't have your aunt coming and going as she pleases."

Polly's eyes narrowed. "I'm adamant on this. If I'm stuck with you, then you're stuck with this reality. You must have contingency plans. No one wants my aunt kept safe more than I. However, you have to admit this waiting around could be for nothing, or it could take days."

Twittering birds distracted him. He looked up to where a pair of robins sat on an overhead branch. "No, I'm certain Grayson will show. It's his mode of operation. He's under orders to produce the jewels when the higher-ups say to. Or else he's in trouble."

Polly looked out over the placid scene, then back at the hard-nosed impossible man who'd chopped off her creative juices. Worse, he showed no remorse for having ruined her afternoon.

"Despite what you say, Detective Cameron, it's supposition. My aunt Martha is not. She's real. We've always been close, but more so since my parents died. She's visiting a friend overnight, but she'll be back tomorrow. Her normal routine is that she comes over here every day to see me and her pets. Several nights a week we dine together. That way I'm assured she's eating some nutritious meals. Martha's into causes, you see. She's a member of various clubs and organizations. She reads palms and tarot cards, and casts astrological charts. She's a uniquely wonderful person, but she's not into food preparation."

"I don't care if she reads tea leaves. She stays away."

"No. I let you bully me about your staying here, since you insist Grayson's hidden the jewels here. I don't believe it, but even if

I did, I won't allow you to dictate to my aunt."

She lifted her chin and refused to speak when he repeated his orders.

"All right," he almost shouted, obviously having reached the end of his patience, "then tell your aunt you're going away."

"Open your ears, Detective Cameron! I can't. Either we tell her the truth or be prepared for her visits. If I have to suffer you disrupting my life, then you must give a little. She knows I haven't planned a vacation."

"Pretend you're ill."

"Do I look ill? Aunt Martha saw me yesterday afternoon."

Once more, he made a thorough inspection of her. Her body tingled as his gaze rose up her bare legs and over her hips, lingering briefly on her breasts. When he finally reached her face, she told herself she was flushed and breathless from anger. She wasn't sure she convinced herself, though.

The corners of his mouth twitched. "Ms. Sweet, saying you're ill isn't a good idea. The fact is, you look abundantly healthy. We'll have to think of a plausible excuse."

She let out a strangled breath. The man was deliberately fractious. Hotly aware of his innuendo, she knew her skimpy attire didn't help. What she saw in his eyes, though, wasn't flirtatious foolishness, but an implacable irrevocability.

"I don't want my aunt in danger; therefore, we'll pretend you're my gardener."

"A high school boy mows your lawn once a week."

"How did you know?"

He merely raised his brows.

"Then pretend you're my plumber."

"Do you usually ask your plumber to sleep over?" When her shoulders slumped, he suggested she pack up and visit a friend until he said she could return.

She thought of her computer, of her marvelous plans. "You're not throwing me out of my house. I'm not moving my computer, my research, all my papers, on the chance this isn't all just a wild goose chase."

"Why do I get the impression you aren't taking me seriously? Kindly remember, my job is to protect you."

"Hah! You're here to catch a thief. Who may or may not be a

phantom, as far as I know. Who may or may not have hidden diamonds on my property. Your job is to 'protect me' only because I happen to be here. That's the scenario, and don't think I don't know it. If Grayson has been here, I'm all for letting him come back as quietly as he came the first time, take his loot, and leave. Arrest him down the road, or over in the next county. I wouldn't be the wiser."

"Are you through?" he asked in a tone that said her arguments fell on deaf ears. "If for some reason the surveillance teams report Grayson isn't coming tomorrow, Fran won't stay during the day. I will."

"Why not? What will she be doing?"

"She drew the lucky straw. She'll split her time with another case we're working on until we know Grayson is closer. It's easy to palm Fran off as your friend. But if I'm under your roof for any length of time, I need a viable reason. I'm open to suggestions."

He folded his arms, leaned back against a maple tree, and waited.

Polly bit her lower lip. What excuse could she give for having a muscular hunk in her house? She smiled and snapped her fingers. "You're my butler."

"Get serious," he drawled, giving the impression he was letting her wind down before he told her what to do.

Whatever suggestion she came up with in the next few minutes, he discounted. All for valid reasons. When she ran out of ideas, she stared mutinously at him.

Even several feet away from him, she felt his powerful impact. He was physically impressive. He spoke in a quiet, authoritative voice. Even leaning back against the tree, his thumbs tucked loosely into his pants pockets, he was not a man a woman could ignore. And that, she admitted, included herself.

"All right," she said, "if you refuse to be a gardener, a mechanic, a plumber, or anyone else I suggest, then you come up with an idea, smarty. Let's see how your creative juices work."

He was silent a moment, then straightened away from the tree. He looked into her eyes and made a suggestion that had her heart beating like a drum. Her reaction was instantaneous.

"Never!"

CHAPTER THREE

Reid didn't respond, he simply watched her as she went on, as if he was once again waiting for her to run out of steam.

"I may be a writer," Polly said, "but what you're asking requires an imagination even I don't possess. To pull it off, I'd need a lesson in Method acting."

His eyes darkened. "Pitching my butt on a farm with a hostile hostess isn't my idea of a heavenly assignment."

"Don't blame me. I simply can't do as you ask. You're not my type."

"You're not mine either. We're not talking marriage. We're talking about a way for me to protect you and your dotty aunt, who calls her pet milk cow Horace. A cantankerous, obstinate bovine who won't give milk unless she's listening to Guns N' Roses. And then there's Cuddles, short for Barracuda, who is not a fish but a Chihuahua!"

He kicked a stone. It sent a squirrel running. Polly realized then that he had barely been holding his temper in check.

"Why wouldn't I be delighted," he went on, "to be stuck on a farm getting bored to my eyeballs, sleeping under the same roof with an uncooperative teacher- romance novelist, who spouts how she values her time, but who, from the abundant goodness of her heart, wastes a fraction of her hallowed hour devising a stupid list of inviolate rules of behavior? Did you think I'm going to check what's on it, or do you expect me to memorize the damn thing?"

"Are you through?"

"Yes!" he thundered. "Unless I left anything out."

"One thing," she said sweetly, as she bent down to pluck a daisy.

"Which is?"

She twirled the stem beneath his nose. "Horace has a pinup poster of Axl Rose in the barn."

Reid stalked away, letting out a string of curse words that flowed back to her on the wind. He stopped abruptly, his attention caught by something at the base of tree. Following him, Polly saw a pair of possums actively mating.

"Remarkable," Reid muttered. "Wherever you look. What do you add to the water here?"

"Nothing. It's a lovely warm day in June. We're in the country. Nature is taking its course."

"Which reminds me. I omitted one thing. You're the only writer I know who has to experience a role before she writes about it."

Polly's insides were shaking, but she refused to let him see that he'd gotten a rise out of her. "I never said that. I said for me to get into the mood where you're concerned, I'd need a lesson in acting. I could, however, easily picture myself madly in love with Ashley Wilkes."

Reid scowled. "The wimp from *Gone With The Wind?*"

"Don't you dare call Ashley a wimp. He's sensitive, kind, brave, loving. Gentle. I'm sure he read poetry to Melanie."

He hooted. "Wilkes was a wimp. A wimp portrayed by Leslie Howard, a British actor who wore a pained expression on his face throughout the entire movie."

To hear Reid denigrate Ashley Wilkes sorely tested her composure, which already was marginally held together by sheer willpower. And he thought she could pretend to be his lover!

"We better settle this," he said. "What about when you acted in a school play? You used your imagination then, didn't you?"

She regarded him with impassive boredom. "For your information, the last time I acted in a school play, I was nine years old. I played a bunny rabbit. Furthermore, you can't lie about the look a woman gets in her eyes when she's in love. Other women recognize it. Sensitive men do too."

"And that is?"

"A dewy radiance. A softness. Her very soul vibrates. She longs to be alone with the man she loves. One look shared between them across a crowded room is enough to make her tingle with desire. Him, too, I might add."

"Good Lord. Is that the sort of stuff you put in your books?"

"I didn't think you'd understand. For your information it's not stuff. It's romance. It's what women dream of. It's obvious you don't know what I'm talking about, which says a lot about you as a lover. Not that I care. Let me put it this way, lovers are expected to want to make love. A lot. As far as I'm concerned, that lets you out."

"I'd be ecstatic to pretend we're on the verge of a nasty divorce. However, we'd first have to have been married in order for that pleasurable event to occur. May I remind you that your aunt didn't attend our wedding?"

"There is a point to this, is there not?"

"You bet there is. If you insist on letting her come here daily, she'll see me."

Polly frowned, feeling she had to come up with a workable solution. "You can hide."

"No, that's out. Now, I've tried the nice approach. It didn't work. I'm not going away. If you value your aunt's life the way I value mine, I need a logical excuse for her seeing me here. For the last time can you think of an acceptable excuse?"

"No."

"Then use mine."

"I am not enjoying this conversation, Detective Cameron."

"Neither am I, Ms. Sweet. But whether you like it or not, you're going to pretend you're in love with me. In love. The whole sloppy enchilada. Every soap opera you've seen rolled into one. Dewy radiance. Heart palpitations. If your aunt sees us together, you damn well better pretend the sun shines over my wonderful head. Bat your eyelashes like a windmill for all I care."

"I will not!"

He propped his fists on his hips. "Ms. Sweet, if you value all you say you do, then whenever your aunt Martha's around, I strongly suggest you treat me as if I'm your own personal dream Adonis!"

Her mouth open, Polly stared at him. His dark eyes glowered beneath furrowed brows. His mouth was set in a tight line.

Some Adonis!

She smiled a cool, serene smile. "Detective Cameron, you're out of your mind."

"Ms. Sweet, am I giving you the impression I'm happy?"

He looked as if he was ready to strangle her. She lifted her chin. He lifted his. Standoff, she thought. Apparently, whatever game she played, he would too.

"Ms. Sweet, you placed this obstacle in my way. I'll give you one minute to decide. Either your aunt stays away, or you agree to my plan."

"That's not much of a choice."

"I agree." He stormed away.

Polly weighed her options. If Reid Cameron were an ordinary crazy man, she could take her shotgun and shoot him for trespassing, for forcing himself on her, for his deranged behavior. She'd find a reason to hold up in court.

Unfortunately, the Pennsylvania State Police had sent him. He represented law and order. The government. Big G. At his funeral state police from the entire nation would send uniformed mourners, representatives to honor their own. The media would take pictures of their black armbands. Cameron's likeness on TV would taunt her. What support would she have? She knew the board of education wouldn't approve of a kindergarten teacher-murderer.

She stole a glance at him, and a shiver ran through her. He stood on a rise overlooking the river, one leg bent, the foot resting on a rock. His hand was absently rubbing the thigh. From this distance he looked formidable.

She was back to square one, between a rock and a hard place. If she told Martha not to come, she'd distress her aunt. Martha had had a minor heart scare last year. Polly wasn't going to do anything to push it into the major column.

If she visited Martha instead, Martha wouldn't see Horace, and that would distress both her aunt and the cow. With a miserable sense of inevitability, Polly realized that much as she'd like to tell Cameron to take a flying leap off that bluff, she couldn't.

He was right. Arguing was silly if it endangered Martha. And her aunt, bless her heart, thrived on gossip. The telephone grew out of her ear. With her vast circle of friends, each would know within the day that a lawman was camped out in her niece's house. Then, too, what if one of her own friends dropped in?

26

She was about to go to Reid and surrender, so to speak, when he turned and walked back to her.

"Time's up," he said. "Suppose we rehearse."

She blinked. "Rehearse?"

He rubbed the back of his neck. "You pretend I'm Ashley. I'll try fooling myself into thinking you're Scarlett. One kiss ought to do it. Consider it your Method acting lesson."

She laughed outright. "Oh, that's rich. Actually it's sickening. What a line! Let me get this perfectly clear. You want to kiss me—"

He slammed one fist into the other hand. "No. I don't want to kiss you. I want to catch a thief. I want to leave faster than you want me to. But we need to convince your aunt and Grayson I'm here for personal reasons. So consider this your acting lesson, Ms. Sweet. See if you can manage to get the glazed look in your eyes you claim lovers share."

She poked his chest. Her finger hit brick. "Wait! Aunt Martha won't be home until tomorrow evening. You could be gone by then. Grayson might not see me."

"I can't chance it. Not with her, not with Grayson. He's not calling me on the phone to let me know his exact time of arrival. Suppose he sees us?"

"So?"

"I enjoy living. I need a cover too!"

"Don't yell at me. Suppose the worst happens, and I'm stuck with you for a few days? Then how do I explain your sleeping here to my aunt?"

He shrugged. "Let her think we're resuming an old love affair. Or let her think I'm a new man in your life. I don't care what you tell her as long as you make it convincing."

Polly muttered an impolite word under her breath. "All right. Get it over with."

Reid put his hands on her shoulders. She puckered her lips, squeezed her eyes shut, and shuddered. "What are you doing?"

Her eyes popped open. He'd cocked his head and was frowning with puzzlement.

"Getting ready," she said tartly.

His mouth pulled into a sour line to match hers. "Getting ready? How do you expect me to pretend you're Scarlett when you purse your lips like some damn fish? And what's with this shivering

27

and scrunching your eyes? Is that how you kiss a man?"

She didn't bother to respond. Anxious to get it over with, she raised up on tiptoes, brushed her lips across his cheek, and stepped back.

"There," she said. "The Method acting class is over. Thank you for your edifying lesson. I've never had a more illuminating kiss, or one that left me hotter. Now, if you'll excuse me, Detective Cameron, it's nearing dinner. I'm eating light tonight. A tuna sandwich and iced tea. I don't suppose you want a sandwich?"

Without waiting for his answer, she whipped off in the other direction. She hadn't gotten ten steps before his ominous, silky voice rang out.

"Aren't you forgetting something, Ms. Sweet?"

She swiveled. "Sorry. What kind of bread do you like?"

"Come back here. We're not through."

"Really?" she said airily. "I am."

"Stop acting as if you're writing a scene for your book. I'm serious." He walked toward her, stopping less than two feet away. "You said a woman gets a certain look in her eyes. Whatever it is, you look the same as you did before. You wouldn't fool anyone into thinking we're lovers."

She could feel his sharp eyes issue a challenge. Allowing Martha to visit was her idea. Now he was daring her to go through with their agreed-upon plan.

There was a hint of coiled restraint about the way he stood, his feet apart, his hands at his waist, pushing his jacket back. There wasn't an ounce of fat on his lanky frame. He was a big man, in height and, she suspected, in strength. He also was obviously a man used to getting his way.

She blew a lock of hair from her face. "Why do we need to rehearse? If Grayson comes here, I guarantee you I won't be thinking about a lover. The look on my face will be fright."

Reid raised his head skyward as if willing God to give him strength to deal with her.

"But," he said, "this still leaves us with Aunt Martha's daily visit. Unless you tell her to keep away, you have to convince your aunt we're lovers. Which means you need another lesson. I hope this is the last."

Before Polly registered his eyes were hotter than coals, before she could utter a whimper of protest, he yanked her to him, cradled her head so that she couldn't move, and kissed her. She opened her mouth to demand he stop, but he boldly swept his tongue inside, and with a ruthless possession, explored her mouth.

Polly was in shock. His warm breath mingled with hers. Spreading his legs a bit, he aligned their bodies, then he placed his hands on her hips, bringing her forward. Aware of all of him, she knew she should slap his face, or lift her knee for a well-aimed jab, but she couldn't. Instead, she kissed him back.

Texture and taste melded. His hands slid over her buttocks, held her to him. Then he suddenly lifted his head. His astonished breath hissed from him, as if he too, were experiencing an instant shock.

"Damn," he muttered, shaking his head slowly. "Ms. Sweet, you're one hell of a big surprise. Who expected this?"

She tried to speak, but she didn't know what to say. He didn't give her the chance anyhow. He lowered his head and began kissing her again, pressing his hips forward at the same time.

The heady kiss sent liquid heat coursing through her to the pit of her stomach. Surprise. He'd called her a surprise. That was mild compared to how she felt about him at that moment. Her heart did a little flip-flop, then a series of somersaults.

Slipping her hands around his neck, she threaded her fingers through his thick hair. She was aware of the steady beating of his heart and knew the second its speed matched hers. She clung to him, searching her brain for the perfect excuse to be answering his kisses.

Research, she thought disjointedly. The rational idea of gathering research for her romance books settled her mind as she arched her neck provocatively. He growled low in his throat, then kissed her neck. When she purred, he left a hot trail of kisses on her face, her eyes, her cheeks. His hands roamed from hip to rib cage, then downward to touch and knead the bare flesh of her thighs, as if assuring himself of her feminine curves.

Polly was flabbergasted by the amount of research she was getting for her novels. Detective Cameron kissed the way the hero of a hot romance book should kiss. He pulled her roughly to him and planted a tantalizing kiss on the sensitive spot at the base of her throat. For herself, she would always prefer a tamer man, a caring man who asked, never a macho type who took. But, she thought, pulling Reid's head back up for another soul-shattering kiss, if this man succeeded in sending poor Ashley to second place this fast, it proved just how paltry her love scenes had been. No wonder she'd received five rejection letters. Each editor had said her love scenes needed more punch.

She mated her tongue with his. She molded her body to his. Excusing her wanton behavior, she promised to describe the stirring sensation in her next love scene. She wiggled closer, marveling at the way his muscular arms enfolded her. At the way his thighs cradled her. At the way his hard body quivered with life. How wonderful for the opportunity to investigate Reid Cameron's masterful method of seduction. All in the name of gathering research.

Reid wasn't gathering anything in the name of research. He was hoarding moments of exquisite, unexpected pleasure. Somewhere in his fogged-up brain, his conscience reared up to mock him. He knew damned well what had prompted him to silence her sassy mouth. She had driven him up the wall, then refused to listen to reason. With her nonsense about needing a Method acting lesson, he'd decided to show her.

Only his scheme had backfired. Who was giving whom the lesson? He wasn't kissing her to save old aunt what's her name's life in case she dropped in when Grayson made his appearance. He wasn't even kissing her to fool Grayson or the aunt into thinking he was her lover. He was kissing Polly Sweet for purely selfish reasons.

One he could get fired for in a shot.

Hell! He deserved to be fired for it.

He kissed her incredible mouth with a ferocity that didn't begin to calm his desire. He now knew how it felt to be hit by a Mack truck speeding out of control down a steep incline.

And speeding out of control was exactly what was happening to him. Exerting more willpower than he'd thought he'd need, he softened the kiss. It was light and heady and, oddly, much more potent. Knowing he had to stop now or let nature take its course, he reluctantly ended the kiss. Cradling her face in his hands, he gazed down at her.

Her breathing was ragged, and her cheeks were flushed with passion. She dropped her hands from his neck and opened her eyes. They were languorous, dewy, and she stared at him as if she were waiting for him to explain the mind-boggling kisses they'd shared.

His gaze dropped to her lips. They were swollen from his kisses, and as he watched, she dragged her tongue across them. He ruthlessly suppressed the hot urges of his body. A man knew when a woman's needs matched his. He and his reluctant pupil would be good together. Better than good. Dynamite. How dare she do this to him? He was stunned by the craving he felt. He knew instinctively that on some deep level they were connected. Almost as if their meeting had been preordained.

Stop! Warning bells rang in his head. The wisest—the only acceptable—course of action for him was to remain focused on his mission. Get in. Get out. Minimize risks. Leave no emotional trails. He steeled himself against temptation, against her beckoning rosebud lips.

Hiding his internal struggle, he slapped a grin on his face.

"I think you've got the dewy look you were aiming for. If I meet your aunt Martha, remember what we did to get it there. It's on your head if she knows too much."

Polly flinched, the sensual haze that surrounded her shattered by his callous words. Her voice trembled, but she managed to speak through her humiliation.

"Detective Cameron, I had my own reason for kissing you back. I was gathering research for my book."

His grin only broadened. "I'm sure we could research ourselves into having a great time with a mattress beneath us, but I'm not here to help you with your writing. I'll have tuna on rye. If you don't have rye, white's fine. Not too much mayo, I'm watching my figure."

Berating herself, she spun on her heels, putting as much distance between them as fast as humanly possible. She didn't want him seeing the tears brimming in her eyes. Idiot! she scolded herself. Was her life so barren, she would kiss a man she didn't like?

She fled to the pasture. Horace lifted her head, mooing as Polly approached. "Come on, girl. It's lovely outside, and you want to stay here, but I'm stuck with unwanted guests, so in you go."

Horace didn't care for her excuse. Polly coaxed the cow into the barn, leading her past the wooden barrels she'd set around to catch the water from the leaky roof.

Cuddles lay snoring on a tiny mound of hay. The dog and cow were great friends, and Cuddles often trotted into the barn to visit Horace. But he disliked the pasture, so he would sleep inside while Horace was out. Polly lifted the sleeping dog up in her arms. In a few minutes the portable radio on the shelf would click on for the evening Guns N' Roses show. That would settle Horace down for the night. She'd tried the Grateful Dead and Bon Jovi, but Horace was strictly a Rose fan.

Cuddles snuggled in her arms. Routines, she thought, kissing his soft neck. Nice, dependable routines. Far better for her emotional well-being than Reid Cameron coaxing a lovesick look into her eyes by kissing the socks off her.

She carried the dog inside the house and put him in the basket she kept for him in the laundry room. Glancing at her watch, she saw it was almost six o'clock. Good grief! Where had the day gone?

She had just entered the kitchen to make dinner when she heard a car out front. Walking to the front door, she saw a tall blond woman getting out of a gray station wagon. She wore tan slacks and an attractive cotton sweater.

Stepping outside, Polly introduced herself, thinking Reid's partner was one of the prettiest women she'd ever seen.

Fran smiled warmly at her. "I'm Fran Mohr, Reid's partner. I'm sure he's explained the operation. You can feel safe with us. We're a good team."

"He mentioned it."

"I jabber. He's the strong, silent type, but we're both dedicated to protecting you."

"What a great place," Fran went on, admiring the two-story white farmhouse. The shutters were Wedgwood blue, and brass carriage lamps hung on either side of the tall oak door. A wide veranda ran along the front of the house, and sitting on it were redwood tubs of showy white, red, yellow, and purple petunias and blue-and-white wicker rockers.

"You have a fabulous view of the Allegheny Mountains," Fran added. "It's so quiet, too, not like Pittsburgh, where I live." A smile lit her warm hazel eyes. "I hope you don't mind my sharing your bedroom. It will only be for a short while."

She turned back to the car. "I stopped at the supermarket, and I took a chance that you own a large refrigerator. We don't want you to worry about feeding us. We'll try not to disturb you too much.

We'll clean up, make our beds, make sure there's no hairs in the bathroom sink."

On her first trip into the kitchen toting the bags of food Fran had bought, Polly snatched the list of rules she'd made off the refrigerator and tossed it into the garbage pail.

"Have you and Detective Cameron been partners long?" she asked when she and Fran had finished carrying in the groceries.

"About two years. He's terrific, really wonderful. I trust him with my life. The women in the office are nuts about him. I'm regularly pestered to put in a good word for them."

"Do you?" Polly asked, curious as to the extent of their relationship.

"No. Reid and I prefer keeping our private lives separate from work. Did he tell you I'm going to be working on another case until we know Grayson's nearby?"

"Yes," Polly replied. Apparently Fran and her partner were a hot item, which made his kissing her an awful thing to do.

"I bought a variety of foods," Fran said as she started unloading the bags. "I'm a good cook. Ask Reid. If you like, I'll make dinner tonight."

"Be my guest, although I was just going to have a tuna fish sandwich. You will be here at night, won't you?"

"Of course. And before it gets dark tonight, I'd like to familiarize myself with your house and grounds." Fran's bubbly nature was contagious, and Polly quickly decided she liked her. While Fran chatted, she opened two cans of tuna and chopped some celery, then let Fran take over while she made iced tea.

"I add a dash of relish for zest," Fran said. "Mustard or lemon works as well. The trick is to control the amount. Reid prefers his tuna with lemon."

Fran sliced a lemon. "He's okay in the kitchen, but I'm better. Some things we like to do together." Polly easily imagined what those things were. It was clear the two maintained a close, perhaps intimate, relationship. With dinner under control she excused herself and went into the den to shut off her computer. When she looked up, Reid was lounging casually against the jamb.

She felt a tremor of excitement, as if he were dwarfing the room with his size, pulling her toward him. "Your partner is very nice."

"I'm glad you like her."

"I'm sure you do too."

He stared at Polly's mouth. "I do, very much. She's a highly capable professional. She has a wonderful sense of humor. Best of all, she's agreeable."

"She's so agreeable, she's fixing your tuna the way you like it."

"How's that?" he asked.

His unruffled demeanor strained hers. "With lemon."

"Tell me, Ms. Sweet, what would you have put in my tuna?"

"Poison."

He chuckled. "I thought so."

"Detective Cameron, are you deliberately trying to get my goat?"

A half-grin lifted one corner of his mouth. "Is that what I'm doing?"

"You're trying to."

"Am I succeeding?"

"Of course not!"

"Did you enjoy the kiss?"

Very much. Too much. "Don't be silly!"

"It bothers me to say I did."

"Then consider it research. I am."

He scowled. "So that's what you're still telling yourself?"

She swallowed. "Naturally. What else could it be?"

"Beats me." Suddenly his scowl switched to a smile. "But I'm a true proponent of educational research." He pushed away from the doorjamb and started toward her. Slowly and boldly, his gaze slid down over her body, before rising again and focusing on her eyes with a sizzling look.

"So, Ms. Sweet," he drawled, "let's see if practice makes perfect. In the name of research. Naturally."

CHAPTER FOUR

Reid kicked the door shut.

Polly gulped. "This is my sanctuary. I'd appreciate it if you'd knock first."

"I will. Next time."

"See that—"

He cupped her face. "Next time." His kiss silenced her. His mouth was hotter, wetter, a more deliberate sensual trap than before.

She was shaking when he released her.

"Why did you do that?" she demanded.

"I wanted to see if kissing you elicited the same response it had before. It did. I'm beginning to get used to that look in your eyes. Coming?" he asked, opening the door.

She pushed past him in a regal huff. He was vile, she thought, fuming. Why had she responded to his kiss a second time? More research, she told herself, but how dare he bait her? She was getting angrier by the second. She swore she wouldn't give him the satisfaction of letting him know how much he bothered her. Especially with Fran waiting.

In the kitchen Reid greeted Fran warmly. He then led her toward the front of the house, leaving Polly alone for a long while. She presumed they were either updating each other on their cases, or they were sharing an extended kiss hello. Damn him. He was alarmingly sexy. Little wonder the women in his office panted for him. But not her. She was on to him. A man like him could never be for her.

35

If it weren't for her need to gather research for her novels, she would never be able to explain her outrageous behavior. In all her life she had never acted so brazenly. On the other hand, their fiery kisses didn't appear to have affected him. She supposed she ought to be grateful he hadn't made a big deal out of it. If he had, he would have made it impossible for her to talk to him, let alone have him sleep in her home.

Her friends Grace, Joan, and Lonni would be amazed if they knew what had transpired between her and the state trooper. She'd never tell them, though. They couldn't understand her fixation with Ashley Wilkes instead of Rhett Butler.

"What does that placid man do for your juices?" they asked.

Not much, Polly realized. She had been hot for the lawman. Annoyed at the thought, she filled a glass with cold water and was finishing drinking it just as he strolled back into the kitchen.

"Are you all right?" he asked, leaning close to her. "Your face is flushed."

"I'm fine. Let's eat."

The three sat at the kitchen table, Reid across from her. "I asked Fran's opinion about your bridge. She agrees with me. It needs to be checked."

"My bridge is sturdy, Detective Cameron. I'm certain what you both heard are normal creaks from expansion and contraction. Wood breathes."

"I'll check it anyway," Reid said.

Polly didn't answer, using the excuse of eating as a reason to remain quiet. She was a bundle of nerves. More than once, she caught Reid's hawk like gaze on her, and she was thankful when Fran drew her into the conversation. A half hour of pleasant conversation flew by as Fran talked about her Victorian doll collection and Polly recounted several stories about her students' funnier antics.

"I could never be a teacher," Fran said.

"I love kids. I could never be a police officer."

"Fran," Reid said, "Ms. Sweet disapproves of our tactics."

Polly turned to Reid. Her heart was beating so loud, it was a wonder he couldn't hear it, or that Fran didn't sense the tension between them.

"Your tactics, Detective Cameron. I can't judge anyone else's in the Pennsylvania State Police, only yours."

His eyes narrowed. "Is that so? Then you ought to know that sometimes my tactics switch. Sometimes they depend on the hand I'm dealt."

"Sometimes," she said, "the game is so new, the rules are hard to understand."

He leaned forward. "That's why it's better to discuss the rules in a civilized manner. Then again, things can get out of hand when people allow their emotions to get in the way."

Polly grimaced. "Which should remind a woman to stay on guard, lest an unwelcome situation arises. Wouldn't you agree?"

"Definitely. Although sometimes a woman isn't honest about her feelings. When she lets go, it stuns her. The man too."

Fran's gaze was shifting from one to the other. "What's going on?" she asked. "Am I missing something I should know?"

Polly dropped a clenched hand from the table to her lap. With effort she broke eye contact with Reid and looked at Fran.

"What Detective Cameron means, Fran, is that when he first explained his reason for coming here, I didn't believe him. I asked him to leave. Repeatedly."

Fran turned to Reid, eyebrows raised. "That's new for you, isn't it, Reid? Most women take what you say as the gospel."

"Not Ms. Sweet."

"I wasn't gracious," Polly continued. "I resented him interfering with my work. I still do. He has a way of forcing his opinions on a person. My summer break is very important to me. It's a time when I can write without interruption. But," she sighed resignedly, "now that I understand he won't leave without arresting Grayson, I'll do whatever I can to help."

Fran nodded. "From your perspective I can understand our presence is difficult to accept."

"I don't mean you, Fran." She flashed an angry look at Reid. "Detective Cameron came into my den before dinner to remind me of my role."

Fran dabbed her mouth with her napkin. "As long as we're going to be together for a while, shouldn't you two call each other by first names?"

"That's fine with me, Polly," Reid said. "Especially under the circumstances."

Polly inclined her head. Once again, she was stuck between a rock and a hard place. If she refused, Fran would become suspicious. "Me too, Reid."

Reid scowled as Polly angled her chair away from the table, presenting him with her profile. She folded her arms over her chest, which only made him more aware of her breasts, and crossed one leg over the other. Despite himself, his gaze fixed on the smooth bare flesh of her thigh. How dare she pretend he didn't exist? Pretend that kiss in the den hadn't been dynamite!

He suppressed a wild urge to lift her from her chair and give her a firm talking-to. He'd invested a lot of hard work and many years building his career. He comforted himself that in a week or two, he'd forget he met her.

Turning to Fran, he told her about Polly's aunt. By the time Fran heard the list of her interests, learned she lived across the road and stopped by daily, she grew concerned.

"Don't worry," Reid said. "Polly and I worked it out. To minimize the risk, and should Grayson slip through our net and see Polly with me, we're going to pretend we're involved."

"In what?" Fran asked.

"A romance."

Fran choked politely. "You two?" She looked at them both with obvious doubt. "Do you think it will work?"

Reid shrugged. "It's the only gimmick I could come up with that might keep her aunt from gossiping that the police are staying here."

"I'm hoping Grayson comes and goes before my aunt returns tomorrow," Polly said.

"It's novel, I must say. What made you think of that, Reid?"

"I got the idea from the romance book Polly's writing."

Fran turned to Polly. "If you have to be convincing, do you think you can pull this off?"

"What Fran is asking," Reid said, his tone casual, "is, are you willing to kiss me in front of your aunt?"

Polly stood and carried her dishes to the sink. It took all her willpower not to smash them, to respond in a calm voice.

"Only if absolutely necessary, and only if you remember it's an act."

"Naturally."

He managed to fill that one word with all sorts of innuendo, and she turned to glare at him. Her attention was caught, however, by Cuddles padding into the kitchen, heading straight for Reid.

"Watch out!" she said. "My dog's right under your foot."

Reid's head shot down. "What the——?"

Cuddles was short-coated, with overly large ears, soulful chocolate-brown eyes, and a little tail that spun like a top. The dog climbed onto Reid's sneaker, heaved a sigh from its exertions, then lifted his face to stare at Reid.

Reid threw back his head and roared. "I take it this is your guard dog."

Polly snatched Cuddles from Reid's shoe. She held the dog high, giving it a playful shake. "Meet Barracuda. Cuddles, for short. The way he acts, you can see why we call him Cuddles."

She explained to Fran that her aunt had presented him as a watchdog. "Translated, that means his mother had another litter. Cuddles was jealous, so I inherited him."

She handed the wiggling dog over to Reid. It promptly transferred its affection, lavishly licking his face. Reid ducked when it aimed its tongue at his mouth.

"Some watchdog," he said. "I noticed that you keep your doors unlocked. You invite burglars, then you expect this pip-squeak to protect you."

Cuddles aimed another lick. Reid chuckled and scratched the dog's warm belly, setting off another round of mad tail wagging.

Polly smiled as she watched. When Reid handed the dog back to her, their eyes met. They both had been laughing at Cuddles' antics, but now their smiles vanished. As Reid gazed at her speculatively, she watched the intriguing play of emotions on his face. Her cheeks warmed, and she was the first to break their eye contact.

She cleared her throat. "Come on, Cuddles, down you go."

Reid cleared the rest of the dishes from the table. He and Fran loaded the dishwasher while Polly wiped off the counters and table.

"Thanks for the meal," he said to Polly. "Fran, you're handling the checkbook. Please compensate Polly for whatever we use. She shouldn't pay the state's bill."

"It's okay," Polly said. "Fran brought groceries."

Reid nodded. "Now that we've got that settled." He opened the back door. "Polly, I'd like to talk with you, please."

She heard the change in his voice. He was asking, not demanding. Still, she hesitated. "Can't it wait? I planned to work for a while, to make up for lost time."

He held out his hand. "Please."

When she couldn't think of another reason to delay, she followed him outside.

They walked across the yard to where a small bench sat beneath an oak tree. They both sat, their shoulders touching. Polly heard him sigh, then he picked up her hand, almost as if he didn't want to but was afraid she'd bolt otherwise.

"Polly, there's something I want to say to you, without Fran hearing."

She was acutely conscious of her hand in his, of his hard thigh pressing her bare leg.

"I didn't mean to step out of line. We need to discuss that kiss if we're going to work together." His grip tightened.

"I'd rather not."

He nodded. "Then I will. I don't push myself on women. Also, I appreciate how much your writing means to you. If I've given you the wrong impression, I'm sorry."

She looked at him and saw he was serious.

"I meant what I said about your dad's talent too," he added. "It wasn't a ploy to get you to cooperate with me."

She smiled and relaxed back on the bench. It was nice, she decided, holding hands with him. Not threatening in the least. "I know. You couldn't hide what I saw in your eyes, heard in your voice when you spoke about his paintings."

"Then I'm not all bad?" he teased.

"No." He was dangerous, she thought, feeling heat emanating from his body. Dangerous, but not bad.

"Truce? Again?"

She looked up at him, surprised to see his head so close to hers. If she moved just an inch this way, and he moved just an inch that way, their lips would meet. She was tempted, strongly tempted, to move that inch, but her common sense reasserted itself just in time.

"Truce," she murmured, drawing back from him. "I hope you catch Grayson," she added.

"We will. It's only a question of time."

They sat in silence for several minutes, enjoying the evening quiet, then he asked, "Do you like living alone?"

"I'm never totally alone. I have my job, which keeps me busy, my aunt, and my animals."

Reid studied her. He could smell a non-answer a mile away. He wondered about her love life, but held his counsel. If he opened that can of worms, he'd lose her goodwill, which, he realized, he wanted very much.

"Sitting here," he said, "it's hard to visualize the ugly underbelly of life that I see all the time. It's easy to see why living in the country suits you."

"Did you always want to be in law enforcement?"

"Yes, for the present. No, for the long term. I have a law degree. When I tire of this, I'll put it to good use."

She nodded. "What does Fran think about your plans? It affects her too."

He shrugged. "I guess Frannie's supportive."

"You don't know?"

Polly was shocked. If she were intimately involved with Reid, she'd give him her wholehearted support in starting a law practice. Surely a life outside of the line of fire was preferable to packing a gun, living in constant danger. Then again, Fran had chosen the same profession as Reid.

"I'm sure she's supportive," Reid said. "Fran's a terrific woman."

Polly told herself it made no sense to get involved in his and Fran's private affairs. He'd apologized for any misinterpretation about his kiss, which ended it as far as she was concerned.

She stood abruptly. "If that's all you wanted to talk about, I'll leave you and Fran to do whatever you do."

He walked alongside her to the house. "Don't worry," he said, apparently interpreting her sudden mood shift as concern about Grayson. "I won't let anything happen to you."

Inside the house Polly went straight to her den, but she couldn't concentrate on her writing. After an hour of fiddling, she called it a night.

She found Fran and Reid playing a fast game of double solitaire in the living room. The TV was on. Cuddles sat on Reid's lap, acting as if he owned Reid. Polly joined them. When the *Tonight* program ended, they decided to go to bed.

Polly invited Fran to use the bathroom first, then Reid. Fran didn't loiter. Within minutes she was back in Polly's bedroom, saying good night as she crawled into her bed.

Polly undressed. Wearing her pink short nightgown, she waited for what she thought was a decent length of time. Not hearing Reid, she padded into the bathroom, washed her face and brushed her teeth, and walked back out into the hall.

And straight into Reid. His shirt was open, giving her a free view of his broad chest. As his gaze flashed over her body, her nerve endings flashed danger signals. Thinking she was safe, she hadn't bothered with her robe. It hung in her closet, but the closet door squealed, and she hadn't wanted to disturb Fran. She should have, she thought as she saw Reid's eyes darken with passion. And she really wished he hadn't unbuttoned his shirt.

"Excuse me," she said, flustered. The hallway suddenly seemed steamy, close. She moistened her lips. "My robe... Fran's sleeping. The closet door squeaks, and I didn't want to disturb her. I thought you were through in the bathroom."

"I was waiting for you to finish first."

"Oh. Well, I'm done. Good night."

As if rooted to the spot, each waited for the other to make the first move. As if in slow motion, Reid reached out and lifted a lock of her hair, letting it sift through his fingers. She held her breath.

His hand lowered to her shoulder, almost completely bared by the scoop neck of her nightgown. The feel of his warm skin on hers jolted her back to reality. And reality was that he would only be in her home for a few days while he did his job.

"Please let me pass," she said. "We should get a good night's sleep."

Nodding, he stepped back. "Good night, Polly. Sweet dreams."

She smiled fleetingly at the small joke he'd made with her name, then slipped around him, heading for her bedroom. As she shut her door, she wondered if she'd only imagined him whispering after her, "For my dreams will certainly be sweet."

As early as Polly rose to milk Horace, she found Fran's bed empty, the aroma of coffee wafting up the stairs. She dressed quickly in shorts and a sleeveless blouse and went downstairs to the kitchen.

Reid was sitting on a chair, with Cuddles riding on his shoe.

"Good morning," Reid said. "How did you sleep?"

"Like a log. Where's Fran?"

He put Cuddles on the floor and stood. "She's out walking. And I can tell you didn't sleep any better than I did."

His voice sounded so intimate, it quickened her heartbeat. "Then why did you ask?"

"I wanted to see if you're as truthful as I am. You're not."

Their eyes met and held. Goose bumps rose on her flesh. She had the answer to the tormenting question that had kept her up long into the night. She hadn't imagined the strong sexual pull between them. If she just steered clear of him, she told herself, everything would be fine.

She asked what he wanted for breakfast, but he said breakfast was on him.

"We're going out?" she asked, surprised.

"No, I'm on duty. I'm the official breakfast cook."

The specter of Grayson loomed before her.

"Yes, of course," she said, wishing her emotions weren't running so high, wishing he wouldn't watch her so intently. "I'd love whatever you're fixing. Should we wait for Fran? I'm lucky the rain held up last night. It should help dry out the barn before the predicted deluge."

She turned away in embarrassment as Reid grinned at her. She'd never babbled in her life. What was it about this man that made her act so out of character?

Deciding a tactical retreat was in order, she headed for the barn to milk Horace.

During breakfast Fran reported that she had phoned headquarters. Grayson wasn't expected to show up until Monday. They'd learned from the tap on his phone that he'd decided to spend the weekend in Ohio at his girlfriend's.

Polly treated the news as a mixed bag. It meant another night with Reid sleeping in the next bedroom, and her aunt would definitely meet him.

After they'd cleaned up the breakfast dishes, Reid walked to the back door. He paused there, his hand on the knob, and casually said to Polly, "I'm sorry about making you change your plans again today. I'd like to search the barn for the jewels. Could you meet me there in, say, half an hour?"

She was stunned, and she stared at the screen door for a full minute after he'd left. She'd planned on writing that day. She hadn't planned on searching the barn with Reid. Was he crazy? Even if she hadn't anticipated finishing the love scene he'd interrupted the day before, the barn was the last place she wanted to be with him. Barns had haylofts, and she knew what the hero in her book would do with the heroine in a hayloft.

Alarmed, she ran outside and caught up with him. "I don't see why I should poke around the hayloft too. Maybe you have nothing else to do, but I do. Doesn't my work count?"

He kept walking. There was no use arguing with him. He didn't put her romance novel on an equal par with his work. Men! she thought. Had she been writing a thesis on devious-minded criminals, or just plain devious-minded men, or one stubborn Pennsylvania state trooper whose initials were R.C., she bet she'd get his serious attention.

"Reid, did you hear me?"

He stopped and faced her. "Who wouldn't? I know what you're thinking, but you're way off base. I thought we cleared everything up last night."

She clenched and unclenched her fists, mumbled under her breath, then opened her mouth.

"Don't say it," he told her, walking back to her. "You'll do me an enormous favor if you stopped grumbling. Think ahead to the time when Fran and I will be gone. It'll come sooner than you realize. In the meantime, please accept the fact that we're tied to each other for the duration. And don't bother telling me you'd rather be tied to Ashley Wilkes. I already know that." He glanced behind her toward the house. "And if you're smart, you'll keep from flying off the handle with me in front of Fran. Otherwise, she'll think there's something going on between us."

Polly pulled herself up tall. The insufferable man was too blasted close. "We wouldn't want that, would we? Not considering your relationship with Fran."

"Fran? Fran Mohr?" His brows and his voice rose.

Exasperated, she said, "How many Frans do you know? Yes, Fran Mohr."

He set his hands on his hops. "Frannie's a friend and a

partner."

"She's your—your… girlfriend."

If possible, his eyebrows rose even higher. "Did she tell you that?"

"Not in so many words. She admitted she likes working with you more than any man she knows."

Reid grinned. The tension eased off his shoulders. Polly had the distinct impression she was providing his morning's entertainment.

"Fran Mohr is a fine woman," he said. "A true professional. I hate to bust your romance novelist's plot line, but I'm serving as best man at her wedding next month. She's marrying a buddy of mine, Tom Meredith. Frannie thinks everyone should be married. I don't. Her wedding is as close to the altar as I care to get."

He wasn't marrying Fran. It pleased her to know he hadn't come on to her while in love with another woman. "Scared of women?" she teased.

He rested his hands on her shoulders and gave her a smile so full of blatant sex appeal, it could light a city. His gaze drifted to her lips. "Last night, Polly, did I give you the impression I'm scared of you?"

"Don't bring up last night. If you're trying to earn points as the macho man of the century, I'll give you five. Which doesn't stop me from thinking you're afraid of a commitment."

His smile switched to a scowl. The air between them was ripe with sexual tension. Her eyes blazed, her lips beckoned. Cursed with knowing her taste, he wanted to kiss the smirk off her ruby-red lips.

"Put it this way," he said, his tone stretched taut as a guy wire. "When I want unnecessary prattle, I'll find a woman like you and get married!"

She hooted, shrugging his hands off her shoulders. "Don't flatter yourself. I wouldn't marry a cynical cop like you if you were the last man on earth."

He gave a harsh, humorless laugh. "Don't push me, Polly. Get your kicks writing your romance novel."

"If you're implying writing romance fills my lonely life, you're wrong. I have a date tonight."

That was a lie. She didn't have a date. But if she had to sit in the nearby town's one movie theater and see the picture three times, she'd do it, anything rather than let Reid think she hid from life behind her computer.

"Break your date. You're staying here."

"I will not!"

He shoved his hands into his pockets. "What were you going to do?"

"Horizontally or vertically?" she asked sweetly. His glare became frigid, and she decided it would be wise to stop the teasing.

"Our usual," she said. "Dining and dancing."

"Where?"

"Wherever we please. We don't live in the boondocks. There are places in town. What kind of inquisition is this?"

"You're right," he said. "I apologize. Nevertheless, you're well known in the community. Therefore, the chances are fairly high you'll be recognized. Won't it look odd if you're falling all over one man while you're in love with another?"

"But I'm not in love," she said, giving him a sincere but baffled look.

He trailed his thumb across her lower lip. She slapped his hand away. His mouth twisted in a wry smile.

"So excitable," he murmured. "Have you forgotten so soon? You're madly in love with me. And don't tell me you didn't feel what I did when we kissed, because I know better."

Her eyes widened in shock at his arrogance. He just smiled at her. "I'll try to control myself when we get up to the hayloft," he said.

She half expected him to kiss her again, but he didn't. She was furious with herself for feeling disappointed. It didn't take a rocket scientist to know that whatever she might think of him personally, her body wasn't listening.

As she walked beside him to the barn, she decided that sparring with Reid Cameron was a no-win fight. The best thing to do was help him find the damn jewels, so he would leave her alone.

Midway to the barn, she heard the radio playing. Stopping, she glanced at her watch and frowned.

Reid wheeled around. "What's wrong?"

She bit her lip. "It's odd. I'm positive I reset the timer this morning. I left Horace in the barn after I milked her so she could hear her program. The station moved it up an hour. That's why I changed the timer, but the radio should have shut off by now."

Reid's gaze swept the grounds, taking in the barn, the field, and following the line of fence posts. Nothing struck him as out of the ordinary, and he was confident that the surveillance team's information about Grayson being in Ohio was accurate. He looked back at Polly. "You probably set it wrong."

"I guess," she muttered. She walked alongside him for a few steps, then grabbed his hand. "Ohmigod! I just thought of a horrible reason why the radio is on. Grayson might be in the barn. It's conceivable he switched off the radio while we were eating breakfast. Horace would get so upset she'd make a racket. Grayson would turn the radio back on rather than chance our hearing Horace's fussing."

Reid marveled at her accurate deductions, but he was more concerned at calming her than worrying about Grayson.

"I doubt if he's in the barn. You heard Fran say he's miles away, but just to make sure, I'll check. You walk, don't run, back to the house. Tell Fran what's going on."

Panic seized her. "I can't."

He searched her face. He could take her anger at him—he'd asked for it, pushing her the way he had—but fear was another thing. Tenderness welled up in him. He hated Grayson for putting fear in her eyes.

"I'll walk you back."

"No." She shook her head. "It's not that."

"Then what is it?" he asked gently.

"You might get hurt."

He smiled, and something in his heart softened. She sassed him, could be a spitfire, until she thought he was in danger. "I promise I'll do my best to stay in one piece."

She shook her head, sending her hair in a swirl. Her blue eyes were enormous. It was all he could do not to pull her into his arms and hold her tight. Other than his mother, he couldn't think of a woman who'd ever been afraid for him. It was a potent feeling, one that touched him more deeply than their kisses the day before. He realized he was entering dangerous territory, but before he could pull back, emotionally and physically, she spoke again.

"You mentioned a policeman who stopped a bullet meant for a woman."

"So?" he asked carefully.

Her lower lip quivered. "Don't you see; I don't want that

47

happening to you. True, you sometimes irritate me, and I wish you weren't here, but you are. If I suddenly leave now, and if Grayson's in the barn spying on us, he'll wonder why I've gone back to the house. We must not raise his suspicions. Look at you. It's a very warm day, and you're wearing a jacket. I'm in shorts and a top. Wouldn't you wonder about you if you were Grayson?"

She was watching him with an anxious appeal, and her tone of voice, the muscles working in her jaw, alerted him. He didn't know her well, but he did know that if she broke down and cried, he'd have his hands full. He was no good with crying women. The last time he'd consoled a sobbing woman, she'd formed the mistaken idea be came with the comfort. The time after that, when he hadn't offered a woman his shoulder, he'd felt like a louse afterward. He'd have to halt Polly's possible tears before they got started.

"Grayson's under constant surveillance," he said, trying to sound calm and logical. "I'd know if he was here."

"Could you guarantee me that? Can you?" she demanded.

He hesitated, then admitted, "Anything's possible."

"There, you see! You're ready to chance walking into the barn like a lamb to slaughter. What is it with you macho men? Don't you realize he could shoot you? You're unfair. You barge into my life, order me around, and now you could get killed on my property! Under my nose!"

He sighed. "I don't plan on getting killed."

She waved aside his objection. "It's ghastly. Think of the legacy you'd leave. Imagine how I would feel if I see your blood splattered on the ground. My ground. How do you think I'd feel if I had done nothing to prevent it?"

His hand came up to cup her cheek. "How would you feel?" he asked softly.

"I'd be a basket case. You'd ruin my life. Forever. I'd have unbearable nightmares. I probably wouldn't be able to hold on to my job, let alone finish my book. All because of your selfishness. Is that fair? Heck, I'm scared of thunder. When it gets too loud, I yank the covers over my head. I'm a certified coward. If I watch you walk to your death, I'd have to sell the family farm. The memories would be too painful. And then what would happen to Aunt Martha? Not to mention Horace and Cuddles. Well, Cuddles I could take with me, but a cow? Hardly."

Reid suspected she was winding up to some grand finale. He hated to interrupt, but he did. "Aren't you jumping to conclusions?"

She gripped his arm. "Please! We need to set the scene. Both of us."

He exhaled slowly. No point stopping her when she was on a roll. He'd never seen a woman more hell-bent on having her say. "Okay. How should we go about it?"

Encouraged, she eased her death grip, but not by much. "Simple. We outsmart him."

"How?"

"Imagine you're writing a thriller or directing a movie."

Golden sunlight shimmered in her hair. Her eyes were fired with passion. Pity, he thought, it wasn't for him.

"At the rate we're going," he said, "I'm having a hard time remembering I'm a cop."

Missing the humor and intent on advancing her theory, she said, "If Grayson sees us out here, he's going to feel like a cornered cat. He'll probably be trigger-happy. We need to give him time for his adrenaline to slow down."

Reid saw she was dead serious. Her voice was trembling, her chin quivered, but she was bravely trying to cover her fears. He casually took her hand, pressing one finger over the pulse in her wrist. It was tripping like a jackhammer. He definitely needed to get her back to the house.

"If you don't turn around and walk back to the house," he said, "I'll get angry. Which do you want? Grayson's suspicion or my anger?"

She didn't hesitate a heartbeat. "I'll chance your anger. I'm beginning to get used to your bite. Besides, I know how men think."

"So, you're a woman of the world?"

She blushed. "I wasn't born yesterday. Besides, writers are students of human nature. It's a trait creative people share. You said yourself that you can't guarantee Grayson isn't in the barn."

Seeing he had no choice but to play along, Reid said, "If he is in there, don't you think he's wondering what we're doing here?"

"All the more reason for us to fool him into thinking you're not a threat," she said in all earnestness. "What do you propose we do?"

She gripped his arms. "The only thing we can do. Go into our act."

CHAPTER FIVE

"Act?" Reid asked, unsure of her meaning.

"Our kissing act."

He regarded her in amazement. She didn't particularly like him, but she was ready to kiss him on the gamble it would save his life.

"Stop wasting time," she said. "And for goodness' sake, stand sideways."

"Why?" he asked, his voice strangled.

"It's obvious. If you do, you'll be able to sneak a peek at the window in the loft, see if you can spot him. He'll be in the loft," she added confidently, "if he's in there."

"If Grayson is in there, wouldn't he sneak out the window on the far side of the loft?"

"Are you willing to chance it?"

"I see why you're a writer," he said, aware anew of her vulnerability. Her eyes beseeched him, and he knew if he refused her, he'd heighten her anxieties. She'd talked herself into this scenario. For her sake the least he could do was magnanimously play his part and kiss her.

The thought pleased him enormously. His mind raced ahead, triggering a response in his groin. "You have a wonderful imagination."

"Why, thank you," she said, momentarily distracted. "However, this isn't a plot."

"It should be." He cleared his throat, and with a clear

conscience, pressed his advantage. "How do you propose we do this? Shall I put my arms around you first, or should you initiate the kiss?"

She frowned with concern. "Is it important?"

"I'm not sure," he said gravely. "They never trained me for this situation at the police academy."

"You're a cop. You're supposed to think on your feet."

He kept his expression as serious as he could. "Believe me, I am. All right. Your plan is best. Standing sideways allows me to whip my gun out faster and get a bead on him."

He saw the look of horror on her face and realized his error. "Don't think about it. Particularly now."

She gnawed her lower lip. "I can't help it. I know your job is dangerous. I mean, I know what I read, what I see on TV and in the movies. But with it happening here—"

"Polly."

She quieted, gazing up at him.

"Before we kiss," he said, "please remember I'm certain you're mistaken. I want you to relax. Block every man from your mind but me." Including the jerk you have a date with tonight. "When I release you, walk, don't run, back to the house. Lock the doors. Tell Fran to check upstairs. Then I want you to go into your bedroom and lie down on your bed. Don't leave until I come to get you."

She bobbed her head. Her lids fluttered closed. "You may kiss me now. Don't worry. This time I swear I'll cooperate. I'll do my absolute best."

A smile tugged at his lips. "Thank you. I swear I will too." His fingertips lightly caressed her cheek. He kissed her neck.

Her eyes snapped open. "Kiss my lips!" she hissed. He cleared his throat to mask a choking sound. "I'm getting there."

"Grayson could shoot us before you do."

"I doubt it. Besides, if we're lovers, he'd expect this. We're playing a game of cat and mouse."

Reid ran his hands up the sides of her rib cage, his fingers straying to the undersides of her breasts. "If you're right, I want him to see us holding each other. Tightly. Melt against my chest."

She instantly plastered herself to him, starting a meltdown in Reid. Groaning inwardly, he rubbed his hands up and down her back.

"Yes, that's right, Polly. Now put your arms around my neck.

Good. You're very receptive. I'm going to kiss your chin, then nibble a little on your ear. Feel free to do whatever you think will convince Grayson we're no threat to him."

She kissed his neck.

"My earlobe would be a good place too. Mmmm. That's wonderful. Do you like this?" he asked, returning the favor.

"Stop wasting time," she wailed, dropping her hands. "Remember Grayson's adrenaline."

Reid tilted up her chin and gazed into her sparkling eyes. Despite her apprehension and mounting fear, she insisted on putting herself in possible danger to help him. He kissed her temple.

"I'm thinking about your adrenaline." He brushed his mouth over hers. "Your adrenaline," he whispered, demonstrating his expertise in feather-light kisses on her lips. "I want your adrenaline soaring to the stratosphere. We only get one shot."

Polly shuddered. Dutifully, she let her hands creep up Reid's muscular chest. Considering that Grayson might be in the barn, she couldn't understand how Reid could be this cool, this calm. Did ice water run in all policemen's veins, or just in his?

"If it helps," she said, "pretend I'm Scarlett."

He cupped her face in his big hands. "Polly, please shut up so I can kiss you."

She flung her arms around his neck. Having decided that only her convincing performance could keep Grayson from suspecting Reid's true identity, she pressed her lips to his. His arms encircled her, and she slid her tongue into his mouth. A groan rumbled deep in his chest. Worried she'd gone too far, she tried retreating, but his tongue raked across her lips, her teeth, before tangling with hers.

Polly forgot about Grayson, forgot this kiss was supposed to be an act. She clung to Reid, joining wholeheartedly in his mind-blowing kiss. When she felt his hands on her derriere, she pressed even closer to him. He kissed her neck, her eyelids, her cheeks. She could feel him straining against her and dimly wondered if he was still acting, or if he, like she, had been caught up in the unexpected explosion of passion between them.

He broke the kiss, and his breathing was coming in short pants. "My God!"

"What?" she asked dazedly, stunned by her reaction to him.

Reid grazed her lower lip with his thumb. The first time he'd kissed her, he'd attributed his instant sexual reaction to his irritation at her goading him. He'd kissed her the second time because he couldn't believe the first time. Thanks to her generosity, she'd initiated this kiss. So what did he make of his reaction? Of how aroused he'd gotten?

"Damn," he said, awestruck, "you're either a hell of a convincing actress, or I'm so far gone I don't know it."

She frowned up at him, apparently still lost in the heat generated by their kiss. Then she blinked and stepped back. "Oh." She glanced at the barn. "I changed my mind. If Grayson's up there, let him stay. Come back to the house with me. Don't be a dead hero."

The radio clicked off. Silence. Then they heard a series of loud, long moos. Horace.

She sighed with relief. "If anyone were there with her, Horace wouldn't moo. She's finicky. You must have been right. I must have set the timer wrong."

She looked so happy, he resisted the urge to pull her into his arms and kiss her again. He had to play the scene out. "I'll check. Go back to the house. I'll come for you when it's safe."

"Be careful," she said, her eyes going soft and luminous. "It still might be a trick."

He gave her a brief hug. If he didn't get hold of his emotions, he told himself, he'd be in danger of becoming as mushy as Ashley Wilkes. "You're one terrific partner. Now go on, I'll be fine."

The barn, a traditionally designed building with grayed boards, had a set of wide, high doors at either end. Before entering, he checked the outer perimeter and found it safe. Inside, the barn smelled of leather, wood, hay, and animal. Shafts of light filtered through the slats and the open door. Dust motes danced in the air.

Horace, who Polly claimed acted finicky around strangers, greeted him with brown-eyed curiosity, several swishes of her tail, and a mooed hello. Then she tried to lick his face.

"Stop it! I'll kiss your mistress anytime, but not you."

So much for Horace acting nasty toward strangers, he thought. Or else the cow had seen them kissing by peering out the window near Axl Rose's poster, and figured if he was good enough for Polly, he couldn't be bad. His theory couldn't be nuttier than a cow being a fan of Axl Rose.

Walking to the center of the barn, he looked around. It could best be described as the neatest mess he'd ever seen. Old and rusted machinery was shoved up against one wall. On another hung various large and small gardening tools. Near a metal cabinet was a lawn mower, plus bags of fertilizer, bundles of hay, and an aluminum ladder. Close by the door leading to the pasture, he spotted a pile of roofing shingles and a tarpaulin.

His downstairs inspection over, he climbed up to the hayloft. Remaining on the top step, he let his gaze sweep the interior. Finding it empty, he stepped back down to the main floor. Remembering that Polly had been about to take Horace to the pasture, he led the cow outside. After checking the barn once more, he sat down on a bale of hay and dropped his head in his hands.

He'd never been in a crazier situation. He started to chuckle, but remorse abruptly cut off his laughter.

One fact was irrefutable. Polly had set aside her fears to save him. The more time he spent with her, the more he appreciated her rare and special qualities. He strode from the barn, his pace quick, eager to see her face when he told her the good news.

"False alarm," he shouted as he entered the house.

Polly flew downstairs, her eyes shining with joyous relief. The brilliant smile on her face filled him with delight. Reid had never seen anyone glow with such happiness. Without thinking, he picked her up and twirled her around. Her hair brushed his cheeks. Then, realizing he was holding her longer than the situation warranted, he put her down.

"Thank you for caring," he said quietly.

"You're welcome," she said, just as quietly.

Fran entered the room. "You two look happy. I take it Grayson's not in the barn. I didn't think he was."

Reid gave her a stem look. "Polly was right to warn me to take precautions."

Fran's eyebrows rose at her partner's serious retort, but she only said that she was off on their other case. "Don't plan on me for supper," she added. "And Reid, I'll need to borrow your car, please. My battery died."

He handed her his car keys. "Bring a new battery back with you. I'll install it."

As soon as Fran left, Reid hugged Polly again. "You were

wonderful."

Their gazes met and held. Reid was acutely aware that they were alone for the rest of the day, and perhaps part of the night too. He'd never before gotten involved with a woman who was part of a case he was working on, yet Polly was a nearly irresistible temptation. Against his will, his gaze drifted to her breasts. He wanted to taste her there too. Fortunately, she spoke, forcing his mind away from her delectable body and back to his job.

"Don't you worry about putting your life in danger?"

He took a step back, attempting to put some professional distance between them. "Every sensible law-enforcement officer worries, but you can't let it stop you. When and if I leave the force, I'll become a prosecutor, help put the bad guys behind bars for a long time instead of merely arresting them.

"Polly, we didn't finish talking about your date tonight. I'd appreciate it if you would break it. It could blow my cover." He cleared his throat. "To make up for it, I could take you out instead. Just to dinner. Since Fran won't be here."

Polly studied his disconcerted expression with great interest. The cool, always-in-control Detective Reid Cameron seemed unusually ill at ease. Was he asking her out to dinner as a way of apologizing for the havoc he was wreaking in her life—or were his reasons more personal? And which was safer for her?

"All right," she said, trying to banish from her mind the delightful image of her and Reid dancing to a romantic melody. She took several steps away from him. "Now, if you'll excuse me, I'm going to get some writing done."

She went into her pine-paneled den, but if she thought she'd be free of Reid with a door between them, she was wrong. He filled her thoughts. At first she had resented him. Now she viewed him in a new light. He hadn't taken advantage of her fears out by the barn. Though he'd tried to convince her that Grayson wasn't nearby, he'd treated her with kindness and consideration, even going along with her crazy plan. Going along with it? He'd put one-hundred-percent effort into it. Her face heated as she remembered their passionate embrace, the way their bodies had almost gone up in flames as they'd pressed close to each other.

Turning abruptly to her computer, she tried to attribute her heightened awareness of him to the drama his presence had brought into her life. Her orderly existence lacked the elements of danger that attracted a man like Reid to the police. By contrast, teaching kindergarten must seem drab to him. She was better off in her little world, where she knew the schedule, took pleasure from her teaching and writing. When she wanted electrifying, nerve-shattering experiences, she found them in the theater, movies, and books.

She switched on the computer and brought up the chapter she was working on. As she struggled for an hour, her mind kept wandering to Reid. Did he think she was rude, ignoring him like this? Or, even worse, did he think she was afraid of him?

At best her writing efforts were sluggish. She didn't need an editor to tell her the love scene lacked fire. Pushing her chair back, she rose and walked around the room. She did stretching exercises. Hearing Cuddles scratching at the door, she let him in. He flopped down in his usual position on a square of shag carpeting she'd placed for him near her chair.

She thought about making herself a cup of coffee, but discarded the idea. Sitting down at the computer again, she told herself writing was 90 percent perspiration and 10 percent inspiration.

Closing her eyes, she pictured her lovers. In her mind's eye she saw the tall, dark-haired hero's smile, as intimate as a kiss. Much the same as the smile Reid had given her when he'd swung her around. Then he had grinned broadly. She had, too, for she'd felt grateful he hadn't met with harm. She thought again of how Reid had treated her concerns with respect, while tempering her worries.

Her hero would show her heroine similar consideration. Their eyes would share a special secret, triggered by emotions too powerful for her heroine to deal with in this one scene. Her heroine reacted purely on the shock of discovery, on the sensual pull of the hero's potent presence, the private message his body communicated to hers. Polly knew her heroine's emotions, for like the fictional woman, she'd experienced firsthand the magnificence of a man. Her heroine would respond to the hero with a sense of urgency, brought about as the hero's hands and kisses awakened each sensory nerve ending.

Polly felt herself transported. As she gave her heroine desires she couldn't deny, evocative words and images flowed from Polly's brain. Pages filled the screen as the love scene vibrated with emotion.

When she finished, she read what she'd written.

She paled. She hadn't written fiction. She'd chronicled her turbulent fears, which had led to her kissing Reid, and had ended the scene with the heroine in an emotional turmoil, knowing her life would never again be the same.

Polly copied the chapter onto another disk and switched off the computer. "Girl, you're nuts," she muttered aloud. "You're foolishly sentimental and grossly dramatic."

It was time for her to put Reid's mission in its proper perspective. If she could assist him to leave more quickly, she would. Her decision made, she went in search of him. She wanted to know more about Reid. If Grayson posed a threat to her, he posed a greater threat to Reid. A shiver ran through her. She could shut off her story a lot more easily than she could control the turbulent events in her real life.

Reid heard Polly moving around in the den and resisted the desire to storm her hallowed sanctuary and confess he was as stunned as she. Whenever he got near her, sparks flew. He couldn't deny the way she made him feel, or his surprise at how quickly his attraction to her was growing. But what could he do about it?

He strolled into the bright kitchen, deliciously scented with potpourri and made cheerful by the little touches that attested to Polly's home-loving care. He took a can of soda from the refrigerator and popped the lid. As he sipped the soda, he admired the rough-hewn elm kitchen table, on which she'd placed a blue earthenware vase filled with a bouquet of spring flowers. He sat on the cushioned window bench, which displayed Polly's needlework talent. Gazing out the window, he saw a line of darkening gray clouds in the east shrouding the sky. It was beginning to mask the mountain peaks.

Finished with his soda, he rinsed and tossed the empty can into the recycling pail, then wandered into the living room. Here the furniture consisted of oak and mahogany pieces, comfortable couches, chairs, and a recliner. An upright Baldwin piano stood against one wall. On the occasional tables and the fireplace mantle were family pictures.

He peered at them. The first was of a crying Polly. She looked about two and was sitting on Santa Claus's lap. Her hair was coming loose from her pigtails, her knees sported Band-Aids, and she'd clenched her little hands into fists.

He shook his head, smiling. "Santa, she's still clenching her fists."

Another picture had him laughing aloud. Taken when she was about six years old, wearing pigtails that defied their clasps, the imp was missing her two front teeth. She was standing in front of her parents, sporting a shiner on her right eye, and grinning into the camera.

There were a few snapshots of her father and mother, several others that obviously captured special celebrations. A more serious photograph showed Polly in cap and gown, holding her high school diploma, her parents flanking her. Too bad her parents weren't alive to see their lovely daughter now.

Polly stood in the doorway, taking a moment to study Reid. He exuded a sense of raw power, yet with lithe grace. He combined authority and sexuality. He had eyes like a midnight avenger. A penetrating gaze capable, she suspected, of seeing beyond the obvious, to the soul.

As if sensing her presence, he turned. He gave her a long, heated look, then smiled.

Wow! she thought. His smile could kindle a fire. It lit a warmth throughout her body that flashed to a fiery heat as she remembered his arms crushing her, his lips covering hers.

"All finished?" he asked.

"Yes. I'm sorry if it seemed I was running out on you before. I wanted to get a few pages done. About tonight, Reid… My aunt will be coming over later this afternoon, and since I haven't seen her for a couple of days, I'd like to ask her to stay for dinner. We can go out after she leaves, maybe to a movie. Do you think Fran will be back by then? We could ask her to go with us."

"I don't need a chaperone." His keen look asked the silent question Do you?

"I didn't mean that you do," she said, marveling at his uncanny ability to read her mind.

"Yes, you did. Polly, be honest with yourself. Whatever is happening with us has you as flabbergasted as it has me. You're as amazed as I am."

Rather than answer, she led him out onto the screened-in porch that ran the length of one side of the house. The back wall was painted sunny yellow, with white trompe-l'oeil trellises on it. Like the front veranda, the porch had wicker furniture, including a graceful Victorian rocking chair.

"This room gets the afternoon sun," she said. "My mother dubbed it our solarium. She said it sounded grand."

"It's better than grand," Reid said, feeling an immediate affinity for the spacious enclosure. "For all its size, it's cozy. Makes me yearn to put my feet up on a footstool, lean back in one of these chairs, and enjoy the scenery."

"Fran made a similar comment. She said it's a far cry from city noise. My parents installed storm windows and heat for use year-round. The front porch gets the morning sun. Between the two, I watch both sunrise and sunset."

"What's your favorite time of day?"

"Sunset. There's a sighing softness to it, like the closing pages of a good book. Everything is tinged with feeling. The mountains glow."

"Like your hair," he said. It rested on her shoulders, curling upward like fingers reaching toward the light. Resisting the urge to touch that hair, he bent down to examine the Victorian rocker, whose reeds showed signs of distress. "Sun damages wicker. The rays dry the reeds. They get brittle as a result."

"Where did you learn about wicker?"

"Mostly from my mother. She repairs wicker furniture. After my dad died, she turned her hobby into a business. I often help her ready chairs for restoring, checking and re-drilling existing holes for her to weave and seamlessly blend new reeds with the old. Tension and moisture are critical for weaving wicker."

"You surprise me."

He looked up at her. "Why? Didn't you think cops have private lives?"

"Sorry. I didn't mean to pry into your affairs."

He squeezed her hand. "You're not. It's okay. I noticed it's clouding up. As long as we have time before your aunt comes, how about if I set some of those loose shingles inside the barn on the roof?" They were standing close to each other. Awareness flowed through him. Her scent tantalized him. She started to lean toward him, then she pulled back. "Polly, I…"

"Don't," she pleaded. "Nothing is happening to us. I won't allow it. Maybe going out tonight isn't a good idea."

"Polly, Fran isn't coming back until very late. We're alone, whether we go out or stay here. And personally, I'd much rather go dancing with you than sit in a dark movie theater watching some summertime action-adventure film."

His gaze dropped to her hands. They were clenched so tightly; her knuckles were turning white. "Just forget it," he said. Muttering a soft oath, he shoved open the porch door and walked away.

At the barn, he lugged the ladder outside, set it up, then went back in for the shingles. He began carrying them up to the roof, making several trips.

When he descended for his last batch of shingles, he saw Polly standing at the foot of the ladder. "What are you doing here?"

"Reid, this is silly. I got to thinking about the diamonds."

He drew his arm across his forehead, wiping away the sweat. "What about them?"

"If you find them, I think you should leave them alone. Don't switch them with cubic zirconia. How can you arrest him for carrying fake diamonds? The most you can arrest him for is trespassing."

"I can arrest him for a string of burglaries, selling drugs, and more. Including prostitution."

"You never told me!" she said, her voice rising. He pursed his lips. "I wasn't aware I had to. The only order of yours I'm aware of is not to make love to you." If she wanted to lie to herself, fine. He wasn't going to. He'd felt her passion. She'd felt his.

"Do you want the reward money or not?"

"Of course I do. I just don't think you should waste time hunting for the jewels."

"If I know where he's stashed them, it makes my job easier. I'll know where he's headed. It eliminates the guesswork."

That seemed to satisfy her, but then she stepped up onto the ladder.

"Where do you think you're going?" he asked. "With you. I want to help."

"Do me a big favor, don't."

"Don't be silly. Two of us will work faster. I'll hand you shingles. Afterward, I'll help you search."

"Go away. Polly. In case you haven't noticed, when we're near each other, fireworks start. I don't need distraction."

61

"I'll also be your lookout."

"I told you Grayson won't be here before Monday or Tuesday."

"You also told me the police bugged his car. Can you guarantee he won't change automobiles? Can you?"

Reid gave up. He couldn't guarantee squat. Including what was happening to him. The longer he remained with her, the more he wanted to make love to her. He nearly lost his balance thinking of what he'd like to do with her in the hayloft.

It wasn't easy for him to put down the temporary cover without the aid of the wooden crossbeams roofers use for footrests, but he managed.

"Have you done this before too?" Polly asked as she handed him several more shingles.

He wiped his face on his sleeve. "No. I watch *This Old House* on TV. One of the programs was devoted to putting down a new roof. This is the wrong way, but it won't hurt what the roofer will do later. I'm not gluing or nailing."

He looked over his job. "Without supports, that's as high as I can go."

They climbed down. He put the ladder back where he'd found it, then they both washed their hands at the sink inside the barn.

"Now what?" Polly asked.

"I'm going diamond hunting. You do what you want."

"Reid, please."

"Don't 'Reid, please' me. I'm in a lousy mood. I'll get over it."

Her gaze bounced nervously from him to the loft. "I insist."

"Suit yourself."

"What makes you think the diamonds are up there?"

"It's a hunch. I have to start someplace. Put yourself in Grayson's head. He doesn't know how often you move things around, but he grew up on a farm. He knows Horace grazes in the field. Her added feed is down here; plus, the hay you've got stacked down here is enough to last several weeks or a month."

Polly stared at him with respect. As well as being tall and handsome and wonderfully fit, with the most expressive eyes, he was good at his job.

The hayloft occupied a space approximately half the size of the barn. The afternoon heat coupled with the sun that streamed in through the window made the loft a good eight degrees warmer than the barn below. Reid opened the window. From that vantage point, he had a clear view of the house.

He extended his hand to Polly. "Take a look at the angle."

She joined him at the window. For her to see out, he stepped behind her. Polly stared out the window, but his presence was too distracting. Her inner temperature soared even higher than the loft's, and arousal raced through her veins. Turning her head, she swallowed when she found him looking at her lips. "What should I be seeing?"

"Your bedroom window. When Grayson comes, don't go in there. If he has a high-powered rifle, he'll have a clear shot."

"Oh, dear," she murmured.

He reached into his pocket and withdrew a bracelet with a colorful stone in its center. "Wear this, starting Monday. In an emergency depress the stone. It's a transmitter. Either Fran or I will respond."

Polly could feel the tension in her neck. "You have all the modem trinkets."

"This is so I can keep you safe."

She bobbed her head. "You want Grayson for more than stealing jewels, selling drugs, and dealing in prostitution, don't you?"

He drew a harsh breath. "Yes. We think he's connected to a murder. Would you rather I pretend there's no danger, like I'm pretending I don't want you in my arms now?"

She leaned back against his chest. He wrapped his arms around her. "I think," she whispered, an involuntary shiver running through her, "that I'm very glad you're here."

For several moments they stood in silence, then she whispered his name.

"Mmmm?"

"This isn't a bit like one of my romance plots." He pressed his lips to the sensitive spot behind her ear. "Turn it into one after I leave. By then you'll know the outcome of your story."

That was fine for her heroine, she thought, but what about her?

CHAPTER SIX

With effort Polly stepped out of Reid's embrace and turned her mind back to the reason for Reid being there. "If Grayson isn't due until Monday, technically you could go home and come back Sunday night, couldn't you?"

He gazed into her eyes. "Wasn't it you who told me I can't give you guarantees?"

"Yes, but you seem sure about his movements. Why not take a break, send another trooper, then return?"

He reached out and brushed one hand down her hair. "I'm on assignment. Are you ready to go diamond hunting and cash in on your reward?"

"What about your share?"

"There is no share. This is part of my job."

They worked as a team. Marking off the loft in thirds, Reid raked the hay aside. Laboriously they sifted through hundreds of pieces of straw. Doing only one section took over an hour.

Her back aching, Polly stood to arch it, then pointed to a section of the hay, saying, "I'm going to hunt through this area alone. Maybe it will go faster."

He didn't argue with her. She dropped to her knees and began searching. "Do you know if the diamonds are set or loose?" she asked.

"Both, according to the jeweler's manifest."

She nodded. They worked for another half hour but didn't find anything. As she started to search through another section, Reid happened to glance up. He froze when he spotted the thin, nearly invisible wire. It could only mean one thing. Grayson had rigged a charge! The selfish bastard must have figured if he couldn't have the jewels, no one could, even if it meant maiming or killing innocent people.

"Polly." Reid's voice was low, assertive. Any sudden move on her part could shift the straw around the base of the charge and trigger the mechanism.

She looked up. Bits of straw clung to her hair. "It's futile, isn't it?"

"I think we should quit for today. Polly, I'm about to tell you what to do. Please don't ask questions. Do exactly as I ask."

She heard the warning in his voice, saw his taut expression. "May I move my head?" she asked, her voice as tense as his face.

"Yes, but first put the straw in your hand down. Don't stand. Stay on your knees. I'm coming over to get you."

Her eyes went wide. "What is it?"

"There's a colorless wire to your right, about five inches from you. It resembles fishing line. I don't trust what it's connected to. I don't want to take any chances. It's probably nothing, but just to make sure, please, don't move."

Fear clogged her throat. "It's a bomb, isn't it?"

"I won't lie to you. I'm not certain."

She clenched her teeth. "It is a bomb, isn't it?"

"If it is, it's a crude one. I'll dismantle it."

"No. Let's get out of here." Her words were barely audible. Just yesterday morning her biggest worry was writing a love scene. Compared to the terrifying possibility that the slightest wrong move could set off a charge, her plot problem dwindled to nothing. Bile reached her throat. She bit down hard on her lip and tasted blood.

She concentrated on Reid's voice encouraging her. He said it was probably a groundless worry, she was doing fine. He was proud of her, he said as he inched his way toward her, carefully moving aside hay.

He positioned himself at her back, placing his hands on her waist. Nothing in the world had ever felt as welcome as his strong hands, or his lips near her ear, murmuring how proud he was of her for following his instructions. She knew she was a basket case, but he never raised his voice.

"I'm going to slide you away," he said. "This way it displaces less hay. You'll be on your knees, sweetheart, but I can't help that."

She bobbed her head as his endearment echoed in her mind. Her insides were liquid. Trusting him implicitly, she did as he asked, letting herself go limp as he drew her backward.

"Stay with me, sweetheart, you're doing fine. Only a few more inches, then we'll rest a second before standing."

When they reached the edge of the loft, he helped her stand, then made sure she climbed safely down the ladder. He led her quickly outside, wrapped one arm around her quaking shoulders, and walked her to the house. "Go inside. I'll be right there."

"Where are you going?"

"To diffuse the mechanism."

"Don't!" she pleaded, flinging her arms around his neck. "Let the old barn blow up. Horace is outside. A pile of wood is replaceable. You're not."

He cupped her cheek, his heart reaching out to her. "Polly," he replied, his voice strangely husky to his own ears, "I was sent here to do a job. Please don't interfere. I know what I'm doing."

"Can you guarantee that?" she demanded, the words exploding from her as she stared at him with terror-stricken eyes. "If you destroy the bomb, Grayson will know, so what have you gained?"

"Your safety, which is as important to me as mine is to yours. Do you think I'd let you run a risk if I can help it? I can rig it so it looks as if it wasn't touched. Anyway, Horace needs her stall."

"My neighbor can take her."

"It will ruin my cover. Please, I know what I'm doing."

"I hate Grayson! He's not worth your getting killed."

"I can't stand here arguing." His arm slid around her waist. "I'd rather kiss you than talk anyway."

She stamped her foot. "Sex! At a time like this, you think of sex?"

He chuckled. "Only a kiss. We'll take care of the rest later."

Clenching her fist, she looked into his drugging dark eyes and rated her chances of knocking him out cold. In a flash she understood why he wanted to kiss her.

"I'm on to you, Cameron. You think you can divert my attention. It won't work. If you kiss me now, I'll bite off your tongue.

You're a damned fool!"

A flash of respect came into his eyes, and she knew she had guessed his intentions. He wanted her to feed on her anger, preferring it over her fears for his safety.

She turned on her heel, her feet crunching the ground. Inside the house she picked up Cuddles, ran upstairs to her room, and flung herself on the bed.

"God," she prayed. "Keep him in one piece. Please."

Trying to console herself that Reid knew what he was doing didn't help. She gazed around her dream bedroom, decorated in white. She'd let her imagination and her talented fingers transform it into an intimate boudoir.

It had a canopied bed, with a white rosette-embroidered Indian cotton bedspread, and pillowcases ruffled in layers of lace.

How could this be? How could she idly do nothing? Wait to possibly hear a deadly explosion? If she phoned the police, they couldn't arrive in time to help.

She willed herself to think of anything but Reid searching through shifting straw for a bomb that might explode before he rendered it harmless.

She started getting off the bed to go to him, then sagged against the pillow. He'd asked—correction, he'd ordered—her to wait. If she disturbed him, she could break his concentration, possibly cause him harm. Her stomach churning with apprehension, she decided she'd give him a few more minutes. In the meantime, she curled her knees to her chest, closed her eyes, and prayed for his safety.

That was consoling for only a couple of minutes. Fretting, she glanced at the clock on the dresser. What was taking him this long? Maybe the charge had gone off and his body had muffled its sound? Maybe he wished she could hear him?

Maybe she was driving herself batty?

For the next ten minutes she asked herself unanswerable questions, most of them foolish, but all of them focused on Reid's safety. An ache of sadness gripped her. Scalding hot tears streamed from her eyes. So awful was the thought of Reid wounded or worse, she had to forcibly wipe it from her mind.

Finally, she couldn't stand it any longer. Rolling off the bed, she inched to the window that looked out on the barn, rising on her knees to peek outside. She strained her eyes but saw nothing unusual. If Reid were in danger, he was in it alone. He and Grayson. Dammit, she felt helpless. She hated that feeling.

Despite his attempts to play it down with Polly, Reid faced an extremely dangerous situation. One false move would set off the charge and blow him to kingdom come. His thigh ached, but he stayed rigidly still as he took a few minutes to mentally review the steps he had to follow. Saying a quick prayer, he began. He directed his fingers to move slowly, carefully, and with perspiration beading on his face, he dismantled the timing mechanism.

He sat back on his haunches, waiting for his breath to even out. He held his hands in front of him. Steady before, they now shook. Wiping his face, he dropped his head forward and rolled his shoulders to relieve the kink in his neck.

In minutes he located two soft bags stuffed with loose and mounted diamonds: brooches, earrings, necklaces, and rings. As he held a necklace up to the light, the gems blazed with fire. Grayson knew what to steal. Polly's reward should be substantial. Setting the bags aside, he fixed the wiring to make it appear as if it hadn't been touched. As he rose from his crouched position, he caught sight of a diamond ring on the floor partially hidden by straw. Grayson must have dropped it.

Reid pocketed the ring, grabbed the bags, and descended the ladder. For the second time in less than a year he'd been lucky to stay alive. As he headed for the house, he wondered what sort of mood Polly was in.

He'd hoped to alleviate her fears but knew he'd failed. Her eyes had told him all he needed to know. She had been deeply worried, and the thought of her caring what happened to him appealed to him.

Inside the house he found her curled up on her bed in a fetal position, her dog sleeping beside her. Her hair hid her face, and one fist was slowly beating the bedspread.

"It's okay," he said, putting his hand on her shoulder and turning her around. He tried to smile at her, but what he saw in her wounded blue eyes nearly sent him to his knees with regret for what she'd been put through that day.

He sat down beside her and laid his hand against her cheek. "It's over," he said as tenderly as he could.

Her gaze swiftly covered his body from head to toe, looking for signs he'd been hurt. Her hands slid up his chest to his shoulders. "You okay?"

"Yes."

He framed her face, his thumbs wiping away her tears. "Honey, I'm sorry. Grayson's an idiot. He didn't rig a smart charge. It was a piece of cake to dismantle. And look."

He grinned with triumph as he held up the bags of jewels. "You're going to get a hefty reward."

When Polly saw his delighted expression, as if he'd come from a walk in the park, while she'd nearly died with fright, all her emotions exploded into anger.

"How dare you pacify me with this? Do you know how worried I was? Do you know what you put me through? Then you come here with this... stuff! Go away," she spat contemptuously, her eyes fiercely accusing as she dismissed a fortune in diamonds.

Reid put the bags on the bed, unperturbed by her outburst. He understood that her concern for him was behind her release of tension. And he was even sorrier he hadn't been able to give her guarantees. Though he had expert training, accidents happened in the best of circumstances. She'd gotten the scare of her life. With good cause. The fear she'd kept inside her while wondering if he'd be injured or killed had terrified her. She'd said she was afraid of thunder.

He wrapped his arms around her and pulled her tightly to his chest. "It's okay," he murmured, stroking her hair.

Her tears wet his shirt. "Go away. I don't want anything to do with you. Play cops and robbers somewhere else. I wish I'd never met you. You took over my life."

"Have I?" he asked, feeling absurdly happy that she cared enough to cry over him.

"Yes. From the minute we met. I don't like it! I don't know how you do it, Reid. How do you stay so calm?" Her voice rose with accusation. "It's a piece of cake to you. That's what you said. Your typical day's work."

"No, I promise you I don't do this every day."

"No wonder there's such a high divorce rate among cops."

He was silent for a long moment, then said, "Maybe it's better if you go away until this is over."

She shook her head, drawing in a ragged breath. "I can't. There's Martha. She's an old lady."

"Why should it matter? Show me how to milk Horace, and take Martha away with you. I'll let you know when to return."

"We've been through this. Martha has a doctor's appointment Tuesday. She's secure in knowing she keeps her visits. I'm staying," she said belligerently.

Sighing, he rose to bring her some tissues. She blew her nose.

"Feel better now?" he asked gruffly.

She pushed back her hair. "No. I won't feel better until Grayson's locked up. That tawdry rat took away my most precious possession. My peace of mind." She plucked at the bedspread, sliding him a sidelong glance. "Thanks for saving my life." She sounded so reluctant, he laughed.

"You're welcome. I was glad to do it."

She stared moodily at the canopy above her bed. "I'm sorry I yelled. I shouldn't take my anger at Grayson out on you. And I'm sure Horace thanks you too."

Relief and amusement rushed through him. What a woman! She insisted on acting as his lookout on the roof, helped him hunt for the diamonds, demanded he let the barn blow up rather than risk getting hurt. Bright color dotted her flushed face. Her thick hair tumbled about her shoulders. She shifted her gaze, facing him with smoldering eyes.

"Keep looking at me like that," he said huskily, "I'll forgive you anything."

"Looking at you how?"

"Like a woman who can't decide if she wants to throttle me or make love to me. You've done the first. How about if we—"

"That's another thing," Polly interrupted before he could finish. He was lethal, worse than the dynamite charge he'd dismantled. He was a walking, talking, broad-shouldered, narrow-hipped, devilish sex bomb, who looked better in jeans than any man had a right to look! "This constant kissing," she went on, "must stop. It's disconcerting."

"Disconcerting? That's what you call what we're feeling? I've got a better name for it. And as I recall, you started it the last time, I didn't."

They exchanged smiles. Whom were they kidding?

"You're impossible. I'm glad you're safe, you big lug."

They heard the front door open and a birdlike voice call out, "Hellooo. Polly, are you upstairs?"

Reid groaned. "Martha?"

Polly rolled off the bed and stood. She glimpsed herself in the mirror. "I look a fright. My eyes are puffy. Martha must not see me this way."

Calling down to her aunt that she'd be right there, she dashed into the bathroom and washed her face. She applied fresh makeup, stepping aside for Reid to use the sink. He washed his own face and combed his hair.

She picked up her hairbrush, then caught him studying her in the mirror. He gave her an engaging smile, one packed with lazy sensuality.

"What?" she asked.

"Have you noticed whenever we're together, sparks fly?"

Their gazes clinging, he took the hairbrush from her hand and drew it through her hair. Sparks of static electricity crackled in the air. He dipped his head and kissed her neck. His breath sent shivers down her spine.

"Electricity," he murmured. "We make our own."

"Martha's waiting," she said, her voice a low whisper.

"Too bad."

When she was almost out the door, he caught her wrist. In the flash of a second she was in his arms.

"Don't stop me," he said. "I've got a good reason. I'm preparing us for our act."

Before she could protest, his mouth captured hers, moving insistently over her lips. He boldly pressed his hips forward. One hand sank into her hair, holding her head still.

The kiss exploded into a fiercely wild mating, partly as a result of the dreadful fears she'd experienced and partly because she was unable to resist him. When he lifted his head, he looked at her with stormy passion darkening his eyes, murmured her name, then kissed her again.

A fire raged inside Reid. This one woman was capable of making him care deeply, while sending his blood to a boiling point. He released her and forced himself to sound casual as he said, "You've got that dewy radiant look. Remember, sweetheart, we're

71

supposed to be madly in love."

She only stared at him dazedly, and he smiled as he steered her out of the bathroom and down the stairs.

Aunt Martha reminded Reid of a tiny general in a polka-dot red dress. She had a cap of blond curls, twin dimples, lively deep blue eyes, and a sprightly bounce to her walk. She was Polly's father's older sister by twelve years.

"I never guessed," she exclaimed, after she was introduced to Reid. "Imagine hiding this gorgeous man. I forgive you."

Polly exchanged helpless looks with Reid.

"I wasn't hiding him, Aunt Martha. We... we knew each other a long time ago."

Martha went on for her. "You broke up but you found each other again. It's in the timing. You weren't ready before. Now you are. I can see it in your eyes."

"It's wonderful, isn't it?" Reid said. "She's got that dewy radiance love brings out."

Martha nodded. Polly rolled her eyes. Reid winked at her.

"When did you know Reid was the man for you?" Martha asked.

Polly didn't answer, and Reid finally said, "She's still getting over the shock. We're engaged." He pulled the diamond ring from his pocket and snatched her left hand.

Polly gasped as he slipped the ring on her finger.

Martha beamed. "Oh, how wonderful. Since you're getting married, it's okay that you're staying here. Otherwise, it wouldn't be right. I like a take-charge man. Show me your ring, dear."

Polly's hand was still captured in Reid's, so he thrust it toward Martha for inspection. The round solitaire was set in platinum. Diamond baguettes were set on either side of the stone, which had to be at least three carats. Amazingly the ring fit perfectly.

Engaged! Polly thought. To a man she'd known little more than a day. Wearing a stolen ring—hot ice—as the promise of his sham affections. A daredevil lunatic who disarmed bombs. A lawman who kissed like a dream and made her sizzle. A slippery, sexy eel who would never be like Ashley Wilkes in a million years!

"To think," her aunt gushed, "I'm witnessing a momentous occasion."

"I'd say we all are," Reid said dryly.

Martha nudged him. "Aren't you going to kiss her?"

He chuckled. "Aunt Martha, you read my mind."

He took a stunned Polly in his arms and kissed her for Martha's benefit. When he lifted his head, she kept her back to Martha and hissed, "Stop this farce!"

His lips brushed her cheek. "Shut up, darling," he whispered. "It was your idea to let Martha stay. You're not acting like a woman in love, though, and you might have raised her suspicions. I couldn't have that."

He turned to Martha. "Look at her, Aunt Martha. May I call you Aunt Martha?"

"Please do. You're family now. You were saying?"

"Polly has a dewy radiance in her eyes."

Martha peered at her niece. "I see what you mean." Polly suddenly realized that Reid was crazy like a fox. He had Martha eating from his hand, approving of his sleeping in her house.

"When is the wedding?" Martha asked.

Polly coughed. "We haven't set the date."

Martha put on her glasses. "Let me have your hand, Reid. I want to see what your palm says."

She studied his palm for a few minutes, then smiled with delight as she wiggled his pinkie finger. "It's here. One marriage. That's good. I see twins. Boys, I think. Then a boy and a girl. Polly, give me your hand."

While Reid sat with his mouth open, Polly smirked at him. Martha bent Polly's pinkie finger, examining a crease, then read her palm.

"Yes!" she cried. "This confirms it. You and Reid are going to have four children." Polly protested, but Martha insisted she was right.

"So," Martha said to Reid, "when you came back, you knew immediately. Just like that, you both knew, didn't you? You couldn't deny your feelings. Oh, this is too astounding for words." Martha gave him a coy look. "When did you know you were in love with Polly?"

"Umm, the first time we kissed. Wasn't it then, darling?"

"I wouldn't know," she replied tightly.

"Yes, I would say then. If not the first time, the second time. It hit me between the eyes. It gets better and better. I shouldn't be telling you this—"

Martha inched her chair closer. He gave her a roguish grin. "I don't mind telling you, she's quite a woman. I love holding her."

"Reid."

"Oh, shush, Polly," Martha said. "I want to hear this. Go make dinner. Reid and I want to get to know each other. It takes a real he-man to state his feelings. Too many men hide behind them, as if they're ashamed of having them."

"Like that wimp Ashley Wilkes," Reid said.

"You're absolutely right!" Martha exclaimed.

"Reid."

"Hush, Polly," Martha said. "You'd think you were as old as I am. People think," she added to Reid, "that when you reach your late seventies, you're over the hill. Go on, Reid."

With an ease Polly hadn't known was possible, he reconstructed their fantasy love affair. He supplied details, hinted of wonderful things they had supposedly done together in the past. Her knees grew weak His imagination equaled, maybe even surpassed, hers. She dropped into a chair to listen to his pack of lies, knowing that if he put them on paper, he'd have a sizzling romance novel.

But what really amazed her was her aunt's reaction. She clearly was eating it up. Every once in a while Martha's blue-veined hands would fly to her mouth. A faraway look would come into her eyes, as if she were reliving a love affair herself. When she did, Reid slowed the story, giving her time to savor her memories. Other times, she giggled and bounced on her chair, clapping her little hands in glee.

Unable to stop him, Polly gave up trying and started dinner. She took a package of chopped meat from the refrigerator, slit the plastic wrapping, and dumped the contents into a plastic bowl with such force, the bowl bounced on the counter. She hacked an onion with a butcher knife and added more parsley than she normally would. With Reid adding relish to his recital, she slapped and formed hamburgers and thought about hurling one at his head.

While he fed Martha more whoppers, Polly washed and snapped string beans, then set them to cook in a pot of water where she normally steamed her vegetables. She tore lettuce leaves and sliced tomatoes, then set them on a plate, which she nearly dropped as she carried it to the table.

"What do you do?" Martha asked Reid as Polly set the plate down.

"He's an attorney," Polly answered quickly.

Martha's eyes glowed, and her dainty rosebud mouth formed a little O. "Why that's wonderful. Simply wonderful. And so practical. We'll have a teacher and a lawyer in the family. I want to make an appointment to update my will."

She giggled. "Polly knows I adore children. You do want them, don't you, dear?"

Torn between wanting to strangle Reid and not cause her aunt disappointment, Polly valiantly responded in a way calculated not to dim her aunt's enthusiasm.

"Of course. Maybe not so soon, though."

"I could be wrong about the exact timing," Martha said, "although I think it will be ten months after the wedding." She touched Reid's hand. "It's only natural that you and Polly want to concentrate on yourselves at first. And you should. But I do hope I'll live to see the little ones."

Polly caught her aunt's determined use of the plural. She tensed at the idea of making love with Reid, of nights lying in his arms, his soul-destroying kisses leading to the exquisite sensation of lovemaking with him. Of having his babies growing in her womb.

Martha said, "I want to set aside a gift for my grandniece's and grandnephews' college educations."

With a tremulous smile Polly knelt to hug her aunt. Martha's funds were limited. She lived on Social Security, a small pension from her husband, and the modest income from the interest on a few bonds. By no means was she rich, except in her heart.

Martha wrapped her arms around Polly's neck. Her own smile wobbled as she said, "This means you'll move, dear. Horace and I will miss you."

Polly took both her hands. "No, Aunt Martha. I couldn't leave you. We're not moving. Reid will practice law in town. We've decided to live here. Isn't that right, sweetheart?"

Turning to Reid, Polly saw his jaw tighten, his eyes narrow. She prayed he wouldn't say anything to hurt her aunt.

He didn't. He nodded and said in a gentle, reassuring voice, "That's our plan."

Martha dissolved into tears. She sniffled, rummaging in her

purse for her hankie. "My dreams are answered. Forgive a foolish old woman. I'm crying from happiness. Polly, I wish your parents had lived to see this day."

She turned a fond gaze on Reid. "I'm her surrogate mother, you see. I have been since her dear mother passed away. Every mother wants to see her daughter in a good marriage. I've been sneaking glances at you when you're looking at Polly, and it's obvious you're devoted to my niece. And your love has been tested. You came back for her."

Polly choked up. "I'll get wine," she said, and fled to the dining room, where she kept a wine rack on the sideboard.

She leaned her forehead against the wall, then jumped when she felt a hand at her shoulder. She whirled around.

Reid stood there. She tipped her head back, her face tight. For once he appeared as disturbed as she felt.

"I hope you're satisfied," she said in frustrated misery. "You drummed up this chicanery. I should never have gone along with it. When you leave, you can have the pleasure of knowing I'll break her heart."

"Then don't tell her. Let her go on thinking we're engaged."

Polly's mouth dropped open.

CHAPTER SEVEN

Polly recovered from her shock in record time. "For how long? Until our twenty-fifth wedding anniversary? Exactly how do I accomplish this miracle with a phantom fiancé? Where do you dream up cons like this? Do they come naturally?"

Reid ground his back teeth. "No, they don't. I should have insisted you follow my orders. But no! Out of the goodness of my heart I thought this up as an alternative."

"So now it's my fault?" she blasted.

He snarled a curse that ripened the air. "As much as it's mine, and don't you forget it. I was for keeping that sweet old lady off the property. If necessary, I'm for yanking out her phone so she can't screw this up by telling the world who I am."

Polly's whole body started to tremble. Her heart twisted in panic. He expected her to continue this absurd charade. She closed her eyes and swallowed.

"We can't stay here arguing. It's begun to rain. After dinner I'd appreciate it if you'd drive Aunt Martha home. You can use my car."

During dinner Martha entertained Reid with stories of Polly as a little girl. Polly finally put an end to it. Undaunted, Martha asked Reid about his family. When she learned that both he and his mother lived in Pittsburgh, and that his mother repaired wicker furniture, she said she wanted to ask her to look at her wicker.

Polly grabbed her glass of wine, tilted it back, and drank it down.

Rain was falling steadily by the time they finished dessert. Polly packed up the leftovers for her aunt, then told her not to go out the next day if it was still raining. She and Reid would visit her instead.

Martha's parting comment was that she planned to write Axl Rose and invite him to the wedding. Why not? Polly thought, slumping back in her chair. Since she'd met Reid, nothing would surprise her.

He was gone for about twenty minutes. When he returned, his expression was somber. Twirling the stem of her wineglass, Polly looked up at him from where she still sat at the kitchen table.

From her perspective he looked formidable. His shoulders were powerful, his thighs hard, his legs long. He wasn't wearing a jacket or a gun at his waist. She could attest to the fact that his stomach was hard and flat. And so was the expression on his face when he saw her sipping a glass of wine.

"Congratulations on your Oscar-winning performance," she said. "You overdid it; don't you think? Dating is one thing. Where do you come off telling her we're engaged?"

"The same place you came off telling her I'm going to practice law in this town and live in this house."

"I had to say something. You left me no choice."

"You might have tried sounding ambiguous."

"Hah." She wiggled her ring finger. "What's your excuse? This isn't ambiguous. I can get arrested for wearing stolen jewelry."

She examined the twinkling solitaire. "Arrested by you! Oh, that's funny. My bogus fiancé steals the ring from a jewel thief, then he puts it on my finger to seal a sham engagement. What happens to my reward? Will it be delivered to me while I'm in jail?"

He shrugged. "The ring leaves when I do. I got caught up in the act. It slipped out."

"I'll say. Until I met you, I lived a nice, quiet, predictable life. I like my routine life. To a man like yourself that's boring. You dismantle bombs. You catch crooks. I catch colds."

He hooked a chair with his foot, slid it backward, and sat. "Colds?"

She nodded. "A metaphor for a normal life. I plan my days, then you barrel into my life and in little more than twenty-four hours we're engaged. Pass the wine bottle, please."

He peered at her. "You've had enough. We're going out."

"I still have to change. You drive me nuts. I've never had a man drive me nuts before."

His lips twitched. "This from a woman of the world."

"We live in different worlds. Either you're kissing me or you're pulling a nutty stunt. My poor aunt. She just relived her romance with my uncle. How could you?"

"You know why. To keep her from telling the world I'm a cop. And there's one more thing you should know."

She dropped her chin on her palm. "Whatever it is will keep until Monday. I'm taking the weekend off. My shock limit is filled."

She started removing the ring, but his hand covered hers. "I'd leave that on if I were you."

She sent him an exasperated look. "No, thanks. There's no reason to keep up this pretense. I've decided to tell Martha the truth."

He fit the ring back on her finger. "You can't tell your aunt."

"Of course I can."

"Even if I allowed it, which I won't, it's too late."

"What do you mean?"

"When I walked your aunt inside her house, she asked me if I was sure that I was leaving Monday or Tuesday. After I said yes, guess what she did? Guess what she's doing even as we speak?"

"I haven't the foggiest idea. What's more, as long as I know she's safely home, my brain is off duty."

"Are you getting drunk?"

"No. I'm nursing a second wine."

"Good," he said with infuriating calm. "I can't have my wife drunk."

She hooted. "Get off it. I'm not your anything. We're not engaged." She pulled off the diamond ring. "I'm breaking our engagement. I believe this bauble is state's evidence."

"Polly," he said flatly. "Put the damn ring on."

Suddenly she understood the look on his face. "You're about to tell me bad news, aren't you?"

"That depends on your definition of bad news."

"Stop trying to soften the blow. Talk!"

He gave her a weak smile that threatened to collapse into laughter. "Take my advice. Stay calm. On a scale of one to ten, it's only about a five."

A sense of foreboding crept up her spine. "What?"

He took a deep breath. "Your aunt Martha's throwing us an engagement party."

Polly shot him an incredulous look. "Tell me you talked her out of it."

"I couldn't. It might blow my cover."

Aghast, she leaped from her chair. "I'm going to strangle you. No! I'll blow your brains out instead. Give me your gun!"

A flicker of humor danced in his eyes. Easily restraining her, he anchored her against his powerful frame. "Be sensible." He nipped her ear.

"Sensible!" The screech turned into a moan as his tongue bathed the lobe. "When? When is the party? Stop kissing me!"

He chuckled. "I can't. You know what happens when we're together. Brace yourself. Your aunt's a sly fox. She's a faster worker than I am."

"Impossible! No one works faster than you do!"

"She was calling your school-staff list when I left." Polly squirmed uselessly. Reid was kissing her neck, his breath doing crazy things to her nerves.

"Sunday," he went on. "Even Nature is helping her. The rain should be over by then. We'll have a lovely day for our festivities. Your aunt's calling it my debut. Her word as she kissed me good-bye."

"Heaven help me."

"She showed me lists of names. 'Oodles of names' is the way she put it. I haven't heard that word in years. Oodles. Each 'oodle' is a person. A guest bearing good tidings for our happy future."

"Happy future. You're ruining mine, you louse. You and your award-winning act. Let me go!"

He smiled into her eyes. "Promise not to shoot me?"

She grinned, and he released her. "I'm calling her. Maybe she can reverse the damage before it's too late."

He caught her shoulders. "You'll do nothing of the kind. You'll see this through the same as I will. Your aunt's a terrific woman. I'm not breaking her heart."

"All of a sudden you care. She's my aunt, not yours Why didn't you think about her feelings before telling her we're engaged?"

"In my wildest dreams I never thought she'd throw us a party. Incidentally she's decided on having it here. She says your lawn is ideal for a garden party. It's larger and flatter than hers."

Polly let out a yelp. "That can mean only one thing. She's inviting the world. She'll fill every inch of grass with people. Martha knows everyone. How am I going to explain my one-day engagement? People will descend here like an army with feasts of food and good cheer. Not only will she invite them to the wedding, I have no doubt she'll tell them we're having twins in ten months."

He stroked her back in gentle strokes. "Mmmm. I love your perfume. Don't forget the other two kids. It's wrong to play favorites."

She shook her head, trying not to purr at his soothing caresses. "What a miserable mess. I hope Grayson is worth this."

Reid rested his chin atop Polly's head. What he'd hoped was a plausible reason to keep Martha away from danger had snowballed into a huge problem. He had no alternative now.

"I can't let Martha know why I'm here. Let's go out and have some fun. You deserve a break from this tonight. While you dress, I'll check the bridge. When I'm through, I'll change my clothes. I want to go dancing tonight before anything else happens."

The phone rang, and he groaned. "I bet it's your aunt asking me for a list of my friends and relatives."

He was wrong. It wasn't Martha. It was Fran. She sounded strained and upset as she asked to speak with Reid.

Polly handed him the phone, then started loading dishes into the dishwasher. She didn't pay attention to the conversation, but when Reid replaced the phone on its cradle, he was shaking his head, muttering, "It can't be."

Polly glanced at him, but said nothing. Police business didn't interest her at the moment.

He sat down at the table and shook his head. "Brace yourself. I have news."

"You're leaving."

"Hardly."

He seemed to be struggling to keep his face straight.

"Then what?" she asked, drying her hands.

"Fran's stuck."

"What do you mean? How stuck is stuck?"

"I'd say stuck overnight."

Stuck overnight. As in spending the night alone with Reid.

At first Polly thought she heard wrong. "Tell me this isn't true."

"Fran's fiancé's car was rear-ended when he stopped for a light. Tom's home with a neck brace and medication. He says he's okay, but she wants to stay with him. As long as Grayson isn't expected tomorrow, she received permission to be relieved from duty tonight."

Polly felt a bead of perspiration form on her upper lip. Reid picked up her hand, his thumb idly stroking her palm. "It's been an interesting couple of days," he said. "I came here to catch a crook, but what happened? I met you. You refused to tell your aunt to stay away. I'm a nice fellow, so I let you have your way. When I felt guilty for calling off your roofer, I patched your barn roof as best I could. Afterward, I diffused a dynamite charge. The next thing I know I'm engaged and your aunt is throwing us a party. You've told her I'm quitting my job and opening a law practice in a town where I don't know a soul, present company, Martha, Horace, and Cuddles excluded."

He sighed. "If your aunt is right, and pinkies never lie, I'm fathering twins, then a boy and a girl. But do I worry about the price of milk? No. Why should I? Not with Horace ready to do her part. And Martha wants me to draw up a new will for her to bequeath our children money for their college educations."

He massaged his thigh. "Have I summed it up right?"

Hearing his bleak but amusing assessment, seeing the grin tugging at his gorgeous mouth and the devilish light in his eyes, Polly couldn't contain herself. She collapsed into her chair, laughing.

"Except for one thing." She raised her hand, flashing her temporary engagement ring. With an impudent toss of her head, she declared, "Reid Cameron, you're no Ashley Wilkes!"

He leaned forward. Lifting a lock of her hair, he let it slide through his fingers. "But you, my dear, are better than Scarlett."

A pleasant, cozy peace filled the room, while outside rain pelted the ground. Polly made coffee, and they traded stories of their childhoods, especially what it was like for both of them to be only children.

"I learned to depend on myself awfully fast," Polly admitted.

"It's too bad you didn't have a brother or sister. Keeping up this place is a tremendous responsibility."

"There have been times when I've hung on by the skin of my teeth, but it's worth it. The reward money will pay off my bills."

"Then I'm doubly glad I came."

"Doubly?" Her heart skipped a beat. His character, his sense of morality, coupled with his humor and caring, made him more than merely a handsome man. Cuddles trotted over to him and climbed onto his shoe.

Reid took her hand. "You're the first reason."

"Who's coming in Fran's place tonight?"

"No one."

Her pulse skipping, Polly fought to hide her feelings. "No one?"

"That's right," he said with one of his devastating smiles. "It's just us. Would you call this the hand of fate?"

From the moment Reid had walked into her home, Polly thought, Fate had conspired to play tricks on her. Suddenly the atmosphere in the room became highly charged. One thin wall would separate them and the powerful sexual attraction between them. She was a responsible adult; so why should it matter if she had a house full of guests or just one? On the other hand, her body reacted to his like a charge of dynamite waiting for ignition.

He swung his foot side by side, giving Cuddles a ride.

"It's raining," he said. "Would you prefer staying home?"

"No! I've got cabin fever."

He put the dog on the floor. "You don't say."

"Mmmm. Yes. A most horrible case. I'm keyed up."

He rose, then bent over her. His long fingers curved around her nape. She saw the brilliant glitter in his eyes, his sensual smile, and she knew he wasn't fooled.

"You mean restless?" he said, drawing her out of the chair and into his arms. There was no mistaking the blatant look of arousal in his eyes.

Polly inhaled his manly scent. Heat radiated between them. He was rapidly becoming too important to her. She swallowed. "Exactly."

He was kissing her ear, his warm breath spiking the level of intimacy to a higher degree. "Martha claims it's destiny."

"Not if we stay out late dancing."

"Silly girl." His mouth was a fraction from hers. "We still have to come back." His voice held a soft but potent promise.

She didn't need him to spell it out. The message in his dark eyes held her mesmerized. We want each other, he was saying silently. You decide.

Feeling hot and a little breathless, she eased from his embrace. "I'm going up to change."

He let her go, then said, "I'll check the bridge. Where do you keep your flashlight?"

"Can't it wait for daylight? Why grope in the dark?" she argued, bewildered by her need to protect a man who obviously didn't need or want her protection.

"I'd rather not wait until tomorrow. It shouldn't take me long. If I find loose planks, I'll phone headquarters, and they'll send a repair crew tomorrow. We don't want to hamper Grayson from his destination to a jail cell."

Grayson! Of course he'd be uppermost in Reid's mind. She'd gotten the reminder she needed. Reid and Fran, and whoever else was coming from the police department, would arrest the crooks, then Reid would leave. His reminder gave her a much-needed dose of reality.

"There are flashlights on the shelf in the front hall closet. Take one of the umbrellas too. They're in the stand near the front door."

Upstairs, she chose a yellow dress with a scooped neckline, formfitting bodice, and a bias-cut skirt that flared out over her hips for easy dancing. She attached pearl studs to her lobes and brushed out her hair. After slipping into a pair of multicolored-leather strap sandals, she went downstairs.

Despite the rain and darkness, Reid was obviously going over the bridge with a fine-tooth comb. He wouldn't want to call a repair crew out for nothing.

When fifteen minutes had elapsed, her excuses rang thin in her ears. She was worried. Changing her sandals for running shoes, she grabbed a flashlight and an umbrella and hurried out to look for him. The wind whipped at her back. She angled the umbrella to protect her face from pinpoints of driving rain. The flashlight barely cut through the gloom of the night.

"Reid!" she called, sweeping the light before her.

She was met by silence. She called his name again. Silence. Worry etched its way up her spine. Could Grayson have slipped through the police net? Could he be holding Reid prisoner? Spears of genuine alarm knotted her muscles. Reid would have answered her if he could.

She was halfway across the bridge when she spotted him. "Oh my God!"

She felt the blood drain from her face. Her heart pounded mercilessly. No wonder he hadn't answered. He had fallen through the bridge; only his upper torso was visible. His arms braced on planks on either side, he was trying to free himself. Each time he moved, the wooden planks groaned.

"Stay back!" he warned. Rain spattered his head and dripped down his face.

She halted, panic gripping her. It would have been hard for him to hang on in dry weather, but with rain-slippery hands, it required superhuman effort. Sudden pressure or one false move threatened his precarious position.

Polly couldn't stand idle. If he tumbled into the swollen river, he risked crashing onto one of the many boulders directly below. If he was maimed—or God forbid died!—she wouldn't be able to live with herself. She took a step forward on rubbery legs.

"Don't!" Reid yelled. "For God's sake, don't try to save me."

"What can I do?"

"Pray I don't fall through and hurt my precious hide."

His feeble attempt at humor plummeted her into despair. Assailed by guilt, she assumed full responsibility for his accident. With each scant inch of freedom he gained, she agonized. With each breath he labored, hers expelled in strangled hope. Biting down hard on her lip, she mentally shared his terrible ordeal.

The wrenching sounds of wood echoed in the night as he tried to shimmy backward. Only his lower legs remained hidden now. Adjusting the angle of his torso, he freed more of his legs.

She shone her light to aid him. "Reid, I see what you can't. The planks can't hold your weight much longer. Don't fight me. Please, darling. It's your only chance."

She closed her umbrella and dropped it on the bridge. Getting down on her knees, she crawled over to him, positioning

85

herself behind him. From his grunts and groans she couldn't begin to imagine what the pain of hanging on was doing to his back muscles, in addition to his legs and groin.

He offered a feeble protest. "Go away. We'll both go down. Let me do this myself."

"Argue later," she said as she slid her arms under his and around his chest. "You saved my life in the hayloft doing this. Now, hush, darling. I know what to do."

He eased his grip, allowing her to pull him backward. When they felt solid wood beneath them, he sat motionless while Polly crawled around to the hole to help free his feet.

She lay down at right angles to his legs. Reaching forward, she gently freed one foot, then the other. Reid braced himself on his elbows, angling his body away from the hole.

When both legs were free, she scooted back and grabbed him under the shoulders again. With his help she pulled him toward safety. Drenched and panting, she clung to him, rocking with him, shielding him with her body.

He pushed the thick wet strands of hair from her face. She was weeping, raining kisses of joy over his face.

"I owe you my life," he said hoarsely.

"Thank God, you're safe," she murmured over and over, the shock of his near death setting in as the splintering sound of wood being released from its mooring tore through the night.

She shuddered. Reid had come within a hairs-breadth of hurdling to his death. "If not for my stubbornness, you wouldn't be hurt."

"Don't blame yourself. I should have been more careful."

His attempt to suppress a groan knifed her heart. She didn't have time to waste. "I'm taking you off this bridge, out of the rain, or you'll get pneumonia."

"Help me up."

"I've got a better idea. There's a flatbed cart near the barn, the one with the long wooden handles. You'll ride back."

He shivered, and she hugged him more tightly. "You can't pull me," he said. "I'm okay. I'll walk."

"Horace!" she cried in a fit of brilliance. "You saved her from drenching her hooves and from being blown to smithereens. The least she can do is help you in an emergency."

Refusing further discussion, she dashed for the umbrella, sprang it open, shoved the handle in his hand, then ran toward the barn.

"Horace," Reid muttered. Rescue by a cow would have brought a smile to his lips if not for his aching muscles, exacerbated by the dull throb in his thigh. He'd cut himself on his sore leg. Cursing his rotten luck, he waited for Polly.

Light-headed, he thought for a minute he was losing it, when he heard an ungodly noise. As it grew louder and louder, he identified the source of the racket.

"In a million years," he said aloud, "the guys would never believe this."

Polly, an adorable, bedraggled, defiant angel, her dress and hair plastered to her, was walking toward him lugging Horace's makeshift reins. The incredible sight reminded him of a marching band gone haywire. Polly led the cow onto the bridge, leaving her where she knew it was safe. Horace's bell clanged to the accompaniment of Guns N' Roses.

Reid stood up. "Tell me I don't have to listen to that."

"Horace refuses to budge otherwise. You know she hates getting her hooves wet. Good thing I keep a battery-powered tape recorder in the barn in case of power outages."

Leaning heavily on Polly, Reid made his way to the cart. With effort they managed to get him in it, then Polly turned Horace around, and they headed for the house.

Reid wished she'd thought to bring him some earplugs.

"Do you think anything's broken?" Polly asked as she helped him down from the cart.

"Nothing's broken. The legs are fine. I'm okay." He caught her worried expression. "Believe me, I've had worse. A hot shower will fix me up in no time."

Her expression guarded, she wrapped an arm around his waist and helped him into the house. Once inside, she eyed the staircase.

"Reid, I can bring down a mattress. But if you decide you'd rather sleep down here, I'd have to put the mattress on the floor. In this old house that's drafty. And if you need to use the bathroom during the night, it would be hard for you to get up. Personally I think, if you can make it upstairs, you should. You can take a soothing shower, then lie down. You'd be better off in my king-size bed too."

Hearing her nervous babbling, watching her bite her lips, he knew she didn't think much of his chances of making it upstairs.

"Polly, stop worrying. Of course I can manage the stairs. I'll take a hot shower, and I'll be fine. Just give me a second to recoup my energy."

While he mobilized his strength, Polly raced upstairs, flipping on lights. She whipped off the bedspread and yanked down the covers on her bed, then flew into the bathroom. Turning on the shower, she left the shower door open a crack so the steam could warm the room. She set out clean, thick terry-cloth towels and a washcloth, along with a bottle of peroxide and a box of Band-Aids. As she sped downstairs, she was amazed at how well she was coping with the change from her routine life to a life that was unpredictable and more eventful than anything she'd ever known. She was changing in ways she'd never expected, not the least of which were her turbulent emotions.

Reid finished his long, hot shower, the soothing water easing the muscle strain as he'd thought it would. After drying himself, he put on a clean pair of briefs, then leaned against the washstand in Polly's pink-and-white tile bathroom. Before he'd used the bathroom without loitering, but now he took stock of Polly's personal items. Lady's shaver, deodorant, lipsticks, mascara, brushes. Bubble bath and bath powder sat on the counter. Nice feminine things. Not one sign of a male occupant, which suggested that no man shared her bedroom on a permanent basis. Not that it was his right, but the thought pleased him.

He glanced in the mirror. "Cameron, you look like hell."

He closed the lid on the toilet and sat down, then reached for the bottle of peroxide. Immediately he shouted in pain.

"What's wrong?" Polly yelled from the other side of the door. She had just come from her bedroom, where she had changed into her nightgown and robe.

"Nothing," he answered. "I'm okay."

"Are you decent?"

"Yes."

She opened the door, and her eyes swiftly examined him. He was wearing next to nothing—not exactly what she would call "decent." She couldn't help staring at his wide shoulders, at the line of dark hair that weaved down his broad chest and disappeared inside his underwear. She had never seen such a lean, hard, magnificent body.

Not even in her dreams.

He looked wonderful. With a trembling smile she laid one hand on his cheek, trying to offer solace. He turned his face into her hand and sighed.

"I swiveled to grab the peroxide to pour on the cut. Don't mind me. When it comes to pain, I'm a coward."

"You are not," she said stoutly. "You're the bravest man I know. Here, I'll do it."

As she bent over him, she saw a small scar on his thigh. "What caused this?"

When he didn't answer, her breath caught. Dawning awareness had her looking up.

"You were the cop who stopped the bullet, weren't you?"

"Yes."

"I saw you rubbing your thigh today. You were hurting before the accident."

"Twinging," he amended, with a tenderness that melted her heart. He was trying to comfort her. Her eyes stung.

"After all I've put you through, I'm not letting you lift a finger."

"The shower took the pain away. This was just a twinge. I'm fine. I want you to know that under fire you're marvelous. You saved my life."

"Marvelous." Her voice quavered. "I'm so marvelous I nearly got you killed. I'm so marvelous, I disregarded your warning."

In his line of work Reid had seen people collapse under stress. A trembling Polly tore at his heart in ways he'd never before felt. Taking her hands, he drew them away from her face. Tears glistened in her eyes.

"Don't," he murmured huskily. "It's okay. I'll prove it. We'll go dancing tomorrow night."

"Oh, please! We both know why I suggested that. Now look what I've done. I've rendered you useless."

He grinned. The result of her nearness was plainly evident. "Better take another look."

An embarrassed flush crept up her cheeks. "You know what I mean."

He touched her face, idly brushing his thumb over her cheek. "Will you dry my hair, please?"

Obviously attempting to dispel the sexual tension rising between them, she dried his hair vigorously, first by toweling it, then with the blow dryer. After fluffing his hair with her fingers, she stepped back to observe her handiwork

"There. I'm through."

He caught her wrist, pulling her closer. A feeling of intimacy pervaded the steam-filled room. "You really haven't met a braver man?"

"Absolutely not, darling. You're as brave, if not braver, than Rhett Butler." She winked. "Far braver than Ashley Wilkes."

He rewarded her with a broad smile. "Good, I like that."

In the bedroom he asked for the phone that sat on a table near a wing chair. He needed to report to his headquarters. After talking for a few minutes, he covered the mouthpiece of the phone and told her a crew would fix the bridge in the morning.

"Any new developments?" he said, returning to his phone conversation. He was given the latest on Grayson's movements. He had arrived at his girlfriend's house. The police would arrive at Polly's Monday to seal off the exits and help with Grayson's arrest.

Reid hung up. "Everything's under control. There's nothing to worry about."

She took a deep breath. "I'm so grateful you're all right, Reid. If anything had happened to you…" She choked up for a moment. "I'll say good night"

"No, please don't go. Stay." His intense gaze held her as forcefully as his softly spoken appeal. "Stay."

He held out his hand.

She nodded and took the steps her heart couldn't deny. When she sat on the edge of the bed, Reid lifted her hand and kissed it. His were strong hands, she thought, capable of diffusing a dynamite charge, or of tenderly stroking her as he was doing now.

Rain beat at the windows, but there, in the confines of her canopied bed, nothing mattered but Reid. A lock of dark hair had fallen over his forehead. Giving in to her impulse, she pushed it off his forehead, then kissed his temple.

"I'm having a wide-awake dream," he murmured.

Her gaze roved over his face. The stark raw emotion she read in his eyes compelled her to ask, "Is it a good dream?"

"The best. In it, we're making love."

"Are we, darling?" She felt her senses awakening as his thumb languorously brushed the pulse point on her wrist. Could he feel her heartbeat leap?

"Polly," he said, his voice low and throbbing with intensity. "You can't possibly want me as much as I want you."

She could have told him he was wrong, that her heart was bursting with love for him, but she didn't. Instead, she pushed the thought of sad tomorrows from her mind. He hadn't lied by offering commitments or by pretending to have fallen in love with her. He wanted her. She wanted him. In two days they'd lived through more than most people faced in a lifetime, and they'd triumphed together.

Reid looked up into her beautiful face, at her eyes fringed with thick lashes, at her luscious red lips that tasted like fine wine. He craved her with a surging passion greater than any he'd ever felt before in his life. In a humbling realization he knew why. His overwhelming need stemmed from more than his heated desire to join his body with hers. She had touched his soul.

"Will you share the dream with me?" he asked.

His searing gaze reflected Polly's innermost feelings. From the first she'd felt the sparks of electricity between them. She placed her hand in his, giving him her answer.

CHAPTER EIGHT

"Polly." Reid whispered her name on a sigh of benediction. Kissing her hand, he shifted onto his side, making room for her as she lay down beside him.

"Now I understand the passage I read from your book," he murmured, enfolding her welcoming warmth in his arms.

Polly's heart swelled with tenderness. She stroked his bare chest, kissing the hard, flat planes of his body where her fingers left their sensitive trail. "I was so afraid for you."

He tilted up her chin and kissed away her tears. "Shhh. That's over. We'll celebrate life. Together."

As she slipped off her robe and nightgown, he lit the lamp on the nightstand. Then his arms encircled her naked form, and his mouth met hers in a searing, erotic kiss that sent sparks of pleasure through her.

Cradling her face, he said hoarsely, "It's already better than my dream." His heated gaze traveled down her slim body.

"You're beautiful," he murmured, kissing her lips. He scattered kisses down her body, not letting her hide any part of it from his view or taste.

Astounded by her feelings, she pulled him close, burying her face against his shoulder, kissing him there and on his neck.

Igniting her with fire, claiming her for his, his hands swept over her body. He cupped the nest of curls at the apex of her thighs, and she arched upward, pressing against his palm.

She ran her hands down his arms, then sank her hands in his

hair. As he slipped one finger inside her dewy, pulsing flesh, she moaned with pleasure.

She reached for his hard shaft, stroking him and heightening both their needs.

It was his turn to moan. Even as he pleasured her, she was driving him wild. He trailed kisses along her cheek and neck, before returning to devour her lips. Their tongues tangled, while his hand shaped her breast. He shifted her upward, his rougher skin branding hers. When he took her breast in his mouth, sucking first one nipple, then the other, her body vibrated with a response greater than any she'd thought possible.

A liquefying heat flowed to the pit of her stomach as he tormented her with exquisite mastery, worshiping her with his mouth and touch. Just when she thought she couldn't take more, he wrapped his arms around her, holding her flush to his naked body, giving her a brief respite before beginning his tender assault again, showering her with adoration.

His hands played over her silken skin, driving her upward, higher and higher, until she writhed in his arms, begging for release. "Reid now, please. Together."

He reached for the packet of protection he'd placed on her nightstand. After slipping the sheath on, he shifted on top of her. Wanting to go slow, reining back his instinctive need to take her in one long thrust, he entered her by degrees. But when she clutched his hips and clamped her legs around his waist so that she could take all of him, he slipped past the point of self-control. Again and again, he thrust into her, burying himself fully, feeling her inner muscles tighten their hold, contracting, quivering.

And then he could hold back no longer. Drugged on her alluring scent, her thrilling kisses, the wine that was Polly, he drove into her heat. With bodies pressed close, with lips kissing, with hands eliciting sighs of rapture, Reid's hoarse shout rumbled from deep within his soul. Hurled into her own blinding explosion, Polly cried out too.

Reid bowed his head beside hers. "This is our dream, Polly," he whispered. "No one else's."

Much later, when their breathing had calmed and their world had tilted upright again, he shifted to his side, still joined to her in an intimate embrace. She gazed at him, and in the afterglow of love, his words came back to her. *This is our dream, Polly. No one else's.*

Dreams, she knew, were fleeting, forgotten in the light of day. For now she wouldn't think of tomorrow. Snuggling in his arms, she kissed his cheek. She understood exactly what he had meant.

Awake, Reid lay on his side, his hand drifting over a sleeping Polly's hip to slide upward and cup her breast. She sighed contentedly. What a surprise, he thought, thinking of this amazing woman who snuggled against him. Making love with her affected him to his core. She enriched him, made him feel as if he were ten feet tall, a better human being than he was. After their lovemaking had ended, he'd half expected her to talk about the future, one that included him. She hadn't.

She had smiled at him, kissed him softly on the lips, thanked him for letting her share his lovely dream, then teasingly commented he had a radiant look in his eyes. He hadn't been surprised. She'd bowled him over. From the first moment they'd met, sparks flew around them. Yet she seemed to accept their lovemaking as simply a celebration of life, a culmination of the intense attraction they felt toward each other, coupled with the dangers they'd faced.

What should he say? Making no demands, she'd touched his soul. Always before when he'd made love, it had ended with satisfaction. With Polly he'd reached the heights of heaven. And now what?

Now he went on with his life. Polly was more than a dream. They were lovers. They faced a farce of an engagement party, where he'd mingle with people who loved her and would wish them well. Martha would be in her glory, fluttering among her guests, introducing him to everyone.

No matter how noble his intentions, he was in a mess of his own making. He didn't want to think about Grayson or the hurt Martha would feel when she learned why they'd set up this ruse. But if they didn't tell Martha, then she, Polly's co-workers, and everyone else they'd meet would think they were engaged. How could they develop a normal relationship in the face of that? The answer was, they couldn't.

Polly stirred. "Can't you sleep?" she murmured drowsily. "Would you rather I leave?"

"No. That's the one thing I don't want. Shhh, go back to sleep."

Gathering her closer, he nuzzled her neck. She sighed deeply, snuggled against him, then drifted back to sleep.

In minutes he joined her, breathing her delightful scent.

At 6:30 A.M. Polly eased Reid's arm off her breast and slipped out of bed. Much as she hated leaving the warm cocoon, Horace awaited her. As soon as she'd awakened, the reality of her feelings for Reid had threatened to overwhelm her. She needed time to put them into perspective so she could steer her life back onto its safe, normal course. The first thing to do was put last night into focus. By acting adult about it, not making more of it than it was, she could lessen the pangs of loneliness she would feel after Reid left.

Who was she kidding?

She loved him. When love was one-sided, it was doomed to end. Last night she'd made the decision to spend the night with him, to make love with him. Though she knew she'd have to let him go, she wouldn't change a single loving moment they had shared. She would never find such closeness of spirit with anyone but Reid.

Silently gathering her clothes, she paused to look at him. With his hair tousled, the blanket slipped down to expose his broad chest, he appeared as sexy as he did when he was awake, and that was saying something. Maybe it was because they'd been intimate. When he woke up and looked at her, she knew his dark eyes would fill with heated memory, reminding her that only a few hours earlier, he had made love to her for a second time.

Even as she watched him, his hand snagged her pillow. Wrapping his arms around the pillow, he burrowed his face in it and slept on.

So noise from the bathroom wouldn't awaken him, she washed and dressed in the kitchen. After making a pot of coffee, she headed for the barn.

Either Horace wasn't in the mood to fuss, or she was unusually happy to see Polly. Polly was able to milk her without benefit of music, then Horace lumbered docilely out to the pasture.

The morning was flawless, making last night's danger seem surreal. A slight breeze shook raindrops from tree leaves. The cool morning temperature would rise into the high 70s. She made her way over to the bridge, surveying its span as she walked onto it. She remained clear of the section that had nearly claimed Reid for a victim. Her heart constricted when she thought of his close call.

Retracing her steps, she walked home. In the kitchen she poured a mug of coffee for Reid and went upstairs to her bedroom. After setting the mug down on the dresser, she drew the curtains aside. Sunlight streamed through the windows.

Reid stirred and blinked. "Mmmm. I like waking up and seeing you."

"Do you?" she murmured.

"Yes. Is that coffee for me?"

She brought it over. "I'm glad to see you've regained your health."

"Thanks to last night's special treatment. Have you milked Horace this morning?"

She nodded.

"Then you're free?"

"Yes."

He kicked aside the light blanket and lay naked in her bed, a magnificent, fully aroused male animal. As his heated gaze singed her with longing, he all but declared he wanted to devour her in the most succulent way. "Let's not waste the best part of the morning then."

Polly's breath caught. They had so little time left. She wondered if he could see everything she felt for him in her eyes. Her hands went to the buttons on her blouse.

"No," he said. "Come here. I want to do that."

He turned the simple act of removing her clothes into an erotic experience, kissing her breasts, laving her skin, awakening erogenous zones until she writhed in his arms, begging him to take her.

He brought his mouth down on hers. She met him in a demanding kiss. Reid felt the warmth of her lips in pleasurable torment. The breath hissed out of him when she also cupped him intimately. Her kisses, her touch, roared him to life, slamming into his loins with unbearable tension.

They made love on rumpled sheets with the sun warming their bodies. They showed each other exactly how and where to please, discovering even more pleasure than they'd found the night before.

"I love the feel and taste of your body," Reid murmured. He kissed her greedily, then traced the tip of his tongue around a nipple. "You like this?"

"You know I do," she said, arching against him.

He buried his face between the sweet valley of her breasts, and she shuddered, delighting him with her response. Swiftly he prepared himself, then entered her. She met his driving strokes with a sense of urgency, and he wondered if she, like himself, was achingly aware that in a few days they would go their separate ways. To do otherwise meant continuing the fabrication that they were engaged, and the stress would be unfair to both of them.

He made love to her fiercely, sweeping her into their special sensory world. Polly surrendered to him completely, letting him take her soaring to the highest peak. But when she floated down, she rolled away so he couldn't see the tears in her eyes.

He gathered her in his arms. "Did you know you called me darling, both last night and this morning?"

"Yes," she whispered.

He kissed her shoulder. "Words of endearment are common for engaged couples."

Or couples in love, she could have added. Reid was offering her an out, though, a polite way for her to state the obvious.

She did. "We're not engaged. If I tell Martha about the bridge, it gives us and her an excuse to cancel her party. What do you think?"

Subdued by her suggestion, Reid was silent for a minute. The bridge did offer a plausible and perfect excuse to cancel the party. So why wasn't he leaping to agree with her? Polly's reasoning was as sound as his. Why wasn't he urging her to make the phone call?

He saw himself playing the intended bridegroom, kissing and hugging Polly, grinning and shaking hands with the people congratulating him. While the idea was attractive, the subterfuge wasn't. Polly deserved better. Like her, it disturbed him. But what really agitated him was lying next to her, spent from their loving, and thinking about their impending separation. Could he really give her up?

"I think it would be unwise to cancel," he said.

She frowned down at him. "I've got a lot to lose, Reid. First, my friends meet you, then they hold my hand when I tell them we called it off. It's wrong."

"Your aunt won't cancel. She'll postpone the party. Last night she asked me for a list of my friends and relatives. I told her not to bother, that no one would be able to make it on such short notice. If she postpones the party, though, she'll want to call them. It adds another wrinkle."

"It's all the more reason to phone her and tell her the engagement's off. That eliminates complications."

"I dislike secretiveness as much as you, but your aunt's blabbed to half the town. So that's out for now."

Polly felt on the brink of hysteria. She couldn't be as dispassionate as Reid. Why couldn't she see it from his practical point of view?

She couldn't because she was in love with him.

"Then you want to go through with the pretense?" she asked.

"I do," he replied, regarding her closely. "I don't think we have a choice. When I said that Martha would reschedule the party for next weekend, I thought you understood. By then we'll have captured Grayson."

"And you'll be gone."

"Yes."

She struggled to keep her voice impersonal, as if she were negotiating a business deal. "Okay. We'll do it your way. We'll get through the day. I hope people won't bring presents, but if they do, I'll return them."

Reid got up. "We should dress. Much as I wish the bridge remained impassable so I could have you to myself, I know that's impossible. The construction crew should arrive soon. Also, I've got to hide a camera in the loft, so we can record Grayson in all his thieving glory. When he comes here, I want you to remain in the house. I know you have this tendency to save my life, but don't interfere. By the time he arrives, this place will be swarming with cops."

And that, Polly told herself, was how Reid switched back to being a cop on duty.

Later, when she and Reid were in the kitchen, she phoned her aunt. She told Martha about the unsafe bridge, assured her both she and Reid were fine, and added that a crew would arrive soon to repair the bridge.

"The important thing is that you're both okay," Martha said. "Oh, Polly, we're going to have a marvelous time tomorrow. There's no rain in the forecast."

"Aunt Martha, how many people do you expect?" She prayed Martha would say ten or so, fifteen at the most, but somehow she knew the number would be far higher.

"Sixty. Maybe more. It's short notice."

"My Lord!" Polly sank down in a chair. She hadn't dreamed so many would attend. "You made over sixty phone calls! How was that possible without staying up for hours?"

"I didn't make all the calls myself," Martha said. "I phoned Grace, Joan, and Lonni. They were as amazed as I was. You never told anyone about Reid."

Martha giggled. "Grace bet he's slight of build, with blond wispy hair, like Ashley Wilkes. I didn't tell her he's more the Rhett Butler type. I'm saving it for a surprise."

Polly groaned.

"Anyway, I let your friends split up the names on the snow list rather than try to contact everyone myself. Then I phoned the head of the PTA."

"Oh!"

"Oh, yes, and I gave the girls permission to ask the parents of your past and present students. I called your principal myself. What a nice man!"

The room swam before Polly's eyes. "You called Mr. Grant?"

"You're excited, aren't you, darling girl? I can hear it in your voice. It's to be expected. Mr. Grant volunteered to phone his ex-secretary. He said she likes you very much. He wouldn't miss the party, so I told him to bring his wife. As long as it's outdoors on your lawn and the weather's predicted to be great, the more the merrier. Everyone's offered to bring some food. Tell Reid the tables and chairs will arrive tomorrow morning."

Polly shook her head. Her aunt might as well announce it on the local TV station. "What tables and chairs?" she asked weakly.

"The ones I rented, which Reid insisted on paying for."

"He what?" She covered the mouthpiece and whispered to Reid, "You didn't tell me you offered to pay for the tables and chairs. She's invited at least sixty people!"

Martha's happy voice brought her back to the phone. "Grace is giving you a bridal shower. It's no surprise. Pick a suitable date. I told her at the rate you two got yourselves engaged, to expect a wedding soon."

Polly's neck muscles went into spasm.

"Don't worry," Martha added. "She knows you're not pregnant."

Polly's mouth dropped open. Standing, she shoved the phone into Reid's hand.

"Talk to my aunt."

Reid tried not to laugh at Polly's disgruntled expression as Martha asked if Polly was taking good care of him. Maintaining a solemn tone, he assured Martha he'd never had more personalized or more loving attention in his life.

After he'd hung up, Polly sat back down at the table. "The world is coming here tomorrow," she said, sounding totally demoralized. "This has gotten thoroughly out of hand."

Privately he agreed with her. Aloud he said, "The numbers may make it easier. This way Martha will drag me from group to group. I won't be stuck in long conversations."

"Her short conversations are damaging. I guarantee you she'll announce our four future children."

"I'll stop her."

"Good luck. If you can, you're the first."

"I'll tell her beforehand we feel it's too personal."

"Aunt Martha has got a great batting average with her predictions, and she likes to let people know that."

Reaching across the table, he rubbed his knuckles against her soft cheek. "She'll listen to me. She wouldn't do anything to hurt you. For the record, Polly, you're an intelligent, caring, loving woman. I think you'll make a wonderful mother."

"Let's make breakfast," she said briskly.

While they did, Reid kept talking to Polly, offering reasons why the large numbers of guests would help, not hinder. She noticed that he acted as if it was all in a day's work, a day that would pass quickly. As she made pancakes, he set the table and poured orange juice in their glasses. He disappeared outside for a minute, then came back with a rose he had plucked from the bush near the back door. Her spirits lifted. She couldn't blame him for his honest feelings. Why should she expect him to pretend he was in love with her?

During breakfast Cuddles trotted in and took up his position on Reid's shoe. Reid wiggled his foot, and the dog wrapped his front legs around Reid's ankle. Laughing, Reid asked, "Does Cuddles act this way with everyone?"

Polly smiled. "I've never seen him do it before. He loves you."

"Smart dog."

When he'd finished eating, Reid played with Cuddles. He swung his foot from side to side, giving the dog a ride and laughing when Cuddles wagged his tail like a metronome. Their play was interrupted by a knock at the back door, followed by a voice familiar to Reid.

Cuddles growled when Reid put him on the floor so he could greet his friend Jim Hager, who often worked with the state police. Reid introduced Jim and Polly, and the three left the house. When Reid unthinkingly started to put his arm around Polly, she stepped to the side, shaking her head.

Swearing under his breath, he took note of Polly's subtle warning. He shoved his hands into his pockets, knowing it wouldn't be right for Jim to see him with his arm around a woman while he was on duty. Not only had he forgotten his professional restraint by automatically reaching for Polly, it had felt right and natural to do it. Still, he owed it to Polly not to leave her with emotional baggage. He just wished he didn't feel so rotten about all this subterfuge.

They walked out onto the bridge, toward where Jim's crew was setting up. When they reached the gaping hole, Jim asked Reid how he'd managed to avoid falling.

Reid looked down at the boulders and rushing water beneath the hole. Had he crashed onto one of those rocks, he'd be maimed or dead.

"Polly pulled me to safety. The weather was awful. Besides the rain making it hard for me to hang on and to see, the two of us were soaking wet. Without her I doubt if I could have made it."

Jim looked from Reid to Polly. "He owes you a lot."

Thinking of all they had shared in the past two days, Polly disagreed. Her senses were attuned to Reid, and she was aware of him on so many levels; his scent, the size of him, which made her feel cherished and feminine, the texture of his skin, the way his eyes lit up when he teased her, or darkened in passion. "No, it's I who owe him. I should have had the bridge inspected."

The look Reid gave her said he understood and shared the depth of her feelings. Despite her silent warning to him a few minutes earlier, she was tempted to take his hand. A loud hello forestalled her. Glancing up, they saw Martha at the foot of the bridge, waving. Reid casually pulled the tail of his dark shirt out of his trousers to conceal his gun. Polly sent him a grateful look.

"How long do you think you'll be, Jim?" he asked.

"Can't say for sure. If we can't finish today, we'll shore up the bridge and return later. We'll leave it safe for you, Polly."

"Will we be able to drive across the bridge?" Reid asked. "From what I've seen thus far, the damage seems confined to one area."

Polly saw her aunt start walking toward them and squeezed Reid's arm. "Martha's coming."

They excused themselves, leaving Jim to return to his work. Reid shouted to Martha to stay where she was. Polly knew he was thinking the same thing she was. Jim knew Reid was a state policeman. If Martha joined them, he might, in the course of conversation, allude to Reid's profession, unaware Reid wanted it kept secret.

Martha was a colorful sight in a bright red dress and a fringed red shawl Polly had given her for her birthday. As Polly and Reid reached her, she raised up on tiptoes, craning her head to see what the men were doing.

"Are you certain they'll finish today?" Martha asked.

"I've been assured they'll do their best," Polly answered. "So far it looks like it's nothing more than replacing loose boards from one section."

"How did you manage to get them here on such short notice?"

Polly gazed at Reid. "Reid knows the right people to call in an emergency."

"You're so lucky, Polly," Martha said.

I wish I were, Polly thought.

"Aunt Martha," Reid said, obviously wanting to change the subject, "you've been busy. I hear you've invited an army."

She playfully poked his arm. "How many times will I get to give my niece an engagement party? I'm not through. This morning I phoned a few friends. We don't have a snow list like Polly's school does, but we have our own grapevine."

"Really."

"Yes. Most of us are widows. We check up on each other. All I did was ask a few friends to call around, then let me know who can come. Everyone is dying to meet you, Reid. Isn't it wonderful? In no time at all you'll be part of our community."

Polly was absorbed in looking at a flock of lucky blackbirds flying overhead. She felt an overpowering urge to learn to fly so she could join the birds as they headed toward the horizon. People adored her aunt, tiny, good-hearted tornado that she was. Hordes of guests, ready to cheer, eat, and be merry would descend there tomorrow, not wanting to disappoint Martha.

Martha went on. "I know there's an overabundance of lawyers today, but not in this part of the state. Parents send their kids to law school, and you'll never guess where those ingrates practice law today."

"Where?" Reid asked.

"Beverly Hills and Seattle. Don't worry about drumming up trade. I'll tell everyone the reason you're moving to our town is out of love for Polly. My friends will be impressed. Then I'll drop the hint that it's time to update their wills."

Polly caught Reid's grim smile. The longer Martha prattled, the more fantastic ideas she came up with. Polly was having some bizarre ideas herself of what the engagement party would be like.

Huge numbers of women would cram into her kitchen, carrying platters of food, with their battle slogan: "This dessert needs refrigeration!"

With the ground muddy in places, her floors would be a mess. Cuddles would be in an excited dither. Which, now that she thought about it, was the least of her worries. She envisioned a long procession of vans from the Let's Party Rental parked in her driveway. Drivers and helpers would set up banquet-size tables and hundreds of folding chairs on the grass. Not to mention a sea of colorful umbrellas and the matching paper goods Martha must have ordered. As commander in chief, Martha would direct her troops, transforming her yard into a magical party.

"Toilet paper," Polly mumbled. "I'll run out of toilet paper."

Martha heard her. "It's taken care of."

Polly muttered thanks.

All Reid could do was stare at the diminutive lady who was cheerfully turning his life upside down. But when he thought she had finally run out of steam, she patted his arm and said the worst thing he could hear.

"Reid, it's only right I contact your dear mother. I'd never forgive myself otherwise. If she can't attend, at least I will have done my duty."

"I'll tell her," he said quickly. "Save you a phone call."

"No," Martha said adamantly. "It's my obligation to issue the invitation. I'm the hostess. Etiquette demands it. Trust me."

Her little hands created tiny windmills as she wound up to ram home her point. "Polly's parents would never forgive me."

"They're dead," Reid said. Forgetting Jim might be watching, he swept his arm around Polly's shoulders, more for support than out of affection.

"In this life," Martha said, "but not in the hereafter. Polly's parents are watching you from heaven this minute."

Reid blanched.

"You think they see everything we did—I mean do?" he asked.

Martha missed his strangled innuendo. "Of course I do. Let them enjoy their only child's engagement party as much as you two dears will."

Polly's knees buckled. She grabbed on to Reid. Martha produced a pad and pencil from her pocket and handed it to him with a flourish. "Write down your mother's phone number."

Martha had him, and Reid knew it. To refuse would be rude, and it would hurt her feelings. He scratched the number across the pad.

"It's best if you phone her this afternoon," he said. "She's usually out in the mornings."

"Thank you. If I think of anything else later on, I'll call you." Martha gaily took off like a gyro.

Polly and Reid gaped at each other. Since she couldn't sprout wings, Polly very sincerely wished for the ground to open and swallow her up.

"What a little dynamo." Reid said. "The president should appoint her to his cabinet. Who can say no to her?"

"Not many. When Martha calls, people adjust their prior plans if at all possible. There isn't anyone she hasn't done a favor for over the years. She has a heart of gold."

"I've got to speak with my mother first."

"Make sure she doesn't come."

"That goes without saying. But can you imagine her surprise if she isn't prepared for Martha's phone call?"

Polly couldn't.

CHAPTER NINE

Polly tried to find a silver lining in her aunt's enthusiasm. As she walked away, she glanced at the mountains and the surrounding countryside and its spectacular palette of rippling shades. All right, she scolded herself. The party was one day out of her life. If she didn't dwell on its ramifications, she'd do fine. If the charade got too tough to handle, she could always escape to the pasture, hide out with Horace for a few minutes.

"Can you imagine anything nuttier?" she muttered to Reid.

He inhaled harshly. "Yes, as a matter of fact I can."

She looked at him pleadingly. "What?"

"It'll come to me. Give me a few minutes."

The joke fell flat. They walked on in a somber mood with no particular destination in mind. Finally, they ended up at the old apple orchard. Polly perched on a large boulder at one end of the orchard while Reid leaned against a tree.

"This is awful," she said. "All of it. Martha's enthusiasm. The party. Telling your mother. I wish I could take it back or make it go away."

She looked up at him. "We should plan a counteroffensive."

"What do you have in mind?"

"How do I know? This is your department, not mine."

"I'm fresh out of counteroffensives," he said tightly. "It's one thing to need a cover story, but who expected this?" He rubbed a hand across his knotted forehead. "I never involve my mother in my affairs."

Polly rested her chin on her hand. "I don't know why you're complaining. Your mother knows you're in law enforcement. How can telling her this is a charade, a cover for your protection, bother her?"

He grimaced. "I'm not in the habit of lying, so it bothers me. How do you think I feel about Martha throwing us a party?"

Polly shrugged. "You can't possibly feel as rotten as I do."

"I do. I feel like a louse. Once my mother knows the reason I'm asking her to go along with this, she'll start thinking like a mother. She'll empathize with us, but she'll also put herself in Martha's place and wonder why we didn't come up with a better ruse."

"Why you didn't come up with a better ruse. Leave me out of this."

He didn't answer, and she shook her head.

"Oh, hell, I'm sorry I said that. I'm as culpable as you. Please forgive me."

He smiled at her. "You're an unusual woman, Polly Sweet. Would you think I'm out of bounds if I asked you to kiss me, just to take the edge off my worries?"

Grinning, she got up and walked over to him, pressing her body to his. As she slid her hands around his neck and raised her face to meet his lips, she decided that the riskiest situations could have a silver, if temporary, lining.

Then she stopped thinking as she threw herself into the kiss. His body warmed, from the sun, pressed into hers. His hands roamed over her buttocks, urging her closer to his male hardness.

He groaned when she slid her own hand between them to find him. "You're driving me crazy. I wish the men weren't here."

She kissed his neck. "Good. I like driving you nuts. Why should it all be one-sided?"

He nibbled on her lower lip. "I like hearing you say that."

She pulled back enough to see him. "Tell me about your mother."

"You should have seen her after I was shot. As soon as she found out I was going to live, she campaigned for me to practice law instead. She said it was time for me to get out, but I didn't agree with her. Now I'm not so sure. Yesterday when I disarmed the bomb, I wanted to be more than Grayson's arresting officer. I wanted to be the prosecuting attorney who convinced a jury to send the scum up for a long time. I couldn't stand the thought of you getting hurt."

He had so many wonderful qualities, Polly thought. He could be hard as nails or as gentle as a lamb. He could be a tender lover or a demanding one. She'd just scratched the surface of knowing this complex man.

"Thank you," she said. "I couldn't stand to see you hurt either."

A lazy smile replaced the hard frown on his face when he mentioned Grayson's name. Polly's heart skipped a beat.

"When will you phone your mother?" she asked.

"Soon, Polly. I'm sorry. I really am. Hindsight is twenty-twenty vision. I should have come up with another alibi."

Her fingers traced his lips. "We'll get through it."

"Meeting you and making love with you is the only part of this I'm not sorry about."

"Me too," she whispered, meeting his lips for a long kiss. His arms were her refuge. It seemed incongruous she would seek solace in the arms of the man whose sheer audacity had caused her such misery. Yet when they drew apart and started back toward the house, she held on to his hand, as if clinging to an elusive sanctuary.

Activity on and off the bridge hummed with an array of men, trucks, and machinery. One burly, T-shirted man directed the forklift positioning the new planks. There was noise everywhere, men shouting, hammering, sawing, pneumatic drills.

Spotting Jim in the distance, Polly disengaged her hand from Reid's. "We better not."

Reid set his jaw. Just seeing Polly took his breath away, and all he wanted to do was touch her. Her sun-kissed hair, thick and falling in waves below her slim shoulders, made him want to bury his hands in it, as he had when they'd made love. Her cheekbones were high, her skin a creamy rose, the color of the finest porcelain. Her wide blue eyes, surrounded by a lush fringe of lashes, had a slight almond shape to their outer corners, giving her an aristocratic air.

He shoved his hands in his pockets and tried not to think of his impending engagement party. His supposed fiancée was so beautiful, all he wanted to do was grab her by the hand and hustle her into the house, straight up to the bedroom.

As if she'd read his mind, she smiled up at him and

whispered, "We'll have time alone later."

"I need a scorecard," he grumbled. "In front of your aunt, touching is not only permissible, it's advisable. After all, Martha sees us producing a passel of babies."

"She is rather amazing."

Reid bit back a smile. "Rather is hardly the word. She believes implicitly in tarot cards, astrological charts, palmistry, and Axl Rose."

"I envy her passion."

Reid stopped in his tracks as he saw the wistful, faraway look in Polly's eyes. "Don't," he said. "She's living in her fantasy world. Unfortunately, I helped bring it about. I accept the blame. But as far as you're concerned, Polly, you're the most passionate woman I know."

His lips tightened as he suddenly thought of Polly in the arms of another man. He had no claim on her. What she did in her private life after he left was her business. For himself commitment was merely a word beginning with the letter C.

He cleared his throat. "Then," he continued, his hands jammed in his pockets, "there's Jim. He's worked for the police long enough to know that if they pull him off another assignment, this one takes a high priority. Professionally it's a no-no for me to show you affection. You were right to remind me. I'm going to like tomorrow a damn sight better than today. At least kissing you or holding your hand will be expected of me then."

Polly stared up at him as yet another unpleasant thought struck her. Not only would kissing be expected tomorrow, but surely her friends would ask all sorts of questions about her future husband. She didn't know his age, his favorite movies, his favorite ice-cream flavor, or his shirt size. She didn't know his hobbies, what sports he played in high school.

In short, she knew him mainly carnally!

While they pretended to be an adoring couple, none of the groom's side would be in attendance. Unless she counted Fran. Fran and Reid would be the only two people there walking around with concealed weapons. A bubble of hysterical laughter erupted from Polly's throat.

"What's so funny?" Reid asked.

"Funny?" She stared at him, agog. "Funny? Funny!" The word caught on a sob. Tears pooled in her eyes. "I'm laughing to keep from crying, you silly man. Can't you see how happy I am? Tomorrow promises to be your everyday garden-variety engagement party. It's every girl's dream. I can't wait."

She broke down sobbing. "Poor Martha."

Reid didn't give a damn if the whole world saw them. All he cared about was not upsetting Polly. He held her while she cried her "tears of happiness."

"I'm sorry," she mumbled. "I don't want you to see me acting like a fool."

"What should I say?" he asked, his lips on her temple.

She didn't answer, and he let her cry it out, turning his body to shield her from prying eyes, should anyone look their way.

The consequences of his actions weighed heavily on his mind. On the one hand they were strangers. On the other hand, they craved each other intimately.

They were engaged.

Engaged to be disengaged.

He didn't want to give her up.

He had to give her up.

Swiftly. A clean, surgical break. He should be used to them by now. Circumstances had thrown them together. Circumstances would part them.

When she finally stopped crying, he lifted her face to his with one finger under her chin. He kissed the sheen of tears from her lashes, her cheeks.

"Better?" he asked softly.

She wiped her face. "Yes. Now that I think about it, it won't be so bad. I'll put tomorrow to good use. Writers use their experiences in books. This one will end up a scene in my book. In fact, I'll write down everything that's happened since we met. I'll watch you when you mingle with the crowds, then adapt your actions for my book. So you see, nothing in life is wasted. Consider yourself important to my research."

It wasn't exactly what Reid wanted to hear, but at least she had stopped crying. They continued on to the house, and he tried to call his mother. Her line was busy. He tried several times with no luck, so he decided to make lemonade for the crew. Polly told him where to find paper cups and a few boxes of chocolate-chip cookies on a pantry shelf.

As they carried the lemonade and cookies outside, Jim came to meet them. He'd finished his inspection, and as he'd suspected, the bridge was safe except for one rotted section.

Polly smiled in relief. "Thank goodness! If I had to replace the bridge, it would cost a fortune, which I don't have."

Jim wiped his sweaty brow. "You're getting away lucky too, Polly. New bridges are outrageously expensive. Especially without state aid, and this being private property, I doubt if you'd qualify. The men will support the braces. By leaving the old ones in and drilling new ones, it makes the bridge sturdier. I said it before, Polly, but after seeing a few of those rotted boards, I'm amazed you didn't fall through."

Reid looked down at the rushing river and was grateful for Polly's safety.

"Whoever the guy is you're after," Jim went on, "he might have fallen through and saved you the trouble of setting a trap."

As Reid joined Jim to inspect the repairs on the bridge, Polly returned to the house. Since only a miracle would now prevent half the town from coming to her house the following day, she threw herself into a frenzy of cleaning. She was on her knees, attacking a stubborn spot on the kitchen linoleum, when Reid entered the house about forty-five minutes later.

He paused at the kitchen door. "Do you want some help?"

She shook her head vigorously. "No," she said between gritted teeth. "I'm pretending this damn floor's a punching bag."

He watched her for another minute, then turned to go. "I'll try my mother again."

"Use the phone in my office. When you're through, switch on the answering machine."

The phone had been ringing to distraction. Her closest friends were thrilled, surprised, and, she learned, hurt that she hadn't mentioned Reid. Grace Waters teasingly accused her of holding out on her, but there was a note of disappointment in her voice.

"We're best friends," she complained. "Best friends talk."

Polly apologized. She promised they'd get together for lunch, and she'd tell Grace everything.

After she figured it out first for herself.

Lonni Landis's congratulations ended in a scolding too. "Why didn't you say something? We're best friends. Best friends talk."

Polly promised they'd get together for lunch, when she'd tell her everything. She'd use the same story she would tell Grace.

Joan Daniels said they'd known each other since grade school. She came right out and asked Polly why she'd held out on her.

Polly told Joan what she'd told the others, adding, "I didn't want to jinx our romance."

Lying to her friends pained her. She hoped when she was able to explain, they'd understand. If not, it would strain friendships with people she loved and admired.

She could hear Reid's voice in the den and assumed he'd gotten through to his mother. He returned to the kitchen doorway about five minutes later.

She sat back on her haunches. "How did it go?"

"You're wearing out the same spot."

She hadn't realized. She rose and picked up the mop. "What did your mother say?"

"Everything's fine. When you're through, let's talk."

She flipped her hair back and gave him a level stare. "No. I'm through dissecting the nuances of our sham engagement. We've talked it to death."

"If you need me, I'll be in the barn, setting up the camera."

By afternoon Polly had finished cleaning. She'd scrubbed the kitchen, bathroom, and pantry, and she'd vacuumed. Since Reid still had not returned, she took advantage of his absence to do a little writing. She had barely switched on her computer when she heard his voice.

"Polly."

She turned to see him standing in the doorway. "All through?"

"For now. Polly, we need to talk."

His worried expression alerted her. "The last time you said that, I didn't like the conversation. Am I going to like this one?"

He gazed at her steadily. "I doubt it."

"Then go away. I don't want to hear it."

When he walked into the room and put his hand on her shoulder, she knew the news was bad.

"I started to tell you before," he said, "but you were so upset, I thought I'd wait. Honey, my mother is coming."

His announcement hit her like a hammer, rapping on her chest. Slowly, and with the utmost deliberation, she forced herself to talk. She spoke only one word. "Why?"

"She thinks with your aunt knowing she lives in Pittsburgh; it could raise questions if no one from my family comes."

"But she knows it's a make-believe engagement."

"It's the principle, she said when I reminded her that this is a cover. Furthermore, she's worried that if she doesn't attend, she won't do her bit for our safety. Then there's Martha and you."

"She doesn't know us."

"True, but my mother feels your aunt's friends may think she doesn't approve of you."

Drawing a ragged breath, Polly stood up, her hands clenched into fists. "How can she disapprove of a stand-in fiancée she's never met?"

"It's more than that. If Martha asks you about your future mother-in-law, you won't know what to say since you don't know her. I understand where she's coming from. I wish you would," he said moodily.

As her spirits drooped, Polly's voice rose contentiously. "Reid, I ask myself why life is dumping on me in catastrophic proportions. I can't come up with the answer. Why is it that when I'm around you, one disaster ends and another mushrooms?"

His own temper flaring, he snapped back, "How about remembering who refused to keep her aunt away? Dammit, I'm here to catch Grayson."

"Fine. Everything is my fault! I still don't want to meet your mother! Can't you stop her?"

"No!" he bellowed, stalking around the room like a caged lion. "She's a grown woman. I'm not responsible for her actions. Can you stop your aunt? She's the one making this shindig. Do you think I'm looking forward to it any more than you are?"

"But none of it's real. Call your mother back. Tell her again."

"I already told you she knows, and I've told you why she insists on coming. My mother is covering the bases. I don't agree with her, but I'll be damned if I'll stop her. How will it look when your aunt invites her to her own son's engagement party and she refuses to attend? Not very nice. Besides, she's worried your aunt may be a loose cannon."

"She is not!" Polly cried defensively.

"I know that, and you know that, but how many women name milk cows Horace? Or turn the cow on to Axl Rose's music? Or read your future in your pinkie finger?"

Polly couldn't argue with him when she considered how the scenario sounded to his mother. Frustrated, she threw up her hands. "This is great! In addition to all that, I'm engaged to a man I don't know."

"You know me intimately," he reminded her.

Her mouth dropped open. Even though she was furious with him, she knew he was right. They'd talked a long time after making love the night before, learning more about each other than their bodies, but still not enough to carry her through a multitude of questions. Not the sort of questions her friends would ask. She knew he was so handsome, he could make the most casual clothes look elegant, and she knew how he looked with no clothes on. He was a proud male with warrior instincts and the ability of a masterful lover. A jolt of memory ran through her, and she ran her tongue over her lips.

"What happens tomorrow," she said, "if people ask us things about each other and we don't know the answers?"

"Like what?" he asked.

"Our preferences. Allergies. Hobbies. Favorite colors, movies, actors, TV. Mundane important things that stamp a person as unique. You don't know if I color my hair."

"Do you?"

"No."

"Then why in hell should I have known that?"

"Because," she said ineffectually.

He snorted. "Anyway, I knew it's natural."

"How?"

His gaze traveled downward. "Guess."

She gasped, her cheeks blooming with color. "Get out of my office."

"Not until we have this out." He grabbed a pad and pen from her desk, then lifted her easily and carried her upstairs.

"Put me down!"

"No!"

She pounded his back as he mounted the stairs. She might as

well be flicking a fly for all the attention he paid to her.

He strode into her bedroom and dumped her on the bed, then walked back to the door and locked it. She scrambled to sit up. "You are crazy!"

He planted his legs apart, put his hands on his hips, and glowered at her. "Yes, as a matter of fact, I am. Since meeting you, I have been completely crazy. You're the most irritating female I've ever met. On the other hand, you're also the bravest. Regardless, my sweet, we will stay here until we know each other better. Fire away with your questions." He tossed the pen and pad to her. "Write down my answers."

Her temper spiked. "I don't have to do a damn thing. Go to hell. After you leave my room."

He took off his belt. "Not a chance. You said we didn't know the important little things about each other. We're going to talk. And while we talk, we'll strip until we're down to the bare essentials."

"You're mad. Absurd. A lunatic."

"I'm all of that. Take off your clothes."

"I will not. Put your belt on. Fran's liable to walk in any minute."

"She's not coming today."

Polly's eyes narrowed. "How do you know?"

"I called her a few minutes ago. Tom's still in pretty bad shape, and I told her to stay with him. I assured her I had everything under control. If we hear from the surveillance team that Grayson's changed his plans and is coming today or tonight, she can be here before him. If not, she's coming first thing in the morning. By the way, she knows we're 'engaged.'

"So, Ms. Sweet, we're alone. Before this day ends, there won't be much we don't know about each other. My favorite ice creams are mocha chip and rocky road. What's yours?"

"Vanilla."

His shirt sailed to the dresser. "Vanilla." He shook his head. "No imagination. Are your eyes cornflower blue?"

"So what if they are?"

"Good, then that's my favorite color. See how easy this is? Write that down."

"You're insane."

"We've established that. And remember, we're starting out

even. The blouse, Polly. Your hair is the shade of sun-ripened flax. Put that down for my second-favorite color."

"You lied to Fran."

"I'm getting to be an expert at it where you're concerned. I amaze myself. I'm an honest person who lies like a trooper. No pun intended. I wear white underwear. I prefer socks a solid color. Write that down in case your friends ask."

"If you're so damned honest," she yelled, "why did you tell Fran to stay away?"

"In this whole ludicrous, cockeyed scam I can't stand the thought of sleeping without you tonight. I'm a man who prefers sleeping alone, so why do I want you in my arms? Maybe it's because you're the most responsive woman I know. Maybe it's preordained. I'll be damned if I know why." He sat in the wing chair to untie his shoes. "But you tell me. Do you like the idea of us sleeping apart tonight?"

She felt her cheeks flame. He was angry for wanting her. What should she say? She lifted her chin. "If you're waiting for an answer, you won't get one."

One of his shoes hit the floor. "I already know the answer. Either take off your blouse or say good-bye to it. I like chicken soup, split-pea soup, not too thick, and tomato soup. Nothing creamed."

"You're seducing me!"

He smiled grimly. "Wrong. You're seducing me. You have been from the first moment I kissed you. Probably from the first moment you opened your sassy mouth. Fate, in the person of your aunt Martha, brought us together, so don't blame me. I'm carrying out higher orders. Besides, I asked not to come here."

"Are you sorry now?" she asked, her heart hammering so wildly she could hardly think. Suddenly his answer was the most important thing in the world.

His keen gaze grew serious. "What do you think?"

She tried and failed to keep her aplomb. "I... I don't know."

"Polly," he said, seeing the slightest trembling to her lower lip. "No, I'm not sorry. That's the one thing I'm clear about."

When a glow of pleasure warmed her eyes, he smiled and reverted to teasing her.

"Why aren't you writing down my words of wisdom? You said the little things are important. In case anyone asks, my favorite late-night talk-show hosts are Jay Leno and Arsenio Hall. I read Tom Clancy and Dean Koontz, among others. It's safe to say I love books. Fiction, nonfiction. When yours is finished, I'd like to read it."

His other shoe hit the floor.

He stood and unfastened his pants. As she stared at him, he dropped them on the floor.

"You can tell your friends," he went on, "that I prefer casual clothes. Jeans and sneakers, when possible. My dress suits are mixed: gray, blue, brown. My dress shoes come in two colors: black and brown. I'm an expert swimmer. I'm not very neat. Don't tell them that. It's too personal."

Polly's eyes widened in appreciation as his briefs landed atop his trousers. It was getting hard for her to think about mundane things with Reid naked. Her fingers itched to touch him, to feel his male beauty inside her. But she sat upright, thoughts of lovemaking evaporating, as he turned and started rummaging through her dresser.

"You're messing up my neat drawers," she exclaimed.

"I'm learning the important things about you. It might come up in conversation."

He flipped through her lingerie, pausing to hold up a shimmering emerald-green teddy accented with black lace. "Wow! I bet you look terrific in this. Later, you'll try it on for me."

Flabbergasted, she watched as he tossed it aside and picked up another. He held up a one-piece animal-print teddy that wrapped around like a diaper. "You're full of delicious surprises."

"Put my lingerie back where you found it. What do you think you're doing?" she demanded.

"Getting ready for tomorrow. You're the one who's worried I might be asked a question I can't answer. This is my crash course." He faced her. "I can tell everyone about your underwear. It's one of the little important things. Right?"

When she only gaped at him, he continued. "If there's a lull in the conversation, be sure to tell your friends I broke my right arm when I was ten. In the summertime. I couldn't swim. It'll raise my sympathy level, especially with women. Write that down."

She didn't, nor would she admit he was making a mockery of her worries, showing her in his unorthodox manner how insignificant they were.

"Cat got your tongue?" he asked. "No matter. I love Chinese

food, but I can't master chopsticks. That should go over big. Write that down."

She saw his point. She had stressed the trivial. Maybe tomorrow wouldn't be so bad. Maybe it would be good. Maybe Reid would come back to see her after this was over, and they could date like normal people. Then again, maybe he wouldn't! If he did, they'd have to keep up the pretense of being engaged.

He sat down beside her, his weight indenting the bed. Taking the blank pad and pen from her lap, he set them on the floor. "Where was I?"

Without waiting for an answer, he kissed her fingers, then sucked each one. His tongue found nerves she didn't know she had.

"I see you have writer's cramp. We'll talk instead."

She giggled. "You're stark naked."

He wiggled his feet. "Except for my socks. I can't be entirely naked. I'm courting you." He put his arm around her.

Her heart slammed against her ribs. She hesitated a moment. "This is your idea of courtship?"

He kissed her neck. "What did you think I was doing?"

"Seducing me." She glanced down at his magnificent form. "With your socks on."

He lifted one foot. "You object to my socks? Or is it the color?"

"Most men send flowers."

He snuggled closer. "I'm speeding the process. However, I'm going to feel like the worst kind of damned fool if I stripped for nothing."

The tension over the party slipped from her shoulders as another kind of tension took its place. She felt hot and cold. A shiver ran through her as she remembered his skill as a lover. Arousal made her shakier than she'd been when he'd mentioned courtship.

With one hand he flung her hair back over her shoulder, then he trailed kisses from her neck to the valley between her breasts.

"You're slow, Polly. I'll help you." He unbuttoned her blouse, then slid it over her shoulders. As if he were a magician, it and her bra sailed onto the floor. Her shorts went next.

He kissed her bikinis off, sending her wild. "Who's your favorite actor?" he asked. "Aside from old Leslie Howard. Anyone from this century?"

He was sucking her breasts, moving from one to the other and driving her mad. She gasped out a name. He wasn't listening, though. He flicked his tongue against her nipple, and she moaned, rubbing herself against him. His hand slid down her body to between her legs, and she arched against it.

He lifted his head, his eyes searing hers. "Talk to me," he whispered.

"My favorite color is…"

He kissed her lips, then trailed a hot path down her neck to her breasts. He came back to murmur against her mouth. "Tell me what's important. What were you saying about colors?"

She tugged his hair. "I don't know. Whatever I happen to like at the moment. Not brown. It makes me sallow."

He blew in her ear. "You?" He chuckled. "You couldn't look sallow if you tried. In your romance book what happens to the hero?"

She licked his lips. "His life is changed forever."

He kissed her stomach. "Mmmm. You taste delicious. What about the heroine's life?"

"Who?" she asked, sinking into a sensual haze.

Reid positioned himself between her legs. "The heroine."

"Who cares?"

"I do. Talk to me, sweetheart."

He slipped inside her. At the first stroke her eyes flew open. "In a romance you can't have the hero and heroine riding off into the sunset in opposite directions."

"What about real life? Will the romance novelist listen to her heart and let nature take its course?" he asked, trapping her with words as surely as with his body.

Her muscles tightened around him, giving him her answer.

Many hours later, long after the bridge repairs were finished and they'd said goodbye to Jim, Reid and Polly spent a quiet evening curled up on the couch.

Reid's hand drifted to her breast, and she snuggled closer. His mind wasn't on the movie showing on TV. It was on Polly. It had happened again. Each time he made love to her, it got better. Hotter. Spiraling out of control. Which made it worse. Dangerous. Combustible.

His gun lay on the floor in its holster. He couldn't tell her why the word "courtship" had slipped out. His life was taking a strange and powerful turn, thanks to his having met this one brave, beautiful, glorious woman.

Polly spelled the C word.

Commitment.

CHAPTER TEN

Unable to stop the clock, Polly and Reid got out of bed the following morning with more than a little reluctance. Polly looked out the window. The sky was a blast of blue, perfect for a blast of a party. Leaving Reid, she went to the barn, milked Horace, then returned to bathe and dress in shorts and a top. For the party she would wear the animal-print teddy—for Reid—but she couldn't decide which dress to wear. She wanted to look her best. She and Reid would be judged that day by a jury of her peers.

The first peer who judged her was herself.

She was in love with Reid. A complicating but true fact. He said he loved seeing the radiance light up her eyes. He said he loved making love to her. He hadn't said, "I love you."

She loved everything about him, even if she didn't know all there was to know about the nonconformist who'd stolen her heart. She knew the essentials, though. He was a man of character. He wouldn't purposely hurt anyone. He had a sense of humor. He was intelligent and kind. In reality, she was the one who had gotten them into this mess. She had insisted on her aunt having access to her home, and he had gone along with her, coming up with what seemed to be the best solution. She had never considered the additional strain she placed on Reid. He hadn't wanted the engagement party, nor did he look forward to his mother's arrival.

In effect, he was caught in a juggling act, trying to calm her and put a good face on a bad bargain. There was no doubt he was attracted to her, but only wishful thinking and the wildest stretch of her imagination would mistake infatuation for love.

He'd used the term "courtship" in the heat of the moment. He had no intention of leaving the force, settling down in a big old house, marrying her, and fulfilling Martha's prediction.

At least he had taught her a valuable lesson: Don't sweat the small stuff. Concentrate on what's important. Character counted, not the mundane unimportant things one learns over time.

Provided one had the time. They didn't. His primary purpose was to apprehend Grayson. In a day or two he'd be gone.

Fran had arrived while she was in the shower. Polly was brushing her hair when Fran came into her bedroom, carrying two mugs of coffee. Reid, thankfully, had made the bed and removed all traces of himself from the room while Polly had been milking Horace.

"Hi," Fran said. "Reid sent this for you." She handed Polly one of the mugs.

"How's Tom?" Polly asked.

"He's fine. I fussed over him sufficiently and left him with a pot of chicken soup. It's good for everything. Not necessarily for the patient, but for the nervous friend who has to be doing something."

Polly understood completely. Picturing Reid in the line of duty could easily send her to cooking for an army.

"What does Tom do?" Polly asked.

"He owns a toy store. We met when I asked him for suggestions for toys for my three-year-old niece. She and I had made out a list, but after one look at Tom, the list stayed in my purse. He took my breath away."

Fran sipped her coffee, winking at Polly over the rim of the mug. "He still does."

"How does he feel about your profession?" Polly asked as she chose several outfits from her closet and laid them on the bed.

"I'm sure he wishes I were doing something else, but this is what I chose. He knew that when we met. It didn't stop us from falling in love or planning a wedding. We want children too. If I change my mind about working in the field, I'll ask for reassignment. There's lots I can do inside."

"Do you see yourself doing that?" Polly set a chartreuse linen-blend sheath next to a floral dress. "Which do you prefer?"

Fran cocked her head, looking first at Polly, then at the two outfits. "Wear the flowery dress. It's romantic, perfect for a garden party."

Polly agreed. Made of cotton with a print of roses on a white background, the dress had a fitted bodice, gently scooped neckline, and full, flirty skirt.

"In answer to your question," Fran went on, "if I ask for a desk job, it won't be easy. I'm like Reid. We relish excitement, the charge of adrenaline. He may be tiring of it, though. He plans to practice law. I thought he might make the jump after he was shot. Yet here we both are, still arresting the bad guys."

She turned to leave and paused at the door. "Polly, I know today will be hard for you. Reid told me about your Aunt Martha, why you're both going through with this. I think it's noble of you not to want to hurt her feelings. But your aunt's predictions aside, any woman who tries to change Reid is the wrong woman for him. If it's meant to be, he'll come around on his own."

Message received, Polly thought. Having decided on her attire, she hung the clothes back in the closet and went downstairs. Reid was on his way out the front door, and he told her some men from the department had arrived to set up more surveillance equipment in the barn. She watched out the screen door as he and Fran joined three men beside a plain gray van parked in the driveway, then all of them started walking toward the barn.

While she had the house to herself, Polly began making ice, emptying the ice trays into plastic bags, and refilling the trays with water. She cut flowers from her garden for the kitchen and dining-room tables, then she escaped into her den. To her surprise she was able to forget everything but the story. When Reid knocked on her door some time later, she was amazed that two hours had passed.

"All done," he said. "Everyone is ready. The guys rigged lights that operate on sensors, plus recording equipment."

He smiled and pulled her out of her chair, wrapping her in his arms.

"Be careful," she warned, though she was unable to resist him or the quickening of her pulse. "The doors open. Fran will see us."

"She's in the other room. Besides, she knows we're more than casual acquaintances."

Polly's stomach dropped. Fran had issued her friendly warning for a reason.

"How can she suspect anything?"

He framed her face in his large hands. "Polly, she's my partner. It's bad enough to pretend with strangers or your aunt and my mother, but there's no way I'm going to jam my hands in my pockets when it's just Fran. It's hard to be near you and not want to touch you."

She felt herself blush as she remembered all the touching they'd done the night before. To his delight she'd taken the lead and had made love to him with complete abandon. Looking up at him, she saw he was remembering, too, but then his expression became serious, professional.

"Tomorrow," he said, "I want you to spend the day at your aunt's. If necessary, you'll sleep there. Tell Martha your plumbing's not working. Tell her anything, but I don't want you here."

"Grayson's one man. You said you'll have other police here. Since he left the jewels in the barn, he'll return there for them. I'm perfectly safe in my home."

"Don't argue with me on this," he said firmly. "There's been a change of plans. Grayson isn't coming alone. We picked up a conversation between other members of the gang. They suspect him of skimming jewelry for himself. On his last robbery he didn't deliver as much merchandise as they'd expected."

"If they didn't do the actual stealing, how would they know?"

"From others who'd cased the store beforehand. The network of thieves spying on thieves is long and deep. It's a question of Big Brother watching over your shoulder, in this case, Grayson's. If it's true, and if the mob is on to him, they won't let him out of their sight. When he comes, he'll have company. Of course, that's good news for us. It saves us the trouble of rounding these guys up on our own."

Cold reality washed over her. A few hours ago they'd been making love, oblivious to everything but each other. Now he was saying he'd be putting his life on the line again. She found it hard to swallow.

Instinctively she clutched his arms, ready to beg him not to be part of it. Then she relaxed her hold. She wouldn't add to his worries. Priorities, he'd said. Concentrate on what's important.

She bit her lip hard. "All right. But I'll have to make arrangements for Horace." She thought a moment. "Craig Bucher lives down the road. You'll meet him today. He owns cows. I'm sure he won't mind caring for Horace."

Reid nodded. "Okay, but don't ask him at the party. People will be using the bathrooms this afternoon. They'll know the plumbing works."

"I'll call him an hour or so after he goes home."

"That's my girl."

She knew it was a figure of speech, but she wished it weren't. She wished he'd meant it. She wished it with all her heart.

Making a big production of looking at her watch, she gasped and said it was time for her to get ready. She raced past him and up the stairs. Half an hour later, as she was applying her last touches of makeup, he knocked on the door. When she called for him to come in, he opened the door and stepped inside the room. Her eyes widened in appreciation when she saw that he had changed too. He was wearing a blue linen blazer, off-white linen slacks, and a matching shirt, open at the neck. He might prefer casual clothes, she thought, but he looked dynamite in more formal ones.

"Everything okay?" he asked.

"Everything's fine."

She stood up, and his glance slid to her left hand. "Don't forget the engagement ring. Where is it?"

Her stomach turned over. The fabulous diamond set in platinum signified nothing. She'd be thrilled if Reid put a diamond chip on her finger.

"It's on the dresser."

He picked it up and handed it to her. "Here." Apparently seeing the reluctance on her face, he added, "It's part of the act, Polly. It's just for today."

She slipped it on her finger. "When do you expect your mother?"

"She's here. So's Martha. I left the two of them downstairs." He squeezed her hand. "Don't worry. She'll think you're as lovely as I do."

Thinking he meant the dress, she pirouetted. "Fran likes it too."

"I meant you, not the dress," he said gently.

Awash with emotion, she touched her lips to his.

"All right," she said as she stepped back. "I'm ready to meet your mother."

"I'm not." Cupping her face, he placed his mouth over hers. "This," he said an eternity later, "is no pretense. It's real."

Reid let her precede him from the room. He stole a parting glance at the canopied bed, then followed her downstairs. Hearing voices, they went to the screened-in porch, where they found his mother on her knees inspecting the Victorian wicker rocker. Martha sat on a chair near her. The women were jabbering like old friends. The sight made him smile.

"Mom, you never could resist damaged wicker."

Betty Cameron's head swung around. "You caught me!" she said. She got up as easily as a twenty-year-old, and he introduced her to Polly. Betty Cameron was a stylishly dressed auburn-haired woman with lively green eyes. She wore a green-and-white rayon challis dress with a single strand of pearls.

Betty held on to Polly's hand. "You're the young lady who saved my son from falling into the river. I'm forever in your debt."

Polly and Reid exchanged startled looks. "How did you know?" Reid asked.

"I told her," Martha said as she stood. She looked like a flame in a bright red silk dress, a gold belt, gold bangle bracelets, and red enamel drop earrings.

"How did you know?" Polly asked, astounded.

"That nice man, Jim, told me when I brought the men drinks and cookies. Jim said you beat me to it, Reid, and we got to talking."

Reid saw his elaborate cover ruined. "You were supposed to stay off the bridge."

"I know, but after I saw you and Polly walking on it, I figured it was okay for me too. I was being neighborly."

He gritted his teeth. Jim hadn't mentioned Martha when they had spoken again. Now Polly was sending him a silent warning not to hurt her aunt's feelings. In shock he saw his mother's lips purse in warning too.

"That was a nice thing to do," he said to Martha. "What else did you and Jim talk about?"

Martha tapped a pink-frosted fingernail on her chin, her face a study in concentration. Reid held his breath.

"He's married. His wife's name is Alice. They have two children. I told him I read palms. I read his. His pinkie too. Poor man. Two children are his limit."

Reid blanched. Polly gripped the side of a chair. Betty Cameron smiled beatifically.

"Isn't that nice?" Betty said. "I've always wanted to be a grandmother. In the usual order, of course. Marriage, then children."

Martha agreed. "I didn't tell Jim about your twins, Reid, or the son and daughter who follow the twins."

"That was very considerate of you, Aunt Martha. Please don't tell anyone about your predictions."

Polly couldn't meet Reid's gaze. What must his mother think of her and her aunt? She didn't need a mirror to know her face was crimson.

Reid took her elbow, forcing her to look at him. His smile warmed her heart. He was telling her to leave it to him, and she would. Gladly.

"Honey," he said, "my mother would love a tour of your charming house. Aunt Martha, why don't you and I go outside and direct the workmen where to set up?"

Without waiting, he swooped Martha up. Her feet skimmed the floor as Reid whisked her from the room. Her voice floated behind her as she called Reid a naughty boy. She sounded as if she loved every minute of his attention.

Betty was laughing. "She's an original."

"Martha has a heart of gold. I love her," Polly said, letting Reid's mother know she wouldn't allow her to speak unkindly of Martha.

"I meant," Betty said gently, "that I think she's charming. She's fortunate to have you for a defender, but I don't think she needs one. When I said she's an original, it was with the greatest respect."

Flustered, Polly sought to make amends, but Betty shook her head.

"I'd think less of you if you didn't defend her. It says a lot about your character. Your aunt is a very bright woman. We had a long talk. She's convinced Reid loves you."

Polly's cheeks flamed again. "Please don't take her seriously. Naturally she'd speak freely with you. She thinks our engagement is real. We'll get through today, and by Wednesday Reid will be gone. In no time he'll have forgotten his enforced engagement party." Her voice caught. "It may provide him a few laughs in the future."

Betty reached for her hand. "I seriously doubt that. I saw the way my son looked at you."

Not sure what to say, Polly turned and led Betty into the kitchen. The older woman ran her hand along the highly polished tabletop. "Your father was a talented man. I'm eager to see his paintings. You have your own talents as well. Reid mentioned that you made that needlepoint cushion on the window seat, that you're a teacher, and that you're writing a romance novel."

"He's told you a lot about me," Polly blurted out in surprise.

"Not the little unimportant things. He's obviously proud of you."

Polly ducked her head so Betty couldn't see the sheen of tears in her eyes. "Is he?" she asked, her voice choked.

"Yes. He made sure I know of your talents. Why do you suppose he wanted me to know?"

"I haven't the faintest idea," Polly murmured. Her mind was racing with possibilities, none of which amounted to much. Maybe to put his mother in an agreeable frame of mind, help her get through the day.

"May I sit?" Betty asked.

"Please."

"Has Reid told you how his father proposed to me?"

Polly wet her lips. She had no idea why the conversation was taking such a highly personal turn, nor why Reid would tell her that story. "No."

"Reid's father was tall and impressive, like his son. When Brad and I met on a blind date, the last thing on his mind was marriage. He slipped that in on the phone. I told him I agreed with him. At my age I wanted to do things, see the world, make a career for myself. Marriage and babies weren't on my mind. After we set the date, I learned that he was on the rebound. He had been engaged to a girl, but she had broken it off some months earlier. I asked my sister to call him back and cancel the date, to say I'd broken my leg."

Polly leaned forward. "What happened?"

Betty laughed. "Fate. My sister said not only wasn't there anything wrong with my leg, there was nothing wrong with my mouth! If I wanted to cancel the date, I should do my own dirty work.

"I chickened out and kept the date. When Brad picked me up, we took one look at each other and laughed from relief. That night Brad announced he intended to marry me. He never asked."

"What did you say?" Polly asked, intrigued.

Betty smiled impishly. "I told him he was crazy. Then he kissed me. If he was crazy, then so was I. I found heaven in his arms. We were married a month later. Our lives were gloriously intertwined until Brad's death two years ago." Betty sent Polly a meaningful look. "Reid takes after his father."

Polly swallowed.

Betty took her hand. "Did you think my only reason for coming here was to support Reid's alibi?"

"Wasn't it?"

"No. I wanted to meet the woman who would cause him to concoct such a ludicrous excuse. You must have gotten under his skin fast. When I asked him who'd thought of the idea to say you two were engaged, he admitted he did. Were you surprised?"

"Shocked. When we first met, I couldn't stand him. I let him know it too."

Betty grinned, her smile so like Reid's. "What happened to change your mind?"

We kissed and I found heaven in his arms.

"He's very persuasive."

"But not that persuasive." Betty laughed merrily. "No, I think whatever is transpiring between you must be rattling the cosmos. Martha told me that."

Betty gazed intently at her. "It's interesting that each of you saved the other's life. What do you make of that?"

"If this were a plot problem," Polly said, "it would be simple to manipulate a happy ending. Issues in real life, though, aren't easily tied up in neat bows. Reid's career is law enforcement. It's not living in a small town practicing law and having four children, a milk cow named Horace, and a dog named Cuddles. It lacks excitement."

Betty stood, smoothing the folds of her dress.

"There are all kinds of excitement. Some last far longer than others. Now I'll take the tour of the house, please."

They were just leaving the kitchen when Reid walked in the back door. "Martha's in her glory," he said, chuckling. "After telling the men from the rental company where she wanted everything set up, she brought out Horace's tape recorder. She figured the men should have some music to work to."

"Oh, no!" Polly said, a giggle escaping her.

Reid hugged her, his eyes glinting with amusement. "Yup. I never saw men move so fast. They carted tables, set up umbrellas and chairs, and were long gone before the tape ended."

As she relished Reid's embrace, Polly realized he wasn't hiding his feelings before his mother. He'd hugged her as naturally as if they were alone. She caught his mother's eye. Betty was smiling.

Looking up at Reid, Polly felt her heart fill to overflowing. There was strength and steel and determination in him. There was also softness and empathy and consideration. She very nearly blurted out that she loved this man whose slick, hard body turned her nights into sheer wonder, and whose tenderness had touched her very soul.

The festivities started at one with streams of cars driving across the now-safe bridge. The lawn was a sea of brightly colored tablecloths and umbrellas. Long serving tables displayed a smorgasbord of delicious foods. Desserts with whipped cream crammed Polly's refrigerator. Guests gathered everywhere across the lawn in ever-changing groups.

Polly needn't have worried about Reid's mother. Betty charmed her principal, his wife, and everyone she met, including Polly's closest chums, Grace, Joan, and Lonni. As if born to the plot, Betty, and Fran as well, did their parts. When a comment was called for, Betty said she was delighted Reid had fallen in love with Polly. Fran said she was a longtime friend of Reid's family, and was now a friend of Polly's too.

For their parts Grace, Lonni, and Joan basked in Reid's sunny warmth, his teasing smile. He poured on the charm, always keeping Polly at his side. When he hugged her or kissed her—which he managed to do often—it elicited smiles of approval.

"He's a damn sight better-looking than Ashley Wilkes," Grace murmured to Polly. Smiling at Reid, she suggested that he and Polly and herself and her husband should have dinner together sometime. There was a great Chinese restaurant in town, she added.

Reid winked at Polly, then asked Grace if she knew how to use chopsticks. She said she did. He replied he'd never mastered the art. Polly, who already knew about the chopsticks and could recall vividly the setting of that absurd conversation with Reid, nearly choked on her iced tea.

Reid clapped her on the back. "Wrong pipe, darling?" he asked solicitously.

She swallowed, corralled the first man she saw, and introduced Reid. "He broke his arm when he was ten, isn't that a shame, John? In the summertime too."

"Women," Reid said to John. "You never know what they'll say when they're in love."

John nodded, as if in perfect agreement.

Polly took Reid's arm and walked him on to the next group of guests. Among them was Municipal Court judge Fred Joyce, and she could feel Reid stiffen as she introduced them, as if he were moving into high alert.

"Martha tells me you're an attorney," the judge said.

He asked Reid where he'd gone to law school, and was impressed when he heard Washington University. Joining the conversation, Betty volunteered the information that Reid had graduated third in his class. The judge congratulated Reid, then asked him about some of his teachers, whom the judge knew.

As they spoke, several other attorneys came over to them. All handed Reid their cards and told him to phone. The judge said he'd like to lunch with him. "We'll talk about the town," he added.

As soon as was polite, Reid eased away from the group, taking Polly with him. She walked to the far side of the lawn with him, to where a split-rail fence separated the grazing land from the road.

"What's wrong?" she asked. "Everything is going well."

He shook his head. "My mother goofed. I wish she hadn't talked about me to the judge. She knows I'm not staying here. If I didn't know better, I'd think she was in cahoots with your aunt."

Polly's heart plopped. She felt wretched. Leaning on the fence, she stared out at Horace grazing in the pasture. She had let herself hope Reid would say something about a future. Their future. He obviously never intended to. She'd let her heart chase a fantasy.

Reid remained focused on his goal. To keep Martha out of his hair so he could do his job. And leave. The searing passion they had shared could never compete with his mission. She had served her purpose. She was his weekend in the country.

She turned and walked rapidly toward the barn. If she didn't get away from him, he'd see her cry. She wouldn't give him the satisfaction. She was enough of an idiot as it was, letting his mother lull her with stories. For all she knew, Betty had told them to ensure Polly's sterling performance.

She heard footsteps crunching gravel behind her, then Reid grabbed her arm and spun her around. "Where do you think you're going?"

She gave him a scathing look. "Take your hands off me, or I'll fling this ring in your face."

"For the love of heaven!" he thundered, an instant wariness about him. "What's with you?"

"Nothing. I'm tired of this farce. Poor Judge Joyce was trying to be nice while you gave your mother dagger looks. It's a wonder he didn't see them. Is it okay with you that I prefer to be alone?"

"No, dammit, it's not. You'll ruin everything. If you don't care for your welfare or your aunt's or mine, think of Fran's."

"Why did you ask me to pretend we're lovers? Pretend we're engaged? Surely you could have dreamed up another reason."

"Not at the moment!" he snapped.

She poked his chest. "I'll tell you why, you big, brave macho man! It fed your ego. And in the bargain, you got me."

"If that's what you think, you know nothing about me."

"Bingo!" She heard her voice rise in hysteria. "Now you see my point. I don't know enough. Your mother thinks the sun rises and sets over your head. Martha's bamboozled. I was too. You're good, Reid. If you need a reference, I'll vouch for you as a lover. But one weekend of you is all I can take."

He stiffened. "Then we're both lucky I'm leaving. Isn't that right?"

"You bet we are. I can't wait for this stupid, idiotic afternoon to end."

She heard his teeth grating. He shoved his blazer back and jammed his hands in his pockets.

"Do you intend to come back to the party with me, or is it your intention to blow my cover?"

She looked into his angry face. How could she love him and deny his safety? She wanted nothing more than to melt in his arms and beg him to take care.

"I'll keep my bargain," she said curtly. "But don't you dare touch me."

Something like pain flashed in his eyes. His mouth grim, he buttoned his blazer and nodded. "Tomorrow you go to your aunt's. I'll let you know when it's safe for you to return."

Miserable, she returned to the party. They mingled. They spoke. They laughed. They accepted plates of food and sat down to eat. He gathered up their empty plates. She poured his drink They smiled. They did all the things expected of a newly engaged couple madly in love with each other.

Except for one thing.

Not once did they touch.

As hostess, Polly saw to everyone's comfort. She made certain all had plenty to eat and drink. With each wish for a happy and prosperous future, she pasted a smile on her face and thanked the person. By eight that evening the last of the stragglers departed amid a string of good wishes. To Polly, her face frozen in a smile, it seemed an endless parade as she stood at Reid's side, shaking hands, bussing cheeks, promising to phone friends to firm up dates to get together.

"Reid," Martha said later as they were cleaning up the kitchen, "wasn't it nice of Judge Joyce to take you under his wing?"

"Very," he said, watching Polly.

Martha, her face aglow, her bangle bracelets offering a punctuation to her fluttering hands, praised him on the fine impression he made.

He listened as long as he could stand it. After thanking Martha for the wonderful party, he left.

Polly, citing a headache, excused herself shortly afterward. In search of aspirin, she fled upstairs to the bathroom. She took two tablets, then twisted the engagement ring off and marched into Reid's bedroom, leaving it atop his dresser.

She bumped into him as she left the room.

"Polly."

The moment was awkward. His hands reached for her automatically. Despite her heart hammering in her chest, she coolly said, "I returned the ring."

There was awareness in his gaze, as if he was measuring her underlying meaning. "Stay, please. I want to talk to you, explain about this afternoon."

She looked him in the eye. "You needn't trouble yourself. I hadn't realized how difficult it would be for you. We both couldn't wait for it to end. Thank goodness, it has."

"Your aunt was in her glory today. She's still on a high."

"Your mother wasn't doing too badly herself." Because that had sounded mean in her own ears, she added, "I like her. She's a nice woman."

"She likes you too."

"I've got a headache. Good night, Reid."

To her surprise he blocked her path. She'd have thought he'd be only too glad to shed the pretense. She started to brush past him but found herself locked by a strong arm propelling her into his bedroom. Before she could protest, his mouth was covering hers, and he was kissing her deeply. His hands swept down her spine, crushing her close. She tried to pull away. Afraid to make any noise that the others might hear, she was locked in a silent battle for supremacy.

He lifted her and kissed her sensitive neck, then pressed his lips to the underside of her jaw. "Don't shut me out," he said roughly.

She twisted from his grasp before her traitorous body sought the one man it couldn't resist. She kept her arms at her sides, lest she slip them around his neck, or delve her fingers into his hair. She needed no more aching memories to quell, no more reminders that his arousal signified lust while hers meant love.

"Go away," she said.

"Not until you hear me out. I think we should remain engaged for a few weeks..."

CHAPTER ELEVEN

Had Reid suddenly declared his undying love for her, Polly couldn't have been more surprised. Or more hurt. She closed her eyes, fighting for control, then snapped them open.

"May I ask what scheme you've concocted now that has prompted your impetuous desire to continue a counterfeit engagement?"

"You heard Martha. You saw how happy she is. Why douse her happiness? She's old. It's unfair for us to swing her emotions like a pendulum."

Polly didn't bother to hide her fury. She was wounded. Deeply. He wanted a few more weeks of enjoyment with her and was using her aunt as an excuse. He couldn't even be honest about it.

"I'm flattered as hell that you're concerned for my aunt. Since I'm younger, I guess it's okay to swing my emotions. Is that it? You stick around for a few weeks, then you drive off into the sunset. Permanently. On your next case, if your luck keeps up, another woman will succumb to your charms as quickly as I did. You win, I lose. No thanks."

"That's a cheap shot," he retorted, reacting swiftly and angrily, his fierce expression revealing his irritation. "Making love to you was the only time I've mixed business with pleasure."

It took her a moment to grasp his meaning. "I'm glad I measured up to your standards," she said, deaf to his explanation. When he tried to touch her, she shook him off with a quick wave of her hand. "All of which is beside the point. I'll do what I think is right. I'm a practical person. Usually. I'm orderly, not given to…"

"To what?" Reid asked gently, seeing her wounded eyes.

She drew herself up straight. "The next time I allow myself to become involved with a man, I won't let emotions rule my behavior."

"Hear me out first," he cajoled. She should know that emotions spurred the practical, the orderly, especially when two people became involved. "I never intended for you to face Martha alone."

He still didn't get it, Polly thought. He had no idea the hurt he'd caused her by saying his mother was in cahoots with Martha. She crossed to the window and stared outside at the lawn that had held the garden party. Floodlights shone on the grass. A breeze picked up a deflated congratulatory balloon and skirted it across the lawn.

Her arms wrapped around her waist, she asked, "What did you intend? To substitute an identical engagement ring for me to wear until you think my aunt's ready for a major disappointment? Forget it. I'm telling her the truth. She'll adjust. She's lived a long time; it won't be her first disappointment."

He stood behind her, not touching her. "Polly, I'm trying to make this right."

She was dying by degrees, even as she was resolved to find the strength to make her position clear. Her senses, however, were almost overwhelmed by his nearness. "Are you? Let me help you out. Don't concern yourself about us. Martha is a wise woman. She knows as I do that love is more than the heat of the moment. It's a commitment for the good times and the bad. It's meeting your partner halfway, often more than halfway. It's building a life anchored on trust and respect. On common goals. When I fall in love, it will be with a man who loves me too. A sham engagement to capture crooks is not my idea of a dream come true. One day maybe Martha's predictions will come to pass."

She drew herself up tall and turned to face him. "Once Martha learns why I agreed to this deception, she'll understand and forgive me. Because she was kept in the dark, her guests will pardon her. I hope they'll understand my decision in keeping silent. Your conscience is absolved, Reid. No one's hurt. You've had an interesting experience. You'll earn another medal. Fran said you've earned many."

As Reid stared down at her for an endless moment, Polly hugged herself to keep from splintering apart. "Are you through?" he asked.

"Yes."

"Good, because I'm not." His hands went to her shoulders, his dark gaze riveted to her face. "Stop talking drivel. I can't give you up."

Her heart plummeted another notch. "So we come to the truth. This isn't about Martha. It's about you. We're terrific in bed, so why end it? I've got a news flash for you. I'm not yours to give up. I'm mine to share if I desire."

"What is it you want from me?" he asked forcefully.

"A permanent breather. Beginning now. An end to this charade. You accused your mother of being in cahoots with my aunt. Cahoots! As if my harmless aunt and your mother, who hadn't met her before today, had mapped out a campaign to trap you."

"That's not why I said it!" he shouted.

"Lower your voice! I don't want them up here."

"I'll shout to the rafters if I want to. I was worried that too many people would know too much about me too soon. When you work undercover, the last thing you want is publicity."

"So go away!" she said, making the hardest speech of her life. "If we're seen together, you'll get plenty of publicity. I can't abide this subterfuge and refuse to put myself through any more unnecessary stress. I insist on having my life back the way it was before I met you. There's no room for discussion."

Reid was stopped by the finality he read in her beautiful eyes, and he knew a hurt sharper than the shock of a bullet. "Tell me one thing. Are you sorry we made love?"

She exhaled on a long sigh. "I'm not that good an actress. But it's past. Over. Until you catch Grayson and the others, you'll be in my prayers. I hope it goes well for you and your team. By the way, I phoned my neighbor. He'll take Horace in the morning. But don't come for me when it's all over. I won't be at my aunt's."

He inhaled sharply. "Where will you go?"

"I've earned a few days for myself. When I return, I'll explain everything to Martha. Good-bye, Reid. Good luck."

Reid watched her leave. It was as if she had taken the sun's rays with her, leaving him to grope in a dark tunnel. All day he'd watched each word he uttered. He'd played the intended groom, grateful for Polly at his side as they spoke with her many friends. But when the attorneys and Judge Joyce had accepted him as one of their own, he'd been on his own. And he'd handled it badly. He couldn't blame Polly for being angry with him.

If he declared his true feelings, though, she would think him nuts. After all her talk about how long it took for people to know one another, he didn't dare say he loved her. How could he have fallen in love this fast?

This deeply? If he found it overwhelming, and if he questioned it, then Polly, with her practical sense for the orderly, would think it another one of his ruses to continue an affair.

From the top of the stairs he heard Martha discussing catering halls with Fran and his mother. Little wonder Polly had fled from them. For the first time in his life he envied Ashley Wilkes. If he were Ashley Wilkes, Polly would be running toward him instead of away from him.

Polly was ready to leave early the following morning, the same as Betty. She put Cuddles in the car, then hugged Fran.

"I've written down where I'll be. Call me after you've arrested Grayson. Let me know how you are." She pressed the slip of paper into Fran's hand.

"Shouldn't you give this to Reid?" Fran asked, pocketing the paper.

Polly glanced to where Reid was speaking to his mother. "No, we've already said good-bye." She got in her car. "Let him know there's a lemon-meringue pie in the refrigerator. He told me it's his favorite. Help yourselves to anything else you'd like. There's food for an army. And when you go, leave the house keys in the planter near the front door."

Fran thanked her and said good-bye, and Polly turned her attention to Cuddles, who was in his dog carrier. She had phoned her aunt earlier, saying she needed to do research for her book and would be gone for two days, that Horace was at their neighbors, and she was taking Cuddles. Martha had assumed Reid was leaving too.

After assuring herself Cuddles would survive the short drive, she straightened in her seat. Reid was standing beside her door, one hand on the roof of the car. She let herself drink in the sight of him, caught up in a swirling tide of familiar emotion, wishing she could put her arms around him and feel the magic of him inside of her again. She had spent a restless night, missing him. But he didn't need her for more than sex, not the way she needed him.

He reached in the open window, and his knuckles briefly touched her cheek. "Take care of yourself, Polly. Cuddles, be good to her."

"Reid…"

"Yes?"

Her heart thrummed. She bit her bottom lip. "Take care. Don't be a dead hero."

His hand tapped the car roof. He nodded, then stepped back. She could swear she felt his potent male power recede like the tides.

She turned on the ignition and put the car in gear. How shallow her parting words sounded. Twice they had faced danger. From her rearview mirror she saw Reid and Fran talking. Both wore guns. As she turned onto the county road, a van passed over and crossed over her bridge. She knew it contained police personnel. The waiting game had started in earnest.

Reprimanding herself for her rotten timing, for the way she'd spoken to Reid right before he faced more danger, Polly died a thousand deaths in the motel room. Afraid to leave and miss Fran's call, she resisted the temptation to drive home and stay with her aunt. But she hadn't expected distance would magnify her worry.

"Cuddles, you miss him, too, don't you?"

The dog cocked his head, as if trying to understand the reason for his mistress's sad voice. As the sun went down on the longest day of her life, she tossed the pad of lined paper back into her overnight case. Attempting to write had proved futile. She tried reading and then watching TV, but she couldn't concentrate. Food was no problem. She couldn't eat. She imagined Grayson and whoever else was with him, their guns drawn, shooting it out with the police. She spent the night bouncing from the bed to the bathroom.

Worried she might not hear the phone if it rang, she didn't shower all day Tuesday. By late that night she was ready to climb the walls. Cuddles, who missed Horace, their playful routine, and his padded wicker bed, fussed and whined. She piled towels on the floor for him, but without the cozy sides of his basket, he hated it. Finally, she picked him up and held him in her arms until the exhausted dog fell asleep.

She kept an eye on the digital clock and imagined all sorts of horrible scenarios. Why hadn't she told Reid she loved him? Why had she been so stubborn? In time he might have fallen in love with her too. Instead she'd paraded him before strangers, ignoring the fact that he was on duty and didn't want people knowing too much about him.

At midnight the phone rang. She knocked over the lamp in her lunge for the phone, grabbing the receiver on the first ring.

"It's over, Polly," Fran said. "We got them. The whole lousy bunch of thieves." She sounded excited. "For a while we worried Grayson changed his plans. He was riding in the car with the head of the ring, only our guys lost them." She bubbled on, but Polly only wanted to hear if Reid was all right.

"Fran!" she cut in more sharply than she intended. "Is everyone safe?"

"Polly, I'm sorry," Fran said, obviously aware of who Polly meant. "Reid's fine. He was marvelous. He tricked them."

Polly heaved a sigh of relief. He was safe. That was all that mattered.

Fran was laughing so hard; she could barely talk. "After you left, Reid rigged up Horace's tape recorder to blast out a Guns N' Roses tape when he pressed a control attached to a lead wire. We knew when the crooks were in the loft defusing what they thought was a bomb. Reid turned the tape on at the perfect moment." She laughed again. "We got it on video. You should have seen them all jump. They thought they were being blown to bits accompanied by Guns N' Roses. Hang on a minute."

Polly heard voices in the background, then Fran was back on the line. "The press is here taking down the story."

"How do they know?"

"Police reporters file stories from headquarters. Besides, they know most everything that's going on. News crews descended here like locusts. It's going out on all the wires how Reid tricked those dopes. Catch it on the news tomorrow morning. Reid's filing a report right now, or else he'd speak with you himself."

Polly knew better. "Tell him congratulations. You too, Fran. Does Tom know?"

"I called him first. I can't wait to see him. We're going to watch the news in bed tomorrow morning."

After she had hung up, Polly sat on the bed, her head in her hands. "Thank you, Lord."

Reid was fine. The last chapter was closed. She could go on with her life. Too drained to drive, she lay down on the bed to wait for morning. After she watched the news, she was going home. Back to her nice, orderly life. Without Reid.

She lay on the bed, Cuddles curled up at her side. She was crying softly. Cuddles was snoring loudly.

Sometime in the middle of the night Cuddles started making a racket. His barking awoke Polly. The room was pitch-dark, only a slant of light coming through the slit where the drapes failed to close. In her sleep-fogged state, she thought he was barking awfully loud. Then she realized the racket wasn't coming from Cuddles alone. Someone was banging on the door.

She sat up fast. She groped for the phone to call the police, but knocked it onto the floor instead. Who would be banging on the door at this hour? Disoriented, she switched on the lamp near the bed and leaned down to grab the phone.

"Open up, Polly," a male voice shouted from the other side of the door. "It's me. Open the freakin' door before I bang it down."

Holding the receiver, her hand froze in midair. She'd know that silky, imperious, autocratic cop voice anywhere. Her heart skipped into overdrive.

"Why should I?" she shouted, dropping the phone on the nightstand.

"Because."

"Because is no answer." She raced into the bathroom and splashed water on her face.

"You want the whole world to hear me, fine! I've had a long time to think over our future."

Our future. "You call two days a long time?" Frantic, she dived for her purse. She dumped the contents onto the bed. Shoving aside her lipstick, comb, food coupons, wallet, credit-card holder, penlight, pad, pencil, address book, she found her perfume atomizer. Arching her neck, she gave herself a spritz.

"You're damned right," he answered. "Stop this nonsense. I'm in love with you."

Her heart stopped. When it restarted, she flew to the door and flung it open. Reid stood there, grinning sexily, one arm propped high, the other twirling a rose.

She yanked him inside the room and shut the door. "What did you say?"

He crushed her in his arms and began kissing her before she could say another word. When he released her, he rubbed his cheek against hers. "I couldn't lose you."

He felt wonderful, warm and vibrantly alive. "Not that part. What did you say before then?"

"I understand you know the story of how my father didn't propose to my mother."

"Reid, go back to the beginning."

"My pleasure." He gave her a soul-deep kiss that curled her toes.

When her eyes opened, he was smiling at her. "Before then," she murmured, her hands racing over him, making sure he was truly all right.

"Oh, you mean the part where I said I love you."

She grabbed his face between her hands. Her eyes devoured him. "That's the part. Say it again."

He kissed her, murmuring over and over that he loved her. "Sweetheart, I know times have changed. I respect feminism, but you'd better know right now, this isn't a proposal."

Her head reared back. "I will not—"

"You will. Calm down, tiger. We're getting married."

She opened her mouth. He kissed it shut, sending shock waves of desire pouring through her.

"No, there's no room for discussion," he said, repeating the words she had used with him. "While I waited for Grayson and those goons to show, all I could think about was catching them so I could be with you."

"Fran told me about the Guns N' Roses tape."

"I didn't think Horace would mind. This was my last case. I'm putting in my resignation papers from the state police. I hear the Prosecutor's Office in town is looking for a good attorney. I'm applying. I'm also contacting Judge Joyce. He loves cops. He'll especially look kindly on one who helped catch Grayson and his boooes red-handed. We have an airtight case."

She wouldn't think of interrupting him. He was handing her, her dream.

"I know," he went on, "that you've got this crazy notion that people need to know everything about each other first, but you're wrong. In fifty years we'll still be discovering things about each other. You're exciting. You're wonderful, and you're mine."

"Yours?" she repeated, loving the way his hot gaze roamed over her body.

"I can't help the way I think. I'm selfish. We found something rare and beautiful. Why let it go? Tell me before I go crazy. Do you think you can learn to love me?"

Her arms held him tight. Her lips trembled with mirth. "No."

His eyes narrowed. "No?"

"No."

He shook her. "You're serious?"

"Mmmm, yes. Very. I'm afraid you're too late," she said merrily.

He groaned. "Don't tease me. I can't take it. I was more afraid driving here than I was capturing the crooks."

She stroked his face and gazed at him in adoration, thinking her life was as thrilling as the heroine's in her romance book.

"I already love you, Reid. I've loved you since before we made love. It broke my heart to leave you."

His mouth came down on hers in celebration. "Martha's going to get her wish," he said, his voice husky.

She snuggled in his arms. "Is she, darling?"

He picked up her hand, linking their pinkie fingers. His eyes shone with love. "Mmmm. Shall I prove it?"

"I thought you'd never ask…"

Diamond
In The Rough

Doris Parmett

CHAPTER ONE

It was too darn hot to play cops and robbers. The scent of citrus from a nearby orange grove hung heavy in the Florida air. At 8:00 A.M., the temperature was eighty-five degrees and climbing.

Detective Sergeant Daniel J. Murdock was slouched down in the seat of his unmarked police vehicle, waiting for the Goldberg grocery store to open. His seersucker jacket, worn to conceal his weapon, made him hotter. To top it off, the car's air conditioner was on the fritz.

Only Murdock's anticipation of locking up Louie "The Juice" Simono made the wait palatable. Willing to do anything the mob asked, Louie led a charmed life. For services rendered, he had received their blessing to "juice"—extort money—from elderly store owners. As an added bonus, the mob gained an outlet to launder money.

Dan popped two Chiclets into his mouth, wishing they were Swiss chocolate instead. Sucking the sugar coating from gum didn't rate the same sensual thrill as letting a piece of candy melt in his mouth, but it would have to do. He'd lost five pounds in one week. He intended to shed another three; then he'd be back at his fighting weight. One hundred eighty-five pounds of muscle—if he didn't count the slight pinch of skin at his waistline. Not bad for an old man of thirty-six.

Without thinking, he reached into the inside pocket of his jacket. Yielding to another one of life's pleasures, he lit an unfiltered cigarette, filled his lungs with two deep drags, and broke out in a fit of coughing. He wiped the tears from his eyes and waited for the burning sensation in his chest to clear. He hadn't smoked in a month.

"Damn," he mumbled, crushing the cigarette in the ashtray. "Nothing's fun anymore."

He glanced toward the store. He couldn't see anyone, but he knew that the Goldbergs were inside, along with his partner, Ben Jackman. Ben was wearing a wire so they could tape everything Louie said. Thirty-four years old, Ben was a tall, redheaded Irishman, and the freckles on his face added to his boyish charm. He and Dan had been partners for years.

Even before he heard the automobile's tires making the turn into the lot, Dan's finely tuned reflexes warned him of an approaching car. Louie. He welcomed the surge of adrenaline in his veins, the rush that would carry him through.

He glanced in the side view mirror, already imagining collaring Louie. But... "What the hell!"

Louie didn't drive a red convertible with the top down. And by no stretch of the imagination did he resemble the attractive, dark-haired woman behind the wheel.

He wasn't about to let her screw up his operation. Louie's early morning visits were understandable. He arrived an hour before the stores opened because he didn't want witnesses. What was she doing here?

Parking right in front of the Goldberg grocery, that's what!

Dan yanked the mike off its clip under the dashboard. He read off her license-plate number to the dispatcher, then waited for the computer to run a check on the plates. Dan knew everything was in the timing, and he swiveled to keep the woman in his line of vision.

He groaned. His hopes for a nice, uncomplicated arrest sank as she made no move to get out of her car. Instead, she produced a hairbrush and began to brush her thick mane of hair.

Under other circumstances he'd study her elegant profile—her straight nose, her high cheekbones, the sweeping line of her jaw, and, from the tilt of her chin, her equally elegant neck. When he was on stakeout for long, tedious hours and he spotted an attractive woman, he'd usually let himself daydream. It helped kill the boredom. Sometimes he'd fill in the blanks, harmlessly providing her with a whole family history—if she had what it took to interest him.

The woman turned her head, giving him his first opportunity to see her face clearly. Stunning.

The word rushed into his mind. Almond-shaped blue eyes, a stubborn chin, and cheekbones a model would envy. She tossed the cloud of chestnut hair over her bare shoulders. Individual strands of nutmeg and amber caught the sunlight, an iridescent symphony.

She definitely had what it took to interest him—but not now. Now he just wanted her out of there.

With a growing sense of desperation, Murdock saw her lean her head back on the red leather headrest and close her eyes. "Lady," he muttered, "be a good girl and scram."

He alternated between checking the seconds ticking by and cursing, then decided to take matters into his own hands. His one overriding concern was to get her out of harm's way. He got on the microphone again and spoke hurriedly to Ben. "There's a civilian parked in front of Goldbergs. I'm going to go to her." Then he issued orders to the officers waiting off the lot in unmarked patrol cars.

"All units, there's a woman in the line of fire. After Louie comes out, make the arrest at the end of the parking lot. Repeat, the end of the lot. We don't want to give the Goldbergs a heart attack or involve the civilian." His command reconfirmed, Dan sprinted out of his car.

He had exactly three minutes.

Millie Gordon sighed with contentment as the warm sun bathed her face. It didn't bother her that Goldbergs wasn't open yet. She'd wait. When she'd gotten up that morning, she hadn't been certain what to do—go to the beach; peck away at her computer as her alter ego, the syndicated advice columnist. Ask Ms. M; or, finally, get back to her book, "Not-Your-Run-of-the-Mill People", a collection of in-depth interviews of unusual people in exciting occupations. The beach won. It was a lovely day, and she meant to enjoy it to the fullest.

"I'm fresh out of intelligent advice and I can't find the energy to work on the book," she'd confided to her agent, Wylie McGuiness, on the phone the day before. "I've roughed out that chapter on the concert pianist, but I'm just not interested in it."

"Take a breather, Millie," Wylie had advised in her thick Brooklynese. "What good is vacationing in Florida if you don't take time to smell the roses? Go work on your tan. It should look great with your blue eyes. Better yet, find a man and let him tell you that you look great."

"The trouble with you, Wylie, is that you think marrying one man after another until you get it right is the solution to everything. I've come to terms with my widowhood. I've had my shot at happiness. Stop worrying about me. I'll be all right. You know you can't keep this girl down."

"That's what I like about you, Millie. You're so positive. Then get back to the book next week. I got an extension on the due date from the publisher, but remember, you've got to make this new deadline."

Millie wasn't sure the timing was right. Yawning into the phone, she had promised to get off her duff. Make some progress. Write.

That was last night.

Today, she'd awakened feeling marvelous, like her old self. Unfortunately, work was the furthest thing from her mind.

She sighed again, anticipating a long, lazy day on...

The passenger door of her car was yanked open. She was more startled than frightened as a man dropped onto the seat next to her.

"Lady"—a shiny badge swept past her nose— "don't be scared... Detective Sergeant Dan Murdock of the Port Rico Police Department. I want you to come with me. If you don't, your life could be in danger. Hurry up, we haven't much time."

Millie glanced around the peaceful lot, then turned back to the man. Nuts, pretenders, and loonies came in all sizes and shapes. Her files were filled with letters proving the world was populated by strange people. Some sent pictures. Some were even handsome—like the man whose gaze was now fixed steadily on hers. She caught a trace of cigarette smoke clinging to him.

For a moment she was tempted to tell him to go take a flying leap for charging into her car unannounced. She'd never been one to scare easily. If this total stranger expected her to leave her car and trot after him like some obedient puppy on this flimsy pretense, he had another guess coming.

"Much time for what?" she asked, stalling, while her brain feverishly sorted out her options.

Apparently her slow reaction time irritated him.

He pointed to his wristwatch. "Lady, just get out of the car and come with me. Trust me."

"Why should I?"

He looked taken aback, as though this were the first time anyone had dared challenge him. The badge flew under her nose again. Annoyed, she shoved his hand away, then reached into her bag. She came up with a can of hair spray and aimed it.

"Hold it, buster. Shove that little tin badge in my face one more time and your eyelashes will have a permanent curl. Now suppose you tell me what this is all about?"

He leaned closer and precisely enunciated every syllable. "You're interfering with police business." In one swift motion he grabbed the can of hair spray. For a moment they simply stared at each other, gauging opposing wills, neither acknowledging that he'd lifted her "weapon" as easily as one takes candy from a baby. "I'm not required to give you chapter and verse," he went on. "Just do as I say. I'd hate to have to drag you out of here."

With a firm set of her lips, she dared him to try. If what he said were true, surely she'd have noticed some police activity. But the streets were calm. All she heard was peaceful silence. As if to verify her thoughts, a flock of birds flew gracefully overhead. Adding up all this tranquility, she didn't believe a word the man said. Unless... Of course! She should have realized the game he was playing right away.

"You're from that new television show, aren't you?" she asked. "The one with the dumb name, *Can We Fool You?* Well, you can't." She had the satisfaction of seeing a red flush creep up the man's neck. He started to say something, but she rushed on. "I've always been good at spotting phonies, mister, whoever you really are. The whole idea for the program is dumb. You may tell that to your producer. Give the money you'd pay me to charity. And take my advice. The next time you concoct a preposterous story, make sure you have the proper setting. Besides," she added smugly, "you couldn't scare a kitten. You're going to need a few more lessons if you want someone to believe your act."

Dan recovered his wits at about the time she stopped spouting her nonsense. He clamped his hand on her wrist, then dropped it, warned off by the stiffening of her shoulders. "Do I look like a television actor?" he demanded.

Millie considered his question, studying his tanned face for ten long seconds. He was good-looking enough to be an actor. In fact, he was so handsome, he could play a leading role. His gray eyes, rimmed in black lashes, reminded her of a turbulent sea before a storm. His nose was slightly misaligned, giving him a certain toughness. Black hair, liberally sprinkled with gray at the temples, curled impudently at his nape. She wasn't afraid of him. If he were going to hurt her, he'd have done so by now.

"How do I know what actors look like?" she asked. "Maybe you are who you claim to be. And maybe you're not." Maybe he was an escaped nut from an asylum, she thought. "In either case, I'm not stupid enough to dash off with a strange man who flashes a badge in my face and makes up an absurd story. I don't even owe money on a parking ticket. You are looking at a sterling citizen."

"What I'm looking at is a fool. Now either move this car fast, or come with me."

"That does it." She didn't care for his bossy tone. "No one, I mean no one, orders me around."

Dan glowered at her. He couldn't fault her logic. Under other circumstances, he'd commend her. "Dammit, lady. Juice Louie and Spike Harvey are expected in less than a minute."

It was those ridiculous names that convinced Millie this attractive man wasn't playing with a full deck. She rolled the silly names on her tongue. They were perfect for the movies. "Juice Louie," she said, trying to keep a straight face. "That's very nice, detective. I should have introduced myself. This week I'm Madonna."

She was treated to a hard, suspicious stare. "You don't believe me?"

A knot of irritation worked its way through the pit of her stomach. She let it out little by little. "What I believe," she fired back, "is that you've been reading too many Damon Runyon stories. What I know is that unless you get out of my car, I'm going to make a citizen's arrest."

A decidedly impolite sound came from the man's mouth.

"Mister, I neither know nor care who you really are or what your game is. Anyone can flash a little tin badge. Everyone's into labels, medals, and badges these days. Since there are no police around here, it can't be as dangerous as you claim. I'm perfectly safe." She returned his stare. She added, "I'd better be."

His hand clamped around her wrist again and stayed there. His mouth was a hard line of anger. "Why are you acting so stupid? You're no kid. A woman your age should know better. Let's go."

"I beg your pardon!" She might be thirty-three, she thought, but she was hardly Whistler's mother. "If you don't remove your hand from my wrist. I'm going to scream bloody murder. If you try to harm me, let me remind you it's broad daylight and this is a convertible."

Bile rose in Dan's throat. How did he get such bad luck? If she screamed, she'd spook the Goldbergs. Not to mention warning off Louie. He gave serious consideration to knocking her out, then dragging her body into the rear of the store. Thinking of the wrongful arrest charges this fiery citizen would probably bring, he cursed liberally.

"That kind of language isn't necessary," she said haughtily.

Dan disagreed. Of all the confounded, lousy dumb luck… Of all the women in the whole wide world who might have parked there, he had to lock horns with a gorgeous Doubting Thomas.

"Thanks to your obstinate nature, lady, we're both stuck. Now it's too late." He pointed to his watch. "In less than thirty seconds, a blue Mercedes with two goons inside will be joining us. I assure you, they'll have guns in their car.

"'Guns' with magazine clips that repeat, just in case they didn't kill the first time. They're not big on conversation, so don't plan on talking to them and driving them crazy, too." He angled his head. "They're going to go into that store and Louie will make his weekly pickup."

Millie felt the first real stirrings of uncertainty. Still, she clung to a lingering skepticism. A woman couldn't be too sure in this day and age. "Weekly pickup for what?"

Dan frowned at her. "Money," he said sarcastically. "You didn't think I meant groceries, did you?" Now why couldn't he be talking to a nice, sensible, hysterical woman who'd run like hell at the first sign of trouble? Ten more precious seconds elapsed. It felt like ten years.

Millie's assurance wavered. "Why should I believe you? I don't see any police here. Where's your backup? Are you wearing a wire?"

He quickly flipped open his jacket, exposing his Smith and

Wesson high-speed thirty-eight. "No, I'm not 'wearing a wire.' Will this do? And lady, believe me, it's no toy. The bullet enters the body, making a hole the size of a pencil point. It exits with a hole big enough to put your head in and not get your ears wet."

Millie shuddered. "You needn't be so graphic."

He ignored her comment. "Look in your rearview mirror. What do you see?"

She looked. She saw a blue Mercedes. It slowly turned into the lot. Her hand lifted to her throat. "Would you happen to know the license plate number?" she asked weakly.

Without a backward glance, Dan rattled it off. Coming abruptly to her senses, Millie slid down in the seat. "And I wasted all this time not believing you."

"You damn near ruined everything. And don't you dare faint on me, lady."

"Millie," she said, swallowing hard. "My name's Millie Gordon. And don't worry, I never faint."

"Good." He softened his tone. "Okay, Millie. Since we can't make a run for it, you and I are going to have to convince Louie we're parked here for a reason other than shopping."

She gazed into his eyes, fighting her rising panic. Her heart beat double-times. "I'll do whatever you say."

"Anything?"

"Anything."

He was already leaning toward her, shielding her body with his, blocking out the sun, blocking out everything but himself. "Okay, sugar." He grinned. "It's show time. Pucker up."

Before she could protest, his mouth covered hers. He pressed her down onto the seat, hiding her so completely with his large frame that a passerby could see only her legs. Stunned, she began to squirm, only to have him breathe a warning about sending Louie the "wrong signal." At first his kiss was tentative, his lips merely resting on hers. Then he began to explore her mouth. His tongue slipped between her lips, and a rocket seemed to hurtle through her. Lightning jolted along her entire nervous system. Sensations of sounds, textures, and the scent of Dan Murdock swirled through her brain. Fear of Louie receded, replaced by something more powerful and dangerous— arousal. A year of loneliness had primed her, left her vulnerable.

Even knowing Dan's kisses were play-acting of the most

serious order didn't stop her body from reacting. The danger wasn't from any crooks. The danger seemed to come from the stranger kissing her, making her tremble with desire. Embarrassed, she struggled against him.

They heard a car door slam. "Help me, Millie," Dan whispered against her lips.

His plea galvanized her into action. She looped her arms around his neck, making it look as though she couldn't get close enough to his warm body. She ran her fingers through his thick, silken hair. Her mind was filled with fear, excitement, curiosity, and the nettling worry that Dan hadn't been telling the truth after all.

Dan moved suggestively, intent on convincing Louie and Spike they'd stumbled upon two passionate people who couldn't wait until they were alone. But Millie's body, pressed beneath his, was making him forget Louie. He felt her softness, her breasts flattened against his chest. He inhaled her clean scent. Even in a situation like this, a man would have to be dead not to be aware of her.

Coarse laughter bombarded their ears. "Hey, Juice." Dan recognized Spike Harvey's voice. "Getta load of those two. It's better than the video we watched with them broads last night."

Juice chortled. "Come on, Spike. Give the guy some privacy. Ain't you got no class? Besides, we got business."

Feeling Millie flinch, Dan tightened his arms around her. He heard the door to the grocery store swing open and immediately eased himself off her. Gazing into her eyes, he guessed he looked as stunned as she did. She'd kissed him, really kissed him. He hadn't imagined the sweetness of her mouth. In the space of a moment this woman had become important to him. Did lightning really strike that fast? he wondered.

Millie struggled to put a clamp on her rampaging emotions. Lust—unplanned, unwanted lust—had betrayed her. "Is it safe?" she murmured, avoiding Dan's eyes.

"Not yet." He didn't want to scare her more than necessary, but he couldn't have her bolting either.

"Why not?"

He smoothed the hair away from her forehead. "They'll be coming out soon. My men will make the collar once they're outside. We don't want the Goldbergs involved." Or you either, he added silently.

She appeared to be considering that while he was considering his own surprising reaction to her. What had started as a ploy to fool Louie had ended up fooling him. Completely. She made his blood race.

"Tell me, Murdock," she said, "why are you acting as though you're enjoying this?"

He ruffled her hair and answered truthfully. "Must be the company. When you're not arguing, you're one helluva woman." He kissed her quickly.

"What was that for?" She heard her voice rise. "We've lost our audience."

"Me. The others were for Louie and Spike. You taste good, Millie." He frowned suddenly. "You're not married, are you?"

She was determined to keep an emotional distance from him and wasn't about to share information about her private life. "Murdock, you pick a strange time to get social." She shifted her cramped body and felt him adjust in compensation. She glared at him. "You can at least pretend for my sake."

"Not in my nature, Millie."

"I gather," she said, beginning to relax in spite of the situation, "that you're not a man who lets grass grow under his feet."

He wrapped a lock of her hair around his finger. "Just taking advantage of an opportunity thrown my way."

She shot him a look of annoyance, amazed that she wasn't in the least bit alarmed. "I could have your badge for this."

He looked affronted. "Why, Millie. After I saved your life?"

"You haven't saved it yet."

He stopped smiling. She was right. They still had a long way to go before they were in the clear. It took only one mistake, and one had already transpired.

The door to the grocery opened. "Get ready, sugar. Act Two's about to begin."

He kissed her again, putting as much enthusiasm into it as before. But the instant Louie and Spike were back in the Mercedes, he eased off her.

"Sony, Millie, I gotta go," he said as he heard the welcome screech of tires from the four unmarked police cars. He unsnapped his holster. "Stay down until I send someone back to tell you it's clear. I mean that. Don't go getting your cute nose where it doesn't belong. I'll see you tonight."

"Just a second, Murdock. Aren't you taking a lot for granted?"

He grinned, looking like a kid about to go to a party. "Maybe so. We'll find out later. Anyway, if you were married, you'd have told me so."

"Murdock, you're a Cro-Magnon so-and-so."

He nodded and kissed her lightly. A quick glance told him his men were reading Louie and Spike their Miranda rights. He hung back a few seconds more, enjoying Millie's laughter. It had the husky, deep sound of a satisfied woman. Her cheeks were flushed; her eyes sparkled with deviltry.

She was something else, he thought, admiring her. She was propped up on her elbows, and her hair flowed over the seat. He wanted to lower her right back down and pick up where he'd left off.

"You don't know where I live," she said with a smirk.

He rattled off her address. At her dumbfounded look, he added, "I even know your bra size. And that I didn't get from running a check on your license plates." He was still chuckling as he ran off.

Millie shook her head. She'd never met a man like Dan Murdock. In a flash of inspiration, she realized she'd just met the perfect candidate for the opening chapter of her book.

CHAPTER TWO

Millie disregarded Dan's orders. After all she'd been through, she wasn't about to miss the grand finale. Besides, her fertile brain was hatching an idea. True, it was a bit vague and in need of refinement, but the perfect person had literally fallen right on top of her. It had to be fate helping her.

Arms draped over the back of the front seat, she watched the arrest as she mentally sketched her opening paragraph. "Police Detective Daniel J. Murdock is dedicated to his job... to the extent that he would use his own body to protect a civilian from danger." That would be a good dramatic hook. Warming to the idea, she decided to let Wylie know about her find as soon as she returned home.

Her creative juices were flowing. She was glad.

The truth was, she'd been away from excitement and people for too long.

The scene before her was right out of a movie. Wylie would love it. Police, cameramen, and reporters swarmed everywhere. Dan Murdock was in the center of it all. A thrill rippled through her, and she brushed a hand over her flushed cheek. On second thought, she wouldn't tell Wylie everything. Some details were better kept secret.

Like her scandalous behavior. She didn't need an instant replay to visualize her body's traitorous response to Murdock. How could she—a sensible woman who made her living from advising the lovelorn, lovesick, and loveless—let a smug, self-satisfied man like Dan Murdock cause a war between her nerve endings and her brain cells?

He wasn't even her type. Actually, it was better that he wasn't her type. She'd be able to write about him in a detached, professional manner. That detached, professional manner surveyed him as he worked.

She let her gaze travel down the length of his trim body. He was tall and slim hipped, with an erect bearing and broad shoulders. He had shed his jacket, revealing his well-muscled arms. She clearly remembered those arms wrapped tightly around her. In her eyes, he became a knight in shining armor.

Some knight! she hooted, correcting herself. Hardly original. Pucker up! Nevertheless, she didn't doubt knight Daniel possessed an impressive bag of tricks. The chapter on him would be a winner.

Neighborhood people, curious to know the source of the commotion, began to cause a disturbance, craning their necks and jostling one another in an effort to get closer to the activity. Dan, looking every inch in control, strode over to them. He issued a terse order that sent the bystanders scurrying to the other side of the street.

She was finally able to get a clear view of Juice Louie as the cordon of officials surrounding him parted. He was spread-eagled against the front of the Mercedes. Her bubble of nervous excitement deflated. Juice Louie didn't look very tough.

Unimpressive was a better word. A small, nondescript man with thinning sandy hair, he wore a red and white striped shirt atop stark white shorts. Pale bandy legs ended in droopy white athletic socks and black shoes. She scoffed at his unprepossessing outfit.

"Absolutely no regard for taste," she murmured, thinking Louie was an ideal candidate for caricature.

Her mouth dropped open in surprise at her first good look at Spike Harvey. His blond hair, courtesy of mousse and hair spray, resembled the Statue of Liberty's crown.

"For this, Murdock tried to scare me," she muttered, gazing in wonder at the punk reject from a grade-B movie.

She tapped her fingers on the back of the leather headrest, mentally rewriting her first sentence to give it more oomph. "I had a brush with death in Florida, thanks to Detective Daniel Murdock." So what if the only thing she'd brushed up against was Detective Murdock's body?

What was wrong with her anyway? she wondered. Why was she blowing the whole thing out of proportion? This wasn't a case of a man and a woman stealing a few kisses because they couldn't stand being apart. The only reason Dan had kissed her was that he'd needed to trick some hood. Strictly police business. Nothing more.

The fact was, she realized, it was a simple case of unused hormones. Hers. Hormones she had refused to acknowledge for months. Understanding that relieved her. But it didn't explain why Dan had said he wanted to see her again.

Unbidden, memories of the heat of his lips, the bold intimacy of his powerful body, assailed her, and her throat constricted. She remembered how he had caught her by surprise with that first, open-mouthed kiss. But most of all—most shockingly and embarrassingly—she remembered the overwhelming betrayal of her own body.

And his...

Face it, Millie, she reasoned, Wylie's phone call unnerved you. When a woman is a ship without a rudder, anything can happen. That was what had caused her reaction. She was a widow who missed her husband. His laughter... even their arguments. She missed the loving. She missed so much...

Catching herself slipping into self-pity, she reminded herself not to be maudlin. Anger was a much better ally. With a determined toss of her head, she slung her net beach bag over her shoulder and stepped out onto the shimmering pavement. She sniffed the fragrant citrus-scented air, delighting in the aroma. Much as she missed working in her flower and vegetable garden at her New Jersey home, nothing could compare to the lush perfume of a citrus grove.

She was about fifteen feet from her car when a plainly vexed Dan sprinted toward her. Blocking her path, he whirled her around, thus preventing Louie from seeing her face. "Millie, dammit! Just where do you think you're going?"

"I'm going to see the Goldbergs," she explained.

He brushed his hand across his forehead. "No, you're not."

"Why not?" The action was over. What right did he have to detain her?

"I've got work to do and I can't be worrying about you, too."

She waved off his concern. "That won't be necessary, I assure you. I'm quite capable of taking care of myself."

"I doubt it."

The gleam in her eye and her thrust-out jaw warned Dan. He recognized the symptoms of a delayed reaction to danger. He'd experienced it many times. Filled with unreleased tension and energized by surges of adrenaline, her body needed release. Magnificent Millie was itching for a fight. If she couldn't get Louie, he'd have to be the substitute. She was primed and pumped, raring to go a few rounds.

He understood how she felt. He could be deadly calm, capable of facing down the most ruthless criminal, going by the book and refusing to use his fists or gun except in dire emergencies. As soon as the arrest went down and the paperwork was done, his knees would start to shake. There'd be so much unexpressed emotion in him, he would feel forced to work out in the gym. Pump iron, swim, anything, until his system returned to normal.

"The Goldbergs are giving testimony to one of my men. Then they're going home. They need to cool down from the excitement. Go to the beach and swim, Millie. The exercise will do you good."

She bristled. "What's that supposed to mean? From what I recall, it was your body on top of mine, not the other way around. You're no lightweight." The quick twinkle in his eye made her blush. She knew what he was thinking.

Dan turned her around, his hands on her shoulders. He was having a hard time not remembering her womanly curves. Tender feelings or not, though, he didn't react kindly to having his commands taken lightly, not in his present mood.

"So far," he said, "you've put both our lives in danger—"

She interrupted him. "That's ridiculous. Louie and his goofy-looking friend can't be so tough. Those twerps hardly look dangerous. They're crude-mouthed creeps who make a living by scaring the wits out of old people. For that, they deserve to be sent up for a long time. But they don't scare me." She looked at Dan with cool, calculating blue eyes. "I'm disappointed in you for trying to scare me, too. Or"—she lifted an eyebrow—"did you do that on purpose?"

Dan scanned the heavens. He wanted to shake her. How could he be interested in this woman?

She'd be a thorn in any man's side. If he had a modicum of

sense, he would say good riddance before tangling with this blue-eyed vixen. "You're nuts! Tell me, Millie, what does it take to scare you?"

She pointed to the crowd of onlookers. "I stayed put. I simply chose not to keep my head down. What did I do that was so different from those people over there? All I did was watch you and your men put the muscle on those hoods. They're a bunch of pip-squeaks!" His mouth twitched. "What are you laughing at?" she asked.

At her thunderous expression, he stifled the laughter bubbling up inside him. "I'm thinking about buying you a dictionary of police terms. Either that or I'll let you hang out in the locker room with the guys for a day."

Shaking off her momentary displeasure, she realized she'd just been provided the perfect opening. "I might take you up on that, Murdock."

He raised his brow, staring at her sensual mouth. He thought of how soft she had felt beneath him, how her fragrance had spun its magic, enveloping him in her trap. How her luminous eyes belied her sassy talk. But mostly he'd never let her get within thirty yards of the locker room.

"Not on your life," he said curtly.

Millie had expected a trite comeback, a remark tossed out in good humor, not the sudden tightening of his jaw or the fierceness of his answer. "You know something, Murdock? I think you have all the fun."

His gaze locked with hers, holding them both in conflicting memories. "You know something, Millie?" he responded. "I think we could have some fun together."

She reacted to the heated sensations rushing through her, to the tingling in her breasts, shamefully aware that she must stop playing the man-woman game with him and simply tell him she'd like to interview him.

He took her hand in his, rubbing his thumb across her palm. He smiled into her eyes. "Millie, listen. I don't want you to get the wrong idea. I told you to stay down before because between them, Louie and Spike have a long rap sheet, including a couple of unprovable murders. This extortion business is only a sideline for Louie."

A tremor raced through her. Louie might look like a reject,

she thought, but he was apparently dangerous. Dan had been trying to protect her and she had reacted unwisely. "But now that you've arrested them, won't they be locked up and off the streets?"

"Let's just say I want you to keep that pretty little nose of yours out of police business. An arrest isn't a conviction." He didn't think it necessary to tell her Louie was already vowing revenge, bragging he'd be out on bail within twenty-four hours.

Millie knew she was keeping him, but her curiosity got the better of her. "Why do you call him Juice Louie?"

"Because he squeezes the juice, the life blood, out of his victims. People have been known to pay him the principal on a loan six times over and still never get out from under. Maybe we'll get lucky and Spike will flip."

"Flip?"

"Turn state's evidence for a reduced charge. The term used to be 'sing.'"

The caravan of official cars began to leave the lot. One of the men shouted to Dan. Lingering another moment, Dan leaned toward her. "You're very beautiful." She was tall and graceful, reminding him of a proud huntress. Her face, honey-tan, beckoned him to stay. "My men are waiting. I'll meet you at the beach."

"The beach is a vast place, Murdock. Millions and millions of tiny grains of sand. How good are you at finding needles in a haystack?"

He rocked back on his heels, grinning. He loved a challenge. "I don't suppose you'd consider making my life easier and telling me where you'll be parked?"

She chuckled. "Let's see how good a cop you are."

"There you go again, Millie. Where's your faith? Don't you know I always get my woman?"

With a last smile, he turned and walked away. Millie returned to her car, her heart thrumming like a wild thing. Life around Dan certainly wasn't dull, she mused. In the space of an hour, her life had been in danger... and she'd been kissed senseless by a dark-haired hero, who carelessly referred to her now as his woman.

Dan was thinking of his foolish slip of the tongue on the drive back to the precinct. He hadn't meant to imply or suggest that he saw Millie as "his woman." He had no intention of making that sort of commitment to any woman. He had been married briefly and young to a woman named Lana, more to get her away from her drunken, abusive father than for love.

Just out of college, he had already passed the exam for the police department and had entered law school on a double-track program. After a year of marriage, Lana had decided she wanted to attend college herself. He agreed, but had to quit law school when the demands of finding the extra money became too great. He had fully intended to complete his studies after Lana got her degree. By that time, however, the marriage was over. She found a good job, and when she fell in love and remarried, he was happy for her.

He never went back to law school. As he advanced in the police department, he decided he preferred to stick to being a detective. Since then, his life had been loose and easy. It worked for him. The stress on marriages within the police community was well documented. In many precincts throughout the country, psychiatrists were on twenty-four-hour call. No, he thought somberly, recalling the tearstained, agonized face of Grant Powers widow, it was better to travel alone in this business. Besides, he hadn't met anyone to make him reconsider his decision. Unbidden, an image of a sassy brunette with cornflower-blue eyes floated in front of his face.

But no one said a little fun on the side wasn't, good for the soul.

*

The ocean shimmered with golden sparks on gentle indigo waves. Millie swam with long, strong strokes, pushing her body through the soft, hypnotic swells. She'd been in the water for half an hour, emptying her mind of all thought. Amazingly, her body seemed starved for exercise. Tiring at last, she flipped over onto her back, floating dreamily for a while.

Finally, she headed for land, shedding the last of her stored-up energy. She dragged herself out of the water and sank onto her blanket. Closing her eyes and flinging her arms above her head, she allowed her mind to drift back over the crazy morning. One image was predominant. Dan Murdock. He was as different from her husband as night from day. Frank had been methodical. He'd had the true nature of a corporate attorney.

A stream of sand trickled onto her thigh. She flipped it away, only to feel it happening again. Kids, she thought, reluctantly opening one eye.

Dressed in blue swimming trunks, Dan grinned down at her. His body, as lean and muscular as she remembered, looked fabulous. What was that old saying? she mused. Tall, tan, and terrific. It fit him. He'd make her readers come back for more.

He dropped down beside her, admiring the sleek lines of her high-cut blue suit. "Hi. That's some suit."

"Why aren't I surprised to see you?" she asked, suspicious of how easily he'd found her.

"Hmmmm. That, Millie, is a less-than-enthusiastic greeting. Can't you do better for an old friend?"

Turning on her side, she dug into her bag for her wristwatch. "By my calculations, Murdock, we've known each other for about four hours, three of which were spent apart."

"Sassy woman. You know you're glad to see me."

She was, but she wasn't going to let him know that. "How's Louie?"

"Squawking mad. The judge set a high bail. Louie doesn't like his rights taken away. Neither does Spike, but he's a lot less vocal."

"Will this be on the evening news?"

"Who knows? Nabbing a two-bit crook isn't exactly earth shattering. Our work has just begun."

"Then why the high bail?"

"It isn't who you are, it's who you know. That's why."

"Will he raise it?"

He thought of Louie's threats. "I hope not. Considering Louie's record, the D.A. asked the judge to set bail at a quarter of a million. Given Louie's mob friends, he was glad to accommodate us. Even Louie doesn't have that kind of clout."

"Good. Then the Goldbergs won't worry." She relaxed. "How did you find me?"

"I'm a brilliant cop," he bragged, his boyish grin taking the conceit out of his remark.

She scuffed sand at him with her toe. "Modest, too. You should be written up. Think of the publicity."

"Not me. There's an advantage to working outside of the limelight. Can we talk about you? I see criminals all the time."

Millie hid her disappointment. She'd have to use more finesse to get Dan to agree to an interview. Smiling, she gave him the go-ahead sign.

"You have a gorgeous face."

"That's what they all say," she agreed blandly. He scowled, which pleased her. "There's something else, Murdock. You put a tail on me, didn't you?"

"Well, you wouldn't tell me where you were going." He shrugged, but his eyes were warm with admiration.

Just then a beach ball landed near his feet, spraying sand. A towheaded toddler came chugging over, tears in his eyes. When Dan gave him the ball, he patted the child on the back, praising him.

"That's a pretty terrific throw you have, young man. How about showing me how you do that?"

The pudgy youngster's face broke out in a broad smile. With his mother watching from nearby, the little boy, who solemnly confided that his name was Bobby, threw the ball. It landed a scant few feet from Dan. He showered the boy with compliments. As his mother led him away, the child called over his shoulder, "See you later."

Millie filed this new knowledge about Dan away for future reference. She told herself she was interested in him only for professional reasons. That didn't quell the warm feeling growing in the pit of her stomach. She returned to their previous conversation. "Isn't tailing innocent people a waste of taxpayer money?"

He agreed without hesitation. "It sure is, and it's all your fault. I ought to arrest you for being uncooperative." He grinned. "You could bribe me out of making the arrest, you know."

The man was mad, she thought. Kind to children, but mad nevertheless. It would be fun trailing after him for a few days to get her story. "Murdock, I think you should jump in the ocean. To quote someone I know, the exercise will do you good."

"I'm going," he said, "but you'd better know right now that I'm cooling off because of you." Without giving her a chance to recover from his bold statement, he ran down to the water and dove in.

Leaning on her elbows, she watched him swim. She noticed she wasn't the only one enjoying the sight. Other women's heads were turned in his direction. He was good, she decided. He swam effortlessly, cutting through the water with an economy of motion.

After ten minutes he emerged, coming back to sink down next to her. His fingers trailed across her arm.

"Mmm, you feel good, Millie."

She rested her hand on his, stopping his exploring. "Don't." She barely recognized her own feathery voice.

"Don't what, Millie?" He lifted his head. His eyes bored into hers. "Don't tell you that I felt something back then, and that I want to see if it's real?"

"Dan, please…"

"We both felt something. Don't deny it."

"It doesn't matter whether we did or not. I was excited. It was dangerous. Danger and sex trigger one another. That's common knowledge."

"Not for me. You were the excitement. You were the 'danger,' not Louie."

She hesitated, surprised at the bluntness of his remark. She turned away, only to have him cup her chin, forcing her to meet his fierce gaze.

"But you're right," he said. "Sex and danger are a powerful mix. So…" He released her and moved back. "What shall we talk about?"

Comfortable now, she said, "Let's start with you."

He nodded. "That's easily taken care of. I'm thirty-six years old. I live alone in an old Victorian house. My parents live in Sarasota. And I've got a sister living in Hernando Beach with her husband Jack and two kids. One's a boy, aged ten; the other's a girl. She's fifteen and always in love. They live near Pine Island. Someday I'll take you there. You can walk out in the Gulf for miles without having the water reach the top of your head.

"I was an all right student in high school. Mostly, I chased girls and played poker. For a while I considered making that my life's work, until one day my dad sat me down and said, 'Deal.' He took me for every cent I had in the bank, six months' allowance, and the use of the car. After that, school was more attractive. I was a positive genius of applied fervor in college. I even won an academic scholarship during my junior and senior years. It helped pay the bills. I attended law school, but quit for personal reasons. I like my job."

"No marriage?" She wanted to know what the personal reasons were.

A shadow crossed his face. "Once, a long time ago."

She recalled his easy way with the little boy, thinking he'd make a wonderful father. "And since?"

He brushed drops of water from his forehead. "And since… I live the way I choose. No commitments, no promises. My line of work isn't exactly the most secure."

How could she argue with that? She'd had plenty of letters from wives and widows of policemen. "You must be hungry. Want some fruit?"

He gazed at her for a long moment. "I didn't take you for a coward, Millie," he said at last. "Don't be afraid. I'm not after anything you don't want to offer." Giving her time to absorb his meaning, he rooted around in her bag, finding a red apple. He took a big bite and munched contentedly.

"Now that I've made my life an open book," he went on, "what about you?"

She folded a towel under her head, using it as a pillow. "What about me?"

"Millie, you know what I mean. None of us materialize out of thin air. Tell me about yourself."

"I'm here on an extended visit, you might say."

He nodded. "Who are you visiting?"

"Myself. I came here from New Jersey to find me again. My husband died a little over a year ago."

He cursed quietly. "Kids?"

"No kids. End of story," she said, deliberately closing down the conversation. Dan nodded, then squeezed her hand.

A luxury cruise liner moved slowly across their line of vision. "Ever wonder where they're going?" he asked.

She was grateful he'd chosen a neutral topic. "Sure I do. Sometimes I think I'd like to be a stowaway."

Their eyes met and held. "Is there someone now you'd like to stow away with?"

"No… no one." Her voice was husky. She turned away from his heated gaze. Rolling onto her stomach, she dug up a handful of sand, letting the warm grains filter through her fingers.

Dan resumed eating the apple, happily making chomping noises.

"You're supposed to chew the apple quietly, Murdock."

He gave her a dazzling smile. "I know. I do it deliberately. I fool myself into thinking I'm eating a chocolate ice-cream sundae with hot fudge, whipped cream, and a cherry on top." At her look of uncertainty, he explained, "There's something about using all your senses when you eat. Makes you think you've had a wonderful meal or an ice-cream sundae."

She poked his stomach, teasing. "Not the way you're doing it."

"Be quiet, sassy mouth. This is behavior modification at its best." Concentrating on the apple, he finished it, stripping the fruit to its core. Then he rooted in his shirt pocket, coming up with a fresh supply of Chiclets. He offered her the box.

"No, thanks," she said. "I've got something better." She reached into her bag and withdrew a chocolate bar dotted with nuts. She flopped over on her back, holding it high for inspection.

Dan groaned. "You're not going to eat all that by yourself, are you?"

"Why else would I be unwrapping the whole thing?" She slowly peeled off the paper.

His mouth turned downward and he pretended to pout. "You're cruel." He sucked the last of the sugar coating from the gum. "I'm on a diet."

She playfully pinched the skin at his waistline, not getting enough between her fingers to count as fat. "As well you should be," she teased. "How long have you been on this diet?"

"Going on my second week." He groaned again as she held the confection near her lips. "Don't eat that."

She took a healthy bite, then said matter-of-factly, "Statistics say you'll gain it back. It's not a matter of diet. It's a change of life-style. Habits, Murdock, habits."

He glared at her. "You're a big encouragement."

She sank her teeth into more of the chocolate. "Mmmmm. Luscious."

"Are you going to offer me any for saving your life?"

She peered up at him, then favored him with an unmerciful smile. "Daniel, it isn't polite to ask. Didn't your mother teach you that when you were a little boy?"

"My father taught me to go after whatever I wanted."

Giggling, she moved the candy bar out of his reach. "I'm sure he'd approve of my trying to keep you healthy."

She minced another tiny bite, dripping some of the rapidly melting chocolate on her finger. She licked it off like a lollipop. "Of course, if you'd like me to be party to your early demise, I could, I suppose, offer you a bite." She raised her hand to offer him some, then recanted as he came nearer. "However, in good conscience, because you saved my life, I can't take yours." She lowered the candy bar. "Sorry, Murdock, you'll just have to live vicariously, wishing you were like me. I never have to diet. Good gene pool."

Growling, he lunged at her, grabbing the chocolate bar. His mouth opened.

"And here," she said with an exaggerated sigh, "I was going to offer you a meal for being so nice."

He dropped the candy onto her sand-dusted body, ruining it completely. Laughing merrily, she tossed it back into her bag and flipped onto her stomach.

"What kind of meal?" he asked.

"A home-cooked meal," she said, blithely stacking the deck in her favor. She'd feed him a good meal, serve chocolate ice cream for dessert, then casually spring her idea on him.

"What did you have in mind?" He gave her a long, smoldering look. She looked better than the sweetest, most alluring piece of chocolate. Lying as she was, her breasts plumped together above the top of her bathing suit, enticing him. That suit, he decided, was sexier than a bikini. Her skin, glistening with suntan oil, made him itch to slide up against her.

"Actually," she said, "what I had in mind was more in the way of a proposition."

"Well, now…" He stood up, dusting the sand from his body, then reached down to pull her up, too. One hand cupped her head. The other anchored her firmly to him. "I like a woman who knows what she wants. I'll bring the wine."

He slowly lowered his mouth to hers and kissed her lightly, almost chastely. Still, Millie felt scorched by the kiss. As she watched him stride away, she realized she would have been wiser telling him exactly what kind of proposition she had in mind.

CHAPTER THREE

Millie phoned Wylie the moment she arrived home. For a while she couldn't tell if her agent was thrilled because Millie's creative juices were running again, or because of the story of the morning 's arrest.

"Millie, he's a gift from heaven. What does he look like?"

When Millie finished describing Dan, Wylie confirmed her opinion that her readers would love to know more about the man who had shielded her from death with his life. The truth was, Millie wanted to know more about him, too.

"Reconstruct the crime," Wylie ordered. "Get policemen to play the parts of Louie and Spike if you have to."

Millie groaned. Reconstructing the scene meant putting herself beneath Dan's body again. He was already expecting a proposition.

"And be sure to take plenty of pictures."

Naturally, Wylie wanted pictures. "Wylie, how do you suggest I take pictures of us when I was hidden the whole time?"

"That shouldn't present a problem. I'll ask one of my friends down there to recommend a good cameraman. Or, if you want, you can ask the detective who was in the store to take the pictures. If Murdock is like most people, he'll jump at the chance to read about himself."

Not exactly, Millie thought. From the look on Dan's face when he'd talked about his life, she'd had the distinct impression he was a man who valued his privacy. "There are still a few details to work out."

"Oh, you mean clearing it with Port Rico's police chief. That's a mere formality. These little towns welcome all the help they can get."

Millie needed all the help she could get. One thing about her agent, she thought. Wylie barreled her way past all obstacles, seeing only what she wanted to see. In this case, a book.

"It isn't exactly that," Millie murmured, wishing she hadn't put the cart before the horse. She should have had all the arrangements made before calling Wylie.

Wylie's exasperation was evident. "Millie, what's the matter with you? Say what you mean and be done with it, for goodness' sake."

"I haven't asked him yet."

"Uh-oh."

Millie could imagine the expression on Wylie's face. She hastened to make things right.

"I'm planning to ask him tonight."

Wylie's relief was audible. So was her approval. "Tonight? You have a date with him, your tricky devil! Good for you. It's about time you took yourself out of your self-imposed celibacy. I've never been one to understand the life of a hermit."

Millie could have kicked herself. Her twin brother Kipp and his wife had been hinting the same thing recently.

"It's nothing like that," Millie said. "The truth is; I think he'll be more amenable to saying yes if I ask him on a full stomach."

Wylie's short bark of laughter ripped through the wire. "Okay, Millie. Whatever works. I have to admit I tried the same ruse once."

"And what happened?"

Wylie chortled. "The usual. I married the guy."

Millie decided Wylie was soft where men were concerned. The only thing that had happened that morning, she told herself, was that she had been provided a fortuitous opportunity to branch out her writing. Daniel J. Murdock was the limb she'd climb on—after she pulled a little joke on him first.

The invitation was for seven o'clock. She hurried to the supermarket to buy steaks, determined to get the best money could buy. Then she stopped for fresh fruit and vegetables. Last, she went to a marvelous Italian bakery that made the best chocolate cheesecake in the world.

Watching the time, she rushed home to make a platter of hors d'oeuvres. She marinated the steaks, then prepared a generous Caesar salad and a wild rice vegetable dish. To keep it informal, she planned to serve the meal on the small patio facing the canal. The idea was that when Dan's appetite was satiated—and he was too stuffed to protest—she'd spring her proposition on him.

She prayed Wylie was right that everyone liked a moment in the limelight. Why should Dan be any different?

Satisfied that her home was spotless, she shampooed her hair and bathed. But the scented bubble bath, which usually worked wonders at relaxing her, failed to deliver its usual magic. The thought of entertaining Dan—or any man—for whatever reason—after years of living as a married woman, set her nerves rattling.

She pulled clothes from her closet and tossed them on the bed, trying on and discarding one outfit after another. She wanted to look nice, but didn't want to look provocative. Why give Dan false ideas when he already had one whopping false idea, courtesy of her? She settled for simple white linen slacks, topped by a short-sleeved tomato-red silk blouse.

By the time she had finished dressing, she regretted her rash invitation. She should have just asked him for an interview at the beach. Then she wouldn't be watching the clock every five minutes.

She nervously sprang off the couch when the doorbell rang. All right, Millie, she told herself, stop acting like a giddy adolescent about to date the big letter man on campus. This is nothing more than a polite thank-you dinner, plus a simple, straightforward business proposition. Act your age.

Dan's insistent knock sent her scurrying through the white-tiled foyer. As she swung the door open, her best-intentioned warnings flew out the window.

Trouble stood in her doorway, a lazy, lambent smile on his handsome face. Trouble handed her a bouquet of daisies, a large gold-foil-wrapped box of Perugino, and a bottle of Beaujolais.

Dan Murdock, in blue slacks and sport shirt, his thick hair neatly combed, was nothing short of a knockout. He was more handsome, if that were possible, them before. Clean shaven, he smelled of soap and musky cologne. It was evident from his appraisal

171

of her that he expected something portentous from the evening.

"Hi. Am I too early?"

"No, no, of course not." She stepped aside, ushering him in. "You look... different." She inwardly cursed herself for what he must assume was a case of unwarranted and idiotic fawning.

He tilted his head to one side, amused. "Different good or different bad?"

"Different good," she admitted.

He gave an exaggerated sigh of relief. Then he studied her so intently, she blushed. "You look different, too. Not that the suit you had on today wasn't a showstopper. When I think of those legs of yours..."

Millie felt her heart trip at the heat blazing in his eyes. So much for her plans not to be affected, she thought. "Come into the kitchen."

"Wait a minute." He touched her arm, making her face him. "Is this the way you say hello to a man after a hard day's work?"

"Hard day's work, my eye." She resorted to teasing as a buffer. It was easier than falling into his arms. "You spent the afternoon at the beach, the same as I did. As I recall, the hardest thing you did was try to steal my candy."

Dan skimmed his fingers over her cheek. He felt the leap of desire within him, the heavy thudding of his heartbeat. He had thought of her while they were apart. Her skin had been so soft, as soft as the petal of a delicate flower. Her perfume drew him to her.

"Not so," he said. "I never told you how my day started." He released her arm and followed her into the sunny kitchen. He stood near her as she put the box of candy on the counter.

"There was this screwball dame," he continued, "who insisted on getting herself in trouble. Scrawny thing, too." He raised his eyes to the ceiling, as if in pain. "The sacrifice I made saving her life—"

"Sacrifice?" She leaned back against the counter, not even trying to work while he was dishing out this line of malarkey. The impish glint in his eyes made her heart turn over.

"Yes, sacrifice." Her lashes were the thickest he'd ever seen. "The things I do for my job. She had a face a man wouldn't look at twice—ouch! Pinching's out."

"Twice, Murdock?"

He rubbed his arm. "Okay. Maybe I went a little overboard

with the numbers. Anyhow, then I had to make sure she didn't drown in the ocean."

Millie sighed. "You poor thing. You really did have a rough day."

He nodded. "You can see how grateful I am to be away from her."

She laughed. His teasing had melted her nervous tension. "These flowers are lovely. How did you know daisies are my favorite?"

"Lucky guess. Actually, they were all the florist had. Stop changing the subject and tell me about your day. Did anything out of the ordinary happen to you?" His hand trailed up her bare arm. She pushed it away.

"Behave yourself or I'll call a cop."

"Go ahead. You'll be surprised how fast one arrives."

"Murdock, are you going to let me answer your question or what?"

He shrugged, giving her permission. "First," she began, "this crazy galoot from a TV show jerks open my car door. There I sat, idling the time away, waiting to go into Goldbergs. Anyway, this awful-looking weirdo piles into my car, waving something shiny under my nose. Then he orders me—doesn't ask, mind you—orders me out or else…"

Dan was watching her lips, making her forget the story she was telling. Her eyelids lowered. "Dan, this isn't fair. The flowers… "

He set them on the counter and slipped his arms around her waist. "The flowers will keep. Now what were you saying?"

She wet her dry lips, and was instantly sorry when Dan's eyes darkened. "This—this big oaf knocked me down onto the seat."

"Did he have his way with you?"

He found a sensitive spot behind her ear to nuzzle. She felt it to the tip of her toes.

"Dan!"

"What? Don't you like this?" He kissed the underside of her chin. "You're gorgeous, Millie. You should always wear red." He touched a silver bangle earring. "I don't like the thought of you putting a hole in this lovely ear." His tone was unnervingly intimate.

This wasn't going to work, Millie thought. They were operating on different agendas. As soon as she posed her request he'd know she'd set him up. Why did her legs turn to jelly when she needed to walk resolutely out of the room and onto the patio?

"Hey." His voice sent a warm thrill through her. "All I'm doing is saying hello."

She thrust out her hand. "Shake. It works just as well." She wished he'd stop looking at her with those X-ray eyes. It was as if he could see her inner struggle. She resisted the urge to melt in his arms and picked up the box of candy, holding it before her like a shield. "Is this for me or you?" He chuckled. "That depends, sassy mouth. Treat me right and I may offer you a piece. I'm not as selfish as some people I know."

Suddenly her stomach growled, making her blush. "Ooops."

"Don't worry about it. If I could growl on command, I'd join you. All I had to eat today was an apple. A certain piggish someone I know almost devoured a whole candy bar without sharing."

Millie closed her eyes for a moment, letting her insides adjust to the war going on. Dan's very nearness unsettled her. Dinner had been a bad idea.

"Ease up, Millie," he said. "You're too transparent." He placed his hands on her tense shoulders, sliding his fingers up the sides of her neck. "Am I the first man you've dated since your husband's death?"

She nodded. "This isn't a date. It's—it's dinner between two people who found themselves in an unusual situation."

"Millie, I'm glad I'm here. I want you to be glad, too." He rubbed his hands up and down her arms, then settled them on her shoulders. He leaned his forehead against hers. "Oh, Millie," he murmured, kissing her cheek. "What are we going to do about you?"

She drew back, managing a wry smile. "Did they teach you mind reading in detective school, Murdock?"

His response was surprisingly defensive. "What they taught me was to keep my guard up. Perhaps you can tell me why I have this unholy urge to lower it with you?"

She couldn't begin to tell him. She was having her own troubles. Starting with keeping her hands to herself. She wanted desperately to touch the scar near his lip, to ask if he'd ever been hurt in the line of duty. "Would you like to go outside?" she asked. "There's an orange and grapefruit tree in the backyard."

He laughed. "Thank you. I've seen orange and grapefruit

trees before. I'm a Floridian, remember? Let me help you prepare dinner. What are we having?"

"I fixed you something special because I was such a stinker before. Cooking gives me a chance to relax, to create, to make a statement about my personality. If you eat my food, you know the real me."

She didn't let him see her broad smile as she opened the refrigerator and lifted out a plate of hors d'oeuvres. It was covered with tinfoil. Atop it lay a sprig of mint. "Could you bring that, please?" she asked, indicating a tray with two wineglasses.

"This is very nice," he said, stepping outside with her. He glanced around. "You get shade in the afternoon? Smart girl. This sun can be brutal." He set the tray down on a round table.

The covered patio was small but attractively furnished. Yellow and blue floral pillows adorned tubular chairs, a chaise, and a cozy swing. Dan chose that and patted the cushion next to him.

"I've always loved these things. Come here, Millie."

She walked over to him, uncovering the foil from the plate. "Have some. I'm very pleased with the results."

Dan's lazy smile of invitation turned to one of questioning as he gazed at the hors d'oeuvres. It was obvious he was trying to be polite. "What are these?" The food was mostly an unappetizing white.

"Oh, they're delicious." Barely containing her mirth, she watched him tentatively pick up a cracker with white topping. He chewed it, then grabbed his wineglass.

"That's sawdust with cottage cheese," he protested, eyeing her suspiciously.

"Diet cottage cheese," she said happily. "You said you have to watch your weight. Here, try one of these." Mischievously, she chose a cracker with a sick, yellowish spread. "Low-salt cheddar cheese, or would you prefer water-packed sardines? Full of selenium."

He frowned. "I refuse to eat anything that wiggles."

She pretended to be affronted. "How can you call this dead fish alive?" Pointing to another tasteless-looking morsel, she said, "Well, if you don't want that, how about this?" She offered him a cracker topped with a green mass.

"Is a clump of grass your idea of gourmet food?"

"Watercress is very healthy for you. Full of iron."

"When I need iron, I pump it. And I'm not teething. I know how to chew, and dammit, I'm hungry. You eat it."

Millie chortled merrily. He had such a gorgeous body, she couldn't figure out why he was dieting in the first place. "Are you telling me," she asked, "that unless I feed you chewable food, you'll leave?"

He got up from the swing. "That's a dirty trick."

He glanced uncertainly at the tray. "This isn't really dinner… is it?"

She flopped down on the swing, laughing. He looked menacingly at her, pretending to be offended. She shook her head gleefully. Her laughter ignited his.

"Enough," she said. It felt so good to laugh, to share. She hadn't realized how much she'd missed the silliness of good plain fun. "I cooked for you. I swear on all my cookbooks."

"Not rice cakes, I hope."

Giggling, she confessed she'd really prepared steaks to broil on the barbecue. He sat beside her, and for a few minutes they enjoyed the soft sounds of the water lapping at the seawall.

"Why in the world are you dieting, Dan?" Millie asked. "You certainly don't look fat."

"Cops shouldn't be fat. Makes it harder to run."

"The newspapers will be full of this morning's events, won't they?"

He shook his head. "No, it was routine."

"But what you do isn't routine, surely. I think the public is entitled to know—"

"The public doesn't give a damn. Their attention span is about as long as it takes to change the dial on a television set. If there'd been a murder this morning, it would have made news. Nothing happened."

Except to me, she thought. "Maybe you and the public need to give a little bit."

"Meaning?"

"Meaning a good public relations campaign could make a difference in the public's perception of your work. I realize Port Rico isn't a major city, but that's all the more reason not to be complacent."

"Frankly, that's not my concern. I do my job the way I see best. Without someone looking over my shoulder. I leave the theatrics to television." A look of annoyance crossed over his handsome features.

"How we'd get from broiling steaks to this?" She'd moved too fast. Dan wasn't ready to discuss her doing a profile on him. She put on a bright smile and stood up. "In this house the guests kibitz in the kitchen with the help."

Dan carried the tray and the remaining hors d'oeuvres into the kitchen. Millie followed with the empty wineglasses. She washed. He rinsed.

"Do you mind if I look around your house?" he asked when they were through.

"Please."

Her home consisted of three bedrooms—one of which she apparently used as an office; a computer was set up on a table—a living room, a den, and a great room that flowed from the kitchen. The rooms surrounded her patio, which featured sliding glass doors connecting it to every interior room. The airy feeling of indoor/outdoor living was further achieved by glass-topped tables, white wicker furniture, and predominately white accents highlighting fabrics in shades of blue and mauve.

"I like it," he said, coming back after a few minutes. "Did you rent this furnished?"

"Yes. I have a three-month lease that I can renew at any time. I've been here a month."

"So you like it here?"

"I'm content."

He noted her use of the word content, not happy.

"When the realtor first showed me homes here," she went on, "I thought a split meant a split-level house. I didn't know it meant having the master bedroom wing separated from the rest of the house."

"Yes. People in Florida tend to have a lot of company. This floor plan gives everyone privacy. Of course, if a couple has a baby, the baby's room can be far away." Dan hesitated, then decided to push. He was intrigued by this woman. "Why didn't you ever have children, Millie?"

The memories of the endless trips to doctors washed over

her. She and Frank had tried everything, but his sperm count had been too low. She'd loved him too much to let him know how anguished she'd been at not having a child.

"The time never seemed right," she said, tossing her hair back, over her shoulder. The defensive look in her eye gave him his answer.

She took the pan of marinated steaks out of the refrigerator and handed it to him. "How are you at grilling steaks?"

"Didn't I tell you it's one of my specialties?"

He donned the chefs apron she gave him, then lit the grill while she finished setting the table.

"Don't look now," he said, "but I think we have a visitor." A heron, moving its long neck in slow-motion time to its equally long, skinny legs, was walking toward them. It stopped and cocked its head. His long, tapered bill opened so slowly that Dan laughed. "Fast critter."

"Come here, Henry," Millie called. She held out an anchovy from the Caesar salad. The heron made its way toward her so slowly, she finally walked over to him.

"Henry?" Dan asked dubiously.

"Yes. We've kind of adopted each other. Henry is a beggar. If anyone along the canal is eating," Henry waits. "no one can resist his begging."

"He's certainly fat."

"He likes chocolate." She smirked, darting out of Dan's reach when he tried to swat her rump with a towel.

"Hey," he said, "I think Henry's in love."

Millie followed his gaze. "Oh, she's beautiful." A white heron, her feathers swept back along her trim body, had made her way to Henry's side. Seeing the two of them standing side by side filled Millie's eyes with tears. "They look so right together, don't they? I'm going to call her Henrietta." She smiled. "Henry and Henrietta Huggins. What do you think?"

"I think you're an adorable nut. Dinner's ready."

The steaks were cooked to perfection. It was a perfect night, Dan thought, watching Millie as she talked animatedly about the area. Boats rocked gently at their moorings pear the docks. The sky darkened, leaving dusk for another day. Stars filled the sky, glittering brightly.

"At home," Millie said, her soft voice filled with awe, "it's so populated and we have so many lights, we don't see the stars this clearly. Certainly not this many." She lifted her face toward the sky. "Beautiful, isn't it?"

He gazed at her exquisite profile. She was enough to distract any man. "You're beautiful," he murmured. He wanted nothing more than to hold her in his arms again, but he sensed she wasn't ready. He heard her small, pleased intake of breath at his compliment. It was enough for now. "I never wanted to live in a big city," he went on. "There's too much of everything. Too much pollution, too many people."

The doorbell rang, surprising them both. Millie opened the door and Ben Jackman, his face grim, came in.

"Ben," Dan said. "What are you doing here?"

Ben glanced at Millie, then turned back to Dan. "Louie's made bail."

Dan emitted a string of curses. Millie looked from one man to the other. Both were tall, both commanded attention, but where Dan's longer dark hair and graying temples gave him a slightly weathered look, Ben's close-cropped hair and freckles made him seem youthful. There were deep laugh lines near his green eyes. As Dan made the introductions he extended his hand in greeting and smiled. A bright, open smile.

Millie liked him immediately, but her attention was riveted on Dan. He had changed before her eyes. Gone was the teasing manner, the easy, comfortable air. He was once again the intensely committed detective, concerned first and foremost for the public's welfare.

"We'd better get over to the Goldbergs'," Dan said.

As they turned to go, Millie touched his arm. "Wait a minute."

"What for?" he asked, now all business, letting her know he was focused on leaving.

"I'll go with you."

"Sorry, Millie," he said with implacable finality. "You'd get in the way. I always work alone. I thought you understood that from our conversation."

She understood all too clearly. She'd failed.

CHAPTER FOUR

Outside Millie's house, Dan jammed his fists into his pockets. So much for weeks of hard work, he thought, kicking up a spray of pebbles. Thinking about the turnstile way the mob made a mockery of justice infuriated him.

Dan and Ben quickly got into the car and clicked on their seat belts. Over the years, they had developed a camaraderie, easing the tensions of their daily routine. Tonight, however, there was none of the usual trading of banter and stories. The atmosphere was subdued. Dan slouched down in his seat, one knee jammed up against the door. He stared out the window.

Ben broke the silence at last. "You were a little short with the lady back there, you know."

Dan, startled by the unwonted reprimand, swiveled his head toward Ben. "What are you talking about?"

Ben glanced at him. "Seems to me all Millie wanted to do was help. And what's this garbage about working alone? What am I? Your chauffeur?"

"Oh, come on, Ben. I didn't mean you or other police personnel. Millie's a civilian. She's got no business being with us. Suppose Louie had gotten a good look at her face? Then where would she be? I'll tell you. Stuck in her house under police protection, same as the Goldbergs are going to be."

When they stopped for a red light, Ben lit a cigarette. Trails of smoke curled upward. "Is that why you're attracted to her? Because she won't take orders?"

Dan gnawed his bottom lip. He was dying for a cigarette. "Who said I'm attracted to her?"

"Hey, are we playing blind-man's buff, pal? You were there, weren't you? And you did have her tailed today."

His life was an open book. "That was strictly business. Anyway, Mike was off duty. He owed me a favor," Dan argued lamely. He'd never been able to con Ben. "She's just a woman I met today who happens to be interesting. That's all."

At Ben's snort, Dan chafed. "Knock it off. She's really a very intelligent woman."

"That's what I said. She's just a nice, intelligent woman you met today. And her little dinner party was designed for you both to exchange compliments about your respective brain power." Ben stubbed out his cigarette. "What does this intelligent woman do for a living?"

"How do I know? It didn't come up." All he knew was that she was a widow. What did she do? he wondered, remembering the computer.

"All right," Ben said. "Stop jumping down my throat. What do we do now?"

"Offer comfort and protection to the Goldbergs, and hope Louie makes a mistake, so we can pull him in again. Ask me, Spike's about ready to cooperate, don't you think?"

Ben turned onto the Goldbergs' street. "He might need another day, but I agree. He's mad Louie's out. Dan, you should finish law school. Maybe you could figure out a way for some of these collars and convictions to stick?"

Shoulda, woulda, coulda. Dan reran his reason for not finishing school. Because it had been more important to give Lana a start. And he honestly enjoyed his work with the force. He found it exhilarating, although lately he had been thinking more and more about returning to law school. Getting the sheepskin.

"Don't talk about the past, Ben." Dan gritted his teeth and wished for a perfect world. "We're short staffed at the department as it is. John Q. Public isn't exactly banging down our doors to give us a budget that will let us hire a public relations consultant."

"What for?"

"You know the chief. He's got some crazy notion that if big cities use public relations firms to boost their cause, then we should, too. Ask me, the chief's wrong. I say let well enough alone."

Both men shook their heads. "And I thought all we had to worry about were the criminals."

Dan laughingly agreed. "Did you ask Natalie if she'll work the double shift?"

Natalie Gershon was a twenty-four-year-old police officer who'd followed the tradition started by her father and two older brothers. They were in police work in neighboring communities.

"Yeah, the little pumpkin said, 'no problem.' She wants to build up vacation days."

"Isn't it about time you quit calling her that? Have you looked at her lately? She's all grown-up."

Ben stopped in front of the Goldbergs and turned off the ignition. "I've been calling her little pumpkin since she was knee-high to a grasshopper and her brothers and I were on the same high school football team. Natalie will always be little pumpkin to me."

"What you don't know about women could fill a book," Dan said as they strode up the stone pathway.

"Look who's talking. I'm not the one who forgot to thank his hostess for a good meal tonight, old buddy."

Dan slapped his forehead with his palm. "I'll call her tomorrow and set it right." He had been planning to call her anyway, but Ben didn't have to know everything.

*

As she cleared away the remnants of their meal, Millie thought about Dan's curt refusal when she'd impulsively asked to accompany him. He had bluntly told her he worked alone. Well, she'd just have to change his mind. Since when did a temporary roadblock stop her? she mused, feeling more like the old Millie who used to play outrageous pranks on and with her twin brother Kipp. But what would work best on Dan?

She mulled over her options as she scooped out small pieces of tuna from a can she kept ready for Henry. She dropped bits of leftovers onto the edge of the patio. The birds cautiously ventured near.

Birds… water…

That's it! she decided with a sudden victorious whoop.

"Thank you, darlings. You're my inspiration."

She hurried into her office and worked on her column, readying three weeks' worth of advice to send to the paper. Then she washed, undressed, and slipped into bed. Her mind at ease, she fell instantly asleep.

The phone jarred her awake at 7:00 A.M. Groping for it, she figured it was either Kipp, checking in, or Wylie. She fervently hoped it was Kipp.

"How'd it go?" The voice was feminine, definitely Brooklyn.

Millie groaned. Starting the day with Wylie was like being poked awake by a drill sergeant. "Wylie, are we in the same time zone? I know you can't be in your office yet. Do you realize I've spoken to you more in the last two days than I normally do in months?" She propped the pillow behind her head.

"I couldn't wait. What did Dan say? I'm dying to know how the evening went. Who's going to do the photography?"

Millie coughed nervously. "It's probably a good idea not to count on Dan."

"In other words, he refused."

"Not exactly. I never had the opportunity to ask him. We were interrupted by Ben Jackman, his partner."

Wylie sighed. "I hope your plan is foolproof, Millie. I hate to put you under stress, but after we spoke yesterday I had a call from the publisher. They're threatening to scrap the book if we don't send them something. They have a schedule, too. I went through the usual delaying tactics, but they didn't buy it this time. They politely but firmly told me a year to mourn Frank was enough. Then they followed up with if you're able to write your *Ask Ms. M* column, you should be able to meet your commitment with them. Honey, I have to agree. It's time."

Millie felt terrible. Wylie rode shotgun for her when she needed her, and she'd let her agent down. With new resolve she promised, "I'll get Dan to come around. I've thought of a great plan." She explained it to Wylie, who, practical to the end, asked the logical question.

"Why beat around the bush? The shortest distance between two points is a straight line. Or," she asked, inspired, "do you need an excuse to see this guy socially?"

"Never," Millie protested, a trifle too forcefully. "Neither one of us is interested in a commitment."

"Got that far, did you?"

Millie kicked off the covers and sat up. It was going to be one of those days. She swung her legs off the bed and paced the room with the phone.

"You have a one-track mind, Wylie. For your information, aside from a few laughs, Dan and I are as different as night and day."

Wylie's laughter came through loud and clear. "That's what I said. Opposites attract."

Millie took the bull by the horns and phoned Dan. He wasn't in his office. A woman named Natalie Gershon answered the phone.

"I'm glad to speak with you, Millie. You made quite an impression on our Dan. He told us how helpful you were yesterday morning."

Dan had given her credit for helping! she thought. That was a good sign. It meant he might change his mind and allow her to ride with him while she gathered research. It would only be for a week at the most. Then, blushing furiously, she wondered if while he dished out his praise, he had also explained what she had done specifically to help!

She left a message for him to call. He did so that afternoon and apologized for not thanking her for the wonderful dinner. When she broached the idea of completing their interrupted date, he immediately agreed.

"Don't bring a thing," she said, "and be here by eight. We'll get an early start."

"Where to?" he asked. His deep, masculine voice still sent shivers up her spine.

"That's the surprise," she answered, dangling the bait.

"Animal, vegetable, or mineral?"

She laughed, happy to get a nibble. "All three." Before he could ask more questions, she hung up and put her telephone answering machine on. No sense pulling in the line too soon.

Millie rushed to the door when Dan rang the bell early Sunday morning. He was dressed in light khaki slacks and a white T-shirt. His deep tan contrasted magnificently with his silvered temple, making him a dashing figure. He'd be a photographer's dream, she thought. A woman's, too…

She wore a short lavender jumpsuit that zipped up the front.

He tugged on the silver loop at the top of the zipper, effectively halting her from turning around. His eyes showed his appreciation of her as he slowly surveyed her from head to toe.

"Where are we going?" he asked, finishing his appreciative appraisal.

"I have a surprise for you." She smiled impishly. "You haven't eaten yet, have you?"

"No. Where's my surprise?" He expected her to pull him into the kitchen for another home-cooked meal.

She tugged him out onto the patio instead. A warm breeze blew gently against their faces.

"There," she said, ready to share her excitement. She spread both arms out in front of her, pointing proudly in the direction of the canal. "Isn't she beautiful?"

She was a boat. A canary-yellow boat with an outboard motor and a freeboard deep enough to stow fishing gear. A twenty-footer.

"Whose is it?" He hoped they were going to be alone.

"Ours!" she boasted grandly.

"Ours?"

"For the whole day." She gave him a provocative, untrustworthy grin. "During dinner the other night you said you love to fish, so I planned this especially for you. It's all arranged, down to the sandwiches and drinks."

The boat was compact, Dan mused. It would keep them in constant proximity. He had visions of a perfect day.

Millie reminded him of a little girl trying to contain herself as she impulsively threw her arms around his neck.

"I knew you'd like it," she said.

He folded his arms behind her back. "I love it. Thanks."

"Come on, then," she said, easing away from him. Once again she wondered if her invitation had been a bad idea. Her body seemed ready to burst into flames whenever she was near him. She had to forcibly remind herself she was on a mission.

"You've done this often?" he asked.

"You bet. I love it. We'll be out of here and fishing in no time."

He smiled. To each his own, he thought. What he planned to fish for was a mermaid named Millie.

She skipped down the steps to the boat, calling over her

shoulder, "Dan, the food chest, please? It's on the patio table."

The herons seemed to sense a picnic. "Is this a family outing, Millie? Do we take the children?"

Good idea, she thought. They'd add a festive and comic touch. She could use all the help she could get.

"Sure, why not?"

They made a strange quartet, Millie skipping to the boat, Dan lugging the food chest, and the herons gracefully bringing up the rear in slow motion.

"It'll be good for you to get away from phones and work," she said as they clambered aboard. "There's nothing like the curative powers of a day at sea." And, she hoped, it would make him more amenable to what she had in mind.

"What are you doing?" he asked, with more than a little interest as she lowered the zipper on her jumpsuit.

"What does it look like? I'm going to work on my tan."

Beneath the jumpsuit she had on the sleek, high-cut blue bathing suit she'd worn at the beach. He didn't know which he enjoyed more: her long, long legs, or the hint of breast peeking out from the top of the suit.

Her hair shimmered in the sun. She reminded him of a long-legged, suntanned sprite. She was laughing at Henry and Henrietta as they settled themselves on the bow of the boat, waiting for the fun to begin.

"I've thought of everything, Dan. We've got fishing rods. The bait tank's over the side. I'll pick it up as soon as you lift anchor. Isn't this fun?"

He could think of only one more way to have a lot of fun, and It didn't include an audience of hungry herons.

"I'll drive," she announced.

"Be my guest." Sitting down, Dan stretched his legs out and leaned back on the railing. To his pleasant surprise, she handled the boat like an old salt, explaining she'd spent summers on Long Beach Island in New Jersey.

The ocean was calm, and the boat rocked gently. Dan enjoyed relaxing and watching her, until the urge to be near her was too strong.

"Need help?" he asked, coming closer to her.

"Sit back and enjoy the scenery."

"I am."

He slipped his arms around her waist. Startled, she turned. His eyes were intense as he stared at her mouth. Then he lowered his head and kissed her softly. Sighing, she pulled back.

"Dan, I planned this day for you to relax."

"I am relaxing," he said. "At least for now. If I stay this close to you, I'm not sure how relaxed I'll be in a minute or so. Shall we try an experiment?"

His thumbs traced the line of her jaw, moving upward to her lips. "What experiment?" she asked, trying not to respond to that light caress.

"I stay here and we see which one of us stays relaxed the longest."

For a brief moment she almost played along. Then she drew back. "Dan, be fair. Remember, you're an officer of the law."

He grinned. "Which is why I'm off duty today. I'm a civilian, with all the desires of a man off duty."

"It's not even noon yet," she protested. If he kept this up she'd forget her reason for inviting him. "Here." She moved aside. "Your turn."

She sat down on the bench, her face lifted to the sun. This was relaxing, she thought. And the farther they got from land, the less urgent her desire to interview Dan became. She recalled Wylie's suggestion that Millie had concocted this fishing trip just so she could see Dan again. Nonsense, she thought. But she didn't believe herself.

"Where do you want to drop anchor?"

She sat up, shading her eyes with her hand. "Kind of over there." She pointed to a group fishing boat. "Might as well use their radar."

"Girl after my own heart," he said approvingly.

She scampered over to the fishing rods while Dan dropped anchor. "Okay, Dan, time to fish. I'll even let you bait the hook. Show me how you do it." Make the man show his skill, she thought. Wylie would approve.

Several minutes later she had the first bite. Dan genially shouted that it wasn't fair for the guest not to get the first bite. He yelled encouragement to her as the rod bowed dangerously under the weight of the fish. "Don't drop him. Give the line slacker. No, dammit, Millie, that's not the way to do it! More slack!"

She wanted to shout back at him that she'd won many a fishing trophy. Wylie's image floated in front of her face. She heard her saying, "Dope, give him the damned pole. Have you lost sight of your goal? You're after a story, not a fish."

"Dan," she said, breathing hard, "take the rod. Please. I haven't the strength to reel him in."

"Sure you do, honey." He stood behind her, bracing her. Covering her hands with his, he gave her the added power she needed. "You can do it, Millie," he said. "That fish has your name on it." As he spoke, a large sea bass broke the water.

Millie screamed, then bit her lip in concentration.

Dan was having a hard time paying attention to the bass. Millie's derriere was pressed against him. Each time she wiggled he wanted to take the fishing rod and throw it down into the boat.

They worked as a team, letting slack out of the line, then bending to reel the fish in, repeating the process over and over until the bass was close to the boat.

"Hold him, Millie. I'll get the gaff."

"He's gorgeous!" she exclaimed as he lifted the fish from the water. She threw her arms around Dan's neck, kissing him soundly. "Thank you."

He put the gaff down and caught her to him. His hands swept up her arms and down her spine. His tongue plunged into her mouth on a foray of discovery. The people from the party boat, who had been watching, clapped and shouted their approval.

Millie knew she was hearing voices. At that moment she didn't care if they were coming from inside her head or from outer space. She forgot about her mission. She knew only that Dan's encouragement, his helpfulness in making sure she had the pleasure of the first catch, and now his kiss of approval all worked on her. She felt free and wonderful for the first time in a year.

He released her slowly. For a moment they stared at each other, both aware something had changed between them, yet neither sure of what to do about it. At last, Millie moved away.

"I'm starved," she said, laughing nervously.

They spent the afternoon loafing, talking about nothing in particular, and eating. When they got hot, they jumped overboard and swam. Back on deck, Dan insisted she slather herself with sunblock. She obediently lay down on her stomach so he could apply lotion to her back and shoulders. That was a mistake. Her nerves were warring once more with her common sense. It was time to try her proposition again.

"Dan, has anyone ever interviewed you about your work?"

"A few reporters have called the office from time to time." He continued to gently massage her back.

"I'd love to read what they wrote about you."

"You can't." He leaned over her, his hands trailing up and down her spine.

"Why not?" she asked, telling herself to cool it. Disregard his hands and pay attention to business.

"There are no articles. I turned them all down."

She shifted onto her side. "Whatever for?"

"Because I'm not interested in reading about me and I sure as hell don't think anyone else will be, either."

"I disagree." She eased into her speech carefully. "Imagine if people knew about the arrest the other day. You were a hero. It's a great story."

"You're right. But what happened between you and me is private. Or don't you care?"

It was great theater, she thought, but she saw his point. She also saw her book going down the drain, and the advance money, which she had already spent, having to be returned. She remembered Wylie's sage suggestion about the shortest distance between two points.

"But, Dan, if it were reported correctly—"

"Millie, what do you do for a living?" he asked suddenly.

"I'm a writer," she admitted.

He frowned. "Newspaper?"

"Yes."

"And you saw a story in me?"

"Something like that," she said, feeling her way through a partial explanation. "Surely a little friendly publicity can't hurt."

Dan's face reflected his opinion. "Talk to my chief. His name is Peter Wasach. He'd probably jump at the chance, but leave me out of it."

"But he's not the one I'm interested in," she protested, wondering what made Dan so averse to publicity.

Dan carefully capped the bottle of lotion and wiped his

hands. "Then the real reason for all this"—he waved his hand to encompass the boat, the fishing rods, the food in the ice chest—" is your interest in writing about me?"

Millie sat up. It was going all wrong, falling apart in bits and pieces. "Don't put it that way, Dan. I didn't need to spend all this money and hire a boat just to ask you a question." Which was precisely what she had done, she admitted silently. From the look of disapproval on Dan's face, she guessed he could see right through her. "What's wrong with combining business with pleasure?"

He scowled. "Nothing, as long as both people know what's going on. I was under the impression this was strictly pleasure."

She wanted to say it was, but bit her tongue. She did want to interview him, yet she couldn't deny she wanted more. And that still unnerved her.

From then on, a pall hung over them. They made small talk. Millie knew she'd hit a brick wall. Dan knew he'd been taken. And quite possibly, he thought, the other night's meal fell into the same category as today's outing. While he was thinking about her in amorous terms, she'd only been interested in him as a means to an end.

"It's time we headed in, Millie," he said at last. "I'm working the four-to-twelve shift tonight."

He was lying, she thought. He'd told her he had the day off. Wylie would be thrilled to hear how her client had bombed out, Millie thought ruefully.

She nodded her agreement, and Dan turned the boat toward home. The herons lifted from the water and flew back to land, leading the way.

The birds had been the only winners, Millie thought glumly. At least they could eat fish. She had to eat crow. For the second time, she had blown her opportunity with Dan.

She wasn't giving up, though. If there was one thing Millie Gordon never walked away from, it was a challenge. Somehow, she'd figure out a way to make him change his mind.

CHAPTER FIVE

Dan leaned over the desk, his face tight with emotion. He was stunned by Police Chief Wasach's suggestion.

"Get someone else. I've already said no."

Wasach shot Dan his rarely used but highly effective I'm-the-boss look. At fifty-five, he'd been the head of the department for ten years. Dan liked him. Mostly because, he realized, until now he'd left Dan alone to do his work.

"Can't get anyone else." Wasach's tone was determined. "She wants you, tiger, and it's good public relations. Which, I might add, fell into our laps. Don't you want to help the department out?"

Dan felt as if he were acting in a bad movie. How could Millie do this to him? The shock of her request was wearing off, but not the disappointment. He'd come so close to really caring for her. He should have realized on the boat yesterday when she was peppering him with department-related questions that she had an ulterior motive and probably wouldn't give up until she got what she wanted. And she wanted plenty.

"Don't lay that guilt-trip on me, Pete. Nothing in my job description says I have to do this."

"It's no guilt-trip—and I realize it goes against your wishes—but I want you to reconsider." He turned on his persuasive voice. "I'm hoping the favorable publicity will make the city council sit up and take notice at budget time. We need some new patrol cars, not the recycled ones we've been driving. You said yourself the air conditioning is on the fritz in your car. Multiply that with dozens of other logistical and vehicular problems and you get my meaning."

"But why me? Ask one of the others. Ask Natalie. Two women should get on better."

Wasach shook his head. "Nope. You're our great white hope, Dan. Thanks to you, people nationwide will better appreciate what we do, and for free. You can't buy that kind of exposure."

"Nationwide?" The hairs on the back of Dan's neck bristled.

"Yeah. I tell you the woman's got clout."

"What in blazes are you talking about?" Dan asked, momentarily baffled. Did more bad news await him?

Wasach tossed a copy of the St. Petersburg Clarion across the desk. "She's syndicated. Page one, second section."

Dan dropped the first section on top of the desk. He skimmed the page Wasach had referred to, but found nothing with Millie's byline.

Wasach leaned over the desk and tapped the paper with his finger. "Millie Gordon's really *Ask Ms. M.* How about that?"

Millie, a syndicated columnist. How about that, indeed. He'd shot off his big mouth to her. He'd told her about his marriage, his dropping out of law school.

He groaned, feeling a fresh surge of disappointment at the confirmation that all she wanted from him was a press-worthy tidbit.

How had she gotten to Wasach so quickly? She had spent yesterday with him. Wasach hadn't been on duty. If she'd come in to see the chief today, Ben or one of the others would have told him. "How'd you find out who she is?"

"A woman named Wylie McGuiness called me from New York." Wasach stroked his chin. "That was some piece of work, Murdock, landing on top of a famous person." A chuckle escaped him.

"Who's Wylie McGuiness?" Dan asked. Everything that had happened between Millie and him in the car was apparently now coast-to-coast common knowledge. The whole episode, locker room fodder.

"McGuiness is Gordon's agent. Do the interview, Murdock," Wasach pleaded. "Get us on the map. McGuiness is shrewd. The way she explained it, it's a case of you scratch my back, I'll scratch yours. 'Course, you also get your name in the book. That's part of the deal. You're going to be promoted as a hometown celebrity. You may even get a guest shot or two on TV."

Dan skipped past the celebrity nonsense. "Book? What are you talking about?"

"The one Gordon is writing," Wasach explained, obviously hoping patience would win Dan's cooperation. "I don't know why you're so annoyed, Murdock. Gordon's book's entitled *Not-Your-Run-of-the-Mill People*. It's about fascinating people doing fascinating jobs. For some reason this dame thinks you're a candidate for fascinating. Beats me what she sees in you."

Dan cursed, quietly but thoroughly. "Does Millie know her agent called?" He'd give her the benefit of the doubt.

Wasach steepled his fingers beneath his chin. "How do I know? I'm no mind reader. She'd have to, though, wouldn't she? All I know is that I've given permission for this Millie Gordon to ride with you for a week. Show her the ropes. Let her see what the job entails. She'll do an honest job of reporting."

Dan closed his eyes for a second. "It's a bad move. If by any chance she gets hurt, what then? Do we wait to be sued by her paper, her publisher, her agent, not to mention Millie herself?" He shook his head in disgust, not caring what the chief thought.

His superior, however, was only thinking about his goal. "Stop being so melodramatic, hotshot. Nothing's going to happen. You'll be there to protect her. From what I hear, anyway, you're pretty good at that."

"Louie's still walking the streets. Suppose he sees her with me? He's been threatening revenge."

Wasach wasn't worried. "He won't. He's not about to violate bail, not if he wants to stay out until his trial. He's got a smart attorney."

Dan frowned. "I disagree. If he hears Spike Harvey's started singing, he'll do something stupid, attorney or no attorney. Louie's more afraid of the mob than of us."

Wasach considered Dan's argument, then offered a compromise.

"I doubt he'll be a problem, but if it eases your mind we'll watch Louie for a while. As for Millie Gordon, do the easy stuff."

"Like what? Deliver babies?" Dan asked sarcastically.

"You did it once; you can do it again. By the way, how is your namesake?"

The glacial expression on Dan's face softened momentarily. "The kid's fine," he said, a note of pride in his voice. "He's seven and doing pretty well in school, last time I checked."

Dan had delivered infant Daniel Lopez seven years ago when he answered an emergency call from the Lopez home. The grateful parents, Manuel and Rosita, had named the strapping eight-pound six-ounce boy after him. Over the years he had kept in touch with the family. Rosita was pregnant again, hoping for a girl this time. The baby was due in two weeks.

"Dan," Wasach said kindly, "I know you believe I'm on the wrong track, with this publicity thing. But think what a morale booster it would be for the staff." He paused, then added carefully, "It wasn't publicity that got your Uncle Jack fingered by the mob when he was working vice in New York."

Dan didn't want to talk about it. His uncle had been gunned down in cold blood. As if that weren't bad enough, Internal Affairs had later proved his father's brother was one of what they called the bad cops. "Murdock On The Take!" It had made all the locals. Since then, keeping his family name clean and out of the news was important to Dan not only for his sake, but out of consideration for his parents.

All that slipped from his mind, though. Now he wanted to see Millie and straighten out this nonsense once and for all. He left the chief's office in a foul mood. Knowing it was better to see Millie with a calm, cool head, he decided he'd go to the cafeteria for coffee. Ben spotted him and carried a sandwich and coffee to his table.

"What's up?" Ben asked. "You look like you're ready to spit."

Dan told him about Millie and her agent and Wasach. "So, what do you think I should do?"

"Go for it, fella."

Ben's response didn't put Dan in a better frame of mind. He glared balefully at his partner and best buddy. "So much for friendship and loyalty."

"You're welcome." Ben picked up the Clarion, then let out a low whistle. "You lucky stiff. I wish someone would write about me."

Natalie entered the cafeteria, her green eyes sparkling. She was a tiny woman, barely tall enough to pass the standard for police officer. Her blond curls bobbed as she sat down with them. She squeezed Dan's hand. "What do you know? We have a real celeb in our midst."

"Bad news travels fast," Dan muttered.

"Hi, little pumpkin." Ben leaned over and slipped his arm around her shoulders.

"Oh, shut up, Ben."

"What's gotten into her?" Ben asked, shaking his head as Natalie stood up and stalked off.

"You figure it out," Dan said. "I've got my own troubles."

Ben was thoughtful for a moment, then said, "I may not know much, but I sure as heck know when a woman's got a man by the tail. You've got a case for this Millie. Why fight it?"

"Don't you get tired of giving advice?"

Ben grinned. "Nope. I think you're nuts. If I had the opportunity to spend a week with a woman I liked, I sure wouldn't be complaining. I'd figure out a way to make it work for me."

Dan leaned back in his chair considering Ben's advice. It wasn't hard to recall the image of Millie reeling in that bass, her body tucked firmly into his, her hair flying in the wind as she squealed with delight. Nor was it difficult to remember her flinging her arms around him and kissing him with abandon after she landed the fish.

"You would, huh?" he asked Ben.

"Damn right," Ben said, munching his sandwich.

Dan drained his coffee in two gulps. "You're not as dumb as you look. Thanks, pal."

"You're welcome, I think. What are you going to do?"

Dan crumpled his napkin and stood up. "Why, I'm going to be a hero."

Ben looked puzzled. "Am I missing the connection? I thought this was about getting Millie and you together."

Dan grinned. "It is—on my terms."

*

Listening to Wylie's explanation, Millie cringed. "Oh, Wylie," she wailed. "You didn't."

"I had to. What's the big deal? His boss is thrilled to death. I knocked his socks off."

"The big deal," Millie said heatedly, "is that you've done something in my interest that isn't in Dan's. He made his wishes clear on the boat." Millie recalled how their excursion had ended. "What was Dan's reaction?" she asked, dreading the answer.

"He wasn't in the office, so he doesn't know yet. I had to do it, Millie. I pitched him to the publisher. It was the only way to save the book deal, believe me. They're thrilled and can't wait to see some material."

Millie shuddered. If it weren't for the advance money already spent, she'd chuck the whole project. "Two days ago they were threatening to cancel the contract and today they're thrilled? How come?"

"Publishers are crazy. You know that. They'll say anything to get what they want."

And sometimes, Millie thought darkly, well-meaning agents, too.

Millie's doorbell rang an hour later. She guessed it was Dan. Almost reluctantly, she opened the door. Dan brushed by her, a copy of the Clarion in his fist. His gaze raked over her. "Did you have to pull rank?"

She sighed. She already had a headache from the phone call with Wylie. "I didn't pull anything, Dan." He was silent as he stalked into the living room. She followed him. "I'm sorry about all this. I had no idea Wylie would call your boss."

"Yeah." He shoved the paper at her. "You could have fooled me, Millie, or should I call you Ms. M?"

She was tired of being sentenced without a trial and stiffened her spine. "Millie will do fine."

He stared at her for a moment, then his gaze dropped to her mouth, forcing her to remember. "You told your agent what happened in the car?"

She blushed. With little effort she could feel his lips on hers. "Only as it pertained to the case."

"Yesterday, why didn't you come right out and ask me instead of pussyfooting around?"

"I tried to, but if you will recall, you closed out the conversation."

"That's why you wanted to go with me to the Goldberg's when Ben came by the other night, isn't it? You wanted to get information for your story." His intent gaze dared her to be up-front.

Millie could feel the tension rising between them. She rubbed her hands together. "No," she said hesitantly. "Well... in a way. I like the Goldbergs. I thought if they saw a familiar face it might help them. And, yes," she added, flaring suddenly, "it would have helped me with background information, too."

"Thank you for being honest, Millie. I was merely curious." His voice was as cool as if he were talking to a stranger, not someone he'd kissed fewer than twenty-four hours ago.

"I imagine you've learned what you came for," she said. She started toward the hallway. His hand on her arm stopped her. She flinched.

"Relax, Millie, I'm not going to jump you."

How could she relax when he stared at her like that? she wondered. She was tense, and she knew it showed. She'd like nothing better than to feel his hands on her neck and shoulders, massaging away the tight kinks. She lowered her lashes, not wanting him to see the flash of desire in her eyes.

"Millie?" he said huskily. She looked up. Their eyes met and clung, giving her the odd sensation of being suspended in time. He cleared his throat. "Pete wants you to ride with me for the week."

"You could refuse. I wouldn't blame you."

His tone hardened. "I want to, believe me. But the chief thinks the publicity will make the city council sit up and take notice. The department's budget has been squeezed lately."

"I see." She saw all too clearly. He was saddled with her. "Then what do you propose?"

"A truce."

Her heart skipped a beat. A truce would give her time. Time to be with him and get the book started. She was weak-kneed with relief.

"Just so we understand each other: I accept that this is strictly business on your part, that whatever transpired between us happened because of circumstances," Dan said softly.

What could she say? she wondered. She'd gotten what she wanted, and in the process had lost more than she'd gained. She wanted to turn the clock back. She wished he'd put his arms around her and kiss her the way he had on the boat. With a sinking feeling, she waited for him to continue.

Dan shoved his hands into his pockets. He'd given her an opening to contradict him, had hoped she would. When she didn't, he went through the motions.

"I'll lay out the ground rules. If trouble starts and I say get down, I mean exactly that. I can't have you bleeding on my hands."

"Agreed," she said formally.

"If we have to go out of town to follow a lead on a case, I don't want to hear any complaints."

"Agreed."

He cleared his throat. "There may be times when you'll have to act as my partner..."

Her face became animated. "You mean that? I'll actually be doing real police work with you?"

He shook his head. "No, of course not. You'll only pretend. On certain jobs, Natalie usually comes with me, but I can't have two women in the car. It'll look strange, since it isn't by the book."

"What sort of pretending?"

"We may need to pretend to be man and wife—if we have to spend a night at a motel."

She gulped. She hadn't considered spending the night with Dan. "Is this kind of thing usually done?"

His mouth curved in a brief smile. "Only when necessary."

She hastened to agree to his conditions before he put an end to the entire deal. "All right."

"Good." He turned to leave. "And"—he casually slipped in the caveat—" I get to approve what you write about me."

Her chin shot up at that. It was enough she'd agreed to his terms like an obedient puppy, but now he was intruding on her professional integrity. Her temper sizzled. She'd always been honest and fair. She'd let him read it, of course, but for verification, not editorial consent. She made no effort to hide her mounting anger. "See here—"

"Take it or leave it," he challenged, holding his breath.

Millie mentally reviewed her options, admitting to herself her position was weak. Dan Murdock held all the cards. It was a question of take it or leave it. She inclined her head, then bit out the alien acceptance. "Agreed."

Did she imagine it or did she see a slight twitching of his lips? Forget it, she thought. Dan was stone-faced.

"Fine," he said. "I'll call you when I need you. Be ready to roll at a moment's notice. Police tend to keep odd hours."

"But don't you work shifts? Surely you know your own hours. Suppose I'm in the middle of a column?"

He smiled. "That's your problem, isn't it? You're the one who got your agent to arrange this."

"I told you that I didn't know Wylie was going to call your chief." She jammed her fists onto her hips. Angry as she was now, she couldn't help but remember the feel of Dan's body pressed close to hers as she reeled in the fish, the feel of his hands as they applied the sunblock to her bare skin.

He was gone before she could protest or negotiate terms. She could hardly blame him—he'd been neatly finessed by his chief.

But so had she been. Then again, all they had to do was spend one week together. What could happen in one week?

The next day at two A.M. he knocked on her door. At first Millie thought she'd left the television on. When the knock persisted, she stumbled from bed and peered out the window. The street lamp shone on a familiar car. Oh my gosh! she thought. Dan hadn't been kidding when he'd said be ready at a moment's notice.

Still groggy, she stumbled out of her bedroom. She flung open the door, oblivious to the fact that she was wearing a diaphanous white gown. "What are you doing here at this hour?" she asked, rubbing her eyes.

Dan took one look at her sleep-flushed face, her sensual lips, the tousled hair curling around her face, the sheer nightgown, and gulped. The ensemble left nothing to the imagination. "Never mind that," he growled. "Why in hell did you open the door?"

Was she hearing correctly? she wondered. Had he actually asked her why she had opened the door? She yawned. "Because you knocked on it and I didn't want to wake the neighbors. They might call the police." In her sleepy state, she collapsed against him, giving into a fit of silliness. "Get it?" She poked his ribs. "They might call the police. That's you. So you'd end up here, anyhow."

Dan was having a hard time keeping from laughing. He wanted to scoop her up in his arms, carry her back to her bedroom, and cover her with his hungry body. He almost did just that as she peered at him from beneath heavy lashes. She yawned again.

"It's the middle of the night," she said. "Is this some kind of a test? I saw your car from the window."

And he could see her nipples and every delectable inch of

her. He swallowed hard. "Lesson number one, Millie. Never answer the door dressed like that. It would give a dead man the hots."

Millie glanced down at herself, then flung her arms in front of herself, covering her breasts. "Am I giving you the hots, Dan?" She lowered her eyelashes seductively, then yawned in his face. "Oops, sorry. Give me a minute."

Dan was grateful she left the room before she saw how obviously he wanted her. He recited the reasons that had brought him there. This wasn't going to work; he knew that with a sense of doom. He wanted her on a sheet; she wanted him on a sheet of paper.

A lousy trade-off, in his book.

*

"I'm ready." Millie, her eyelids still at half-mast, walked back into the room. One corner of her blouse was tucked into her jeans. She wore a pair of thongs. A pad and pencil dangled from her right hand.

"What's that for?" Dan asked, smiling in spite of himself. She looked adorable—and groggy.

She cupped her hand in front of her mouth, yawning once more. "In case anything happens. Notes."

He propelled her out the door, then took her key and locked up behind them. He steered her to the car and got her into it, making sure none of her was hanging out.

Praying for enormous self-control, he fastened her seat belt for her. His arms reaching across her, he closed his eyes and drew in a whiff of her perfume.

She reached up and tugged on the collar of his jacket. "Thank you, Dan. That was lovely."

Lovely. Only Millie would say buckling a seat belt was lovely. He smiled wryly. They were off on a stakeout where, if God was good to him, nothing would happen. He'd even arranged for a backup detail. His plan was simple. They'd stay an hour, then he'd bring her home. Between Millie's sleepiness and his libido, he was having a hard enough time trying to convince himself their relationship was all business.

His attempts at conversation elicited mostly short-tempered

mumbles from her. After a while he gave up and simply drove in silence. With the big deal she and her agent had kicked up about wanting to see how a fascinating cop went about his fascinating business, he'd have thought the least she would do was stay awake.

He announced their arrival at their destination. She didn't answer. Glancing over, he wasn't surprised to see her fast asleep, her head listing to one side. A thick curtain of hair covered half her face. He gently nudged her upright. "We're here, sleeping beauty. Time to see how exciting this job is."

He expected her to ask a million questions and begin to fill up that pad of hers. Instead she mumbled a word approximating "wonderful," scribbled something that looked unintelligible to him in her pad, then seemed to give up. She was out like a light. And no matter what he did, her head seemed to find its way onto his shoulder.

In the close confines of the car, her perfume was an exotic goad, setting his imagination alight. He remembered her as she'd opened the door, barefoot and standing in the light, clothed in a wisp of transparent white. "Oh, Millie," he muttered. "You really know how to play dirty pool." Leaning over, he unbuckled her seat belt. His arm curved around her shoulders, drawing her close. "Don't hate me in the morning. I tried." Like a contented kitten she curled into him, her hand lying innocently on his upper thigh. Her breasts flattened against his chest, proving undeniably that she wasn't wearing a bra.

In good conscience, he did try to move her hand, only to have it flop back again. Beads of sweat broke out on his forehead. Millie's subconscious had a will of its own. She was touching him, teasing him, stoking the flames of his passion.

At this rate, he'd be a basket case by morning.

"What's a man to do?" he murmured, giving in to the irresistible urge to taste her creamy skin. His lips grazed her forehead, then drifted slowly to her soft cheek and the corner of her tantalizing mouth.

As if she'd slept in his arms a thousand times, she turned her face up, her lips seeking his. He felt as though he were caught in quicksand as he lowered his mouth to hers with the barest flutter of pressure. She murmured in her sleep. "Mmmm… More."

He froze. What the hell was he doing, taking advantage of

her? He knew all too well what he was doing and there was no excuse. He was behaving like a horny teenager. What made the whole thing impossible was that while he needed a cold shower, Millie was utterly unaware of what she had said, or even that she had touched him while she slept.

Very carefully, he lifted her hand. All right, Murdock, he told himself, don't go getting any fancy ideas. She wasn't responsible for her unconscious actions or reactions. She'd lived alone for a year. That had to be a tough adjustment. And you, Murdock, he reminded himself, are a chapter in a book to her, nothing more.

"Millie," he said, sitting her upright and speaking more sharply than he intended. "Wake up."

She did so slowly, like a flower unfolding. Her eyes, rimmed by those thick lashes, opened. At first she was disoriented, then she saw him and smiled. She stretched her arms upward, the action drawing her blouse taut against her breasts.

"Where are we?" she asked, regarding him with utmost trust. She didn't realize he was just this side of hell. "I'm sorry I catnapped, but it felt wonderful. I feel refreshed now, raring to go. Did anything exciting happen while I was asleep? Anything I should write down?"

He choked back a strangled groan.

"Not a thing, Millie," he lied, dampening his erotic urgency. "Not a thing."

She smiled at him, an innocent, sleep-refreshed smile. "That's good. I'd hate to miss anything."

CHAPTER SIX

Dan hiked his knee into a more comfortable position. For the first time in an hour, he let his body relax. He'd been playing two ends against the middle. On the one hand he wanted to get to know Millie and have her get to know him, and on the other hand he was afraid to open old hurts lest it wound his family.

Millie awake was as curious as a cat. She badgered him with incisive, intelligent questions that kept him on track, kept him focusing on something other than the way her body had felt next to his.

Until Millie, his life had been uncomplicated and sane—if occasionally dangerous. He hadn't even felt the urge for a woman lately. He'd heard about men who burned out early. Read about it in her advice column, now that he thought about it.

Millie was professional and serious, scribbling a mile a minute on her yellow lined pad. What would she do if he suddenly said, "Millie, I think you might be interested in knowing where your hand was while you were asleep. I can attest to the fact that you have the ability to arouse me in less than ten seconds. If you'd care to experiment while you're awake, we can replay the scene, including the part where you kissed me, then asked for more."

Millie touched his arm. "Dan, you aren't listening."

His patience straining, he told her to repeat the question.

"Do these crooks have priors?"

"Alleged perpetrators, Millie. Everyone's innocent until proven guilty." Himself included. "Yes, they do."

"And do you ever think about the danger?"

He wanted to shout that there was more danger being in a car with her than being out on the street. "I think about being prepared, not taking foolish chances. Cloning Rambo doesn't interest me." Unable to resist touching her any longer, he casually dropped a hand on her shoulder, rubbing the fabric of her blouse over her soft flesh.

Millie repressed a shiver of desire. Dan had no idea what he was doing to her. Yet she didn't want to move and possibly break the mood, not when he'd finally begun to talk about himself. "What interests you, Dan? Apart from the job, I mean?"

"Animal, vegetable, or mineral?"

She grinned. "Keep this up and I'll tell Wasach he runs a boring precinct. He'll love that kind of publicity." Couldn't he tell how arousing his touch was? That his lightest caress could send the fires of passion flaring through her?

He smiled, abruptly sending her into thoughts of dark nights and silvery moonlight. "Be serious," she said. "Do you think of the danger?"

"From time to time. I am now," he said, twirling a lock of her hair around his finger. His eyes were level with hers as he leaned back to watch her. "Have you ever shot a gun, Millie?"

She could feel the tension build inside her. For the past hour her body had been reacting to him nonstop. She'd had letters from women telling her what had happened to them in cars, usually the backseat. She jerked herself back to his question.

"Only the ones at a shooting gallery on the boardwalk in Wildwood, New Jersey. I was trying to win a pink teddy bear."

"Did you?" he asked, remembering how intensely she'd concentrated on reeling in the fish. And how she'd used his body for support.

She pursed her lips. "No. It's very annoying. My brother says he inherited all the sharp-eyed genes and steady hands. It's a good thing, too. Kipp's a doctor. I can't hit the side of a barn."

He noted the disappointment. "I'll have to fix that."

She smiled brightly at him. She'd be able to use the information in her book, and maybe win the teddy bear the next time she was in Wildwood. It didn't matter that she could easily afford to buy one. She wanted just once in her life to pick off a prize with her skill. "You're going to take me to the shooting range and teach me how to shoot?"

Dan hated to dampen her spirits so soon after he'd lifted them. He liked this bubbly, carefree side of her. He leaned a bit closer. "No, I can't do that. That's for police personnel. But I can take you to some property I own up the coast. We'll set up some tin cans on the picket posts and see how you do." He frowned, surprised at how protective he felt toward her. "You really ought to take one of those self-defense courses. A woman should be able to defend herself. Men, too," he added, unwilling to reveal too much.

They were interrupted by a call from the dispatcher informing them of a robbery in progress. Millie immediately buckled her seat belt.

He put his hand over hers. "Sorry to disappoint you, Millie, but we're staying put. The call isn't for us." He checked his watch. His replacement would be along any minute. He reached under his seat, hauling up a thermos. "Have some," he said, unscrewing the top. "There are crackers in the glove compartment if you want."

She took the cup from him, placing a hand over the steaming brew as she stared out at the mostly deserted streets. It would be dawn in a few hours. Day Two. She was eating up her time with him.

"Murdock, you got me up in the middle of the night on a wild goose chase." She flapped the yellow pad at him. "You must admit this makes lousy copy. There's nothing to write about."

He almost choked on the hot coffee. "Not really. You're seeing how a policeman exercises self-control and patience."

Millie gnawed on her bottom lip, thinking. She turned to a fresh sheet of paper, picked up her pencil, and fired off another charge. "I know being a policeman tends to run in families. Anyone in your family in the police force besides you?"

"No." His brows creased over disapproving eyes. He'd lulled himself into temporary amnesia over the real purpose of their being together. He'd talk with his father as soon as Dad and his mother returned from a trip abroad. If his father objected to any publicity that might dredge up his brother's name, he'd bow out of the arrangement.

"Was there?" she repeated.

"Let's keep it on me. Leave out the family tree."

"Dan," she protested, frowning. "I'd rather not. You're part of your family. The chapter will be bland. Why can't you understand

and cooperate?" She'd hit a nerve. She knew it. Whom was he protecting?

Dan noted her high color, the intense way she was looking at him. Wanting to see how far she'd go for her story, he said, "Don't play detective. That's my job. You're the writer. That's your job. I'm sorry if you don't like coffee and crackers."

She backed off slightly, but not enough to keep the edge out of her voice. "How do you suggest we spend our time then? Gin rummy?"

She knew a brick wall when she hit one. Dan was perfectly amenable to having a companion help to pass the lonely hours in the car. He was perfectly willing to chat off the record. Yet the merest hint of on-the-record and he became a chameleon. Keep it general or keep it out.

Why? Was it because he resented having been forced into taking her in the first place? Was this how Murdock got even? Was there more?

She resolved to keep her cool. Ruffling his feathers wouldn't get her anywhere. But asking one of her computer whiz friends for some good, deep background on the Murdock family might give her something to go on.

"Can we at least talk off the record, Dan?"

His eyes narrowed fractionally. "Why? You can't use it."

"I want to know more about you," she answered honestly.

He sipped his coffee. His gaze rested on her lips, then flicked upward. "Do I get to ask questions, too?"

She smiled, thinking, You're not going to get away that easily, my friend. "Of course, when I'm through."

"No ladies first?" he teased.

"No one is interested in the private Millie Gordon. The public knows what it needs to about my other persona, Ms. M."

Intrigued, Dan pushed further. "I'm not your public."

"Dan, this is ridiculous."

"I totally agree. When two grown people who are obviously attracted to each other have to set down rules for discussion, it is ridiculous."

Millie was building herself up to a full-blown fit of indignation. "Who said we're attracted to each other?"

He kissed her quickly, surprising her. Her lips parted in semiautomatic shock, and he took advantage of the opportunity. He kissed her deeply, sending her into a hot, heady spiral. When he broke away, she was breathing heavily, but he seemed totally unaffected.

"Our bodies are way ahead of our conversation," he said. "And they're a lot more honest."

His voice seemed so bland to her, he might have been talking about the weather, Millie thought. Well, she could be blasé, too.

"The only thing I want is a good story," she said, mentally crossing her fingers. "Something that will make the readers not want to read that last word on my last line."

"Are you sure? I believe in honesty, too. Let's see if I can convince you that what's between us is important enough to keep out of print."

His lips moved over hers in savage, sensual domination. She hadn't a chance; he knew how to arouse her. They'd been close in a car before. Their bodies were attuned, and fit together perfectly. She felt her resistance melt just as he dragged his mouth from hers.

She surfaced, still tasting him on her lips, still feeling his hard chest muscles. She gazed into his blackguard eyes, reading in them hot desire and certain he could gloat over what he read in hers.

She shivered, not from the cool night but from the heat radiating from him. Oh, he was clever. She gave him that. If she agreed to confidentiality, he boxed her in. He could spill his guts out and ethically she couldn't use the material. His fingers traced circles on her bare arm, making it difficult for her to concentrate. He looked incredibly calm and controlled and about as guileless as a mountain fox.

How would she explain this to Wylie?

"Millie, I never said I was a suitable subject for your book. Your agent and Wasach cooked that up."

"You're saying this deliberately to discourage me."

His smile almost reached his eyes. "I'm a very deliberate man."

His hand traveled up to her cheek and caressed her. She swallowed. She wanted—needed—to know more about him. So she gambled. "All right. You have my promise. Off the record tonight. Tomorrow, that deal's off."

"Fair enough. Thank you." His hand glided around to the

back of her neck, drawing her closer. "I appreciate that."

"Do you ever lose, Dan?" She'd been finessed and trapped by his smooth talk and her own treacherous body.

He smoothed the hair away from her brow. "Sure. Mostly when I don't particularly care about the stakes." He wondered at what point he'd decided, as far as Millie was concerned, to throw years of caution to the winds. "Do you get the impression," he asked softly, "that putting us in a car together is dangerous?"

"You could shake my hand," she whispered.

Bare inches separated them. "Uh-uh. I like this better."

"You know, don't you?" she said weakly. "I can't write about this."

He chuckled. "I know, but this is a lot more fun than answering questions. Did anyone ever tell you those eyes of yours are an extraordinary shade of blue?" He kissed those eyes shut, a soft murmur escaping her lips.

"Dan," she managed to say, forcing away a swift stab of desire, "you're on duty."

His lips brushed her forehead. "Not anymore. There's an unmarked car about thirty-five feet behind us. He's my relief. He's been here for the last ten minutes. Don't worry—he didn't see us kiss."

Infuriated, she gave a mighty push against his chest. She might have known he'd be in perfect physical condition. "You sneak. You went through all this to prevent me from questioning you."

He laughed and kissed the tip of her nose. "I went through all this, as you put it, to see if I can be in a car with you without kissing you. I can't."

Then he stopped talking, blocking out the world for her as he had in the past. She had a strong sense of deja vu, as if her body were reliving an earlier scene, a scene of soft mists and sensations and heat.

A wild, passionate force erupted within her. Dan's tongue teased and tempted hers. His lips were firm and commanding, yet soft and beckoning. Later, she would wonder why she hadn't had the desire to push him away. Why she had let herself be kissed like a teenager.

She would wonder why she had allowed his lips to devour hers, his tongue to pillage her mouth. Why his kissing her seemed so right, so natural, so familiar. She would also ask herself why her arms had encircled his neck and her fingers had threaded through his thick hair while he pressed his body to hers; ask herself how an otherwise sensible woman who knew the score could let herself in for such trouble. Trouble she didn't need, but which she seemed to court whenever she and Dan were within seat belt distance.

Gradually Dan pulled away, his lips lingering on hers for a moment longer before he moved back to his side of the car. Millie felt twinges of both disappointment and relief. She hadn't wanted him to stop. If he'd continued, though, she knew she'd probably have had some firsthand experience about what could happen in the backseat of a car.

"Definitely off limits," Dam muttered to himself, reaffirming his convictions about being in a car with Millie. He stuck the key into the ignition. "I'd better get you home. We have a heavy day tomorrow."

Millie blinked. She was still feeling aftershocks. He'd silenced her questions with the oldest trick in the book. Male to female. She'd fallen into his arms without a struggle, agreeing to everything he'd asked.

Dan pulled out into the road, signaling to the man in the car behind him. He glanced over at Millie; he wanted to tell her the truth, but knew he had no right to tell her the whole story about Jack Murdock. Not without going against his father's wishes.

"What…" Millie started, then paused to clear her throat. "What's this about tomorrow?"

"Oh, we're going to a game."

"What game?" She stared at him without comprehension.

"Softball. How good are you at catching?"

Was he crazy? She had work to do. Tomorrow, as far as she was concerned, was Day Two. She already knew the score: Dan two; Millie zero.

*

Ben stepped into Dan's office. It was eight in the morning. "Geez, you look like hell. What happened last night?"

Dan looked up. His eyes were strained from the mountain of paperwork on his desk. He hadn't slept all night. Millie had gotten into his blood like a fever.

"Dammit, Ben. Wear shoes I can hear, or else knock. Nothing exciting happened. Mike made the collar after we left last night."

Ben slipped into the empty chair in front of Dan's desk. "Then why are you so grumpy?"

"I'm not grumpy. I'm busy." He tapped his pen on the edge of the desk. "Don't you have paperwork to do, too?"

"Yeah, but I'm not hyper about it."

Ben stretched his long legs in front of him. He was completely relaxed. "What's ticking you off today? You act as if you have a burr under your saddle. How come? Louie's still being a good boy. Aren't you and Millie getting along all right?"

Dan's spirits had plummeted with each hour that passed since he'd dropped Millie off at her house. He was in over his head and he didn't like it. The problem was he and Millie could be getting along famously—provided he gave her what she wanted.

"Sorry, Ben. I was thinking about my dad's brother. I'm trying to figure out why Uncle Jack turned into a bad cop. He was my idol when I was a kid. Finding out he had such feet of clay really hurt."

Ben shrugged. "Who can say what's in another man's head? Things happen. Pressures build. You're not responsible."

"Yeah, maybe so, but I have a clear memory of what it did to the family. It nearly killed my dad. It took him years to work out his shame. He idolized his older brother."

"So that's what's bugging you. You're afraid this book Millie's writing will trigger old memories and reopen old wounds for your dad. And yourself, looks like...?"

Dan rustled a sheaf of papers. "Something like that. Wasach sees me as the great white hope to force the city council fathers to buy us the equipment we need. Hell of a fix I'm in." He smiled grimly. "I never thought I'd live to see the day Pete would use me as a bargaining chip."

Ben unfolded a paper clip and traced its design on paper with his pen. "You could refuse. Or you could take Millie into your confidence."

Dan had considered that at about four A.M., but discarded the idea. There would be no reason for them to be together otherwise. He was pretty sure after his machismo display in the car that she'd say no to a date.

"I can't tell Millie yet," he said. "I figure I'll play this out for a few more days. She's promised me the right to edit anything I don't like."

Ben dropped the clip into an ashtray. "Seems to me that's a pretty unusual concession. Most writers would be irritated as hell at being censored."

"I told her I wouldn't agree otherwise."

Ben nodded as he stood up. "Are we still on for the softball game? The little pumpkin said she can play today if you need another man. That is, if you're still planning on meeting the guys."

Dan leaned back, lacing his fingers behind his head. "Haven't missed a game yet, have I? Ben, do me a favor, will you?"

"What?"

"Call her Natalie and take a good look at her. She's no man. She's got legs and breasts and a cute little rump."

Ben looked affronted, as if he'd just been accused of not knowing the difference between men and women. "Is Millie going, too?"

Dan shook his head. His friend was as blind as a bat where Natalie was concerned. "Millie's going. The agreement was one week."

Ben's smile crinkled his eyes. "Well, cheer up. You have only five more days after today."

The implication that he wouldn't be seeing Millie after five days made Dan wonder exactly what he did want. All he knew was that he hadn't slept well in two nights for thinking about her. He'd be a zombie by the end of the week.

Ben paused at the door, his hand on the knob. "Dan, is it wise, bringing Millie to a game with your group? Suppose something triggers one of them off? You'd have a gang riot on your hands."

"Quit sounding like a mother hen. The guys have made progress. They've got jobs and are contributing to society." His monthly game with the team was important. They depended on him. It had taken a long time to build their trust. "I'll handle it."

"Just so you know what you're doing."

Dan recognized the note of warning in Ben's voice. "I told you, I'll keep them in line. Besides, nothing's going to happen."

"You always were a softie."

"Bull. I'm the guy who arrested them and put them inside."

Millie took a red pen and crossed off yesterday's date on the calendar. Today, she'd bring her tape recorder and wouldn't let Dan off the hook so easily.

She walked out onto the patio. The sky was a bright blue with high cirrus clouds. The water in the canal was calm. The fishing boats had already left. A few people were sitting on their patios enjoying the cool morning air. The weatherman predicted another hot day.

Henry and Henrietta sat on the grass, their necks curved downward. When they saw her they rose majestically, like two statues coming to life.

"Good morning, you two. Guess what? Millie's going to make a fool of herself today. If she's very lucky she won't fall on her face!"

She was wiping the slate clean, she decided as she fed the birds. Yesterday never happened. Today she'd add to her store of information.

She did her stretching exercises, then walked back into the house to dress. Considering the weather forecast and that she'd be playing ball, she dressed in shorts and a cropped cotton top.

When she saw Dan drive up, she hurried to the door, determined not to show by expression or deed that last night meant something to her.

Smiling, she flung open the door. "Hello, Dan."

A long breath escaped him when he saw her fire-engine red shorts, a matching red shirt, dangling red earrings, and sneakers. Her hair was tied up in a ponytail. She could have been an ad for the all-American girl. All wrong.

"Millie, you look terrific. Now will you please change your clothes." He spoke calmly, but there was no mistaking the steel behind his tone.

Color stained her cheeks as her quick anger flared. She lifted her chin in defiance. "Why?"

His shoulders moved eloquently. "Because we're going to be playing ball with a bunch of men."

"I hadn't thought we'd be playing with a bunch of geese," she said huffily.

"Very funny. Please change your clothes. You're half naked.

Suppose you fall?" he said, grasping at straws. She'd have his men at each other's throats.

"If I fall. I'll pick myself up."

"Millie, the team is made up of ex-cons."

"Ex-cons?" she repeated, her writer's instincts smelling a story. "Why are you playing with ex-cons?"

"They've served their time and are trying to go straight. We play once a month, mostly so I can stay in touch with them."

Intrigued by this information, she asked, "How do you know them?"

He looked past her to a point on the wall. "I was the one who arrested them."

Now that was something she could use in her book. "And you play ball with them? How'd you manage that?"

For the first time since she'd met him, he seemed genuinely embarrassed. "Someone has to give them a chance to change. The jails are too crowded." His gaze roamed over her scantily clad body. "Can't you be comfortable in pants and a long-sleeved shirt? I'm not trying to tempt the fates here."

He was standing very close to her, so close that she felt an urgent need to ask a question. "If we weren't playing with ex-cons, would you be asking me to wear something else?"

His hand tarried with a lock of her hair. "Would you want me to?"

She felt the thudding of her heart, the electricity between them. She tilted her head to one side, gazing into his fathomless gray eyes.

He had the face of a Greek god—carved in granite, softened only when he smiled. Strength and tenderness were both there, doled out judiciously.

He'd obviously just showered and shaved. His hair was damp and she caught the waft of his cologne. He wore a pair of faded denim cotton shorts and a matching polo shirt. There was no use denying the attraction she felt toward him. They'd been headed down this path since they'd met.

She realized that he'd answered her question with a question. Ignoring the voice of reason, she twined her arms around his neck. Instantly she was lost in a golden haze. His mouth was the sun and she was reaching for its warmth.

She wanted him to kiss her. The pounding of his heart matched hers. Last night hadn't been a mistake. There was a fire in her blood. When he drew her into his arms and held her tight, she no longer cared why she was there, only that she was.

"Oh, Millie." He buried his lips in her hair. "I want you."

He trailed kisses along her neck and face and felt her quiver. She was where he wanted her to be. He kissed her leisurely, saying hello with his lips and hands. When his fingers cupped her breast, feeling the nipples harden, he cursed the time. Kissing her tenderly, he took her on a trembling journey. He didn't press, he didn't demand, but rather let her show him what she wanted of him.

"I want you," he repeated.

His words penetrated her foggy brain. Want was easier than need. Want was a casual excuse for an affair. She wanted everything. She wanted nothing. She was confused by her own actions. She tore her lips from his. Her chest rose and fell with her rapid breaths.

He let her go reluctantly. His breath came out on a sigh as ragged as hers. He pressed a kiss to her palm, then kissed her lightly on the mouth.

"It seems," he murmured, "an automobile isn't the only place that's dangerous for us to be alone. Change your clothes, Millie. We're late."

CHAPTER SEVEN

Murdock's Maniacs was made up of ex-juvenile delinquents who would have been in and out of jail if it weren't for Dan. They voted to make Millie the umpire, and then explained the rules of the game to her. She flipped the Maniacs' cap backward and offered her first official speech as umpire. "Piece of cake," she said, patting two hulking players on the back. "Let the best man win. Play ball."

Dan rolled his eyes heavenward. The men stared at her for a moment, then laughed themselves silly. The ice was broken.

Dan had been a bit apprehensive about bringing Millie after Ben's words of caution. The men hailed from a tough street world where distrust was the name of the game. But Millie breezed into their midst, behaving as if she'd met his motley crew when they were in the church choir. By seeking their help with the rudiments of the game, she broke down their initial barriers. By the bottom of the second, the entire team was eating out of her hand.

Millie gave Dan a little flak when she first spied Natalie Gershon as they arrived at the field.

"She's wearing shorts!" Millie exclaimed. "Why aren't you telling her what to wear? Do you realize the humidity's awful?"

"Natalie," he patiently explained, "can take care of herself. Besides, these guys aren't about to get involved with a cop. She could drop-kick any one of them and they know it. You're different." And you're mine, he thought, knowing he had no right to tell her that.

Millie glanced down at herself. At least she had gotten Dan to compromise on a short-sleeved shirt. "I'm different all right. I'm the one who's going to roast. Long pants. Hah."

By the top of the seventh Dan's team was trailing by a score of four to three. Dan was at bat. Joe Moreno, displaying the same grace and fluid motion he used to strip a car in three minutes flat, was on the pitcher's mound, peering straight at the catcher. Behind Dan, Tony Graham crouched down, signaling the play with a variation of the code he had used to alert his gang when the cops approached. Joe nodded in answer to the call, reached back, and let go. In the past, his pitch had been clocked at seventy miles an hour.

Dan, with two strikes against him, swung with all his might, his arm, shoulder, and back muscles straining through the delivery. The ball was on its way deep into left field.

Millie silently rooted for him. She knew Dan was doing something with and for these young men besides having fun. He was their role model. They treated him with respect and affection. She pulled the cap off her head and wondered if he'd ever been simply a story to her, or if she'd always been most interested in him as a man.

Dan ran full steam to first base, rounded the corner, took the signal from Natalie, and kept going, his powerful legs pumping hard. In left field Whitey Kane, an ex-cat burglar, scooped up the ball. He threw it to Frank Gargan at second, who caught it on a fast dive just as Dan slid into base.

Flushed with success, Dan stood up, wiped the sweat from his face, and grinned. It was the best play he'd made all afternoon. Excited, he clapped Frank on the back.

"Too bad, Frank. Those are the breaks."

He looked over to Millie to see if she would congratulate him. He figured he'd earned her accolade. And there she was, sprinting toward him. She opened her arms wide—and hugged Frank. Who happily hugged her back.

"You're out, Dan," she said. "Frank's toe was on the bag first. Great play, Frank."

Dan couldn't believe his ears. "I was safe!" he stormed.

"Too bad, man," Frank said. "Those are the breaks." He doubled over with glee.

Millie smiled graciously, as befitted a woman whose word was law. The urge to kiss her was nearly overwhelming, but Dan managed to turn and stalk to the fence where the rest of his team was standing.

The inning continued. Dan watched as Millie trotted to the

pitcher's mound in her self-appointed roles as coach and Mother Superior. Joe's last pitch had been off his stride and he was visibly upset. Disgruntled, Dan saw her turn on the charm. Jealousy was a new emotion for him. He soundlessly mimicked her words to Joe.

"You're terrific, Joe. Ease up just a bit and show me what you've got."

She swung around, grazing Dan with a broad wink. He laughed in spite of himself. He meant to ask her later exactly how long she had been playing softball. Millie clearly operated on her own agenda.

Dan was up again in the eighth inning. In another close play, this time at first, Millie called him out. The Maniacs loved it.

"You're going to make the men think I'm a pansy," he growled in her ear. He desperately wanted to kiss her.

She tweaked his nose. He was sweaty, mean, tough, and oh, so handsome. "Well, Murdock, I can personally attest to the fact you're no sissy. Want me to put that in my book? You'll get all the women after you."

She had miscalculated the effect of her words. He grabbed her and kissed her full on the mouth in front of everyone, locking her in a vise with his arms. Catcalls and whistles cheered him on.

He lifted his head. "Write whatever the hell you want."

The blood was pounding in Millie's head. She drew back until her gaze locked with his. His eyes were flecked with tiny specks of green; his hair danced as he ran his fingers through it. He had the superior look of a man thoroughly pleased with himself. In two days he'd succeeded in keeping her totally off balance.

"Batter up, men," she called, a little shakily. "Murdock's insane."

He kissed her quickly. "You got that right, toots." The game ended in a tie. Normally they played until there was a winner, but Dan saw Millie flagging from the heat. He spoke to a few of the players and Phil, a seventeen-year-old who played first base, walked over to Millie.

"We're bushed," he said, "and we want ice cream. Do you mind if we quit?"

Millie's shirt was sticking to her. She was hot and tired and thirsty. "Let's go."

The owner of the ice-cream parlor knew Dan and the others.

Ben and Natalie split up, each sitting with a different group. Millie immediately realized they were helping Dan. He moved from table to table, spending time with each group. If it appeared one of the men needed to talk, another would get up to make room for Dan.

Millie turned to Joe, sitting beside her in the booth. "What do you think of Dan?"

"He's the best," Joe said instantly. "I hated cops before I met him. And I used to strip cars. That's how Dan found me. Man, I hated that dude back then." Joe slurped the remainder of his chocolate float, poking his spoon to get the last drops. He licked the chocolate off the spoon. "My ma blesses him now."

"What changed your mind about him?"

He shot her an amazed look. "How many cops vouch for you after they arrest you? Dan showed up every day. I still didn't trust him. He was there at the trial. He came to see me regularly, droning it into my head about finishing high school and making something of myself. The guy was a real pest. He'd show up with my mother. She'd say how proud she was of me…" Joe shook his head in wonder.

"I can see why," Millie said. Heroes come in many packages and guises. Dan was a hero. This was her opening hook for her first chapter.

Joe dangled his spoon. "Imagine, my own mother saying she was proud of me. And I was in jail. How could I let her and Dan down? My old man wasn't around."

Pride and bitterness, Millie thought. Bitterness for an absent father. Pride in himself because someone cared. Because of Dan, a mother had found pride in a son. And a son had found pride in his difficult manhood. "What are you doing now, Joe?"

"Dan fixed it so I can go to junior college. I'm doing okay. I'm going on to get my degree." He looked at her with shining dark eyes. "No one in my family ever went to college. But I want to be an electrical engineer."

She put one hand on his arm. "You've got success written all over you, Joe." When he blushed, she asked, "Do you have a girlfriend?"

"There is someone I like. It's not like you and Dan, though."

Millie gasped. She realized that with his kiss, Dan had laid claim to her in front of everyone.

"What's this big lug saying?" Dan asked, slipping into the

booth. He draped his arm around her shoulders.

"Oh, nothing," she said. "We were just shooting the breeze."

For the next few minutes Dan and Joe chatted while Millie listened. Dan didn't preach, didn't lecture, but instead posed thoughtful suggestions. When they were alone in the car returning to her home, she was quiet.

"Penny for your thoughts, Millie?"

"I'm thinking," she said seriously, "that I haven't even scratched the surface of knowing you."

"For your book?"

"For me." The truth slipped out so easily, it astounded her.

He squeezed her hand. "That's easily remedied. I think it's time I showed you how the other half lived."

"Where are we going?"

His gaze locked with hers. "To my house."

"Do you live near here?" she asked, aware of how her heartbeat had speeded up.

"Not too far. We're almost there."

She told herself that seeing his home was important to the story. They could be good friends. She'd be going home to New Jersey soon where she belonged and the time with Dan would be a pleasant memory. She leaned back in her seat and spent the rest of the drive trying to convince herself her lies were the truth.

A charming, relatively old Victorian-style, his house was situated in a neighborhood with stately palmetto palms planted thirty years ago or so, when the houses were almost new. Latticework surrounded a wide veranda dotted with blue wicker rockers. The extended roofline shaded the porch from the hot sun. Hibiscus bushes intermixed with succulents created a natural border along the stone pathway.

"What a lovely house," she said sincerely.

Dan smiled. He wanted her to like his home. He wanted to see her in every room of it. He wanted to be able to breathe her scent and remember her in the cool of the night when he needed her most.

"Thanks," he said. "I like it." He linked his hand with hers. "I'll show you around."

"How rude would I be if I asked to use the shower first?"

"Can I come too?" he teased.

They showered separately. Millie had brought a change of

clothing with her, another bright red blouse and a softly flowing white cotton skirt. She and Dan met up again in the large, cool living room.

"The furniture is comfortably old," he said as she toured the room. "Someday I'll toss it and get new stuff. This is mostly hand-me-downs from family. I think they used me as a replacement for the Salvation Army. It never mattered before." The implication that it mattered now sent her emotions into a tailspin.

The room featured a gold Lawson sofa, a well-used leather recliner, several overstuffed chairs, a standing lamp, and two end tables with attached lamps. Good, serviceable furniture for a bachelor who didn't particularly care about decor. She caught herself seeing the home as it might be, bright and cheerful in light, airy colors.

"Do you play?" she asked, walking over to the upright piano in one corner.

"I tickle the ivories once in a while," he admitted. "How about you?"

It was a house for a family, she thought. A family and music. "A little." In fact, she played very well. She missed her Baldwin.

"Why don't you try it?" he suggested. "See if it needs tuning."

"Maybe later?" She hadn't touched a piano since Frank's death. Had it really been more than a year? And was she really standing in another man's house thinking about wanting him to make love with her?

The shadow was there, fleeting and sad. Dan saw it and wondered. He led her into the dining room. There was an oval oak table and six high-backed chairs. A crystal chandelier hung above a silver candelabra centerpiece.

"Your family gave you very nice hand-me-downs," she said.

"Maybe they're trying to tell me something. What do you think?" he asked quietly.

She tensed. "Probably. Parents usually get over-excited on the subject of marriage and carrying on the family name."

"And you, Millie? What do you think?"

"I think," she said, feeling the heat as his gaze blatantly caressed her, lingering on her breasts, "that it's none of my business." She moistened her lips and stared at the silver candelabra. "You have this nasty habit of doing all the questioning, Dan. I often ask myself why."

"And what answer do you get?"

She flipped on the light, studying the prisms in the chandelier. "None. You're not a man who opens up easily."

He couldn't just yet. They went into his study. The well-used room beckoned to her. She wanted to ask about the wall of bookshelves crammed with books, but didn't.

Dan walked over to the stereo and turned it on, filling the room with the sublime strains of Mozart. He turned back to Millie. The light streaming in at the window glowed on her shiny hair. She belongs in a room like this, Dan thought. A room of quiet beauty and passion.

"Dan, why did you quit law school?"

He picked up a paperweight, palming it from hand to hand. "I needed more money. At the time, I was married and attending school on a double track program."

"Double track?"

"A double-track program allows you to take the same subject in the daytime or the evening, your choice. Not many schools offer it. But the truth is, I was restless."

Millie understood the feeling. She was filled with restlessness herself. She wanted to move across to him, to touch him. She remained perfectly still.

"I'd sit in class," he went on, "listen to the lecture, then go home to pore over books or work my shift. I began to wonder why I was there. I envied the others who knew they wanted to join the best law firm in town and make gobs of money. There wasn't a ladder most weren't ready to climb in the pursuit of the American dream. Money, not law, was the real ambition. I kept thinking life should be more meaningful, more exciting."

Would he always choose a life of dodging bullets? she wondered, sitting down on the couch. She couldn't bear the possibility of his getting hurt. "But what if you want to resume your studies?"

Fate and circumstances, he thought. It all boiled down to that. His had altered in the last week, irrevocably, from the day he'd met her. "If I choose to do so, I can return. If the reason were compelling."

Tiny darts of excitement radiated from the base of her stomach to her throat. She needed to uncover the real Dan Murdock.

She needed...

"Dan, did you quit school because of your wife?" She saw him stiffen and knew she'd touched another raw nerve. What else was in his past?

He joined her on the couch, crossing his long legs. "This is off the record, Millie.

"I was a few years older than Lana. We started dating when I was in college and she was in high school. I was brought up in an old-fashioned way, where the boy picked the girl up at her home.

"Lana always found an excuse to meet me several blocks from her house, though. In those days I didn't recognize the signs of child abuse.

"Her mother had died when she was twelve, leaving her the burden of the housework. One day—she was out of school and working as a clerk in a department store and I was a senior—I was late for a date. She wasn't where we usually met, so I went to her house."

Dan grimaced. Millie felt his temper as he continued. "Her father was drunk, mean, ugly, vicious drunk. Lana didn't want me to see what the bastard had done to her. He'd beaten her. Her eyes were swollen, her lips cut, her face blotchy.

"I wish I had known. She always wore long-sleeved dresses or blouses, even in hot weather. I never knew."

He stared across the room. "I brought her to my parents' home. Her father was so drunk he didn't miss her or even try to find her for three days. Mom and Dad took Lana in to live with us. We had enough cops in the family to scare the life out of her father. My... my Uncle Jack threatened to beat her father up if he came near her."

Millie saw his face tighten as he stumbled over his uncle's name. She sensed there was something he wasn't telling her. The reporter in her filed away the name.

"I graduated from college," Dan continued, "joined the police force, and enrolled in law school. It was an ambitious plan. Dad was retiring early. He had put his time in. Before he started a new career he and Mom wanted to travel. Lana and I eloped."

"Did you love her very much?"

He stood up and walked over to the window, cramming his hands in his pockets. "I cared for her, but after she came to live with us, both our feelings changed. We were more like brother and sister. The marriage was doomed from the start. Our intentions were good. We were just too young.

"We kept the marriage alive while I helped her through college. She's remarried now. She's happy and even has a good job. Makes a hell of a story, doesn't it?"

Millie had dug her nails into her palms to keep from interrupting. Now she rose. She crossed the room to Dan and put her arms around his waist, hugging him. Her head rested against his strong back. He'd taken on so many burdens with that back, she thought. Yet he hurt. Tears filled her eyes for the young man who had bravely tried to right the ills of the world. He'd given her a precious gift with his trust.

Dan felt drained but strangely at peace. At Millie's touch his rigidly held body relaxed. He'd never told another woman the details of his youthful marriage. He curled his hands over hers and pulled her around in front of him.

Droplets of unshed tears moistened her thick lashes. He studied her face, seeing the sadness and the longing there. He knew she wasn't even aware of her longing. It clung to her, as it clung to him. Like him, she had needs. They'd both been denied too long.

"Millie, don't cry," he whispered.

She wiped her eyes with her hand. "I'm fine, really. I won't use the information, but shouldn't we be formalizing this interview? I'll get my pad and pencil."

"Should we?" he asked. "Do you really want to ask me a bunch more?"

The expression in his eyes should have warned her, as should the huskiness in his voice. The musky scent of sexual heat should have warned her that to start with this man meant hitching a ride to his extravagant star.

He touched her with nothing save his eyes—those smoky, intense gray eyes—yet she felt his brand on every part of her body. In her lonely heart and aching breasts, in her most secret places. Wherever his gaze touched, she blazed.

"Wouldn't you rather see where this heat takes us first, Millie?"

Her mind, that safe control center that had served her well until now, shut down as needs stronger than she'd ever felt before tore through her. A part of her cried for what might have been, cried for the young Dan, just as that long-dormant part of her begged for release with the mature man he had become. She felt rooted to the spot, powerless to deny the hunger she read in his eyes.

He brushed his lips across hers. "Tell me you want me as much as I want you."

She did want this man, shamelessly. Now. She barely breathed… "Yes."

What he read in her jewel-like eyes filled him with tenderness. He bent down, grazing her lips in a butterfly kiss. Then another and another, until both strained for more.

He lifted his head and smiled. His gentleness was her undoing. She pressed her body closer to his, sliding her hands up over his shoulders. He felt so good, so strong, so very much alive. She marveled at the hard muscle alive under her eagerly probing fingers.

Pivoting her, he held her against him, her back to his front. He slipped his hands around her slim waist, his fingers pointing downward.

"Since the first moment in the car, I knew I wanted you," he said with quiet intensity. He dipped his head to kiss the soft flesh below her ear. "We'll have each other," he vowed. "We'll make it beautiful."

His touch robbed her of breath. His promise of beauty was like a benediction. She spread her hands over his, moving to his rhythm. He was hard and strong and infinitely tender.

Moaning, she nestled her head back, cushioning it in the curve of his shoulder. She watched, almost mesmerized, as together their hands gently squeezed her belly. Just as hypnotically, he stoked the flames inside her, fanning them into a fiery blaze. Murmuring endearments to her, he spread rampaging embers to every fiber of her being.

She turned and kissed him hungrily. Her passionate response delighted him. He had known this was in her. With Millie pressed tightly to him, he rotated his hips.

"See how much I want you?" he murmured. "Millie, you did this. You have this power over me."

His hands moved upward, feeling and knowing her as a blind man would learn a delicate flower. Her breasts filled his palms, blossoming in his hands.

"I want to look at you, Millie." Her blue eyes shone with absolute trust. Exhilarated by it, he unbuttoned her blouse.

She felt his fingers brush her skin. One button . . . two . . . three… A cool rush of air touched her breasts. Blouse and bra slipped off her shoulders, and Dan looked at her with adoration. "So beautiful."

He bent his head to kiss her. His tongue laved first one nipple, then the other. Whatever he touched, he caressed reverently. He has the soul of a poet, she thought. It seemed the most natural act in the world to hold his head against her. She exalted in his mouth sucking first one breast and then the other. The sucking motion tugged deep—between her thighs she felt a readying moisture. She bent over him, her hair curtaining them in hedonistic privacy.

Sensations flowed through her and raced through him.

Sensual, stimulating, stirring.

He felt them all as he drank of her sweetness. "Ah, Millie. You're magnificent. Let me show you how I want to love you."

He was asking for permission to continue. Again his gentleness stirred her. Life called to life, helping her shed the past. "Yes," she whispered.

He pulled off his shirt. Flesh met flesh and they gasped in delight. This first time. This special time.

Smiling into each other's eyes, they stood pressed together. Neither wanted to hurry. They rejoiced in the sensual gratifications of giving and taking.

Their lips touched. Sweetly. Playfully. Love bites. Soft laughter.

So many delicious places to kiss, she thought. Like the corner of his mouth. "Rough beard."

"I should have shaved."

"No, don't. I like you this way."

"I'll grow a beard, then."

"Silly."

He lingered over her soft cheek, then closed her eyes with tender kisses. "Bluer than the deepest ocean," he said into her hair.

"There's a song there, Dan."

"We'll compose it together. You be the bass. I'll be the high notes."

"Dopey, it's the other way around."

He laughed. "I never knew. Your perfume is driving me wild."

"Really?"

"Really."

"I'll douse myself with it."

"Will you let me put it on you?"

She smiled. "If you like."

"You should have candles, Millie. Scented white candles circling a bed, with a mirror on the ceiling, and a feather boa across your breasts for me to…"

"To what?"

He kissed the teasing smile from her face. "I don't know. I'll think of something."

She was sure he would. "And what do l do?"

"You lie there and let me play." His mouth on hers, he sent his tongue on an erotic journey that left them both breathless.

She knew she was more than a little infatuated with him. Neither could yet say the word of commitment—love.

"I've known you forever," he whispered.

"A lifetime in a few days."

The hair on his chest was silky soft. She ran her fingers through it, then kissed his nipples as he'd kissed hers.

"More than enough time." A glint of humor lit his eyes. "We'll keep this off the record, too."

She rained kisses on his face and neck, then suggestively thrust her hips forward. "Mmm, my pleasure."

She touched his lips, tracing their outline with her tongue.

"Oh, Lord," he said, then groaned. His hands framed her face. The silver in his eyes had darkened to gray-black. "I've never wanted a woman as much as I want you. This kiss will be our first, Millie. The others were just practice."

She steeped herself in his scent. The misery of the recent past slipped from her shoulders. Only the present counted. She wouldn't think about the tomorrows when she'd no longer be there, when her vacation must end. "More. Now," she cried urgently, letting the words tumble into his mouth.

"Now," he breathed into hers, cupping her buttocks.

His tongue slipped into her mouth, and like a flower she

opened to welcome him. They had waited almost too long. The heat was almost too scorching. Their bodies sought each other with an intensity that threatened to engulf them.

He'd promised her memories. She knew she would at least have them.

He kissed her wildly, ecstasy flowing from his inflamed loins to hers, heightening the tensions screaming for release. When he lifted his head, breaking their sustained kiss, his ragged breathing matched hers.

Touching, tasting, neither could say whose heart beat faster. Eyes glazed with passion, he held her close to his side as he led her toward the bedroom. The bed was large and masculine, like its owner. The room held the mementos of a man very different from her husband.

He felt her tremble and temporary panic shot through him. Taking her face in his hands, he looked directly into her eyes. "Millie, don't you want this, too?"

How could she tell him that for all the advice she'd given to women all over the country, ultimately nothing counted for her? She was, she realized, frightened. "There's been no one except my husband," she whispered.

He understood. Millie was vulnerable. "Then you make me very proud. I hope I'll please you."

"Please me?" she repeated in wonder, some of her doubts flowing away from her. "Dan, you—"

"Shh, no more talk."

He stripped off his clothes, then reverently undressed her, kissing each exposed part of her body as her clothes drifted to the floor. "Come here, beautiful." He curved his hand around her nape, drawing her fully against him.

She was sent whirling by the bold touch of his body, his lips seeking hers. It stamped forever a different brand on her psyche. The gentleness he'd shown until now was replaced by white hot passion. He made love to her with his mouth on hers; with his hands stroking her body's pleasure points; with erotic words of love hoarsely whispered.

Desire made him taut as a wire. Need made him hold back. For the first time in his adult life he was as vulnerable as the woman who'd entrusted him with the gift of herself. He was in danger of losing his mind, and, if he weren't very careful, his heart.

He bent to take a nipple in his mouth, teasing it, laving it with pleasure. When she thought she could stand no more, he laughed, then did the same to the other. Her breasts became the center of her being, jolting long-dormant nerve centers into raging life.

She slid her hands up his arms and across his wide shoulders, exploring and charting the muscles underlying his smooth skin. Her fingers curled through his hair. She pulled his face to hers, kissing him until she heard him moan.

Hunger matched desire, driving them both. Millie felt suspended above herself, tossed up in a storm, whirling in its vortex. Dan lifted her onto the bed, and she gasped at the intense heat of his body as he lay on top of her.

He kissed her with a savagery of want. He took all she had, adoring her body as one would pray at a shrine. His fingers found the moist, hot center of her, and he knew she wanted him as much as he wanted her.

"Look at me." His voice was rough. He wanted to watch the miracle of her as he entered her.

She smiled up at him, her blue eyes smoky with passion. "I know," she whispered.

A groan ripped from him as she lifted her hips. He came into her then, and she arched against him, taking him fully. He carried her higher than she had ever been. He made love to her with a raw, primitive force with jungle heat.

She was boneless, melting. Tumbling. Her hips urged him on, racing into a heated climax that swallowed her. Dan felt her muscles tauten. He rocketed forward to a shattering climax, inflamed by the same inferno.

Rolling off her, he wrapped his arms around her. She rested her head in the crook of his shoulder.

He chuckled. "I think after that you can say we pleased each other."

Millie floated down to earth. Reaching up, she kissed his neck. She kissed his chest, too, and toyed with the springy mat of his hair. "And I can't print a word of it."

He tipped her chin up, kissing her full on the mouth. "I give you permission to print the whole thing."

She caught more of his playful spirit. He was making what

could have been a difficult situation easy for her. "All right." She started to get up.

"Where do you think you're going?" His hands remained firmly on her waist, preventing her from leaving. Impulsively, he kissed the base of her spine, then licked the spot with his tongue.

She gasped. "To get my pad and pencil." He hauled her back and she fell flat on top of him. He wrapped his arms and legs around her. "What are you doing, Dan?"

His hand skittered up and down her body. "Frisking you. I must say I've never frisked a woman this way before. Put that in your book, too."

She giggled. He found her ticklish spots. "No fair." She rocked on top of him, finding any part of his flesh she could, giving him back the same treatment. Playing, and not sleeping after sex was a new experience for her. Everything with Dan seemed new.

He rolled over and pinned her beneath him. "I claim my prize."

"It's not over until the fat lady sings." she said, nipping his neck.

"Oh, yeah?" In a flash her arms were above her head, her wrists clamped in one hand. He stared down at her with stormy eyes. "Now, let me show you what it's like to mess around with the law." He knew her body, knew what made her writhe beneath him. He used this knowledge to his advantage.

"Oh, no…" She moaned. "You're not fair."

He showed no mercy. "It's a tough world, lady."

She arched toward him. "Very—tough," she agreed, kissing him.

As quickly as it started, the play erupted into passion. This time he took her swiftly, masterfully. She loved it, matching his thrusts with a wildness she didn't realize she was capable of. He took her up, suspending her on the edge, then buried his face in her breasts as they fell into the abyss of ecstasy.

"Bells. I hear bells," she murmured, smiling.

He heard bells, too, and silently swore. It wasn't bells. It was the phone.

He kissed her brow, then leaned his forehead against hers, waiting for his breathing to return to normal.

"I'm sorry, Millie. I have to answer it." He liberally hurled oaths at the invention even as he lifted the receiver. "Yes," he snapped.

The jumble of words in his ear was almost incoherent—and reminiscent of another time. Wasach had put a curse on him.

"Stay calm. This isn't your first. Did you call the ambulance? Good. They'll probably get there before I do. Just hang on. I'm on my way." As he hung up, Millie hurriedly handed him his shirt.

"What happened?" she cried frantically as she struggled into her own clothing. "What's wrong?"

Dan zipped up his pants, swearing. "The baby's coming more than a week early." She finished dressing and he grabbed her hand, propelling her out the door.

"What baby?" she asked.

"We're about to become parents, Millie."

Baby? Parents? "Whoa there, Murdock. Have I missed something here, or are you a faster worker than I thought?"

"Millie." He tugged her toward the car. "I'm the slowest worker in the world, couldn't you tell? This is one man who's going to need a lot of rehearsing."

In a pig's eye, she thought. "I'll take notes."

He laughed and got her into her seat. "Like hell you will. Buckle up."

"What about my book?"

"Forget it. We'll write our own."

But she couldn't forget it. Or the life she led, which had nothing to do with chasing crooks, outfoxing an extortionist, umpiring a team of ex-cons, or racing through the midnight streets to deliver some premature baby.

She could only wonder what other surprises Dan had in store for her.

CHAPTER EIGHT

Dan told her about Rosita and the possibility that her second might be born at home, too. He boasted proudly about his namesake. They discussed almost everything they could think of—save the most important topic.

Each other.

It was as if the phone call had broken the tenuous link they'd forged. Dan's frustration took many forms. He wanted to tell her why he'd been dancing around most of the questions she had asked. It wasn't like him to be indirect, especially since by being with her, he agreed implicitly to talk with her. He was pretty sure Millie would do her homework. If it were up to him, he'd tell her about his Uncle Jack, the stain on the family name, everything. But it wasn't up to him.

Aware that her interest in him stemmed from a business arrangement, his needs surprised him.

But for Lana, he'd lived alone all of his adult life. He'd had his share of women—nice ones and demanding ones, pretty ones and not-so-pretty ones. A long-term relationship to him meant a series of stages one went through. After Lana, marriage hadn't been important. The years had drifted by, piling one on top of the other.

Aimlessly.

With Millie it had been different from the first, he realized with a shock. He'd never thought of her as a date or as someone to fill a vacancy in one of his temporary relationships. By reason of avoidance of the "love" word, they seemed to have elevated Topic A to an extreme significance, putting off the inevitable for a better time.

Millie was also experiencing a surge of another emotion. Guilt. She'd forgotten everything when Dan was making love with her. She'd let her body be played like a violin by a virtuoso. And she'd begun to realize that she could still feel, could still yearn to be loved by a caring man.

Sighing, she closed her eyes and tried to conjure up her husband's face. She'd deeply loved him—but now couldn't get a clear picture of him. From the years of advice she'd given to widows in her *Ask Ms. M.* column, she knew letting go of the guilt was part of the process of acceptance after a spouse dies.

How often had she responded to the anguish and guilt in letters by surviving spouses? Let it go, live your life, you have a right to find your happiness. She'd written it all, believed it when she wrote it for millions of readers.

Now all she had to do was convince herself.

With its red light flashing, Dan's car sped through the streets. He hoped the ambulance had arrived and that there'd be no need for his services. "Have you ever witnessed the birth of a baby?" he asked Millie.

Did he think she lived in the dark ages? she thought. She'd seen countless women sweat, grimace, scream, clutch, push, groan, and scream at their husbands—on television. In the movies. On stage.

"Are you kidding?" she boasted, glad to have the conversation directed to a neutral topic. "Lots of times."

He let out a long whistle, then took a curve well past the speed limit. "Rosy will be glad to see you. As a woman, you can probably appreciate that. You can help me then, if the ambulance hasn't arrived."

Millie sat up with a start. Her stomach did a queasy nosedive. She admitted the truth about her so-called television "crash course" in birthing. "Especially on late-night reruns of *Ben Casey*. I'd only get in your way."

Dan shook his head. Millie bit her lip. She folded and unfolded her hands, as if trying to keep them warm. He squeezed her leg. "Don't freeze up on me now, honey. Giving birth is the most beautiful act in the world.

"Tell you what. Well make believe this is a television show.

Rosy's the star, you're the supporting cast. I'm the director. I'll coach you through it."

The image was too real. Maybe Dan and her brother didn't think anything about delivering babies, but it wasn't her game. What happened if the baby was a breech? She prayed the paramedics had already whisked the laboring mother to the hospital. Failing that, she fervently prayed, let the mother-to-be order her out of the bedroom.

Millie tossed her hair back with shaky fingers. She managed a wobbly smile, ashamed of herself. "Does this sort of thing happen often?"

He laughed. "Lord, no. This is only my second delivery."

"And here I thought all you did was apprehend hoods and thugs. You're going to make a terrific midwife."

He pulled around a car, then gunned the motor. "No, I'm not. And yes, most of the time I do arrest criminals, or push paper, or give testimony at trials."

"And then the Pied Piper rehabilitates them," she said, patting his arm.

He sailed through a red light. "Better than arresting, booking, and prosecuting them all over again. Costs society too much."

"Bull, Murdock," she replied, again in possession of her intellect. "You do it because you're an old softie."

"Bull, Millie. I do it because cops are trained to protect society. Don't you dare ruin my Humphrey Bogart image. Keep this out of your book."

She practically leaped off the seat. "Enough. I've got my agent breathing down my neck on one side and you breathing down the other side. I've long since spent the advance money, and so far you've given me nothing. The deal was that you agreed to see the chapter. Before you know it, though. I'll be going home…"

He felt a tight ache in his throat. Their lovemaking meant more to him than to her. "What are you talking about?"

She heard the despair in his voice. "I live in New Jersey. My family is there. My life is there. You knew I was renting."

He struggled to keep quiet, then exploded. "Millie, your timing stinks!"

She made an effort to joke with him, to ignore the censure in his tone. "Oh, for goodness' sakes, what are we arguing about? Here we are about to become parents."

Privately, she agreed with him. Her timing did stink. So did the woman's whose baby decided it needed Dan to repeat his Dr. Casey routine.

The Lopez house, a two-storied white clapboard, was located in a middle-class neighborhood, not far from the beach. A fanning breeze riffled through her hair as Millie closed her car door and glanced around. The homes were situated on neatly tended plots. Instead of grass, many of the lawns were painted green rock, landscaped with islands of cactus varieties.

"Too much sand around here," Dan said. "Besides, it saves mowing."

He ran up the steps and rang the bell. It was immediately opened by his young namesake. Young Daniel was a handsome, stocky built boy with luminous hazel-brown eyes, layers of midnight-black hair, and two adorable dimples.

"The ambulance isn't here yet," Daniel said. He grabbed Dan's hand, pulling him inside the cool hallway. "Mom's gonna have the baby at home, I think. She went to Lamaze classes, but Dad couldn't make it all the time, and I think he's scared. She should have taken me instead." His reedy voice quavered.

Dan ruffled the boy's hair. "You did fine, Daniel. Wait here, Millie."

Her relief was short-lived. Daniel touched her hand, beseeching her with pleading eyes.

"My mama may need you. Dad's nervous. Please help her." His tears were near the surface.

Millie smiled weakly, gathered her resolve, and nodded. This wasn't like any television script she'd ever seen. But who could deny a child with such beguiling eyes? He'd break women's hearts in years to come.

At the bedroom door, Millie hesitated. Rosita's husband, Manuel, wasn't nearly as calm as his son. In his mid-thirties, Manuel was a handsome adult version of young Daniel. He was also sweating as profusely as the pregnant woman on the bed.

Rosita tried to smile when she saw Dan, but was quickly gripped by pain. He introduced Millie, then timed a strong contraction, then another. Ambulance or not, he thought, this baby was going to be making a neighborhood appearance pretty soon.

He gave Millie a crash course in coaching. Petrified that she might make a mistake, she followed his orders to the letter, coaching Rosita as though both their lives as well as the unborn baby's depended on it. Dan ordered Manuel to bring clean towels and a basin of boiled water.

Manuel fled the room gladly, his eyes close to hysterical. Dan wiped Rosita's face with a damp cloth. "Next time, young lady, you're going to the hospital a month early, if I have to take you there myself."

He glanced at Millie. "You're doing fine, coach. When your time comes, it'll be a piece of cake."

She barely had time to let Dan's words register. He'd intimated that one day she'd be repeating Rosita's experience.

Millie knew if she lived to be a hundred, she'd never forget Dan bringing Rosita's baby girl into the world, or the look of sheer pleasure on everyone's face when the infant let out its first lusty cry, bringing the rest of the family on the run.

Tears streamed down Rosita's face. "Oh, thank you, Dan. You've helped me give birth to the baby daughter I've always wanted."

Dan winked at Millie. Her knees were buckling, her mouth was dry as dust, but her spirits soared. She'd been part of the most wonderful miracle. And she hadn't fainted.

"Piece of cake," Dan said, grinning. "Right, coach?"

She nodded. Her throat was too full to speak.

The paramedics rushed into the room just as Dan was swabbing out the baby's nose and mouth to clear the passageways. He swaddled the infant in a clean towel and laid her on Rosita's stomach. "Rosy, you did great. She's all yours, guys."

"Thanks, Murdock. We owe you a great favor for our precious baby."

They waited in the living room while a paramedic cut the umbilical cord and helped with the placenta. Later, Rosita asked for Millie, who helped her put on a fresh nightgown.

She stroked Millie's arm. "What is your full name?"

"Millicent Dolores Gordon."

Rosita and Manuel beamed. "We will never forget you, Millie," Rosita said. She lifted the tiny bundle. "Meet Millicent Dolores Lopez. Would you like to be the first to hold her?"

Millie bawled all the way home—big, fat, sloppy tears. Each

time she tried to stop, a fresh flood of tears trickled down her cheeks. "Do you realize," she asked, sniffling into a tissue, "we each have a child named after us?"

Dan smiled at her. Her nose was shiny red. Her dark hair was a tangled nest around her face. But her blue eyes gleamed with pride. He thought she'd never looked more beautiful. Millie was lost in the euphoria of what she'd lived through.

"As soon as I'm in New York," she bubbled, "I'm going to empty out FAO Schwarz. Nothing is too good for my namesake. Of course. I'll get an equal number of toys for your little Daniel. Can't have him getting jealous."

Dan's brow furrowed. Was she pushing him to say don't go? "So you're really going back?"

She hesitated. "Eventually. I only came here for a change of scenery."

He stared stonily ahead. "I'm usually a workaholic," she added, sort of as a verbal footnote. "My work's been sliding lately."

He understood her feelings, perhaps more than she did herself. She'd come to Florida to close a chapter in her life. Was she telling him she was eager to be back among the family and friends she'd known all her life? Or was she waiting for him to say the words that would keep her here?

The sun, a fiery orange and red ball, dipped below the horizon. One minute it was day; the next, a soft, soothing night with a vast throw of twinkling stars above them as Dan walked Millie to her door. He kissed her and left. They were both bushed. He wasn't in the mood for small talk—not when he needed his wits about him to plan...

*

Millie lounged on the patio, still floating on a cloud. She'd slept well, alternately dreaming of Dan and her infant namesake. She wrapped the phone cord around her fingers.

"Let me get this straight," Wylie said. "Yesterday you and Dan became parents. And here I was worried about you. What do they put in the food down there? Fertility pills?"

Millie giggled silently. If Wylie only knew! "Not real parents, goose. Rosy named their first son for Dan seven years ago. This baby is named for me. I have a vested interest in little Millie."

She told the story in fits and starts, downplaying her part in the process, extolling Dan's coolness and emergency medical prowess, and praising Rosita's courage.

"I'm beginning the chapter today," Millie announced euphorically. "Dan's an unsung hero."

"You mean it's still not written?" Wylie pounced on the admission. "Hang up and get to work, dammit. I've run out of usable excuses. If you can't work there, come home. Do I have to remind you there's a law against spending unearned money—unless you want to hock your house and give it back?"

Nothing Wylie said dampened Millie's spirits. She waltzed into her temporary office and turned on the computer. She'd never missed a deadline yet.

Daniel J. Murdock's favorite phrase is "piece of cake." This intriguing detective sergeant resembles a silver-tipped Cary Grant, is as closemouthed about his private life as Gary Cooper, and protects his tough-guy Humphrey Bogart image. He is not your run-of-the-mill detective, believe me. I speak from firsthand experience. In the short time I've known the man, he's placed himself in the line of danger to save my life; introduced me to a group of softball-playing reformed ex-convicts proudly bearing the "team colors"—Murdock's Maniacs—on their caps; and coached me as I helped this multitalented man deliver a baby.

And I think I might be in love with him.

Sighing, she stood up, spreading her fingers across the small of her back. She flipped through her Rolodex, found the number she needed, and dialed. Chip Harvey was a computer whiz, a first-rate researcher, and her friend. She quickly explained the book's concept and what she needed.

"Take it you need this stuff yesterday," Chip quizzed shrewdly.

She chuckled, pleased she'd called him. "Or the day before. It's deadline time. You know how hairy that can be."

"Not to worry, Millie, darlin'. As we say in the trade—piece of cake."

Now where had she heard that before? Millie smiled at the reference.

Dan slumped into the chair in front of Wasach's desk and

tried to look exhausted. He crossed his long legs at the ankle and stretched his arms above his head. He yawned, then yawned again. Thank heaven for reflex actions when you needed them.

Wasach narrowed his eyes. "You want a vacation? What for?"

Dan fixed his eyes on a spot above the chief's shoulder. He was being deliberately vague. "Three days. I've got the time off coming. Call it a paternity leave."

Wasach sat back, skeptical. "Everything all right with your folks? Your dad isn't upset about your being included in this Gordon's book, is he?"

"He and my mother are overseas. They'll be back soon. Anyway, I've decided to wait and see what Millie writes."

Wasach nodded. "What about her? You know how important this is for us. How are you going to explain to her she's got to take a few days' break in her schedule?"

"Don't worry," Dan assured him. "You'll get your story. I have an idea she can use the time off. She looked pretty pooped to me yesterday. Besides being in the stakeout, she helped deliver Rosy Lopez's baby. She told me she needs to work on her *Ask Ms. M.* column."

"All right," Wasach said. "Three days. Then I want you back here. Louie's case is coming to trial." He tossed a pink-banded cigar across the desk. "Here, Detective Sergeant Daddy. The guys and I pitched in. Congratulations."

Dan's brows lifted. "You're all heart, Wasach. How about one for Rosy's husband?"

Wasach sat back. "Give him yours. We're on a tight budget."

Dan caught the innuendo. Whenever the chief had something to say, he never missed a trick in selling his case. Now he was saying, take your three days, Murdock, but never forget we're depending on you.

Dan let the insinuation roll off his back. He had something more important to think about. Millie. He knew the perfect inducement to get her away from the computer. But first, he needed to stop at a toy store...

Dan took Millie to the hospital to visit Rosita and her new daughter. As they left, Millie couldn't stop talking about the infant. She'd had little experience with babies and had been awed by the tiny girl's perfection. She stopped in mid-sentence, though, when she caught Dan grinning at her.

"What are you smirking about?" she asked.

He pulled her to him and kissed the tip of her nose. "I was thinking how lucky we are that Rosy didn't have twins."

Millie's brows arched. "I'll have you know that I'm a twin."

"In that case, I take it back," he said good-naturedly. "Do you and your twin look much alike?"

"No. My brother Kipp is tall." She held her hand above her head. "Six-foot-three. He's broad-shouldered." She winked. "He's the one who shaves."

"Sounds identical to me," he teased. "Are you two close?"

She nodded. "Very. I'll be glad to see him again. I miss him."

She didn't notice the shadow that crossed Dan's face, nor was she paying much attention when he commented, "There're always airplanes if you lived here."

"What now?" she asked, rummaging in her purse for her sunglasses as they walked out into the bright sunlight.

"Now," he said offhandedly, "we go bear hunting."

"Bear hunting!" She halted in mid step, intrigued.

He took her elbow. "Close your mouth, Millie. I'm offering you the chance of a lifetime. Think of the publicity for your book, if we were to catch a bear. You can put the picture on the cover."

Millie didn't know if it was fate or coincidence. All she knew was that being with Dan was exhilarating, but at the rate she was going, her publisher would definitely demand repayment.

"Bears in Florida?" She still didn't trust him. He tsked. "Ever hear of *Gentle Ben?*"

Who hadn't? In her best lead-on-MacDuff voice, she said, "Bear hunting it is."

Her only question was whether they had to go to Alaska to snare one. She ignored the scolding sound of Wylie's voice in her mind, demanding that she get cracking.

Dan congratulated himself. He'd passed the first hurdle. Now for the second. "Pack an overnight case, Millie. Oh, and you might want to bring along a dress for the evening—in case the bear is hiding out in a fancy restaurant."

Her antennae flashed on, along with her jolting nerves. This had nothing to do with official business or he would have told her. She was making a decision with irrevocable implications. "Is this bear likely to need a bathing suit, too?"

"Don't be silly." He broke into a spontaneous grin. "Bears swim in the nude."

*

Was it her imagination, or did he linger on that last word?
"Aim."

Millie aimed, sighting down the barrel with a demonic squint.
"Pull."

She pulled. "I can't stand it!" she fumed. "The stupid can is still standing. They all are."

"My fault," Dan said cheerfully. "I should have said squeeze."

She made a move. "It won't help. You can recite the alphabet backward and I'd still miss the dumb can."

She'd been at it for half an hour. Every empty soda can stood up straight and tall on the fence posts. They were in a clearing in the middle of a field. Flanking it were stands of tulip oak trees draped with Spanish moss. Nearby a meandering stream gurgled past a stone waterfall on its way to the Gulf.

They had passed Weeki Wachi on Highway 19 when Dan slowed the car, halting on the shoulder. "Why are we stopping here?" she'd asked.

He had pointed to a sign. "I thought you might like to read that."

She'd gasped in amazement. "I thought you were kidding. There really is a sign warning about bears."

Dan had looked pleased with himself. "Detectives never lie. Put that in the book. We have brown bears in Florida. I bet you thought all we had were alligators?"

As they drove on, he had regaled her with bear stories, each more preposterous than the last. When he'd bragged about people flying in from Alaska to check out whether the Florida bears were really larger, she'd finally scoffed. "You're lying."

He'd winked. "But of course. It's a great tourist attraction."

Tourist attraction or not, she still couldn't hit the side of a barn. If she did see a bear, she'd run for cover. Her shoulders slumped. "Dan, we might as well quit. I'm a total failure."

He wasn't about to. Not with the surprise he planned. "You

need a pith helmet."

Was he mad?

"What for?"

"In case you bag a tiger instead, silly. Wait here."

He went to the car, popped open the trunk, and scooted back with a large bag. With a great flourish, he pulled out a pith helmet. He plunked it on her head before she knew what was happening.

Oversized, it fell over her eyes and nose. She couldn't see a thing. "Very funny," she muttered. "Now I've got a toilet bowl on my head."

"Pith helmet," he corrected her. He tapped the helmet, listening to the hollow sound. "Perfect fit. I wish I had a camera."

The helmet bobbed up and down. She gestured broadly with her hands. "I can't hit a blade of grass," she said, "let alone a bear or a tiger."

"Don't be silly," he said. He was having the time of his life. "I'll coach you through it."

She groaned. "Where have I heard that before? I'm getting tired. Who can shoot playing blind-man's buff?"

"Patience, Millie. One last time."

"What are you doing?"

She felt his chest against her back as his hands covered hers. The scent of his cologne surrounded her. Even if she wanted to, she couldn't think straight, let alone shoot straight.

He extended her arms then tipped the pistol skyward. "Shhh, there's a bear up in that tree. Now I want you to draw gently on the trigger. Squeeze and pull!"

The report of the bullet broke the stillness. Millie jerked backward. Dan steadied her. He plucked off her helmet, twirling her around. There was a big, wide grin on his face. "You did it!" He hugged her. "You bagged your bear!"

In spite of herself, the child in her wanted to believe. Dan made it sound so possible. "I don't see a thing," she said, looking around and feeling foolish.

"Ye of little faith." He scooped up the bag, grabbed her hand, and darted over to a tree. "What do you see?"

"See?" She kicked at a chimp of leaves. "Spanish moss; it's on all the trees... Shouldn't we be going?" she asked dejectedly.

He picked up the dark, round ball of moss. With one hand he

held the clump over her head and drew her to him with the other. His eyes glowed. "Happy New Year, Millie," he said softly. "That wasn't moss you shot. That was magic mistletoe. It grows in these tulip oaks. For a kiss, the mistletoe turns into a bear."

It was wonderful to play his game. She steeped herself in his presence, his scent, the deepness of his voice. She wanted to kiss him, to make love with him.

"What do you say, Millie?" His voice was now quietly serious. His eyes held her mesmerized. "Shall we see if there's magic left in the world?"

He stroked her cheek. She didn't want to think about complex issues, or of going home, or the reasons behind Dan's reticence each time she questioned him about his family.

If he wanted magic, she wanted it, too. She wrapped her arms around his neck, lifting her face to his. When his lips touched hers she let herself believe in magic. Transported beyond mere earth, she let herself feel the magic.

Excitement built quickly. Dan had promised her magic, but found himself enraptured instead. Millie's body, her pliant flesh melding with his, set him on fire. He wanted to stay there with her forever in their private world.

When had the air smelled so pure, the rustling of the trees been so lyrical, the trill of a bird so sweet, or the sky above so blue? He was conscious of everything, yet mostly he was aware of the woman in his arms. And yet he had never been so wary of the fact that her book stood between them.

When the kiss ended, they smiled into each other's eyes, willing to submerge their doubts for a little while longer. Dan eased away from her and surreptitiously reached into the bag. "Voila, your magic bear!"

Millie's throat clogged as she reached for the stuffed animal. Dan had gone to great lengths to give her the teddy and she was touched. "I love her. Thank you."

Dan beamed, although he would have preferred to hear her say, I love you. "You're welcome."

He had scoured the toy shops to find the perfect pink teddy bear. It had round, soulful black eyes, a button nose, and a sweet smile. A shiny red heart dotted with tiny rhinestones adorned its chest; and on its pink, ruffled skirt were the words Love Me. He hoped she'd get the message.

"Now you can forget all those other times when you went home empty-handed from the boardwalk in Wildwood, New Jersey."

A tear rolled down her cheek. "Oh, Dan. She's beautiful. She's my Bernadette." She flung herself into his arms, laughing and kissing him.

"You really are a magician," she said. She gave him a brilliant smile, wishing she had some magic dust herself. She would cast a spell on him to erase the pain of his uncle's death. Chip Harvey had called back. The Murdock name had been dragged through a media circus in New York City some years ago. Detective Jack Murdock had been killed by the mob, then revealed to be a cop on the take.

Dan clasped her tightly to him. He was caught between loyalty to his father and wondering whether the fickle public would remember or care "I wish I were a magician, Millie," he told her silently. "I really do..."

CHAPTER NINE

Dan patted the bear seated in the pith helmet on Millie's knee. She steadfastly refused to be parted from either. They were traveling the last five miles of their trip. He couldn't remember spending a better day.

Neither could Millie. She loved listening to his voice as he pointed out places of interest. She drank in the sight of him, his broad shoulders and chest, his strong arms, the easy manner in which he drove. He was completely relaxed and so sure of himself, she envied him.

"Why Bernadette?" he asked, watching her fondle the bear's pink ears.

She felt a familiar tightness gather in her stomach. Choosing a baby's name was an exercise in futility she'd indulged in a long time ago. "If we'd had a child we'd have named it either Bernadette or Bernard. It means brave as a bear or courageous. You have to be courageous to get through life. They're strong names, good names to live by." She couldn't hide the wistfulness that crept into her voice.

"Why didn't you adopt?" Dan asked. He knew she wanted children. He'd seen the yearning and hunger in her eyes when she held Rosita's baby. She was wealthy in her own right; her husband had been a corporate attorney. It hadn't been money.

Millie gnawed her bottom lip. It was a while before she spoke. "It never came up."

He was moved by the simple declaration, more so since he didn't believe a word of it. He suddenly realized the truth. "Your husband didn't want to adopt a child, is that it?" There was a thread of censure in his tone.

Tears, unbidden and unwanted, singed her eyes. Frank had said he wanted children—his own. She'd come to realize that deep in his psyche his inability to have children was tied up with fears and doubts about his manhood. "Does it matter?" she murmured.

Dan watched her with compassion, his expression gentling. In the late afternoon, the sun streamed through the window, sending shafts of light through her hair. He stared straight ahead again. "I was just wondering where I'd be if my parents hadn't adopted me."

Millie was caught off guard, too stunned to speak for a moment. "You're adopted?"

He shrugged. "Yes. So's my sister. We came as a pair. The Murdock's didn't have the heart to break us up, thank God. I was four years old, not exactly the age when most people want to adopt. Too bad your husband never met my folks."

The more she learned of this complex man, the more she realized how easy it would be to love him. He spoke so naturally, so lovingly, about his adoptive parents. "What happened to your natural parents?" she asked.

He hesitated. His eyes reflected remembered pain. "Dad was a chemist. One night he and my mother went to the small plant he owned. They were on their way to a party, dressed in their evening things. I remember that my mother looked lovely in her yellow gown. Dad had a special government order he wanted to check on. Somehow two vials of chemicals must have been knocked off a shelf. The chemicals merged and exploded. They died instantly."

She squeezed his hand. She could imagine the horrible scene. "Oh, Dan, I'm so sorry. Weren't there other members of your family who could raise you and your sister?" How cruel to compound one tragedy on top of another, tearing innocent children away from their relatives.

A muscle worked in his jaw and a fierce expression clouded his face. When he spoke, his voice was stoic with disillusionment and grief. "I don't know the details, but no. There was no one able to take the two of us."

Knowing the accomplished, caring man Dan had become, her heart swelled with pride. She understood at last the reason behind his passionate protection of his adoptive family. "May I use this in the book?"

"Sure, why not? I'm proud of being a Murdock." Then tell me the rest of it, she begged silently. Trust me not to hurt your folks. She tried to break down the last barrier separating them.

"You know, Dan," she began cautiously, "Other than the history of your marriage, that's the most you've said about your past. You have this habit of answering a question with a question. Why?"

He sidestepped the issue, joking. "Maybe I'm a psychiatrist in hiding.

"I'll tell you one thing," he added, getting back to the subject uppermost in his mind. "If you were my wife, we'd have children, one way or the other." His mouth curved up, lightening the mood in the car. "Not that I wouldn't try my best to have them the old-fashioned way, you understand."

Her nails dug into her palms. She didn't want to think about how it really had been with Frank. She'd begged to adopt a child until she was blue in the face. For a while she had thought he was refusing because of her busy career. She had promised to put it on hold to raise a family. Even Kipp, who normally didn't interfere, had once broached the subject with Frank, assuring him he'd love an adopted baby. Frank had thrown every argument back in their faces. He wouldn't budge. If it wasn't his biological child, he didn't want the headache.

Frank had been a wonderful man in every other respect, and she had loved him, yet clearly part of her still resented his resolute stand. She had nothing to show for all those years of marriage. It would have been different if it had been her choice, too. Plenty of women chose to be childless. Child-free, they called it now. She wasn't one of them.

"Stop it," she said abruptly, feeling disloyal. "You don't know how it was."

Dan frowned. "I can guess," he said, then wanted to kick himself for his faux pas. It was like a sore tooth. He was jealous of a dead man he'd never met, who couldn't defend himself. Wonderful, he thought, disgusted with himself. And that, he supposed, was a new definition of love. After thinking it would never happen to him, he had fallen for Millie like a ton of bricks. He was making a first-class botch of it. He considered telling her, then realized the timing was wrong.

"Sorry," he said. "That was none of my business."

"What are your plans?" she asked, directing the conversation away from herself. "Are you hoping to make chief someday? Readers will want to know."

The answer came swiftly. "I have no ambition to play the budget game with a mayor and city council." He wanted to demand that she tell him about her husband. He didn't give a damn about the book or readers. He wanted to crawl inside her head. "Millie, I know I haven't exactly answered everything you've asked me, but there's a reason."

"What's the reason?" She held her breath, willing him to trust her.

"Give me until next week. One way or the other, you'll have your answer to my less-than-candid behavior."

She dared to hope. "A week, no more. I'm working on a deadline. If I can't get one good chapter, I'll scrap it and resurrect some material I wrote a while ago. My publisher wants results, not excuses."

So does Wasach, he thought. "Fair enough."

They had made a little progress, she mused. She'd settle for that. "What's happening with Louie?"

"His trial won't come up for a while."

Dan slowed the car, turning off the main highway onto a side road. A sign directed them to the Ocean Resort.

Dan chuckled. "But when it does, we've got a little surprise for Louie. Spike Harvey resents being in jail while Louie's breathing the nice outside air with his friends. Naturally, Ben and I have been making regular visits to Spike, seeding his anger. He's decided to cooperate in exchange for immunity. We're keeping him under protective custody until the trial."

Millie stopped playing with Bernadette's ear. This was good news. "But I thought Spike was still in jail."

Dan smiled crookedly. "Can you think of a better place than a jail cell to keep someone in protective custody?"

She punched his arm with the bear, laughing. She looked at him with admiration. "You conniving devil! Spike's in jail one way or the other, and you get Louie, too. With your little scheme you don't have to pay police personnel to work extra duty. That's good, Murdock."

"Yeah," he drawled, delighted to see her in a better frame of mind.

"Is Louie really dangerous or just mouthy?"

"He's unpredictable. The company he keeps makes him dangerous. Now what do you say we skip all this work talk and enjoy ourselves? Here we are."

Here was the Ocean Resort, a sprawling complex on lush grounds. They drove alone a palm-lined road leading to the main building, which looked out over the ocean. There were tennis courts, three Olympic-sized swimming pools, outdoor snack bars, and a complete gym. For the swimmers and sailors, the resort offered snorkeling and sailing, and for the fishermen, rental boats.

"Wait until you taste the food," Dan said. "Culinary masterpieces." He parked the car near the manager's office. "Chef Henri's from France. He fell in love with an American exchange student, followed her here, and made all her parents' favorite dishes. That's what I call strategy. He doesn't work in the kitchen anymore. He prefers meeting the people, but the standards are the same. He rules with an iron skillet."

Millie carried her overnight bag and Bernadette, falling into step beside Dan. Adult or not, she'd been away from the dating scene a long time, and she'd never checked into a hotel with a man who wasn't her husband.

"Do you come here often?" she asked. Lord, she couldn't believe she'd asked such a dumb thing. Dan was a grown man, and she could attest to his sexual appetite.

He gave her a quizzical look. "I plan to." Dry amusement rumbled in his voice.

Jealousy stabbed her, but she managed to keep her voice light. "I can see why." Needing a moment, she paused to admire the vivid tropical flowers.

His lips twitched. "It's a very romantic setting, don't you agree?"

"Very." She smiled until it hurt, remembering her advice to her readers. Whatever you do, ladies, don't show a man you're jealous. She wasn't aware she was clutching Bernadette by the throat.

"You're killing your bear," he remarked casually, then turned to hide his smirk of satisfaction.

Embarrassed at being so easily read, Millie immediately

relaxed her death grip on the bear's neck. Ms. M. would handle the situation brilliantly, she thought, but plain Millicent Dolores Gordon put her foot in her mouth. So much for sophistication.

Dan turned back to her. He put down the suitcase and placed his hands on her shoulders. "My parents love it here. They've been telling me about this place for the past two years." He rubbed his knuckles over her cheek, looking deeply into her eyes. "Millie," he said softly, "I've never been here before. Never had a reason to come before."

Immense relief washed over her. "Thank you for that, Dan." She grinned. "I'm famished."

"Me, too. I phoned for reservations. We can change in our room, then have dinner."

That answered her next question. He expected her to share his room. "Aren't you taking a lot for granted?"

His gray eyes were unreadable. "Am I?"

Who was she kidding? She wasn't a coy adolescent. She knew exactly what his invitation had meant. She'd made love with him and couldn't get it out of her mind. "One room will be fine."

He leaned over to kiss her gently. "You won't be sorry, Millie. I may not write an advice column, but I do understand. Each step you're taking now is a new one. It is for me, too. And," he added, stroking her cheek, "if it helps you, I'm a little nervous, too."

They were given the honeymoon suite. Millie never learned if Dan had arranged it or if the hotel really was full. They had a sweeping panoramic view of the ocean. Sliding glass doors led to a secluded terrace and deck area with a private heart-shaped hot tub. Purple, pink, and white geraniums lined the walls, along with potted palms, cactus, and bougainvillea.

The opulent suite consisted of a large living room that flowed into an enormous bedroom decorated in muted earth tones. A compact kitchen and a bathroom with a sunken tub and indoor sauna completed the suite. But it was the mirrors above the bed that held Millie's attention.

"Dan," she said weakly, wishing she were a trim twenty-year-old. She set the bear and her bag down. "I'm over thirty."

He put his arms around her. "So am I. You promise not to look at the ceiling?" He carefully refrained from giving her the same promise. There wasn't a spot on Millie's body he hadn't seen and kissed, and wanted to kiss again—soon. He silently applauded the decorator.

She sat down on the bed, shaking her head.

He sat down next to her. "What?" He took his gun from his ankle holster and laid it on the night table.

"I was just thinking, if my readers could see me now, they'd say—"

"That I was a very lucky man." He took her hand, massaged the palm with his thumb, then kissed her lips.

Millie's heart began to hammer, and she wrapped her arms around him. She wanted to remember everything about him.

"They've decorated this suite beautifully," she said.

"It's the French influence. You must be starved. It isn't every day you shoot a pink bear. Let's change, or we'll never get out of here."

Wanting to look glamorous for Dan, she had brought along a strapless red silk dress, high-heeled sling-back pumps, and dark patterned stockings. Knowing his preference for long hair, she left hers down, brushing it until it shone. The light caught highlights of shimmering amber. She wore a rhinestone comb tucked behind one ear.

She took special care with her makeup, applying smoky blue eye shadow and dark mascara to emphasize her eyes. She dotted lip gloss over her pale red lipstick. The look on Dan's face told her she hadn't wasted her efforts. She smiled, fluttering her lashes, then giggled. Her femme fatale imitation was ruined.

He slipped his arms around her waist and nuzzled her neck. "You're making it hard to leave this room. Mmm, you smell good, too."

"Dan… I thought you said you were hungry." He was nibbling her ear and she couldn't think straight. He kissed her throat, then lowered his head to her breast.

"I am. I'm starved." He lightly kissed one nipple. "Well, these were made to feed a man's senses." The muscles in her stomach coiled, and she pressed a hand to the back of his head. "Reservations," she mumbled.

"Right." His sigh was ragged. He straightened up reluctantly. "A real man would rip off your clothes and drag you to bed."

She couldn't resist teasing him. "A real man of thirty-six

needs his protein."

Pretending to be affronted, he moved close to her. There was a mischievous gleam in his eye. "Are you suggesting I'm getting old?" He backed her against the wall, pinning her arms to her sides, and branded her with a stormy kiss. His hips ground against hers. "That's not old," he said, letting her feel his rising desire. "And neither is this."

His hands held her in a vise. He opened his mouth on hers, kissing her relentlessly until he heard a moan deep in her throat. He released her suddenly, leaving her breathless. His eyes were dark, his voice hoarse. "On second thought, if we don't get out of here, I'm going to skip the meal and get down to dessert."

Millie needed another kind of nourishment. She'd found it once in his arms. Boldly, she pushed aside his jacket and ran her hands up his chest. Her fingers worked on his patterned silk tie, loosening the knot.

"Not a bad idea, Murdock. Of course, we're all dressed and we do have reservations." As if it were a feather boa, she slid the tie up on the back of his neck, teasingly drawing him close until their lips were a breath apart. She smiled dreamily. "Come here." He willingly did what she asked, letting her fit her mouth to his, taking what she wanted. The tie floated to the floor.

When she let him come up for air, his eyes were glowing with desire. His hands skimmed her rib cage. "I've always admired a woman who knew what she wanted. You don't mind if I return the favor, do you?"

She shivered with delicious sensations. He removed the rhinestone comb from behind her ear.

"Be my guest," she said. He was, tracing the shape of her ear with his tongue until her bones felt as if they'd melt.

"My turn." Her hands dropped to his waist, fumbling with the belt. She kissed his chin, then ran her lips lightly up his face to his mouth. Satisfied that she was driving him as crazy as he was making her, she threw her head back and fluttered her lashes.

"I imagine," she murmured huskily, "in a place like this, at the height of the season and all, they'd be miffed if we didn't show."

Neither moved to the phone. The belt followed the tie. She kissed the pulse beat at the base of his throat.

"You're racing, Murdock?" For good measure she made him

race a little faster by blowing tiny breaths in his ear. "I didn't hear your answer, detective."

He found his voice on a croak. "Think of the happy couple who will inherit our reservation."

His arms went around her and he tugged at the zipper to her dress. She leaned into him, making low throaty sounds. He chuckled, then began slowly to lower the zipper.

He kissed her shoulder, the curve of her neck, and paved a wispy course to her other side, giving it the same meticulous attention. He turned her around, following the line of the zipper with his lips.

"Murdock." His name shuddered out of her. Her dress slithered down her body. She stepped out of it and pushed her stockings off. She wore only a strapless bra and bikini panties.

"Oh, baby, do I want you," he said huskily, turning her in his arms.

Her fingers were busy with the buttons of his shirt. She spread the shirt fabric wide and kissed his chest. Then she pushed the shirt off his shoulders, and it fell to the floor. "You're sure you don't mind missing the meal?" she teased.

"From what I hear"—he nibbled his way along the top of her breasts— "there's eating and there's drinking. Personally, I'd rather drink. I have this terrible thirst." He released the clasp on her bra, and took her breast in his mouth.

At the first touch of his lips hot electricity shot through her, fanning her desire into a full conflagration.

Dan flicked his tongue in erotic circles around her nipples. She could feel the very air heat. Her trembling fingers worked feverishly at his pants zipper. In a moment they faced each other undressed, with no thought of shyness.

Dan sat down on the bed. She knelt behind him, her arms around his waist, and trailed kisses along his spine. "What?" she asked, as he chuckled.

"I just realized it doesn't much matter where we are—car, hallway, hotel room, field, my house— it's going to end the same way. We might as well stay naked."

"What about food?"

He turned to her. Her face was flushed, her eyes glowing.

"The heck with food." He pressed her down on the bed and

leaned over her. "We'll grow skinny together. There's someplace else I'd rather be."

"And where is that?" she murmured.

His gaze traveled slowly from one end of her body to the other. He poised over her, lifting her hips. "In you. Giving to you. Like this…"

Millie giggled, turning her face into his shoulder. "The mirror on the ceiling was a waste."

"A lot you know," he said, shifting her on top of him. "Where do you think I got my inspiration?"

"You promised!"

He shook his head. "No, I didn't. You did." She collapsed on him, laughing. "Are you trying to tell me," he growled, his mouth hovering near hers, "that my lovemaking was a joke?"

They'd made love twice, wildly, passionately, arousing each other until they erupted in a volcanic climax. The sun had long since dipped below the horizon. Except for a small shaft of flickering moonlight streaming through the window, the room was dark.

"No," she said. "I'm trying to tell you I'm starving. Oh, no, you don't!" She pushed his roaming hand away. "I'm really starving, as in let's eat. You shower first. I'll see what can be done with my dress."

"Why don't we order room service?" he grumbled. He trailed his fingers up her thigh. "Then I can eat what I want and you can eat what you want. By the way, I dare you to put this in your book."

The book. She'd forgotten all about the damned book. Forgotten that that was what had brought them together. His hands were incredibly arousing. He made her body tremble. She willed herself to relax, to reason calmly.

Dan wasn't the marrying kind. His bachelor life-style suited him. She wasn't the type to settle for a long-term affair, or a gun on the night table when she went to bed. The sooner she returned home, the better. Vacation romances rarely amounted to anything. If she didn't believe it, Ms. M. did. Right now she'd trust Ms. M.'s judgment over Millie Gordon's.

Dan brushed the hair back from her forehead, kissed her lightly, then patted her fanny. He picked up the phone and called the restaurant. Winking at her, he somberly told the maître d' that they had been unavoidably detained. "Something came up," he said, while she choked. Smiling, he hung up. "He said there was no problem. We have a later seating for thirty minutes from now. Get out of bed, lazybones."

It took Millie a moment to stiffen her jellied legs. Within half an hour they'd showered and dressed and were strolling arm in arm into the restaurant.

The maître d' asked them to wait at the door. Chef Henri, a tall, middle-aged man with a neatly trimmed dark beard, piercing blue eyes, and a firm handshake, came to greet them. He bowed in a courtly gesture over Millie's hand, and introduced himself.

"Your dear parents speak so highly of you, Dan," he said as he seated them at a table overlooking the ocean. "For my friends the Murdocks, I shall, with your permission, order for you." Pleased by the gesture, Dan thanked him.

"To start, you shall have salade Henri, followed by gratinee, fillet of sole duxelle farcie, sauce beurre blanc, julienne of vegetables, rice pilaf, with a dessert of fresh fruit sabayon."

Henri snapped his fingers. Instantly a white-coated waiter stepped forward and handed him a linen-swathed bottle of wine. Henri poured a small amount into a glass and handed it to Dan for his tasting approval. Then he filled Millie's glass.

"To cleanse the palate," he said, "and with my compliments, de Ladquette Pouilly Fum C'est l'amour," he added, beaming. "Toujours l'amour." Dan grinned as Chef Henri left.

"What a character. I like him. Did you understand everything he said? I sure as heck didn't."

She smiled, not answering. She saw that several other women in the room were gazing at Dan with open admiration. She couldn't blame them. Dressed in a beautifully tailored double-breasted dark blue Italian suit, his white dress shirt emphasizing his deep tan; Dan looked both dashing and handsome. For tonight, he was hers, whether he understood French or not.

Dan decided restraint wasn't his strong suit. Millie wasn't helping, sitting opposite him, her lips swollen from his kisses, her face flushed from their lovemaking, her hair tumbling down her back. She was gazing at him as if he were the most interesting dinner companion in the world. But he was always more comfortable with action over words.

He debated acknowledging that he loved her, deciding finally against it. Weren't those her own words of advice that he'd read over and over through the years? The very words that prompted his silence now.

"True love needs time to mature," she'd written so often it was her trademark. Ms. M. was an old-fashioned advice giver. He tried to meld that with Millie, the gorgeous hoyden with the tumbling mass of black hair, who sent his senses into the stratosphere, and whose blue eyes he saw in his dreams. They were one and the same, writing about a society in a sexual shambles, cautioning people not to act out of haste.

If she needed time, he'd give it to her. Another week. No more, he decided. Love made him an impatient man. In the meantime, he'd check with the dean of his law school. He had more important things to do with his nights than sit in un-marked cars waiting to pounce on palookas and hoods.

He'd woo her, then ask her to marry him. If she said no. he'd lock her up in protective custody until she said yes. Of course, protective custody would be his house. First he'd have to come clean with the goods about his uncle. If he didn't, she'd rightfully wonder why he didn't trust her—writer or not.

Pleased with his decision, he dug into his food with gusto. "Great meal."

"Delicious," Millie said. Obviously, he hadn't noticed she was merely poking at her food. She'd been replaying what he'd said in the car: "If you were my wife, we'd have children one way or the other."

She flushed, remembering his next line. "Not that I wouldn't try my best to have babies the old-fashioned way." And his best was very good indeed.

Hours later, Millie again recalled Dan's words. She had assumed she knew all about sex. If she'd felt excitement with Dan before, it was nothing to the way he made love with her now. It was as if he'd passed a turning point in his life. He took her, by storm, sheathing himself in her with turbulent ungovernable passion.

The scent of him was rich, compellingly masculine. His body was hard and firm. His fingers found the center of her femininity, trapping her in his power until she could tolerate being held off no longer. "Dan, please," she implored him, digging her nails into his back.

That was what he wanted to hear. She needed his essence.

Increasing the tempo, he exploded with her.

Millie drew the sheet up over her body. Sometime during the night, she'd put on her nightgown. She lay on her back, a languorous feeling creeping over her. Dan had gotten up to use the bathroom. Shifting to her side, she cupped her head in her hand, awaiting his return.

Later, she'd wonder what made her turn to look at the door to the hall. There was just enough light in the room for her to see the handle move. Too stunned to speak, she watched the door open slowly.

Frantic, she tried to scream to Dan, but her throat locked. Oh, please, she prayed, be a mistake and go away.

She bit down hard on her lip. Covering her mouth with the sheet, she reached over to the night table, groping for Dan's gun. She held it in her shaking hands, and aimed it squarely at the bandy-legged figure stealing into the room.

Her breath exploded with recognition.

"Freeze!"

"Stay where you are, Louie."

Louie's eyes were fierce, following the waving gun. He dropped the pipe in his hand. "Lady, I'm harmless." His gaze darted around the room. "Where's Murdock? Ask him."

Never, even in her wildest dreams, had she imagined herself in such a situation. The sweat poured down between her breasts. Her throat refused to function. Her hands were glued to the gun.

And Dan was in the bathroom.

Then she saw the pink teddy bear sitting in the pith helmet. She glared furiously at the crumb who dared intrude on her lovely weekend.

"You make one move before Dan gets in here and I'll blow you to the moon, creep."

"Lady, please put that thing away." Louie, seeing the face of fear in front of him, knew danger. It gave him the bravery to shout. "Murdock, for God's sake, get out here and arrest me! This dame's crazy."

Dan ripped open the bathroom door. "Holy—" In a flash he took stock of the situation. Millie, glassy-eyed and scared out of her wits, was waving the pistol in Louie's direction. It could go off at any time. No wonder he was scared.

"You bastard," he said to Louie. "You're going away for a long, long time for pulling this trick." He eased over to Millie. He didn't want to make any sudden moves.

"Millie, darling, give me the gun."

She barely glanced at Dan. "You have the right to remain silent. Anything you say can and will be used against you in a court of law—"

"Geez, Murdock, can't you get that gun?" Sweat ran down Louie's face.

"Honey, those are my lines. Now be a good girl and give me the gun."

She shook her head. No one was going to harm Dan, she told herself. Besides, the metal had grown into her hands.

"Please, lady," Louie said. "Give Murdock the gun."

"Sweetheart." Dan moved closer to her. "I love you. If you shoot this no-good louse, we'll never have all those little Bernards and Bernadettes cluttering up the house."

"That's right, lady. Don't you want them?"

Dan glared at Louie. "Shut up. For your information, this woman shot a bear today. So it would be a cinch for her to take you out. Now—on the floor."

Dan placed his hand over Millie's, prying her fingers loose. "Honey, I love you. Do this for me."

Millie nodded. The gun fell into his hands. Keeping it trained on Louie's prone figure, he helped her sit down on the bed. Then he picked up the phone.

"Ben, I've got a little surprise for you. Can you drive up where we are and pick it up?" He quickly filled Ben in with the situation, then hung up. "Louie, you made one hell of a mistake trying to get me. I'm going to see to it that you rot in jail. Looks like you bought yourself some bad P.R., pal. Even your mob friends won't have anything to do with you when I'm through."

Millie was coming out of her daze. She found herself giving voice to a string of unladylike pronouncements aimed at the intruder on the floor.

She was still fuming when Ben arrived. Her passionate lover was gone: Dan had reverted to being all cop. He had cuffed Louie to the bed and read him his Miranda rights.

After Ben left with Louie, Dan held her in his arms,

absorbing the shudders that racked her body. "Darling, you were wonderful." He was back to gentle.

She wiped the tears from her eyes. She was shaking with fear—for him. "He could have hurt you. You were defenseless."

Dan smiled indulgently, making light of the potentially serious situation. "That was a heck of a way to be defenseless."

It wasn't funny. "I want to go home," she said.

He couldn't blame her. The room, the entire resort, had lost its special flavor now. "All right, darling. We'll dress and leave."

She hadn't heard him, he thought, when he'd said he loved her or when he'd told her he wanted children with her. Sighing, he slipped off the bed. Maybe tomorrow . . .

The next morning Millie caught the first plane out of Tampa to Newark Airport. When she had said she wanted to go home, that's what she'd meant. She had fallen hopelessly in love with Dan. She simply couldn't face the possibility that he could be hurt in the line of duty. If that made her a coward for not wanting to lose a loved one twice, so be it. Dan had been lucky this time. For her the price was too high.

The real estate agent promised to have someone pack her remaining belongings and ship them to New Jersey.

Kipp and his wife Stacy met her at the airport, their faces mirroring their concern when they saw her puffy, red eyes. Wylie had called to tell them what had happened. "You need time, sis," Kipp said. "Dan Murdock sounds like a good man. Don't close the doors behind you."

She refused to talk about it. She refused to spend the night at their house. She wanted to be alone to nurse her wounds. She left her suitcase by the front door while she wandered through her house.

She removed the protective covers from the furniture as she roamed from room to room, imagining the house as it once was, when Frank had been alive. Now it was empty and silent. As empty and silent as she felt.

She'd gone to Florida to run away. She'd left Florida for the same reason.

Sighing, she sat down at the piano in the living room, letting her fingers drift over the keys. She remembered another house and an upright piano, one that wasn't nearly as expensive as her concert grand. Yet it was that house and that piano tugging at her heart.

Dan's house and Dan's piano.

He didn't know she was running away. She had told him she needed at least a day to catch up on her work. He'd looked at her quizzically, started to argue, then changed his mind. He'd kissed her hard, telling her everything would be all right. She'd held on to him tightly. "Be careful," she'd said.

"Piece of cake, sweetheart." He'd hurried down the path to his car, excited that Louie was not only behind bars, but he'd be staying there for a very long time.

Once inside her rented home, Millie had called Wylie first, then the airlines. Except for her broken heart, it was hard to picture that she'd been away, things had stayed so much the same in so many ways.

She unpacked her computer. She had work to do. She had promised Wylie she'd have the Dan chapter on her desk within a week.

For four days she followed a strict routine, breaking it only when her back ached so much she had to take a walk. The phone still hadn't been re-connected. She was grateful for that. She needed time to be able to speak calmly with Dan and explain why she'd left.

Assuming he still wanted to talk to her after her running out on him!

He made the national news. Louie's arrest this time was significant because of his newly revealed mob connections. She sat sipping a soda as she watched Dan's interview on the evening news. He answered the questions curtly. It seemed to her it was all he could do to bridle his temper. He hadn't shaved and looked as if he hadn't slept in days. Still, he was beautiful to her.

Oh, my darling, she thought. Forgive me for adding to your burdens. If it hadn't been for her, Dan would never have gone to the Ocean Resort. Louie might have stayed away from him and he would never have gotten this sort of publicity. It broke her heart to realize a smart investigative reporter might soon reach into the Murdock past and make the connection Dan clearly feared to make public.

Police Chief Wasach was standing next to Dan. She noticed that Dan tried to hand off the reporters' questions to him. The reporters obviously weren't buying it.

"Were you alone at the time, detective?" one of them asked. "I understand you were in the Ocean Resort's honeymoon suite."

Millie held her breath. Dan looked straight into the camera. He seemed to be sending the message directly to her. "I was with the woman I love and hope to marry... if she'll have me."

She gasped with surprise. "Damn you, Murdock. Stop making this harder for me," she exclaimed as the reporters shouted over one another asking questions about this unexpected and colorful new human interest angle to the story.

Over the next three days Millie finished the chapter. Then she called Wylie. "I can't give it to you."

"What?" Wylie's tone clearly announced she'd been afraid of something like this.

Millie's tears came then. She was powerless to stop them. She realized when she finished the chapter that she'd written it for Dan and only for him.

It was the longest love letter she'd ever written. She had sent it express mail to him that morning.

"I've gone back to my earlier material," she told Wylie. "Remember? About the concert pianist who suffered a stroke? I heard him give a concert last year. If you didn't know he was playing with one hand, you'd swear it was with two. I've already polished that piece and put it in the mail. The publisher should be satisfied. It's a good chapter. I'll send you more in a few weeks." She hoped Wylie wouldn't read her the riot act.

"You sure you know what you're doing, Millie?" Wylie didn't mind.

"No, I'm hoping I know what I'm doing. This is one time I could use Ms. M.'s advice."

"Want mine?"

Millie laughed shortly. "Do I have a choice?"

"Go back to him. With all my husbands I've never felt about a man the way you feel about Dan. You've lost love once. Don't throw it away this time."

The next afternoon Millie stood in her backyard drinking in the beauties of spring. She'd come to a decision about her house, finally. She loved the neighborhood. It was a wonderful area in which to bring up children. She would miss it when she sold it, but it was time to move on. Someone would love this house as she did. But she no longer belonged here.

The gardener had come during her absence, as promised.

Bending down, she picked a bouquet of yellow iris. Purple, white, and deep red tulips grew in brilliant clumps, surrounded by grape hyacinth. She loved the spring.

Dan had been on the evening news again the night before. He'd looked marvelous, strong and commanding. When he'd gazed straight into the camera, she could have sworn he was looking at her. She'd turned up the volume, catching every nuance, loving and missing him more than she'd thought possible.

She'd listened with pride as some local politician praised Dan for exposing a major crime syndicate. Dan was given a special commendation. Pete Wasach had smiled broadly as he pinned the medal onto him. She'd chuckled at Dan's expression. His mouth was compressed in a forbidding line.

He hated notoriety or attention. Thanks to her, now he got plenty.

Watching him on television, she had gradually come to terms with her feelings. Nothing was as important as being Dan's wife.

Only she was too late. He hadn't called. He'd certainly received the chapter by now. Maybe, she thought, annoyed when the doorbell rang, he'd change his mind. What man wants to be married to a chicken?

She walked through the house and swung open the door. A portly, middle-aged man with a bulbous nose and watery eyes was standing there. The sign on his uniform read: We Deliver Anything.

"You Ms. M.?" he asked.

"Yes." She couldn't hide her disappointment. She'd secretly hoped it might be Dan, coming to tell her he couldn't live without her, and was dragging her back to Florida—by the hair, if necessary.

"This is for you." The man shoved a slim package at her, then waited.

"Yes, of course," she stammered, realizing the man wanted his tip. "Wait here." She ran into the living room for her purse and dug out her Visa credit card. "I'm sorry. I know this is unorthodox, but you see, I ran away from someone I met in Florida. I haven't had time to get to the bank yet and I've spent all my money on groceries."

He rolled his eyes. "Lady, forget it. You need it worse than I do." He left, muttering.

Millie fumbled with the wrapping, then stared at the

photograph. She nearly cracked up. It was Henry and Henrietta. They were begging, their mouths open.

"He loves me!" she shouted. She dashed to the phone. Impatiently she counted the rings until the line was picked up. She almost blurted out that she wanted to be the mother of all the little Bernadettes and Bernards they could manage when Ben dryly informed her Dan was away. Another case.

"When will he return?" she asked, crestfallen.

"I'm not sure. All I know is that he said he'll be away until the case is solved. Is there a message? Maybe I can give it to him when he checks in."

"No, never mind. Thanks anyway, Ben." She hung up, feeling glum and miserable. She was still moping when the bell rang again.

"Now what?" She grabbed her credit card, just in case, and yanked open the door.

The young policeman looked very serious and, she thought, nervous. He stood very straight as she stared at him. He coughed, then asked, "Are you Millie Gordon?"

She nodded. Please, she prayed, not bad news about Dan.

The officer stood straighter, if that were possible. His brown eyes were stem. "I have a warrant for your arrest."

She repeated the words soundlessly, unbelieving. "Are you crazy?" she yelled. Thoughts of Dan were wiped from her mind as she stared at the young officer. "I've never done anything wrong in my life. Now please leave me alone. I'm busy."

He squared his shoulders and tugged his cap. "I'm afraid I can't do that. You'll have to come to the station with me to answer the charges."

"What charges?" she asked, frantically trying to remember her lawyer's phone number. This couldn't be happening.

"You'll have to ask that man in the patrol car. He's got the extradition papers."

She pushed him to the side, her glance slicing to the black and white squad car parked in her driveway. The sun's rays prevented her from seeing clearly the face of the man in the backseat, but she'd know the shape of that head anywhere. She had held it to her breast often enough.

"Oh, is that right, officer?" she asked, chuckling.

He cleared his throat again. This was his first arrest. Why, he wondered, did it have to be a gorgeous woman with a glint in her eye that spelled trouble? "Yes, ma'am."

He jumped out of her way as she burst past him, running down the steps as if her life depended on it. He got his wind and took off after her, but he was too late. He groaned as she yanked open the ear door and flew onto the lap of the man who sat there grinning.

Grinning! What kind of a crazy arrest was this? He watched closely, just in case he had to give testimony.

Millie flashed her Visa card. "I'm Millie Gordon of the Port Rico Police Department. You'd better come with me, mister. If you don't, your life could be in danger."

"Oh, yeah?" Dan barely got the words out as kisses were rained on his face and neck.

"Yeah." She waved away the policeman, who had poked his head over the front seat.

Dan couldn't wait to get her alone. "In that case, lady," he said solemnly, "I'll do anything you want."

She wrapped her arms around him, kissing him full on the mouth. "Promise?"

He laughed, kissing her back. "Promise. That doesn't include the mirror on the ceiling, though. My father said I have to make you an honest woman. He's found out no one cares what happened years ago to his brother, and uncle Jack. Well talk about him later. I love you, Millicent Dolores Gordon, and I want to make me an honest man."

Millie stopped kissing him long enough to get in one last order. She turned to the rookie, who had slid behind the wheel. "City Hall, driver. This man has just been given a life sentence."

Dan stopped nibbling her ear. "What?" he growled. "No time off for good behavior?"

"Not a chance, Murdock," she said, sending him a cocky, self-assured grin. "I'm going to be the best cop's wife you ever saw."

His hand strayed to her thigh. He'd wait until later, until she lay naked in his arms, to tell her she'd have to be the best prosecuting attorney's wife he ever saw.

"Promise?" he asked.

"Your best handcuffs, Murdock."

"What about children? How many do you want?"

"For starters? How about trying for twins? We could make our own team of Bernards and Bernadettes."

Neither paid attention to the gasp coming from the rookie in the other seat.

"That might be fun. What about your job?"

"Ms. M. can work anywhere. Give her a laptop and she can even work in the maternity ward."

"Not a chance," he said gruffly. "I intend to be in there with you."

"Okay."

He'd never heard her give in so easily. "You're fishing for something. I can tell."

"You bet." She stroked him between his legs. "Yipes!" he shouted. "Watch it, or we'll be having those twins sooner than you think."

"Driver," Millie commanded, "I said City Hall."

Flabbergasted, Officer Norman Brackman, fresh out of the academy, one week on the force, and taught to show deference to all superiors, even the ones from Florida, asked, "Sir, is this your wish?"

Dan didn't bother to answer. Instead, while the young man shook his head at the antics of the two passengers in his patrol car, Detective Sergeant Daniel J. Murdock of the Port Rico Police Department performed his last official duty.

He lowered Millie onto the seat, shielding her body with his, blocking out the sun, blocking out everything but himself. She was his for keeps.

"In that case, sugar, it's show time. Pucker up."

"Murdock, I thought you'd never ask."

Her throaty laughter wafted into the front seat. It was a sound Officer Brackman wished he'd hear a woman make for him. He started the car, heading for City Hall and the Marriage License Bureau. After all, he'd had his orders.

ABOUT THE AUTHOR

Doris Parmett

Having lived on both coasts and in the middle of the country, I can't remember when a book hasn't been a welcome part of my life. I come from a family of writers and readers; therefore, the progression to set my own stories on paper seemed natural. As a teacher and reading specialist, I've always told students that books are friends. They'll never tell you they're too busy to see you. An author's job is to transport us into another world. A world where characters come alive. We root for them through adversity; hope for the best.

When I wrote my eleven Loveswepts, I kept meeting a number of well-intentioned but rough at the edges, hunky charmers. Fate kept bringing together heroes and sassy-mouthed vixens; heroines determined not to follow orders. Their only problem: love knocks them for a loop. (I could have told them that!)

Regardless of circumstances, books are friends. I wish all of you lots of friends.

13Thirty Books
Exciting Thrillers, Heart-Warming Romance,
Mind Bending Horror, Sci-Fantasy
and
Educational Non-Fiction

Romantic Times: Vegas

The Excelsior Hotel and Casino. Built in Las Vegas in 1960 by mobster Louis "The Lip" LaFica. For decades the towering hotel has been the subject of incredible stories and rumors that have kept it in the public eye the world around. Why have so many lovers been mysteriously, magically, magnetically drawn to this magnificent edifice? And why now have so many bestselling authors at last come together to reveal the adventures of these lovers who have stayed at the glorious Excelsior?

The Third Hour

The Third Hour is an original spin on the religious-thriller genre, incorporating elements of science fiction along with the religious angle. Its strength lies in this originality, combined with an interesting take on real historical figures, who are made a part of the experiment at the heart of the novel, and the fast pace that builds.

Ripper – A Love Story

"Queen Victoria would not be amused--but you will be by this beguiling combination of romance and murder. Is the Crown Prince of England really Jack the Ripper? His wife would certainly like to know... and so will you." — Diana Gabaldon, New York Times Best Selling Author

Heather Graham's Haunted Treasures

Presented together for the first time, New York Times Bestselling Author, Heather Graham brings back three tales of paranormal love and adventure.

Heather Graham's Christmas Treasures

New York Times Bestselling Author, Heather Graham brings back three out-of-print Christmas classics that are sure to inspire, amaze, and warm your heart.

Zodiac Lovers Series

Zodiac Lovers is a series of romantic, gay, paranormal novelettes. In each story, one of the lovers has all the traits of his respective zodiacal sign.

Never Fear

Shh... Something's Coming

Never Fear – Phobias

Everyone Fears Something

Never Fear – Christmas Terrors

He sees you when you're sleeping ...

More Than Magick

Why me? Recent college grad Scott Madison, has been recruited (for reasons that he will eventually understand) by the wizard Arion and secretly groomed by his ostensible friend and mentor, Jake Kesten. But his training hasn't readied him to face Vraasz, a being who has become powerful enough to destroy the universe and whose first objective is the obliteration of Arion's home world. Scott doesn't understand why he was the chosen one or why he is traveling the universe with a ragtag group of individuals also chosen by Arion. With time running out, Scott discovers that he has a power that can defeat Vraasz. If only he can figure out how to use it.

13Thirtybooks.com

facebook.com/13thirty